Afsun Beyond *the* Vineyard

KHATERA TUGHRA

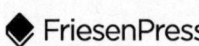
FriesenPress

One Printers Way
Altona, MB R0G 0B0
Canada

www.friesenpress.com

Copyright © 2023 by Khatera Tughra
First Edition — 2023

All rights reserved.

Translated by Yunus Tughra
Edited by Momoye Sugiman

No part of this publication may be reproduced in any form, or by any means, electronic or mechanical, including photocopying, recording, or any information browsing, storage, or retrieval system, without permission in writing from FriesenPress.

Although inspired by reality, this is a work of fiction. The specific names, characters, places, and incidents are either products of the author's imagination or are used fictitiously. Any resemblance to actual persons, living or dead, is entirely coincidental.

ISBN
978-1-03-917162-6 (Hardcover)
978-1-03-917161-9 (Paperback)
978-1-03-917163-3 (eBook)

1. FICTION, CONTEMPORARY WOMEN

Distributed to the trade by The Ingram Book Company

I dedicate this book to Yunus Tughra, my heroic father whom I cannot fit into small sentences. He has a special place in my heart. His boundless encouragement, love, attention, and protection have strengthened me at every stage of my life, including this current journey.

Preface

Although we can act with confidence in our imagination, sometimes we don't know what path we're going to take. We can't predict what's going to happen to us. The story of Afsun is difficult to tell, but it's one I feel morally obligated to share because she is an example of girls and women who never get a chance to have their voices heard.

Inspired by real events and real people, this novel tells the story of one resilient young woman and her family who flee the turmoil in Afghanistan and seek refuge in Russia in the early 2000s. Unfortunately, they do not find what they had hoped for there. After many years, they suddenly go back to their homeland. I thought this real-life drama of return migration would be told most effectively through the lens of an adolescent girl writing in her diary.

Sensitive and strong-willed, Afsun faces uncontrollable sociopolitical pressures. She begins her journey with great dreams and hopes, but she finds herself in situations she never imagined. You will read about a vibrant young woman who is transplanted from the metropolis of Moscow to Faryab, her parents' region of Northern Afghanistan. Once a beautiful, peaceful country, Afghanistan is now corrupted by years of tyranny, war, and foreign occupation. Having grown up in a totally different culture, Afsun struggles to make sense of a society where religion is misinterpreted and misused, where severe poverty damages people's lives—and where women's status is erased, shattering the aspirations of all young girls.

The narrative addresses important aspects of Afghanistan's long history and rich culture, along with its challenges in the twenty-first century. It explores the solidarity of a handful of women and girls trying to hold on to their dreams in the shadow of backwardness. I felt compelled to write this novel to help prevent them from fading from the world's consciousness.

I appreciate everyone who believed in me. I thank Duygu Tughra for being a mother and friend to me. Her ideas, editing, and analysis helped me fine-tune the original Turkish edition of my book under the title *Efsun*. I am deeply grateful to my dear father, Yunus Tughra, who read my work more than I did. I want to thank my two sweet little sisters, Melisa and Aliza—and my beloved Sarwar family. In addition, I want to express my appreciation to Momoye Sugiman, my father's former English teacher in Canada. She guided him throughout the translation and substantive editing of *Afsun Beyond the Vineyard*. I am also indebted to my dear friend, Rubaba Mohammadi, an internationally acclaimed Hazara artist who perseveres in pursuit of her dreams despite the obstacles facing her in our homeland. She has generously poured her passion and talent into the evocative painting you see on the cover of this book.

Finally, I thank myself. I express my love and gratitude for the ability to stand up for good over evil in the world I have stepped into.

Khatera Tughra

What you will read in this novel is inspired by the personal observations and notes of a real-life adolescent girl.

CHAPTER 1

An Ordinary Girl in Moscow

In last year's fire, all the stories and novels I had written perished when our house burned to the ground. At first, I was devastated, but two months later, I forgot all about the writing I had lost. With the emptiness that it created, I wrote a new story, but when I read it in class, nobody seemed to appreciate it. At that time, I thought I'd never write another story.

Normally, I enjoy writing. I write more freely and with peace of mind when I know no one will read it. Anyway, now I've decided to tell you something about my life, the daily life of an ordinary young girl. I'm sure no one will mess with my diary. I just write down whatever's going on in my mind. For example, I describe the events of my day. I even write about what happened at breakfast in the morning, who asked out whom at school, what my mother talked about to her mother on the phone.

There are days when I write aimlessly because I can't find a certain subject. At night, I end up throwing away what I wrote during the day. In the morning, I throw away what I wrote the night before. Sometimes I use the back of the same sheets to avoid wasting paper.

✣ ✣ ✣

It's still 2014. Today I realized I haven't written anything in a while, so I'm writing about my life again. The first thing is the meaning of my name: Afsun. Whenever I ask about it, I get the same answer. Its power seems beyond its meaning in Persian—a charm or spell. I don't know why, but even if I hear my own name a thousand times, it's still inadequate. I love my own name as if it were actually enchanted, and it makes perfect sense to me. Now that I'm a teenager, it's ridiculous that I'm obsessed with this kind of thought, but the pleasure I feel when I hear my name makes me believe that "Afsun" is the most beautiful and mysterious name in the world.

I'm writing these lines at school. Mr. Ivanov, my literature teacher, loves poetry. In fact, if it were up to him, he would read poetry aloud to us every day, finishing each class with a poem. I always get a warning from him because I'm passionate about writing, but I don't participate in class discussions. He's always mad at me for not listening to him. Well, since I don't know much about poetry, I'd better keep writing about my favourite topic: my life.

After I thought about it for a while, it made more sense for me to write the story of my life under my own name, Afsun, as I love my name so much. Sometimes I laugh at my own writing. Even though no one will read what I write here anyway, when I read my writing over and over again, it sounds ridiculous to me, so I begin again. Writing my story is not always ordinary. Sometimes a different story emerges.

I need a turning point. I feel like there's something exciting waiting for me, a meaningful incident, a moment that's going to make my life less ordinary. Although I have no idea what the reason for writing something meaningful is or how it's going to happen, my gut tells me I'm going to make it happen. A while ago, I even tried to "find a boyfriend" that I wasn't at all curious about because I thought my turning point might involve a love story or breakup pain.

My American classmate, Benjamin, is blonde, average-sized, attractive, and liked by the other girls—and he seemed interested in me. We finally started talking. Luckily, the "relationship" didn't last more than two weeks … there was no romantic love. But even this attempt to have a boyfriend and "separate" did not improve my ability to write. On the contrary, my writing has become even more illogical and disorganized. Worst of all, if this relationship had continued, I might have lost those pure feelings in me, the kind of love I dreamed of, and most importantly, my self-respect.

As I think about it now, the sunlight is filtering through the classroom window, warming my body, turning the room a sunny yellow like the fried egg I ate this morning. As my mind wanders, my imagination goes where it's never been before … I love travelling by car. Now if I were in a car, I'd get to where I wanted to go before my dream was over. But class isn't like that. You dream a thousand times. You imagine fighting with people you don't like, what sharp answers you'd give. Still, when you look at the clock on the classroom wall, only five minutes have passed. Finally, you finish the class and every day you think, "This was one of the longest hours in the world."

But something unusual occurred today. My brother hadn't done his homework—again. They called me to his school as if I were his parent. (If my mother had heard about it, she would have been angry enough to note it as a black mark in her children's school life.) There has never been a better opportunity to escape a boring literature class.

Mr. Ivanov always says, "You will understand the power of writing when you cry as you write and the power of poetry when your heart beats rapidly as you read it. It's like having your emotions touched." I wouldn't say anything to the teacher, but did the story I wrote mean nothing just because I didn't cry when I was writing it? Mr. Ivanov has another saying: "If a novel does not make its reader emotional and shed tears on the pages, then that novel is not written very sincerely."

Fortunately, I also know that no one's words should be automatically accepted, especially in these teenage years. I thought maybe I wouldn't cry when I was writing, but if someone else reads my writing (which is unlikely), I wonder if that person would start crying. I recall what my father told us today: "Be careful when I'm on the phone. Don't let your voice be heard at the other end." As I mentioned before, it's clear that my story would not affect anyone. I'm sure of it. Ha, ha, ha.

So, they called from my brother's school, and I left my classroom to look for Aziz. There was an Arab girl sitting next to me in my classroom, and my classmates told me later she went through my notebook after I had left. Since I wrote in Persian, I assume she didn't understand anything. I was a girl who returned to her love of writing after a long pause and wrote in secret all the time. Therefore, everyone who sees me writing naturally wonders what I'm writing about.

I picked up my brother from the principal's office. It's a good thing my mom didn't return the school's calls. She would've made us go hungry for a night as punishment.

"Why didn't you do your homework, Aziz?"

He replied indignantly, as if I had made a huge mistake.

"Our parents were fighting the other day! Dad was saying we were going to Afghanistan! I thought, if we're leaving Russia, I wouldn't need to do my homework, so I didn't do it!"

I laughed because I thought it was something that could never happen. "It can't be like that, Aziz. You know our father always says things he doesn't mean when he's angry. You *must* study. You have to be careful to do your homework because you're twelve years old. You already know that very well. You don't need to hear it from me."

Nevertheless, Aziz concluded, "If we're going to be leaving soon, what's the point of studying here now?"

CHAPTER 2

A New Year

I believe New Year's Eve 2014 will be as ordinary as ever. I haven't made any preparations. A lot of thoughts are racing around in my mind. The most interesting thing about my life is that I was born in Afghanistan and came to Russia with my parents when I was two. My dad's a car mechanic, and my mom's a makeup artist, so if you ask me if they chose their jobs *after* they came to Russia, the answer is yes.

My mother studied until grade twelve, and my father was an architecture student at Kabul Polytechnic University when he married the girl his mother chose before he lost too much time. His mother told him to get married and then go study or else she wouldn't make her milk halal—the common threat mothers use in my culture to intensify their message. It's like saying "or I shall never forgive you!"

Since my father's family was quite wealthy, my mother's father just married her off without consulting her. But my mother loved someone else at the time. Sometimes my parents fight because she still can't forget her true love. I've heard many times that they even reached the stage of divorce, but in Afghanistan, because divorce is so shameful, my father chose to leave the country instead of getting divorced. He even risked everything by dropping out of college.

My father tells this story differently from how my mother tells it. "A lot of things that are strange in other countries are very normal in Afghanistan," he says.

Sometimes I think about the fact that I was born in Afghanistan. I want to know how people live there. But more than anything, I wonder about Faryab—that province my mother told me about. One night, my father found the Afghan channels on TV and called out to me. My mother doesn't like to listen to the news, so my dad always calls me over to watch our favourite shows together. Jokingly, he says, "Girl, let's watch the shows we love."

When I came downstairs that evening, the president of Afghanistan was speaking. I think the combat mission my father was talking about recently, the one conducted by American soldiers, was handed over to the Afghan soldiers. The president was shouting about it. I asked Dad why the president was so angry. Although I speak Persian and Uzbek, sometimes I interpret some expressions differently.

My father said, "These invaders destroyed our beautiful country ... First the Russians, then the civil war, and finally the Americans ..."

In our house, everyone understands three languages, but only my parents and I know how to speak all of them fluently. Aziz and Asra could speak if they wanted to, but I think we *speak* a language better when we can truly understand it. That's why I'm always mad at my siblings. They think they're Russians just because they were born in Moscow. Okay, I don't have any objections if they love Russia, but they should remember where their roots are and preserve our family's culture.

After the president, the young news reader continued to deliver the news from where the president had left off. As I recall, he said, "Tolo TV news bulletin by Yama Siawash." His pronunciation was so good that it became my dream to speak Persian fluently like him. Some men have a special tone in their voice, a tone so clear and deep that it brings the listener closer. When I heard the presenter, I was amazed by his voice.

The news showed the true face of Afghanistan: war, terrorism, poverty, hunger, violence against women, and many other issues resulting from incompetent officials. It was the saddest and most deeply affecting news bulletin I've ever seen. My mother doesn't like her homeland. My father is in love with it. And for me, it has been a dream to see the mountains of Afghanistan and daily life there up close—to visit there just once.

Perhaps the only interesting thing about my life is that I'm from Afghanistan, but I live here in Russia as an immigrant child because war has prevented me from growing up in the country of my birth. My father says that in the 1990s, Uzbek or Turkmen languages weren't spoken in the capital of Kabul. Before coming here, my parents spent two years getting their visas and passports processed. While waiting to come to Russia, we stayed in Kabul for a long time. One day when Mom and I went out, people mocked us when they heard us speaking in Uzbek.

"I don't care if people make fun of me," my father said, "but just because I spoke in my mother tongue, the officials disrupted our paperwork. It was very difficult for me to face this—as if I had committed a sin."

There's ongoing war in Afghanistan. While the powers who start the conflicts can live comfortably in their own countries and speak their own languages, the ordinary people of Afghanistan are the victims. Sadly, they fight and kill each other—even over slight linguistic, religious, and ethnic differences. Sometimes I think this situation will continue as long as all the parties involved in these civil wars fail to resolve their disagreements among themselves. Politicians have not managed to put together a strategy based on mutual understanding and respect. What is clearly missing is social justice and integrity.

In Moscow, while Russians are welcoming in the New Year with parties and fireworks, more than 7,000 people have died in Afghanistan as a result of war. What's going on out there? Why is there always war in Afghanistan? That's all I've seen and read on the news ever since I was a young child. I can't stop wondering why those 2,000-year-old Buddha statues in Bamiyan were destroyed. Why did the Taliban leader order the destruction of those ancient works of art? What harm did they do? Did they take away the people's faith? They were just statues carved into the side of a cliff. They weren't that powerful. What was inside those Taliban heads that made them want to bomb such a historical treasure to the ground? What did they gain? I wish I knew the answers to these questions. In a magazine the other day, I read that if those Buddha statues had survived until now, they would be declared among the greatest wonders of the world, but unfortunately, they're gone forever.

I don't know about my dad, but after that night, I've always followed that news channel. Once a week, at night, I turn on my computer to find out what Yama Siawash will say about Afghanistan today. In between, there are some news presenters who speak Persian better than others. The topics are usually the same, but the specific stories are increasingly heartbreaking—from men whose whereabouts are unknown to the *mullahs* (respected scholars of Islam) who forbid romantic love yet take little girls as their brides, to the sight of people running around after bombings and explosions, children crying and hugging their father's body, and people picking up the body parts of their loved ones. Unfortunately, such gruesome scenes have become part of normal, everyday life in Afghanistan.

Today is March 21, 2015. I wasn't able to watch the news from Afghanistan for two weeks because of the intensity of my studies. I felt like I didn't know anything about the situation there. When I turned on my computer after two weeks, even the background behind the news anchor had changed. The sound of screaming girls was the first sound from my computer. There was a picture of a girl wearing a black hijab. Blood covered her head. I couldn't understand because they used Persian words I'd never heard before. In one video, around 200 men were beating her. They were hitting her all over her head and body with stones. In other footage, they dragged her by her hair. She was crushed underfoot … I thought my heart had stopped. Quickly, I got up and locked the door. I knew if my mom saw what I was watching, she'd take away my computer. At first, I didn't know why they beat up that young woman because I couldn't watch the news all over again. But I saw people protesting, holding banners and photos of a woman named Farkhunda.

I sat down and started researching. The internet was full of articles, photos, and videos about the incident. I think it's one of those events that can rock the world in one day. I clicked the first link that appeared on my screen. It led to a YouTube video. I learned that Farkhunda was a twenty-seven-year-old graduate of the Faculty of Theology. She was a brave woman who had merely questioned the amulets of the exorcist mullahs at the shrine. These guys claimed to be able to cure sick people miraculously by breathing on them. Apparently, Farkhunda had gone with a friend to the Shah-Do Shamshira shrine in the centre of Kabul. The mullah there was taking advantage of the superstitions of the people by selling them amulets written in Arabic. In the name of religion, he was making a profit.

As soon as Farkhunda witnessed this scene, she addressed the women gathered there. As a person who was educated in theology, she said, "There is no such thing in our religion. It is God who will give healing. Do not believe these superstitions." The mullah, fearing the collapse of his business, did what he knew best and started shouting at the people.

"Muslims grow up! Look, this girl burned the Quran! She's an infidel!" The people who heard him—from the beggars to the peddlers, to the bystanders wandering the streets—everyone began attacking Farkhunda furiously, without realizing what had actually happened. Those who could reach her used their fists and feet. Others used stones and sticks. They beat her with whatever they could get hold of. In a few minutes, everyone who was passing through the street got involved and tried to get close to hit or kick the girl. The mob grew like an avalanche.

In the next link, I read a similar news story that offered more horrifying details: Farkhunda, an Afghan woman was lynched in Kabul on March 19, 2015. After an argument with a mullah selling amulets in front of a shrine, she was attacked and run over by a crowd of onlookers. First, she was beaten. Then her blood-covered body was dragged by a car from the shrine to the street and then to the nearby river. The enraged mob didn't stop there. They started hitting her on the head again with rocks. Even that was not enough. In the name of "religion" and "honour," she was dumped into the shallow river. Her body was set on fire with gasoline. In their twisted way, the ignorant mob supposedly saved the honour of their religion.

She had insisted, "I am a Muslim! I have memorized the entire Quran! Muslims never burn the Quran!" But no one heard her cries. So, in less than a few minutes, the world discovered Farkhunda. The police didn't attempt to intervene. They couldn't even reach the scene of the crime in central Kabul. The most painful part was that one of the *female* police officers who was there proudly told the media, "I slapped her myself."

I was watching this news two days after it happened. Eyewitnesses swore there was no such thing as "burning the Quran." The accusation against Farkhunda was a total lie! However, I learned that only forty-nine people were arrested for lynching. The trial at the court in Kabul was settled after only four days. Four of the defendants were sentenced to death and eight others to sixteen years in prison, but eighteen of them were found not guilty, and all the others who were detained were released. Farkhunda's coffin was carried at the funeral by women's rights activists. This scene attracted a lot of protesters.

I couldn't hold back my tears. It was impossible to fall asleep. It's 5:00 in the morning as I write this. I can't erase Farkhunda from my mind. My eyes hurt from crying so hard. My heart can't accept the catastrophic death of a young woman as a result of such brutality and ignorance. I'm sure I'll never forget it. I've been on the internet searching for more new stories from the past two days. Looking at the photos of the poor girl, I first saw her in a black hijab, then her face and head covered in blood, and finally her unrecognizable charcoal body. I was trembling at the sight of those images. I can't help crying about this cruel world and wishing that girls were never born, especially in countries like Afghanistan.

✜ ✜ ✜

Around 10:00 this morning, my mother banged on my locked door. She said whatever popped into her mind at the moment to get a response. She was furious. I quickly slid my laptop under my bed and opened the door. My mother looked me in the eyes and asked me in a slightly calmer tone, "What happened to you?"

"I was asleep, Mom," I replied.

"Okay, but no more locking the door."

She removed the key from the inside of my door and left. With swollen eyes, I went downstairs. Surprisingly, Mom didn't force me to eat. This was a rare occurrence in our family. I was waiting to hear that familiar phrase from her lips: "Come on now, eat or you'll be grounded for a week." But she sensed something was wrong when she noticed my eyes. Maybe she thought I was sick.

When I looked in the mirror, I saw threads of blood in the whites of my puffy eyes. I returned to my bed and managed to fall asleep. I slept for almost twelve hours straight that day. At night, when Mom and Dad got worried and came to wake me up, I finally got up. However, I couldn't admit I'd been crying all night because of Farkhunda, so I lied.

"It's almost exam time," I said, "so I've been studying all night."

Mom was surprised. "Well done, girl. Now let's eat together."

I felt extremely hungry. I hadn't eaten much the night before. I remember telling myself I'd have a snack after dinner, but I realized I hadn't eaten anything at all in the past twenty-four hours. I got up and went to wash my face right away. Since the bathroom is right next to my room, I always hear my family's disturbing bathroom sounds. As the eldest child in the family, I got the single room: a small area of only two square metres. Even though it's a tiny room within hearing range of the bathroom, I always say it's a lovely, peaceful room.

Now I have to erase from my mind those horrifying images of innocent Farkhunda. I have to try to forget them. There's no other way. I know I can't bring her back to life—but I can't live with all my anger and sadness either. Last night wasn't the first time I had stayed awake in front of my computer until morning. I spend four or five nights a week like this, but I don't remember being so sleep deprived before. I was devastated by what I'd seen. Maybe I slept for so long in order to get those images out of my head.

I crept down the stairs. Everyone had already started eating. I hugged my dad and whispered in his ear, "Shall we talk after dinner?" He shook his head as if to say okay. I hugged and kissed my siblings one after the other and inhaled their scents deeply. Since I do this often, they weren't surprised. But this time it meant something different to me. It reminded me of Farkhunda's siblings. They all must have loved each other. They protected each other for sure, but then they were tragically separated from Farkhunda for such a senseless reason. Having this kind of experience in your family must leave you with the worst feeling in the world.

I prayed and thanked God that we were all together at dinner and everyone was talking about something different. Aziz is twelve years old. I get angry when our relatives in Afghanistan refer to him as a little Russian boy. To me, he's a very strong boy with unique thoughts. He doesn't like to be labelled "little boy," so I always call him "young man." However, he doesn't like that label either. "Don't make fun of me, sis," he says, but he probably knows himself that he's still not big enough for certain things.

Then smiling, my mom asked, "So, Aziz and Asra, shall we applaud your sister for sleeping fifteen hours straight?"

My brother and sister started clapping with their hands. My father clapped with his spoon and fork. Pretending to be a lawyer routinely interrogating criminals, my mother questioned me in a funny way. "Afsun, ma'am, we understand that this is the first time you have prepared for an exam. Would you like to tell us about this unusual situation?"

"Mom!" I protested.

Now everyone was laughing. I thought if I told them the real reason I couldn't sleep and showed them pictures of the tragedy, they'd be upset about what they were making fun of. But I can't show them those horrible images. Aziz and Asra shouldn't hate Afghanistan. After all, it's their parents' homeland, no matter what it has become now. Our elders have warm memories of that place. Although it stands out as bad today because of the war, Afghanistan has its roots in a solid culture and beautiful traditions. That's why I've been hiding negative recent events from my siblings.

We need educated people to see the Afghanistan of my dreams. If tomorrow Aziz and Asra get higher education and achieve their desired professional positions, they should go to Afghanistan and serve there. Some people may find my love of this country exaggerated, but I feel not only for my own homeland, but for all countries. I pray especially for Iraq, Syria, Libya, and many African countries that are struggling with hunger. All people who suffer are of the same value to me. May God help everyone. We have responsibilities as citizens, of course. Educated and equipped people can save these suffering countries. Those who are trained abroad should go back to their home country and try to end the ongoing conflicts and help people get out of poverty. Whether the reason is ignorance, a lack of education, or foreign invasion or intervention, I pray every day that the war ends and children will no longer suffer.

Dinner was almost over, so I cleared the table and went to wash the dishes. Then I joined Dad in front of the TV. Putin was giving a speech. As in any other family, one usual source of friction between my parents is the remote control. Will we watch Mother's show tonight—or the news? Tonight, my dad's choice prevailed. Putin began his speech in his usual way: with exaggerated seriousness and self-confidence. Such a cool, controlled manner suits that guy. He likes to project an image of running the whole country as smoothly as a flower. These powerful leaders don't want any turmoil in their own countries, but they don't mind destroying other countries by continuing their antagonistic behaviour. When I turned to speak to my father, I remembered Farkhunda.

"Dad, have you heard about Farkhunda?"

"Yes, how do you know?" He seemed surprised.

"I saw it on the news, and then I looked it up on the internet."

"Don't let your mother know!"

"I'm trying to hide it."

"You'd do well to hide it."

"Is that what happens in Afghanistan all the time?"

"Occasionally."

"Then why isn't the government taking precautions?"

"Here's the difference," my father explained. "Ninety-nine percent of people don't even hear about these incidents. In fact, dozens of women are being abused every day, and the events of people who believe in superstitions are part of everyday life."

"It hurts even watching it."

"I'm afraid there's nothing we can do, girl."

"But why do they kill people in the name of religion? Can't Muslims see these games? Or is this the religi—"

I hadn't even finished my sentence when my father gave me the hardest slap on my face I've ever had in my life.

"You have disbelieved, my daughter! Repent! I never want to hear such words come out of your mouth again!"

My mother and siblings were speechless as they witnessed this scene. In a split second, the father–daughter conversation was over. Now I likened my father to those narrow-minded bigots in Afghanistan.

Despite the slap, I continued. "If there's an answer to that, why don't you tell me? Teach me instead of being angry. Maybe I don't understand because I grew up here. You know that."

My father shut up at that point, and I ran up to my room in tears. He seems like a stranger these days. I know he's been talking with some men who are all part of some group. A few of them are in Russia, but I don't know exactly where. The rest are in Afghanistan. He's been talking with them on chat lines for about a year and a half. During this time, I've noticed some major changes in him. I liked seeing my father praying. He used to be like an ideal father, but now he seems stricter, more distant. For example, he now expects me to wear a headscarf. "Cover your head!"

I'm not against the hijab, but his approach should be more polite. Mom is already wearing a hijab, and we do what is required by our religion, but there should be some room for questions, for dialogue. My father didn't have to slap me. Lately, his behaviour is especially different towards Asra and me. He doesn't hug us or call us his "sweet daughters" as he used to. His entire attitude and tone of voice—and even the way he looks at us now—make him seem like someone I don't know anymore. Actually, I feel sad for him.

CHAPTER 3

Father's News

It was the last day of school for us. Mom and Dad came to pick us up for the first time. My father was unusually friendly. He wasn't even mad that Aziz was making a fuss about which one of us would sit by the window. My mother's face was a little frowny, though. She was talking very little. She seemed upset. Normally, she only looks like this whenever she can't find the lipstick or dress she likes when she goes shopping. I didn't care too much because I had a feeling something was happening. As soon as I got into the car, my dad made an announcement.

"Kids, I have news for you, and that's why we're going to have dinner at a restaurant. Your mother's a little angry, so she won't cook for us tonight."

"I wonder what the news is. Dad, are we moving into a new house?" Asra asked.

"No, my daughter," he replied. "It's something better. We're all going on a trip to a place you love and always want to visit. We're going to Afghanistan! Your grandfather's a little sick, and he wants to see you. You know, the last time we were there, the day we left to come here, Afsun was just two years old—"

"Actually, your grandfather isn't sick," my mother said, interrupting. "This is one of your grandmother's usual tricks to insist that we go there."

"Mom, let's go!" I said. "Look, our school is already on vacation. And don't you miss your family? My grandparents, your aunts, your siblings? Almost your entire family lives there."

"My dear, you do not know what I think."

Suddenly, everyone got quiet. My mother's deep thinking implied something. I could understand her thoughts more or less, but I wanted to know the reasons in detail. For the first time, even Asra reacted positively about Afghanistan. Our life was kind of limited with just our father, mother, and siblings. We were jealous of people who spent time with their grandparents, cousins, and other relatives.

We continued to discuss all this when we got home, but then we had to change our clothes quickly for dinner at the restaurant. As soon as I got out of the car, I caught up with my father.

"Dad, have you thought about what we're going to do if mom says no?"

"Don't worry. I'll convince your mother. You know she misses her family so much. She's just being coy."

My sister is very intelligent. She attributes everything to philosophy and mathematics. She discussed all the possibilities in eight minutes while we were changing our clothes. It usually takes me a long time to get ready, but I got dressed quickly tonight because we were going to discuss the vacation time ahead and our trip to Afghanistan. I called Asra's name a few times, but she had disappeared. *Where is this girl? We're going to be late!* I checked everywhere, including her room. No luck. When I got to the car, I was surprised to discover she was there already. She had somehow beaten me to the car!

As usual, everyone was looking at me as if to say, "You're late again." For the first time, I was glad I was prepared before anyone else, but somehow the expected pattern remained intact. As always, they asked me, "Why are you late again? Is it so hard to get ready?"

I don't know how time passes when I'm sitting in front of the mirror. I like to take care of myself and dress well. It's very important to me to look tidy and special—just like my name. I think every young girl wants to feel special. I know that what I'm saying and what I'm writing are the feelings of a sixteen-year-old teenage girl, but it's like a little neuron in my head has grown too big, and it makes me assume I know everything.

We left our parents alone inside the restaurant and went outside. I couldn't stop wondering about what Afghanistan looks like. My parents have told me sentimental stories about their homeland. Despite all the negative images of the political situation there, I'm attracted by Afghanistan's mysterious, peaceful, and natural places. I've always dreamed of these places. God, I wish my mother would agree to go so I can witness the big family atmosphere I'm curious about! At the same time, though, I'm afraid of the country's instability and injustice—the disturbing images of war and oppressed girls and women. Therefore, I've decided not to pressure my family about it too much.

As in every Afghan family I know here in Moscow, regardless of our many years of living here, the father makes the final decisions. We women are not even asked for our opinions. The men will just let us know when they've decided something.

My mother was calling us. A voice inside me whispered and prayed despite everything. "I wish we could go. I wish, I wish …"

I didn't notice it myself at first, but I had said my last words out loud, which is when I heard my mom say, "Guys, we're going …"

I was surprised. *Yes, God finally heard me! Yay! We can go!*

"… home now," she finished.

"Mom!"

"I'm just joking," she admitted. "Okay, we're going to Afghanistan, but let's be ready by next week."

I'm writing down the good news from today, and now I'm counting down the days. We'll be in Afghanistan in seven days. Oh, I'm so excited!

It's now Monday morning. I've been thinking about Afghanistan all weekend, imagining our first meeting with our grandparents and other relatives. My dad keeps making fun of me. The first thing he said was, "If I had known how you'd react, I'd have mentioned this trip a long time ago. Look, the princess woke up before everyone else. And this is the first time I've seen her get up so early and get ready since she was a little kid."

Yes, it's summer, and we're going to spend a month in Afghanistan with our relatives! Everything's going exactly the way I want it to. My father is happier than anyone else. He has never stopped thinking about his homeland, as if he could no longer bear to stay in Russia for another minute. Dad has worked so hard here. There were times when we didn't even see him for days. So, when we woke up for school in the morning, Dad would still be asleep. This trip is more important to him than to anyone else because he won't have to work when we're there. He'll return to his good old times that he describes as "bay bacha," or rich boy.

Before we left, I managed to meet up with my classmates Benjamin and Katarina in front of GUM, Moscow's famous shopping mall. We sat down for a while and chatted. Then we walked down to Red Square and the Teatralnaya metro. My friends weren't as excited as I was. I think the word Afghanistan intimidates people. As we hugged each other and said goodbye, Katarina began crying. As she boarded her train, she kept turning around to look at me with tears in her eyes, as if something terrible had happened … I tried to express the same degree of sadness, but I couldn't do it. The truth is I'm actually feeling more excited than sad about leaving Moscow for a vacation in the place of my birth.

Asra hasn't seen any of her friends. She doesn't like to say goodbye. She thinks it's unnecessary. Anyway, we're leaving for only a month, not for life. Asra is very smart, but what I don't like about her is that she tries to look cool and show herself as different. Sometimes she's so aloof she seems like a robot. Even so, for some reason, every parent we know wants to have a daughter like her. If she weren't my sister, I'd never want to be friends with her.

We're flying out at 4:45 this morning and we're going to the land of "afsun"—the land of enchantment. I've heard a lot about this country from my parents. Five out of the ten books I've read recently have been about Afghanistan. I know a little bit about the general situation there, but now I'm ready to face it.

We're flying directly from Moscow to Kabul Airport. I'm so excited!

We received our boarding passes at the airport, and our passports were to be stamped at the exit. All our documents were in my father's hands as we went through, and the border police said something to my father. We didn't hear it, but I assumed they were talking about our residence document. We were subjected to a special protocol.

I asked my father, "What's wrong?"

"It's okay," he replied. "They do it because we're holding an Afghan passport."

Luckily, we were allowed to board the plane. As usual, I'm sitting next to my dad. Asra and Aziz are closer to Mom, while I'm "daddy's girl." Despite his recent bad behaviour, I got on the plane with the hope that everything would be fine between us. Once we're back in Afghanistan, we'll be just like we were in the old days.

Our first destination is Kabul. Then we'll travel to Faryab, a large province in Northern Afghanistan. I've heard that Faryab was one of the most important regions of Afghanistan in ancient times, but people living under prolonged wars were deprived of the education and social opportunities they deserved. With a population of around two million, Faryab has a rich culture. Back in the less-developed days, the people lived a hard life. Nevertheless, my grandmothers used to tell some positive, heart-warming stories about Faryab, so I expect a complete paradise with its unique natural beauty.

We're finally here in Kabul. We took a taxi from the airport to the bus station. It took us about four hours in congested traffic, on uneven roads. Although I was exhausted, my attention was caught by the strange looks people were giving us in the hubbub of the big city. Sitting in the taxi, I had mixed feelings about all I'd witnessed so far. I cried and laughed for different reasons. I feel like an introverted prisoner with all sorts of thoughts and dreams running through my head about what awaits me in real life here.

We need to travel by bus to the Faryab region. The bus station is in Saray Shamali, one of the busiest places in Kabul. Along the way, what stood out was the small colourful houses built on top of the mountains. Some of the streets leading to those houses are narrower than a metre. I couldn't figure out how people managed to get through. And from what I understand, there's no water or sewage system, so they have to carry water in buckets for many kilometres. How do they get out of there in snowy weather? It must be an incredible nuisance. I've seen many pictures of these colourful houses on the mountains, and I've imagined visiting them. Finally, I can see them in real life! One of the first places I've seen in Afghanistan. They are more beautiful than I had imagined ... at least from the outside.

Some of the little kids who lived in the houses were rummaging through the garbage. Others were selling food and drinks on huge trays they balanced on their heads as they walked around the streets. I couldn't stop the tears from streaming down my face as I watched these children through the taxi window. What surprised me was their genuine smiles and innocent eyes. They seemed to be doing their job joyfully—despite their circumstances, as if everything in their lives was going great.

I was angry with myself at the time. We don't appreciate enough everything we have and how blessed we are with the opportunities given by life. Instead, we're disappointed about what we *don't* have! When I saw these children, I was angry with myself a thousand times! I learned my first lesson in Afghanistan from the little kids selling stuff on the street. I'm never going to complain again about what I don't have. Despite all the challenges, I'm going to appreciate the beauty of life and whatever is given to me, no matter how small. Wow, it seems like my perspective is changing rapidly.

Carrying things they wanted to sell, some of the children were approaching the cars stuck in heavy traffic. I thought it must be too tiring for them, but they seemed to know their job. One child was coming towards our taxi. I hoped she'd come to my window. Then the taxi suddenly moved forward and came to an abrupt stop. A little girl with a sweet smile approached my window. At that point, the driver asked me to close it.

"They'll bother you with their sales pitches," he insisted.

"No, Uncle. Let me talk to her."

"It's up to you," he grumbled.

When the girl began speaking, I couldn't help focusing on her eyes. They were probably the most beautiful eyes I've ever seen in my life, like the eyes of a movie star. This was the first time I've seen someone so beautiful and sweet living in such extreme poverty. My inner voice was saying, "I wish she could come with us." That's when I realized she was walking away.

"Wait! Where are you going?" I called out to her.

"I see you're not buying anything, sister. I'm in a hurry. Have to finish selling. My dad's sick. He's waiting for me."

"Wait! I'll buy something! Come here. What's on that tray? Give me something."

I opened my bag, found fifty rubles, and handed it to her.

"Hey, sister, what is this? You're giving me fake money?"

I asked my father for some money. Then I gave her fifty afghanis (less than one US dollar). She was about to hand me the change when the traffic suddenly accelerated, and the taxi driver had to move. A little farther away, when the traffic came to a standstill again, a small white hand touched my hand, which was resting outside the window. The hand was white because it was covered in dust. I knew it was the little girl's hand. She had come running several metres just to catch up to me, just to give me my change.

I was moved. Even in her situation, she still had a generous and honest heart. It reminded me of a saying: "People in Afghanistan are very proud. They don't accept any money when they don't deserve it." However, I believe good and bad exist in every society. It may not be right to generalize, but it's what crossed my mind when I watched this angelic girl running back to her spot with the change in her palm. The beauty and innocence of her eyes reminded me of images on some magazine covers. If she had been born in another country under different circumstances, she would turn out to be someone else in the future. Life is absurdly unfair.

Finally, the traffic thinned out, and we arrived at the station where we could catch a bus to Faryab. Allahdad, one of my father's cousins, was waiting for us there. As far as I know, he lives in Kabul. I remember one of the famous traditions of Uzbeks in Afghanistan. They are well known for their overwhelming hospitality. The fact that Allahdad came all the way to ask us to spend the evening with them showed how persistent they were about it. Since we knew our grandparents were eagerly awaiting our arrival, we had to decline Allahdad's invitation. Hopefully, we'll return to Kabul another time. We were exhausted and had come such a long way, so we thought we'd better head straight to our grandparents.

What stood out as my first impression of Allahdad—the first man I've had to deal with in Afghanistan—was his strange attitude towards women. Even though he hugged Aziz, he didn't talk to or even look at Asra and me. It was as if we were invisible. He and Dad went and bought tickets for a bus leaving at 5:00 p.m. Until then, he said that we should stay in the waiting area (which was like an inn) at the bus stop.

As we were leaving, my father's cousin turned to my mother. Pointing at Asra and me, Allahdad asked, "Is this how they're going to go?"

Asra reacted as expected. "Hey, brother, first, we have names. Second, is there anything weird about us?"

Instead of responding to Asra, the young man turned to my mother again.

"No way! There are thieves on the road, plus the Taliban militants. Wear burkas! You're going to go on a bus with young men for God's sake!"

Even if we obeyed his ridiculous command, what I didn't understand here was *how* we were supposed to wear a burka. After we left the airport, my father gave Asra and me *chadors*—head scarves—and I had covered my head as I had learned from my mother. But a burka?

Then Asra said, "Sis, what's wrong with this guy? Why doesn't he speak with us directly? Why doesn't he even look at us? Is there something wrong with his eyes?"

"No, he's looking at everybody else. I think he's just against us. It's kind of an example of respect to avoid making any eye contact with someone's young daughters."

Dad stepped in and said, "Yes, you're right, cousin, the bus leaves in two hours, so let's get something for the girls before then."

They wouldn't let us sit in the waiting room for about an hour just because we didn't have any immediate male relative with us. Unbelievable! We had to wait for my father. He and Allahdad finally returned with these long blue dresses and a bag containing other pieces of material. My father called us to the room at the bus stop where they had not previously let us enter without him.

An old man was cooking kebabs in front of a small white door, and a little boy next to him was shouting loudly, "Kebab! Kebab!" From the outside, it looked like an old house. When we walked in, we were greeted by a fruit-patterned table, a dirty white teapot, and various old cups on the floor covered in dust. I wondered how these people could eat here.

Then I heard my dad's voice. "We're going to be late, so get dressed!"

My mother pulled out a big piece of dark blue cloth from the bag. It was a burka. From that day on, I was sure I'd never be able to say that blue is my favourite colour. And I guess I wouldn't even say that I like the colour of my own eyes because of that.

CHAPTER 4

On Our Way

I had never seen a "dress" like that before. It has a different name in Persian. I had read it as a "chadari" before. So I had no idea what a burka was until I saw it. It was a long, wide piece of fabric. It had floral-patterned embroidery on the bottom hem, but other than that, it was just a flat piece of cloth, with no remarkable features. I don't know why the colour is blue. From top to bottom, it's like a cage with a rectangular mesh window at the front that looks like a fence so the wearer can see out. But if the window is not close enough to your eyes, you can't see anything. Of course, it doesn't look attractive from the outside. It's like they want to wrap us women in it to put us in a grave.

First, Mom put hers on, telling us, "Before we went to Russia, I used to wear it. It was white back then. Now it's blue." She was trying to make this burka business seem so normal.

Dad was getting anxious. "Come on, girls! Afsun, get dressed! Come on, Asra. What are you waiting for? We're late!"

Realizing the extent of the sexism here, I began to worry about this "vacation" in Afghanistan—despite Mom's reassurances that women don't have to dress like this in the cities of Kabul, Herat, and Balkh.

"Those black sheets are usually enough, but on our way to our hometown, there are people who still live with a backward mentality, so we women have to dress like this. There's a belief that if you don't cover up completely, you can't go to heaven."

I couldn't believe my mother was saying such illogical things. Her words made me regret coming here. But I tried to balance my thoughts. I knew my father wouldn't have allowed me to remain in Moscow alone.

As usual, Asra expressed my inner voice when she said, "Dad, I would never wear this piece of burka or whatever you call this thing. We already have black chadors. What's the point of that burka now? It's up to you. Buy me a ticket, and I'll go back to Russia right now, or I'll wait for you in Kabul, but I won't wear it! We can't even breathe in it! I'm only fourteen! I don't know why I should have to cover up like this!"

At that point, Asra burst into tears. Even though there's only a two-year age difference between us, I usually have to accept what she doesn't agree with, mitigate the tension a little bit, and calm things down in order to prevent a family fight. I usually just pretend to accept the situation and then sit down and write out my real opinions. Maybe they'd understand better if I addressed the issue face to face instead of writing about it. I don't like it when I accept everything they say without uttering a single word. I get mad at myself. *Look at Asra and learn! She's defending herself openly, but you just sit down and write what's happening here. Well done, Afsun. Go ahead and be the passive one, and let everyone take advantage of you.*

Mom taught me how to wear the burka, and I felt like I was gasping under all that thick fabric. My mom has asthma. Surely, the burka will make her condition harder to bear. Hopefully, she'll make it all the way without fainting. She can't stay more than two hours in any confined environment. Wearing those ugly tents, my mother and I walked out of the room like Afghan women fighters—in other words, like convicts sentenced to death.

I continued thinking about my mom trapped inside the suffocating layers and how she'd endure a fifteen-hour bus ride with bad road conditions. I had good reason to put up with this uncomfortable journey. A month will pass fast. I took a risk by agreeing to come to Faryab, my father's home province. I had dreamed so much about it that I felt as if peace and happiness were waiting for me there—the peace and happiness that I had dreamed of my entire life. We got on the bus. They gave us the first six seats in the left row, my mother by the window, my father next to her, Asra next to me, and Aziz behind us occupying both seats.

Usually, Asra chooses the window seat, but when we got on the bus, I was closer to that seat. So, for the first time, I got the seat by the window. It was so hot inside the bus that it felt like a sauna. I couldn't even breathe in the burka with all its heavy layers underneath. I was wondering about how to drink water, how to eat food. Most importantly, I was trying to breathe fast as the air was not coming in.

Within the first few hours of the journey, my mom fainted. We panicked. What I learned from some women sitting near us was that I could lift the front of the burka a little bit to get some food and drink. It was a tragicomedy. When my dad wasn't looking, I'd lift the front of the burka and sneak out. Best of all, there was a little space between the seats. I was thankful I could put my feet there.

At some point after the bus left the station, it stopped in a crowded place. Immediately, children and peddlers selling water and food entered the bus. They started pressuring us to buy something. Our bus had stopped near a hospital, and there was an ambulance right next to us. I rested my head against the window and looked outside. Finally, I was in Afghanistan, the land I had fantasized about.

A half an hour passed, but the driver hadn't returned yet. The sound of people vomiting in the back seats and the stench of sweat in the air had reached an unbearable level. I needed to find an escape, so I put on my headphones and started listening to "Get You the Moon." All the things I love were together: music, Afghanistan, and a car journey. But the unbearable atmosphere in the bus did not allow me to enjoy anything.

Luckily, the driver finally returned. He took something like a sheet from the bus, but then he left again. Some of the passengers stood up and objected to the delay. The driver came back—along with a clean-faced young man with amputated arms. Another man accompanied him. The two new passengers sat in the empty seat on the right side across the aisle from us. The man's laboured breathing indicated how much he was suffering.

Glancing around, he noticed the passengers staring at him as if to say "what a pity," so he apologized for the driver's delay.

"I am so sorry. My dressing took a while. I kept you waiting."

We were only about thirty centimetres apart. I could see his movements. I could see that breathing was an effort for him. When his friend made him drink water, I could sense the misery in his eyes. It gave me chills.

We continued the journey on broken, bumpy roads for another hour in relative silence. The bus moved like it was going to overturn at any moment. By the time we reached Parwan Province, the roads had improved a little. The driver turned on the ventilation system, and the atmosphere became a little friendly. People were sharing food with fellow passengers. The conversations began to grow. Except for the wounded man and us, everyone was talking. I could see my father's head. From time to time, he looked back and checked on us. The wounded man with his arms cut off looked at my father. Then his lips were moving, but I couldn't figure out exactly who began the conversation. I immediately took my headset off and heard my father's voice.

"Where are you coming from?"

"Shiraz, from Iran."

"Do you still live there?"

The man took a deep breath and said, "No, I was working there."

Inevitably, my father looked at where there were once arms, as if to say, "You don't have arms. How did you work?"

"I lost my arms," the man said with a wry smile.

"Get better soon ... I'm so sorry ... If you don't mind, may I ask what happened?"

In my head, I was like, *Dad, what kind of question is that? You've already asked, so why'd you bother asking if he minds? How can he 'get better'? His arms can't grow back!* I hate personal questions that require explanations in such awkward situations.

"No worries, man. I don't mind. It was a work accident."

Then my father said, "These things happen."

Again, I said to myself, *What do you mean, Dad? These things happen? What kind of solace is that?* I don't like it when people try to comfort others with such nonsense. They could simply say, "God give patience."

My father turned his body sideways in his seat so he could face the two men directly across the aisle as he continued the conversation. This time it was the stranger's turn to ask questions.

"Where do you come from, brother?"

"From Russia. We're going on a family visit."

"That's great."

"Yes, and these two are my daughters. That young man in the back is my son."

"Mashallah."

I found out the man who lost his arms was named Omid. That's what the other man just called him. I think Omid wanted to sleep, or his friend was becoming uncomfortable with my father's questions, because he asked Omid to switch seats and sit by the window. When the friend was helping Omid, my father tried to help as well by placing little pillows behind the man to make the space more comfortable to sleep in.

From her seat, my mother handed us various snacks. Since it was quiet again, I took my notebook and pen out of my bag. Finally, I was able to write about the events I'd witnessed in Afghanistan so far—along with my own reflections. The bus continued moving forward, but I didn't know exactly where we were. I guessed we were approaching a northern district. I could see the occasional green vineyard through the window.

I heard my father's voice say in a gentle tone, "No, brother, it's okay. I asked out of curiosity."

Omid's friend, who was now in the aisle seat, was talking to Dad.

"It's hard, of course," he said with a shrug. "You see, a month ago, his child was born. He was always dreaming of being reunited with him, hugging and playing with him, but his hopes burned out. He won't even be able to hug his child now."

Since Omid was asleep, the stranger began to reveal more sad details.

"Actually, he's my nephew. He waited at the construction site for a week, wounded. Maybe if he had been taken to the hospital in time, he wouldn't have lost his arms … You see, he had gone to Iran for work … to pay the rest of the *qaleen* and bring his wife from her father's house."

In Afghanistan, if the man can't pay the entire amount of the qaleen (or *toyana* in Dari)—the obligatory, agreed price for his bride—the bride remains in her father's home, even if the wedding has already taken place! She's not allowed to go with her husband until he pays off the debt! Apparently, while Omid was cleaning the elevator during construction, the elevator moved, and his arms got stuck between the floors.

Omid's uncle continued his story. "We waited a month for a visa but no luck. Then we went to Iran illegally. Hospitals in Iran refused to treat him because he had entered the country without a visa. One hospital gave him only medication and painkillers to keep him alive. Then I brought him back to our country through Herat. We had the treatment immediately in Herat, but it was too late. They cut off his arms, and now we're on our way home to Faryab. He was the only surviving child of my sister's four sons. He was carrying the burden of the entire family. His parents don't know he's lost his arms yet. We've got a lot of pain. Sorry, brother, I spoke to you too abruptly at first."

The man told Dad all this as he discreetly wiped away tears. He managed to compress what they had gone through into short, simple sentences. He wasn't able to elaborate. I was witnessing two weary young men.

How strange life is. While a child in one corner of the world is whining and crying just because he can't replace his iPhone with the latest model, we can see another child playing joyfully with the prosthesis replacing his leg that was destroyed when he stepped on a land mine.

According to a story I heard, a little boy was shot in the head, yet he survived because of a small flicker of the gun at the instant of the shooting, while the rest of his entire family was executed. Nevertheless, people still expected him to feel grateful for having survived the tragedy. Life is so complicated and unfair.

As Dad's conversation with the stranger ended, I turned my attention to my phone. I inserted the new SIM card we had bought, but it wasn't active, except for a few zones where I was able to text a little bit with a friend.

Despite my fatigue, the burka's heavy darkness, and the long, bumpy bus ride, I was falling in love with the nature of Afghanistan as much as, say, Majnun falls in love with Layla, and Farhad falls in love with Shirin. These are among our culture's epic love stories. I don't know exactly why I adore this country. Maybe because of its resilient people amid all the misery. For example, despite the pain of the young man who lost his arms, he had occasional heartfelt smiles. The fertile land, the unique mountains, the shepherds who do not think about tomorrow as long as they can find daily food, the natural smiles on children's faces, the old man with ripped clothes who generously shares his only piece of bread—maybe these are some of the reasons for my love of this country.

Although I've expressed regret from time to time for coming here, I can honestly say that I'm happy. Before the trip, I had bits of information about Afghanistan, but now I'm here to get a deeper understanding of everything, to get a closer look at the difficult life here and learn something from it. And now, I understand that the negative events I'm probably going to face here shouldn't make me feel pessimistic. Meanwhile, even though you're not allowed to smoke on the bus, some passengers openly flout the rule. It's disturbing, but no one complains. I guess, even if you did, no one would take you seriously. The funniest thing is the useless "no smoking" signs everywhere.

I didn't know how far in our journey we were, as I drifted off at some point. I had wanted to see Salang and its famous tunnel. It was midnight when we got to Mazar-i-Sharif. Mom woke me up to get ready to get off the bus for dinner. I was still asking about Salang when the bus stopped. We were at the city's bus rest stop: Ada-i Mazar. Many buses resembling ours had stopped for a dinner and washroom break. Some of the passengers got off to pray. A child started washing the bus, the drops of water splashing over my burka. It was actually refreshing. Then when I felt the wind on my skin, I realized how much I needed that relief.

There was another new thing I learned. In Afghanistan, men and women don't sit in the same place to eat. I wonder what kind of mentality they have. Why shouldn't my father sit down with us and eat? Why do women feel obliged to hide even from Aziz? My brother is just a twelve-year-old kid!

The air was still extremely hot. A large sheet was laid on the asphalt a little farther away. It was called a "dining area." Everybody was talking about something different. I was regretting that I couldn't see the places along the way. We sat in front of the chained door of a shop, and I took off the burka. Then my mother went over to the canal and began vomiting. We rushed to her aid, giving her water and napkins to wipe her face. Then we brought her to the dining area.

Trying to help her, Asra said, "Take a deep breath, Mom. It'll make you feel better. Put your head here."

I was so scared. I hoped my mother would be okay. We were huddled around her. Aziz was trying to talk to Mom, but of course, he had to make sure he didn't face any of the female passengers. Suddenly, I felt someone poking me in the back, and a woman's voice said, "Open up. Let her get some fresh air."

Asra, Aziz, and I looked at each other and made some space for this woman who had been sitting nearby. She held my mother's head in her arms and began massaging her chest. When she revealed her face, I saw a beautiful old woman. I had noticed her earlier when she was eating snacks under her burka. Women here are so used to wearing their burkas they've developed creative techniques for manoeuvring inside them.

"Thank you, Aunty," I said.

"You're welcome, sweetie. Don't worry. She's fine. It could be a result of the weather change. Eat something. Look at your face. You look pale."

My mother seemed to be feeling better. My father ordered some food, and it came in less than five minutes. The service was the fastest in the world. I'm glad that even in such a place, our restaurants service is fast. I already feel like such an Afghan girl now, happy and proud of the little things. Perhaps they prepared the food quickly because there weren't many options on the menu: three large trays of Uzbek rice (a dish that my mother always cooked) and two other dishes that I saw for the first time. I called to the woman who had helped my mom, along with her friends. At first, they didn't want to join us. They looked at us as if we were from Mars. But once Aziz left, they came over to us.

Our conversation with these strangers began with a typical question: "Where do you come from?" They turned out to be not what they seemed. Two of the women were nurses. The other one was a teacher. We sat down and chatted for a while. I will remember that time in the warm environment of Mazar-i-Sharif—with its yogurt drink and delicious *Uzbek palaw*, a dish consisting of long-grain rice with lamb, carrots, onions, and garlic. Anyway, that night was one of the most memorable nights of my life.

I've read that Western countries are spending a lot of money in Afghanistan, especially on health and social areas, but it seems all lies because of the corrupt politicians. We went through three different cities in the North. There was no noticeable improvement. Not even proper toilets. Maybe modern toilets exist in other parts of the country, but I've been wondering where they might be if not in public places like this one. Asra and I went to search for a washroom again, but we couldn't find one, so I gave up going to pee and went back. Many of the women we had dined with boarded different buses. We put those heavy burkas back on and returned to our bus.

CHAPTER 5

Welcome to Faryab

It was almost dawn, so we continued our journey. We would soon arrive in Faryab, the fatherland. The bus we took from Kabul Saray Shamali passed the cities of Parwan, Salang, Kunduz, Baghlan, Mazar, and Shibirghan, whose nickname used to be Little Moscow. With the light reflected from the bus, I could see the domed houses of the city. I fell asleep unintentionally because of road fatigue and dreamed that it was my eighteenth birthday. We were having a simple, informal party. I didn't smile in this dream. In fact, I had tears in my eyes. It was an extremely weird dream! And actually, kind of haunting. The atmosphere in Afghanistan was even affecting my dreams.

After another frightening dream, I woke up to the sound of explosions and gunfire. The sun had come up. Our bus was in the middle of the road. We were right across from a shop on the side of the road. It was almost obliterated by an explosion. I froze. Even brave Asra could not hold back her tears as she heard gunshots and the blast of an explosion for the first time in her life. Aziz rushed to my parents. My mother was trying to grasp hold of my burka. The bus filled with cries of terrified people … Blood splattered onto the window where my head rested.

God, what a nightmare this is! Please wake up, please! This time, I heard a gunshot closer to our bus. I saw a soldier lying on the ground. He was covered in blood, with the body of his comrade on top of him. It was *their* blood on our window … I was screaming, "What a nightmare this is! No! This can't be real! Oh, my God!" Asra gripped my quivering hand.

There were around ten Taliban guys. In front of a small shop on one side of the street was an overweight, old man. He had a long beard and was dressed in white local clothes. Holding a large knife, he was sitting calmly on the ledge of a wall. Standing on either side of him were two armed men, like in a mafia movie. Their faces were covered except for their eyes, which were outlined with a natural black substance called *surma* to make them seem scarier. There were a few other men stopping vehicles, forcing out any government officials or soldiers they found and killing them.

Unfortunately, my window was facing right that way. I could see an elderly man and other people being shot. So, there was a reason Asra didn't sit by the window for the first time. I didn't want to see all this. My father told Asra to shut her eyes. My mother had Aziz with her. As usual, I was the only one who had to stand strong in difficult times.

When it came to our bus, two armed youths, aged around fifteen to eighteen, and another man behind them entered the bus. Since they were holding radios, I guessed that someone must have reported our bus. First, they looked at Omid.

"What happened to your arms? Did you lose them in the army?"

"No brother, it's because of a work accident in Iran—"

"Don't lie!"

His uncle next to him intervened. "This young man is my nephew. I'm bringing him home from Iran. He's not a soldier!"

I could sense that Omid's uncle was suppressing his anger when he spoke. I imagine it was harder than he ever thought to have to answer for the arms his nephew had lost. Luckily, he had a document from the hospital. He showed it to them.

"You don't come and work with us like a real man. You go to Iran."

The young Taliban militants seemed tough and ruthless, but the one behind them seemed older and a little sane. He said, "Come on, Makhdum. Move on! Take care, young man."

Then they walked past Omid and his uncle and continued down the aisle. They went through and questioned all the men. They looked at Dad for a long while.

"Where's your beard, filthy infidel?"

Dad was trembling. He started to respond, "Sir—" and was slapped hard across the face. I thought I was going to die at that moment.

"We are coming from Russia. I swear I won't shave anymore."

According to his vow, my father would no longer shave his beard. The man looked at my father again and shouted, "Heretic!"

"Whose woman is this?" His eyes were on Asra, his hand on his gun.

Before my father could finish saying, "My daughter, sir," the old man who had been sitting on the ledge outside entered the bus. He was obviously in charge.

"What's the problem, Yozarsif?" That was the name of one of the young men.

"Commander, I'm talking to this beardless American infidel. He claims they're from Russia. He doesn't have a beard, and his daughters don't wear their burkas properly."

The old man was so overweight that he was struggling to breathe as he spoke.

"Where are you coming from?"

"Sir, from Moscow—"

The Taliban guy named Yozarsif slapped my father again and shouted, "Don't just sit there! Get up and answer! What were you doing in Russia?"

"Sir, I'm a mechanic."

"How many children do you have?"

"Three."

"So, you said, 'Let me bring fewer children like the infidels, and let our prophet's generation go away.' Well, I don't like you! Why'd you come back here?"

"Sir, I came so that my children would grow up with Islam. It was difficult being in Russia. They dress too openly there. We've come here to live with Islam in our own homeland, so my children do not become derailed."

There was a moment of silence.

"Oh, well ... First thing, buy that girl a proper burka."

Then my father said, "I'm a friend of Yusuf Makhdum, sir." The Taliban guy looked surprised. He seemed to recognize the name. He thought about it.

"You come outside. Let's talk. You've got Islam now. You're going to get these Russian kids back on track. Well done."

After this disturbing interaction, my father got off the bus with the Taliban guys. I could hear voices of other passengers behind me saying, "God forbid, man."

Inside the bus, my mother, Asra, and Aziz were still crying convulsively. My mother was going to faint. I was holding her asthma spray in her mouth and giving her air when my father returned to the bus.

One of the Taliban guys had slipped a piece of paper into Dad's pocket. The message was simply "WE'LL SEE YOU." My father looked like he didn't have a drop of blood in his face. He came and tried to calm my mother, and the driver started the bus. My mother, Asra, and I made sure that we adjusted our burkas securely to conceal our entire faces.

As I was taking care of Asra and Aziz, I looked back at where we had just left. I found out the place we had passed was called Faizabad. Although everyone was a little less agitated, I'd say we had just experienced a scene from a horror movie. All the beautiful sights of nature that came my way after that could not erase the images of civilians being killed right in front of me and the blood of that soldier dripping down the outside of my bus window.

We passed the districts of Shirin Tagab and then Khwaja Sabz Posh. When I looked out the window, I noticed an interesting design on the glass. The drops of blood that had splashed on it were scattered by the wind and dried up. It now looked like a red painting, a work of abstract art on glass I had seen somewhere before. The image was like the work of a famous artist, but this time, it was not a painting. That red wasn't paint. It was the blood of someone who would never again meet the loved ones who were waiting for him. Those people whose bodies were covered in dust would never be reunited with their children. The children waiting for their fathers would look at the door of their house hopelessly, with a continuous flow of tears.

The men who killed the poor soldiers as "heretics" didn't even realize they were actually firing bullets at religion and humanity by shouting *"Allahu Akbar"* (God is great) with Russian-made *Kalashnikovs* on their shoulders and American-designed iPhones in their hands. The heartless members of this terrorist organization were also extorting foreign aid meant for the children they had orphaned. I couldn't understand what kind of mentality it was that could slaughter civilians and steal from orphaned children. Did the Taliban militant, whose name I heard was Yozarsif, and thousands of others like him know who they were serving with the killing machines they carried on their shoulders? Couldn't they have chosen to work towards the development of their country and serve its people instead of focusing their energy on terrorism? I was shaking.

My brain was exhausted from the first day of our journey. I fell asleep, but this time when I woke up, we were on our way to push out of our minds the nightmare we had witnessed on the road. We were about to reunite with our big family. When we finally got a phone signal, it was my dad's phone that rang first, and he began talking. All the relatives and friends were waiting for us at the entrance to the city of Maymana. As I looked out the window, the rolling hills and the lambs grazing on them represented a complete rural scene. It was a serene, picturesque landscape—just as I had imagined. Finally, I could see a crowd waiting to greet loved ones.

My father turned back to us and said, "Kids, look over there! Your family is there! You see. They've been waiting for us."

At that point, the driver declared, "Oh, thank God, you've finally arrived here alive."

A few minutes later, the bus stopped. My parents quickly said goodbye to the other passengers, and we got off. I could see how happy the people were that all of us had arrived safely. All the passengers were welcomed with hugs. Everyone had tears in their eyes.

Asra, Aziz, and I just stood there with our suitcases where the bus had stopped, first because of road fatigue, then because we were still in shock. We didn't know quite how to react to the terrible events we had witnessed. It's like we were frozen. While everyone was busy embracing my parents, my paternal grandfather approached us. We used to talk online.

"My Afsun!"

"Grandpa!"

He put his hands on my head, removed my burka, and threw it over the bags. It felt as if an enormous load had been lifted. I was like a newborn baby emerging into the light. The fresh air hit me in the face. The wind grabbed my hair, which remained uncovered. As I looked at my grandfather, I felt the air flowing between the strands of my hair. I tried to kiss his hands, and he kissed me on the head and hugged me. He hugged me so warmly I felt a sense of relief I'd never felt before, not even on my mother's lap.

"How are you, my dear?"

"I'm fine, Grandpa, thank you."

I enjoyed the atmosphere until Grandma, my dad's mom, stepped in. It seemed as if they had brought an entire tribe. The conversations seemed like they'd never end—not until everyone, one by one, was embraced and kissed by all the women, and all the older men were kissed on the hand. If they were younger, we just exchanged hellos. If you're in an Uzbek-Afghan family environment, you know they ask everyone one by one, "Are you okay? Is your mom okay? Is your dad okay? How was your journey? Who is staying in Russia? Is everyone over there okay?"

In turn, we were questioned individually. They started with me and moved on to Asra or started with Asra and moved on to me. Don't ask me to explain. It's a very funny custom. It's called *ahwal porsi* (a meet-and-greet) in the language of this place. Like its name, it's different.

I could see a lot of young men, but no young girls. Another thing that bothers me in this society is that young women are not allowed to step outside the house without permission, while their brothers can walk around freely. If you're a girl, you're obliged to sit at home and cook for others. How frustrating and unfair!

After being on our feet for what seemed like hours, we settled into the cars that were waiting for us. I was next to Aziz.

"You know, sister, ten cars came to pick us up."

"Really?"

I counted the cars. Indeed, there were ten cars. I remembered Putin's convoy. Even though the models weren't the same as his, their flashiness seemed the same to me. I felt like I was in a James Bond movie.

I didn't know exactly where we were, but in the last few minutes, I realized my grandparents couldn't figure out where to go. I thought I'd make a video of our way home, but my plans didn't work out. All four of my grandparents were there. Before the cars started moving, Dad's father turned to us and announced that we would be going to Oncha Arlat, his vineyard. "Ma'am, you go to my sister-in-law's car. We need to get the food we made at home and our supplies for a week."

It was just Asra, my Aunt Nuriya (my mom's younger sister), and me in the back seat of the car. From what I heard from my mother, my aunt is a recent law graduate, the only lucky girl in our family.

"Congratulations, Aunty," said Asra. "You were at the university, so I couldn't call you."

"Thank you, honey," said Aunty Nuriya. "Make some room so I can sit between you two."

From those first few minutes of our conversation, Aunty Nuriya seemed close and friendly. Our destination was near the city centre: Oncha Arlat, a small district of Maymana. My grandparents had several houses and ties there, but I don't remember much after the exhausting bus ride and especially after all the terrible violence we witnessed.

Everyone stared at our convoy as we passed. It was exciting. Uncle Zafar was driving the car I was in, and the people created a fun and crazy atmosphere on the journey. At one point, the asphalt roads came to an end, and we entered the narrow streets full of stones and soil. One car could barely make it through.

Finally, we reached a big gate. When we got to the vineyard, we saw more people waiting for us. My cousins who stayed at the house in the city were also coming to meet us there. At first glance, the lush nature made me feel like I had come to a corner of heaven. I had never seen a vineyard this big and beautiful in my life. In the middle of the vineyard were some slaughtered sheep, large cauldrons, and teapots.

The relatives prepared everything very quickly. Even though I felt drained of energy, I managed to finish the obligatory ahwal porsi with everyone. Asra and I were hardly ever apart during this time. I know she was sleep deprived. By nightfall, we were both ready to collapse.

"I've been looking for a room for us," said Asra. "There's no vacant room."

"Let's speak with Aunty Nuriya. She'll find a place," I replied.

I found my aunt in the kitchen.

"Please find us a place to sleep. We're exhausted."

"Come on, girls. Come with me."

Suddenly, my grandmother intervened. "Take them to the room where we put the presents. I have the key in my pocket. My hands aren't clean. Come and get it."

In a room full of sweets and lots of food, my aunt cleared enough space to lay a mattress for two. We fell asleep immediately.

CHAPTER 6

Gender Divide

I could barely open my eyes. My lips were dry. How many times did my aunt try to wake me up? But I couldn't wake up. She was waiting at our bedside. When I focused and looked up, I saw two other girls in the room with her. Wearing long dresses, they looked like angels of death in a horror movie. They gazed at us as if we were extra-terrestrials. I think I'll have to face more of this awkward attention while we're here. Maybe our clothing style makes us seem different to these curious girls. Everyone's so enthusiastic, asking us countless questions all the time.

I quickly recovered and got up. It sounded like the middle of the night, but I could hear people talking and laughing from outside in the spacious sitting area called the *sofha*. I woke Asra up too. One of my great-aunts saw us through the door, which was slightly ajar. She came in crying and hugged me.

"My sweet angel!" I understood she had been planning to greet us yesterday as soon as we arrived, but her husband didn't allow her to go. She shouted at the girls, "Why are you just standing around here? Get food for them!"

I wondered why anyone would have to cater to us, but I didn't say anything. They disappeared and came back with a huge tray. It was filled with enough food for at least ten people. Asra and I sat and ate for almost an hour as we talked with the girls—although we were disturbed by the yellow light of the room and the mosquitoes flying around it. All the girls took turns introducing themselves. Everyone wanted to participate in the conversation. One of them was the granddaughter of my father's cousin. Whenever Asra and I spoke, the girls smiled and looked at us admiringly, telling us how sweetly we spoke Uzbek. Actually, I was overwhelmed by all this flattery, but I admit that the way they speak is different from our speech.

We went out to the "women's area." Approximately forty women were gathered, as if it were a wedding. They've got a lovely space. The courtyard contains two distinct sitting areas. The sofha extends across the width of the big house, but it is nothing like the sofas in Moscow. It is not a piece of indoor furniture but an expansive elevated slab of concrete covered with thick carpets and then a mattress. Curtains of colourful fabrics separate the men from the women, allowing the women to sit at ease.

Many of our grandparents' neighbours came over just to greet us. I tried to prepare myself for the values and customs of this place. For example, you should stand up for the visitors and kiss them one by one, and then you sit down and remember them one by one. It's a tiring but charming tradition.

After I finished my salutation mission, I went to join my mother. I heard women saying things to each other such as "what a beautiful girl." They commented on our skin, height, eyes, and so on. I asked my mom if she needed anything, and when I was sure she was okay, I went back to the room where the girls were still gathered. Asra was busy with her iPad, and the girls sitting there couldn't take their eyes off her. I love Asra so much, but sometimes she annoys me when she acts like no one else is there. It must be a great skill to be able to treat people this way, without paying attention, acting as if they don't exist. The situation of the teenagers and children in this place is heartbreaking. It seems that the war has taken away everything from them, including the hope in their eyes. Strangely, they examine our every move with a curious gaze.

I entered the room and began talking. That introverted girl in Russia had become someone else entirely in such a short time. It felt good to learn the customs of village life and discover the feelings of the people here. The girls were asking funny and interesting questions. I enjoyed sitting at that time of night and chatting with these genuine, kind-hearted people.

Aunty Nuriya acts possessive sometimes. From the first night, she wanted me to stay only with her even though she was secretly texting with someone at the same time. What could I do? There were still real people who weren't busy texting when I was conversing with them. Those young girls were deserving kids with natural curiosity and love.

As the hours went by, most of the girls left to go to bed, so we were just a few. The remaining girls were wondering about our clothing style in Russia and asked to see photos from there. They were all telling different stories. Although all of us were teenagers, some of them looked a bit older. But just because they look older shouldn't be a reason for getting married. Another thing I learned is that they sometimes call each other "sister-in-law" as a joke.

Curious, I asked, "Why do you call each other that? You're not married, are you?"

The only answer came from Gul Chehra. "Actually, Afsun sister," she said, "from the moment we are born, our uncles, close relatives, and whoever loves us call us 'daughter-in-law,' and from that day on, everyone calls us that person's daughter-in-law. For example, that nut-nosed girl, Guljan, was delivered by my grandmother, and the birth was difficult, so my grandmother said, 'I've worked so hard for this. She's going to be my grandson's wife now.'"

Guljan added, "My father said that if we give a girl, we'll get one in return, so they promised Gul Chehra to my brother."

"What do you mean?" I asked. "Are you really engaged? Fifteen is an extremely young age. Until you grow up, maybe you'll fall in love with someone else. Maybe you'll want to marry someone else."

"No, sister, there is no such thing as marrying someone you choose—even if we love someone. No one can love us because everyone knows we already belong to someone else. No one would ever reach out once they know that."

I was in shock. Girls are exchanged here like goods to be bought and sold or bartered! The two fathers negotiate a deal. You took my daughter, so I take your daughter for my son. What about the dreams of these young people? What kind of future can they have? Why can't these girls fall in love and marry as they please? Will the lives of Afghan girls continue like this forever? Get married at fifteen and spend your entire life serving your husband's huge family? What a pity!

Anyway, let me get back to my conversation with Gul Chehra and Guljan.

"And what do your fiancés do?" I asked.

Gul Chehra replied, "The two of them work in Iran. They save and send money, so the qaleen will be prepared. Then they'll come back to get married and then go back to Iran."

Gul Chehra explained all this as if she had memorized it, like the situation was just routine work that everyone else accepts. She told her story with a smile. Or perhaps she was just pretending to be happy. I don't know. Anyway, it's a disturbing yet interesting situation.

"How old are your brothers?" I asked.

"My brother is seventeen, and Guljan's brother is twenty-six, I think."

"Seventeen years old? School status? How does he work at this age?" I couldn't believe it.

"We're not doing well financially," replied Gul Chehra. "Most people here don't like school very much. If they return to the village after completing their studies, the Taliban calls them heretics and says, 'Your dead body will not be washed.' In other words, no funeral ceremony for you since your body won't be accepted. Girls have no right to go to school anyway, and boys use it as an excuse. But some of them have studied and have good jobs in the government. Some Afghans leave the country, like my brother, at fourteen. He sends money. We prepared the house, and if he sends money this time, we're going to have an engagement party."

Guljan intervened angrily. "No, it's not just your brother and me. It will be *your* engagement party as well!"

It's almost like Guljan and Gul Chehra are in competition with each other. They don't really want to be in that situation, and they try to laugh about it. I don't want to pressure them with a lot of questions, but I'm genuinely curious.

"Girls, are you really happy?" I asked.

I didn't hear anything for a few moments. Finally, another girl joined in. I don't remember her name, but I think she was the gardener's daughter.

"Well, they should toss their hats in the air with joy. Here, many other girls their age end up becoming an old man's fourth or fifth wife. I know a fifteen-year-old girl who is going to marry a fifty-five-year-old man! Guljan and Gul Chehra are lucky they are marrying young guys as beautiful as horses."

As beautiful as horses? This girl is only fifteen, I said to myself silently as I listened, *and her fiancé is eleven years older than her! She doesn't even know him and they're calling her "Mr. Abdullah's bride" rather than her own name. She hasn't even completed her own childhood, and now she's going to become some stranger's wife and spend the rest of her life looking after his many children? I think that's why this society remains ignorant.*

I didn't really believe what that other girl said about a man of fifty-five marrying a young teenager. There's no way any man can have the mentality to marry someone his granddaughter's age. I didn't like that girl. I thought she was lying and making fun of the girl she was talking about. Thinking about what she said and how happy she was for Guljan and Gul Chehra, I couldn't focus on other stories. I was confused. It was time to leave, and the girls were called by their mothers. Oddly, they seemed afraid of their moms. As soon as they heard their mother's voice, they vanished without saying anything. I moved to the group in the other corner of the room. They were cousins and other relatives who lived in the city and were in a better socioeconomic condition. They said those girls I was talking to were "peasants, just maids," and they wouldn't have allowed them into the room if I hadn't been there. I just walked by and sat next to my aunt.

"Oh, finally, Miss Afsun! If you hadn't come … Were those ugly girls more important than your cousins? Anyway, look how much fun Asra has been having with us."

It was my cousin Dilshad who said this. She's the one I can't stand. I didn't appreciate her pretentiousness and sarcasm, but I didn't want to give a harsh response.

"I'm sorry. Those girls are as precious and beautiful to me as you are. They were just sitting there staring at you, so I went over there to be polite."

Then I heard one of the women say, "She's so naïve."

Another cousin said, "Don't worry, she'll be like us in time."

These cousins were busy with only two things: texting and complaining. I understand there's jealousy among them, but I think most of them keep each other's secrets. That evening, I sensed a divide among them. In the first group are those innocent girls who can't do anything for themselves. They're restricted, as if they're tied up, while the girls in the second group are allowed to do many things, but all they care about is clothes and romance. Not all the women and girls in town are as comfortable and free as my cousins. Actually, not even my cousins are completely free. They were texting from their mother's phones or secret phones and computers.

I was so tired. I got up to go to bed in the same room with those smug girls. For the first time in my life, I slept in a room with about twenty other people! In the morning, I woke up so slowly and saw them sleeping almost on top of each other. Although our time here has been tiring, it is still worth exploring Afghanistan and understanding different lives.

CHAPTER 7

Beyond the Vineyard

I've decided to go up to the hills beyond the vineyard. There was a sound of cows coming from somewhere nearby. My grandmother and other women had buckets of milk in their hands. Back in Moscow, I had joined a group of teenagers who said "we don't like milk" to prove that we weren't kids anymore. However, when I saw the white milk inside the buckets, I wanted to take a bucket and drink it all.

As I walked down the middle of the vineyards towards my destination, my grandmother called out, "Girl, where are you going? Watch out!"

I replied, "Don't worry, Grandma. I'll be right back!"

In many regions of Afghanistan, people still use outhouses far from the house. I was beginning to wonder how we were going to get there at night. It's a very different toilet. My brother wouldn't go there at night. He was terrified of monsters attacking him in the dark. I laughed when I thought about Aziz as I passed the outhouse. Grandma couldn't see me anymore by that point. *So, are those other women going to stop me, or is it really dangerous to go up there? Come on, keep walking,* I told myself.

There was only one tree up on the hill. It seemed so lovely standing among green, yellow, and various other colours. How gorgeous were the leaves glistening in the sunlight at that height. I wanted to reach the tree, so I kept walking through the vineyards. As I was sneaking out, someone called behind me.

"Hey, girl!"

I kept going, telling myself to ignore the voice and not look back.

Then the voice said, "Don't go wandering alone! There're young shepherds out there. Anything can happen, and you don't have anything with you to protect yourself."

Finally, I turned around. There was a girl in a long dress. She was taller than me. The sun hit me right across the face, so I couldn't see well. Rays of the sun shone from both sides of the girl's head, making her seem like an angel. The closer she got, the more beautiful she looked. As she approached me, I just stared, admiring her. Her height, body shape, and face came into greater focus, and I thought I was enchanted. Her long dress enveloped her, stretching all the way to the ground. Only the tips of her shoes were visible. A tall, slender girl has a special kind of attractiveness. I thought she must be a model. *What's she doing here? Is she in these clothes because she's a model for a photo shoot or maybe an actress for a movie shoot? No, where would a movie star come from? Then my grandfather's also an actor?* I laughed to myself.

While I was thinking about all this, the girl came and stood next to me. No way! It wasn't only her height. When I looked into her eyes, I could see my reflection in those green and hazel eyes. They glistened like glass, two eyes in two different colours. God, she was beautiful! It was hard not to feel envious. But when I looked at her hands, I saw dough stuck on them. Her hands were calloused as if from hard work. There was a wound, slightly covered by the dough, between her thumb and her index finger, but I could see it from the edge.

She was talking, but I didn't catch everything she was saying. Her accent was so unusual. Actually, I wasn't really paying close attention to her speech at first. All I could concentrate on was her face, her eyes, her posture ... I asked myself how a person could be so beautiful.

"What are you doing here? Are you okay?" she asked.

I shook my head. "I'm good, thank you."

Although I had a lot of other thoughts and questions in my head, all I could manage to say next was "And how are *you*? What are you doing here?"

"I'm fine," she replied. "When I saw you alone up here on the hill, I wanted to ask ..."

"I'm sorry, I don't remember you. It was so crowded last night."

"Oh, but I wasn't there last night."

"What's your name?"

"I'm Birishna. I think you're our gentleman's granddaughter?"

"Yes, I'm Afsun."

"Oh, yes. I've heard your names. Afsana, Asra, and Aziz."

She pronounced only Aziz's name correctly. She mispronounced my name, but it was fine. The way she pronounced it was cute.

"So what does your name mean, Birishna?"

"I don't know."

We were both awkwardly silent for a moment. Although I didn't want to go farther up the big hill anymore, I said, "Let's go. Let's go up higher."

"Okay."

It was damp and dusty where we were sitting. I was all dirty. I grasped my dress and tried to shake the soil and dust off. Birishna didn't seem to care about getting dirty. She got up and helped me. Once again, she was standing next to me. At that moment, I told myself, *Wow, she could be tallest girl in Afghanistan!*

As we began to walk slowly, I said, "Tell me, what do you do here, Birishna?"

"Nothing much. Housework …"

"You didn't go to school, huh?"

"No, I couldn't go."

"Well, so you live with your parents, don't you?"

"Yes, I live with my family. Eleven brothers and sisters, sisters-in-law, mother, father—and a husband."

"Wow—I mean, Mashallah! Eleven brothers and sisters … What? You have a husband? How old are you?"

Now, I understood that age was no issue here. Girls get married so young here, and the saddest part is they're married off against their will.

"My mother says I was born on a snowy night. My grandfather wrote my cousin's date of birth in the Quran, and I'm nine months older than her. Now my cousin is seventeen years old … What age am I?"

I understood the answer right away—between seventeen and eighteen. However, Birishna was still calculating with her fingers.

"Oh, sorry, my calculation is not good," she said. "I'm between seventeen and eighteen."

"And where's your husband?"

"He's moved to his village, but he'll be back next week."

"Good. So, what are these wounds on your hand?"

I wish I hadn't asked. Obviously, the question hurt her. She took deep breaths and her eyes reddened. She seemed to be in pain.

"These wounds? The other wives of my husband made these." Then she rolled up her arms slightly, and there were more wounds. They had made minor injuries to her face as well. I was shocked. I didn't know what to say. Her husband's wives?

"What do you mean?" I asked.

It was unbelievable! She was looking at me, but I was speechless. She was very young, only seventeen, but two years ago, she married a man who already had other wives! How could they let her do that? God, why didn't anyone help her?

It seemed like someone was listening to her for the first time in her life. Birishna's eyes were still red. If she looked up a little bit, the tears would start flowing uncontrollably. I was so confused. I couldn't digest what I had just heard and respond to it.

"I'm sorry, what did you say?" she asked me.

"Nothing, nothing ... How many times has your husband been married?"

"Including me, he has had five wives."

"What? How's that possible?"

"The first wife died in childbirth, God bless her. Now there are four of us."

"So, why are the other women beating you?"

"I don't know. They don't like me. They speak to me sarcastically. Because of them, I can no longer go to any weddings and gatherings. They humiliate me everywhere, and they say to me, 'Look into your eyes. You're the devil. You're the servant that God does not love.'"

Birishna couldn't hold back any longer. The tears came flooding through her beautiful eyes of two different colours, like diamond grains, like a sudden rain. I'm someone who always says a person needs to cry sometimes. I believe crying can relax you, but I think this girl was crying for the first time in her life. Her throat seemed blocked, and the sound of her hiccups hit me hard.

"Don't keep talking if it hurts you."

"It's okay," she said. "I'm always home. I have no one to talk to."

"Why did you marry this guy?"

"I didn't want to. He is one of the richest men of our village ... One night, five of my father's lambs were killed by a fox, and when my father sadly told the story at the mosque, the bastard pulled my father into a corner and said, 'That girl of yours, Birishna, give her to me, and I'll give you fifty lambs in return.' My father agreed. So, within a week, they gave me to that old man for fifty lambs."

"Oh no! How old is this guy?"

"Sixty-seven, I think."

"Come on! Did you have a wedding?"

"No, his other wives came and asked me. Then on the first day, one of them hugged me while she laughed in my face. She pinched me in the back and said, 'There's no daylight for you in this life any longer.' I cried a lot, but it was in vain ... The imam came in the afternoon to conduct the ceremony, and my husband stayed that night at my parents' place. So that's how my life was ruined."

She wasn't talking slowly anymore. We were getting closer to that beautiful tree I had wanted to reach. I wasn't interested in its beauty anymore. I just wanted to give this poor girl a chance to unburden herself and relax in the shade. Finally, we reached the tree and sat under it. I was where I wanted to be. As she wiped away those relentless tears with the edge of her headscarf, I understood how a young girl's dreams could be smashed overnight.

"And then what happened?" I asked.

"A man I had never seen before—he was older than my father, and I secretly loved his son and played with his daughters—well, this older man jumped on me as soon as he walked into the room. He was a wrinkled old man. He was so disgusting! I looked at his beard, and he put his teeth and lips close to my face and said, 'Come on, kiss me, girl ... Oh, you're so soft and white, like bread...' When he kept saying, 'Come on, hug me,' I thought, *God, let's get it over with! God! I know it's a bad dream. It's going to be over. This man is my friend's father! I've seen an old photo in their room once before. It's just a nightmare. It's not real. It's almost over, girl ...* But I'm afraid this disgusting nightmare is never going to be over. I screamed. I cried. My feet, my legs, and my head were shaking wildly as I tried to break free, but it was no use. He pinned me down. His whole weight was on me. I used as much power as a skinny fifteen-year-old girl has, but he was pressing against me so hard. He was biting my breasts. I was frozen from the trauma.

"My mother claims I didn't say a word for a week. I cried, staring at the wall. I remember a week later, when my brother came, I started to pull myself together. When I went to the toilet, I still had blood on my body, dried blood all over my legs … I asked myself, crying over and over again, if that old man wanted blood, then why didn't he go cut one of his lambs and take her blood? I got crazy. It hurt so much. I washed myself. I thought this wouldn't have happened if my mother had been there for me at the beginning of all this. My mother was away in the highlands that day when my father made the deal. Every year, they take the animals to graze there for months. My mother went to help my brothers. She returned on the wedding day. Nothing could undo the deal. Nothing was left to object to."

I was stunned. I listened without commenting. It was clear that Birishna needed to pour out her story. She continued.

"What I don't understand is, what does a kid who grew up picking cow dung until the age of fifteen know about marriage? I had no idea what would happen on the wedding night. My mother was always so tired that we never talked. My sisters and sisters-in-law, along with the other women in my family, asked me only one thing before that night. 'You're a virgin, aren't you?' When I asked what a virgin was, before I could even get an answer, his other wives came and picked me up and we went out into that dark night. How many times did I think about committing suicide in the first week? But in a ruined house where more than fifty people live, I wasn't even free to kill myself. Every time I tried, I'd get caught. Now I just try to lose myself in my books. I hope one day soon his filthy body will be in a grave. Regardless of my age, he used me like a machine. I pray at night, crying that he will go to hell!"

Birishna was still crying convulsively as she unravelled every horrific detail of her story. Not for a second did her tears stop flowing like a river. I was too shocked to respond. Since I've never been in such a frightening situation, I couldn't tell her that I understood what she'd gone through. All I could do was put my hands on her hands and let her go on. It was a relief for her to be able to talk openly about her life. I encouraged her to keep talking.

"You said you didn't go to school. So how did you learn to read?"

"When I was small, we were going to learn the Quran at the mosque. I learned the alphabet, but I couldn't continue. I mentioned my brother earlier. He's different from the rest of us. He dropped everything and went to the city when he was little. He stayed there in a mosque and went to school. When he came to visit us on vacation after the wedding, he was very upset to see me like that, but he couldn't do anything. Maybe he could've, but when thousands of people stood across from him—my father, uncles, relatives, neighbours, and briefly the whole village—he couldn't make a sound out of desperation. Anyway, he spent his whole holiday with me. He taught me to read, but most importantly, when I was feeling terrible, he was a salve to my wounds. From that day on, I'm always trying to read a book. If my dad or my husband sees me reading, they'll be mad, so I read at night by the light of a flashlight I stole from my husband. I have three books. My brother brings me books every time he visits, and I read them dozens of times, even by spelling them out, but with excitement."

"It must've been hard, but I'm glad you learned to read."

When I looked around at the natural landscape from the top of the hill, everything looked like paradise. But by our third day, my initial fascination with this place was starting to wane. Although some of the girls from the city seemed to be doing relatively well, the situation of Birishna and countless other girls like her made me ache. It's already difficult enough being a girl in this world. What I heard shattered my heart. Tears were streaming down my cheeks. My nose was red from crying so hard.

"Have you ever loved a boy around your own age?" I asked her.

"Yes, but he had no idea that I loved him. Actually, he's kind of my son now. That's what hurts so much and makes me like a rock. To be now the stepmother of the person I loved … The last time my husband forced me to go to his home was on a Ramadan holiday. He has forty-seven children and twenty-three grandchildren. I was there for a week. One night, I stayed at the house. I said I was sick while everyone else in the family was visiting a neighbour's house. They insisted that I join them and kept calling my name, but when I didn't get up, they gave up. I stayed at home with only one of my husband's daughters and one of his sons, the one whom I loved, in the other room. It was just the three of us in the house. I was sitting there looking out the little green window at the lights on the mountain when someone entered the room. It was him, Ramazan, my stepson. He stood right at the entrance and simply said 'hi' in a quavering voice. I said 'hi' back, and then he turned on the little light. I could see only his head and face. It was a very faint light, but this is the first time I had ever seen him so close up. He sat down near me. My heart was beating fast. The love of my childhood, the person I dreamed of living my life with, was sitting in front of me now, but he's my husband's son ... Unfortunately, life's greatest pain had been granted."

Birishna continued her story. "We both looked at each other for a few minutes without saying anything. Ramazan was crying. Why? Did something happen to him or was he sick? There was no point in thinking I wouldn't touch a man until I got married. I put my hand on his shoulder and said, 'Are you okay?' He kept quiet for a moment, and then he said, 'How much I loved you, Birishna. I watched you from the corners while you were playing with my sister. I dressed up hoping you'd notice me. I watched your lambs and wandered around. I left for the city to make a good life for you. I studied in the city for two years, but look what life has done to us. How could my father do this? You're the same age as some of his grandchildren. He touches the body of the girl who adorns his son's dreams with her beautiful eyes! I'll never forgive him.'

"At that point, we heard his sister's voice. Ramazan got up fast. As he wiped away his tears and began leaving the room, he whispered, 'I'm going to love you until death, Birishna.' It's been 480 days since then. I die every minute, every second. Every morning, I wake up thinking I'm going to kill myself. On Fridays, that scum comes to us, and every time I cry that there can be no worse torture than this. I never heard the voice of Ramazan again. I could never look him in the eye and say, 'I love you too.' I ended up marrying his father when it was Ramazan I loved. I can't bear to think about what he said. At least, our feelings were mutual. His sister said, without knowing it was me, 'Ramazan is probably infatuated with someone. He repeats that if anything happens to that girl, he's going to die.' I wake up every morning praying that nothing bad will happen to him. I know I can't be with him. For the rest of my life, I will be the widow of this scumbag, his father. Maybe I'll die in the corner of a room thinking of my forbidden love."

CHAPTER 8

Birishna

The sun was so intense that it made me forget about the time. Everyone was calling me loudly from the vineyard. I think they were worried.

"Come on, we'd better leave now. It's been an hour and a half since I left the house unannounced. Everyone must be worried about me."

I ran down the big hill with Birishna. We both had swollen eyes. Now I understood what a painful life this girl has had. I had likened her to a foreign film actress when I first met her. After hearing her story, however, I thought, *Maybe I'll look at life from another perspective. Maybe I'll be able to believe that it's love that connects people. Maybe I can comprehend how good my life is and learn to be grateful. Or maybe I can at least listen to girls like Birishna and do something to help them one day.*

I ran with these thoughts in my head. Birishna stopped on the way and called out, "Afsana!" She was still saying my name wrong, but I didn't care.

"Yes?"

"I love you so much. I'm glad you came here, and I'm glad I finally met the first person to hear me."

Birishna walked me to my grandparents' house. Then she quietly left. Everyone was so angry with me for having disappeared. But for the first time, I wasn't upset about their reaction since I knew they were angry out of worry and love.

Everyone else had finished breakfast. I was the only one left. I went to hug my mother and then sat down to eat. I couldn't stop thinking about poor Birishna. Stuck in my mind was that age gap between her and her husband.

I made a simple calculation—sixty-seven minus seventeen equals fifty—over and over again. Fifty years between them! I sat next to my mother and rested my head on her hands. Thank God my family isn't like Birishna's. At least, I know they wouldn't marry me off against my will, but it doesn't stop there. Just because it didn't happen to me, I can't forget that most of those little girls in Faryab are going to face Birishna's fate sooner or later.

I've been going up the big hill for a week now to meet her. Yesterday I waited for hours for her by our favourite tree, but she didn't show up. We have to go back to the city soon, so this morning, for the last time, I went up the hill again.

Despite the terrible incidents on the road on our way here, my first week in Afghanistan has been enjoyable and eye-opening. New people, new stories. A different fashion sense and different personality types. One is rich, and she sees no one but herself. Another is poor but has a good heart. One is a distant relative, another a cousin. In short, I met about a hundred people in one week, and we had a great time.

It's as if we've been living here for years. Aziz has been bombarding Mom for a week with his questions about Afghanistan. Asra stays in our room most of the time. Mom attends to all the women. Guests keep coming to visit us. During our time here, I think I've seen my dad only once. Although the recent changes in him aren't normal, I haven't really thought about why because of all the activity around me. It's been so busy and intense.

They slaughtered a lot of animals the other day. Aziz was with my father. He saw the whole thing. It affected him badly. I had to sit up at night and console him. I woke up late in the morning. Apparently, Birishna had been waiting for me for a while. I was angry with myself for being late. Finally, I sensed that familiar wounded hand touch my shoulder from behind. I heard her voice, but it sounded different.

"Hey, Afsana."

"Oh, Birishna, how are you girl? Where have you been?"

"I'm fine. I've been waiting for you every day, starting with the trees, walking up the hill, but I didn't see you yesterday. I came to your home one day when you were reciting the Khatam Quran, but your grandmother gave me so much work that I never saw you."

"Oh dear, I'm sorry. I've been dealing with Aziz. They slaughtered animals in front of him. The poor boy hasn't slept at night for three days."

"Oh no! I hope he recovers soon."

"He's not sick. He's just scared."

We both smiled. When I looked at Birishna closely, she didn't seem as upset as on the first day. In fact, she was smiling. I wanted to ask the reason, but it wasn't appropriate. I held back asking because happiness is her right too.

"Afsana, do you know what happened?"

"No, girl, tell me what happened. Is your husband dead?"

For the first time, I knew the news of someone's death would make me happy, and I know it's not right to think like this, but never mind. As long as bastards like him are alive, the underdogs will be crushed.

Birishna answered my question with a laugh. "No, of course not!" she said. "My brother came. We chatted all night last night and I told him about you."

"Hmm. So that's why you're happy. Good for you."

We had to go home today. If I were late like the other day, my grandmother would tell Grandpa.

Birishna's feet never went backwards—like she'd run away if she could, but even if she did, she knew she didn't have a home to accept her. We sat down and had a little chat. She was talking like she was used to it, but I thought maybe she was just pretending to avoid upsetting me. It seemed like she regretted making me cry the other day, but I don't regret it, because she's my first friend here. Besides, I've learned a lot from her. I was also moved by the desperation of the girls living in the countryside, so if I had to go back to that day and listen to this girl, I would do it again for hours.

"Birishna, we're going to the city today. You know, my uncle works for the police, and he couldn't come to see us because of the security situation. He was very upset."

"Well, then I'm happy for you."

She spoke haltingly, as if she were communicating in a foreign language … She was having a hard time speaking Uzbek.

"What people are you from?" I asked.

"We're Kochi, which is nomadic, but since we've always lived in Faryab, we speak Uzbek instead of Pashto. I can read Persian as well."

The Pashtuns are an ethnic group in the south—I know that—but I hadn't heard of the Kochi before I met Birishna.

"Our tribes relocate according to the seasons and do not have a home of their own," she explained. "That's why we have that name."

"Do you keep moving?"

"Normally, yes, but my father was smart in his time and served our master, and he took this land. That's why only we have a house, but we still sometimes go to the mountains with the tribe to feed the animals."

"That's different. Is your husband here?"

"No, from what I hear, his second wife is sick. He's taking care of her. I hope he never comes back."

The two of us joked and laughed, and even Birishna's smile was different. I thought, *What a hard time these beautiful eyes have seen. I wish I could do something for you.*

"Do you have a phone?" I asked.

"What are you talking about, girl? Women don't have phones. They're evil devices. Don't you know they corrupt you?"

For a moment, I was surprised. I thought how naïve this girl was, but then she started laughing and said, "That's what they say about it. It's shameful to have a phone. We had a neighbour who talked to someone on the phone and then ran away."

"Don't worry too much about it," I assured her. "It's a lie. People just do what they want or don't do it. It's not about the phone itself."

"Anyway, my parents think it's evil, so that's why I don't have a phone."

"Never mind the phone. If I come back here, I'll find you somehow. And if you hear me coming, come to see me."

I approached her for a hug, but she was embarrassed by the smell of dung on her body. She kept me at a distance.

"I'm not very clean today."

"No, it's okay. Come here."

I was wearing a dress I had bought in Moscow. She moved towards me, looking at my dress and then looking down at her own dress. I hugged her. Hugging her felt different today. She began crying so much that it was like we were saying goodbye on our deathbeds.

Then she said, "For the first time in my life, someone loves me, and it's beautiful, and I want to see you from now on, Afsana."

"Take care of yourself, princess."

"Princess?"

"It means beautiful girl, like an angel."

Her eyes lit up even more. "Is that me? No way!"

"Of course, it's you, Birishna. That's the truth."

I walked away gradually. I turned around and saw that she was still waving. She waved like a child. She had told me once before that when the NATO peacekeeping forces came to Faryab, she was a little girl, and they gave presents to the kids. The NATO soldiers would wave "bye-bye" as they were leaving. It was from watching them that she learned how to wave. I laughed to myself. What a funny girl. I imagine she had many more stories. As long as some incidents remained just "stories," it was okay. Otherwise, they could become nightmares. As I looked back at Birishna, I felt like I'd left a piece of my heart inside her hands. I felt a pull to go back and hug her one more time and tell her not to worry.

I ran back to her. Maybe it's not right to get so familiar with someone in such a short time, but I knew that our hearts were intertwined as if we were sisters. She had told me everything about her life. I felt like we had a connection from the past. This time, I was really late and ran to my grandparents' house without looking back again.

✢ ✢ ✢

A few months ago in Moscow, the principal gave me a punishment simply for being late for school. I found the courage to protest, saying, "Nothing is normal in this country! They steal our lives. They're unfair. Not even the president and state officials do their job properly here."

Wow! I made such a big deal out of a trivial thing—an undeserved punishment for being late for school. Then I come here to Faryab and see some of the world's *real* problems! Probably, the more comfortable you are, the more ridiculous the things you worry about are. At the time, I thought I was very well educated and knew everything. Maybe I was just an all-knowing person in my small world under Moscow's conditions. It seems like childish nonsense to me now.

Look at Birishna. She's married to someone her grandfather's age, and she still says, "God help me." I've seen all this and I've realized something: I'm going to appreciate what I've got. I'm going to be thankful. But I'm going to fight and never give up. When I complain about my life, I have to remember the determination of the girls who were born into poverty in a war environment and persecuted just because they happened to be born female.

Conditions are different everywhere. Maybe you're telling the truth, but maybe the concept of "truth" depends on the circumstances. Maybe you could have been born in a better or worse place than the country you live in, but you have to remember that even if you were born in heaven, you still may not feel happy. Or you may complain about why the fruit of your trees didn't grow in the shape you wanted. That doesn't mean you're selfish. That's the nature of human beings. They've always told us to change life the way we want, but changing that life doesn't include the society around us. Society doesn't change the way we want it to. We can only love the society around us when we change our own life the way we want … I'm laughing at myself now. My inner voice seems a bit wiser these days.

I'm out of breath. They were waiting for me on the other side of the waterway. I leapt across a narrow portion of the brook to the other side where Grandma was picking fruit.

"Girl, what were you doing out there?" she shouted when she saw me. "Is that how you pass the time? You're a girl, so watch out! Your life depends on it."

The peasant women nearby seemed surprised when they heard my grandmother's warning. I laughed because all I had done was jump across a fifty-centimetre space. Now, according to my grandmother, I might lose my virginity because jumping involved opening my legs. And of course, losing one's virginity meant that a girl's life was over.

"Never mind, don't worry about it," I replied. "Where's my dad?"

Then my mother appeared out of nowhere and pinned me against the wall.

"Where do you disappear to every day?" she demanded.

"I go visit the vineyard. It's a beautiful place."

"God, I hope you finish this holiday with the best of luck," she said. "Hurry up. Get your luggage out of the room. We're leaving now."

Thanks to Grandma, those blue burkas were laid out when I came back with my luggage, and all the women were looking for their own burkas to put on.

"Mom, what's this? Do I have to wear this tent again? No more!" I was defiant.

Asra made fun of me, interjecting, "Yes, princess, the game's over. Come on."

Wearing all those layers of fabric again was a nightmare—and it hurt. How did women walk around wearing these heavy things? I marvelled at their patience.

"It's rude to talk like that! Shut up!" my mother yelled, pulling my arm so hard I almost cried. Reluctantly, I agreed to put the burka on again.

It's hard to describe where we're staying. Life here, despite all its challenges, can be explained by the concepts of purity and naturalness. If I were to ask my classmates back in Moscow to describe this environment, perhaps they'd say, in the words of our literature teacher, "The sun entering through the space between the lush tree leaves warms my body, and the sounds of birds caress my soul." Mr. Ivanov would be surprised to hear such a sentence from me.

We're going from my grandfather's vineyard to the house where my father grew up. I'm excited, but I also wonder when I'm going to come back here and see Birishna again. I put on the burka layers and started walking like a newborn duckling, my mother in the front and me trailing behind. What I'd like to know is whether I have to wear this thing for the entire month.

Wearing those burkas, we waddled to the door and up 500 metres from the vineyard where, this time, four cars were waiting for us.

My "king father," whom I admired two years ago, is a different person now. Here in his hometown, he seems like a tyrant—like many of the men here. When he sees his own wife and daughters, he doesn't run towards us as he did in the past. Mom refers to this change in behaviour as "the Afghanistan effect," but I've observed this transformation in his attitude over the last two years. Sometimes I even think my father might have returned to Afghanistan for other reasons, not just to visit his family.

I was going to ride in the black Toyota we came in the other day. My brother, sister, and I usually rode in three separate cars. Everyone from the city was coming back with us. Just as I was about to get into the car, my Aunt Nuriya approached me. She was also wearing a burka, of course, but hers looked elegant. She was attractive even in a burka. Her hands, the way she held them in the middle of the burka, her fingernails, and her watch suited her. Her hands looked beautiful against the burka.

"I'm mad at you," she said abruptly.

"Why?"

"You didn't like me very much. You always stayed away!"

"No, no, Aunty, it's not you. I just chose to be with nature because I couldn't get used to the sudden change. Everything was so new to me here."

"Okay, but from now on, no more wandering around alone and trying to get used to this place, okay, my dear Afsun?"

"Okay."

I climbed into the car, my mother got in next to me, and Aunty Nuriya followed. I leaned my head against the window. It was relaxing to listen to my music while riding in a car. I love car rides. I was willing to ride in that car for hours or even days in the place I had always dreamed of seeing, but—there was only one "but" in my mind—I just hoped my aunt wouldn't talk too much. I thought that if she could pass this test, I could be friends with her. I prayed she would leave me alone during the car ride, at least, so I could enjoy my music uninterrupted.

We were in the third car. As we slowly left the front entrance, I put on my headphones to listen to the songs I always listen to: "Ta Ki Nabashi Hamdam Jani" from Sarban, "Gülpembe" by Bariş Manço, "Dorogoi Dlinnoyu," "Podmoskovnye Vechera." These songs were on an international compilation album. People were surprised that I also liked Selena Gomez and Yildiz Tilbe. Sometimes they'd ask how I know Turkish, American, and Arabic songs. The album I listened to had songs by artists I had never heard of before. I think listening to music isn't about understanding the language. It's more about feeling the emotion that the rhythm of music provides.

Mulberry trees lined both sides of the dusty, rocky roads where large stones were buried. Full of leaves, the branches hung down so low that they touched the car. Even some of the hanging branches of the extremely tall trees made contact. When you open the window and look up, you know what fresh air means. One street, after another. It was like we were playing hide-and-seek in the streets. I refer to every view I see here as paradise, but at the same time, what's going on here is hell. That stark contrast shocks me.

After the unpaved, narrow streets of Oncha Arlat, where our cars had to struggle to pass through, we headed towards the river. There was no bridge across the river, but cars could pass where there wasn't much water in some spots. Before reaching a spot where we could pass, we continued along the river. Even the sound of the car's tires on the stones sounded good. By the way, as long as my dad didn't see it, my aunt and I could pull up the curtain-like bottom of the burka and look around. Children and middle-aged women carrying water on their backs looked curiously at our convoy. Even though I don't know why, I think we seemed exotic to them. Some of the women were washing colourful laundry in the flowing river water. Little boys were swimming in their *perahan tunban,* the traditional clothes of Afghan men and boys. Some of the children managed to stay afloat when their extremely wide pant legs became like balloons. Dozens of beautiful, naïve, and kind-hearted children manage to be happy here no matter how little they have.

About an hour and a half later, I could finally see paved streets. Kohi Khana is one of the central districts of the city of Maymana. The river's water was running low, maybe due to the small dams on the road. When we came to Kohi Khana, there were two ways to go.

On one side of the river, the Kochis lived a nomadic life under white tents. They reminded me of Birishna. She said they had to move from one place to another, depending on the season. They're always trying to find warm places. It's hard for them to spend the winter under the tents. Since they live in warm places, their skin colour is darker. Other physical characteristics also distinguish them from the locals. Since the majority of those who normally live in Northern Afghanistan are Uzbek or Turkmen, they have small noses and almond-shaped eyes.

I could sense how sad and helpless Birishna was when she was telling me about the Kochis. I remember her saying, "If my father had gone to school and grown up with educated, cultured people, maybe our life would've been different." In fact, I think what's happening in Afghanistan is that a lot of these people are uneducated, so they live with the mindset of a hundred years ago, which leads to conflicts.

The other side of the river—the side where those innocent children were watching us—was the way we were going. The road was covered with dirt and gravel in order to get across the river to the asphalt road. The person driving our car talked all the way. He was one of my mother's many cousins—that's how he introduced himself. I don't know what he said. I was listening to music the whole way. We were going faster now, and the houses looked a little different.

I took off my headphones. I didn't know exactly where we were, but the place names sounded attractive. Maymana seems relatively small. In fact, the entire city is almost as big as one of Moscow's most densely populated neighbourhoods. That explains why everyone knows each other.

I learned that my two sets of grandparents were neighbours in Afghankot. I really don't understand why my maternal grandparents moved so close to my paternal grandparents since my two grandmothers are not too fond of each other. Anyway, it's kind of convenient that they all live so close to each other. At least, I can go visit my other grandparents when one house becomes too crowded. This way, they don't have to compete for our attention and complain that I'm too attached to one side of the family or that I've been spending too much time in one house. Being able to go back and forth between the two houses effortlessly, I can make both grandmothers happy!

The streets seemed to get a little wider, and the houses were very close to the river. Then the streets began to get a little narrower, with shops on both sides displaying their products in the middle of the street. Since merchants occupied the whole street, cars could barely pass. I found this scene fascinating. It used to be the city centre and one of the most important places in Faryab. The paved road petered out, and we turned right on the first street, which led us to a slightly higher level.

My grandparents were the first to get out of the cars. I could sense the rivalry below the surface between my two grandmothers. There was some discussion about which of the two houses we would sleep in, but since this vineyard belongs to my maternal grandmother's family, she won this time. The two houses are about thirty centimetres from each other. One has varnished wooden doors, and the other has black and green doors. Since my grandfathers are friends, they agreed on the selection of wood and the style of the doors. However, when the workers came to paint them, the two women chose different colours.

We were kept waiting outside for a while. Then they burned an herb called *esfand*. It smelled like incense. At that point, they brought out a freshly slaughtered lamb. There was a flame on the tray. They poured esfand on it and directed the smoke towards us. Apparently, according to Persian tradition, it has magical powers. It's supposed to protect us from the evil eye and negative energy.

Arriving at the front door of the house, I saw a winding iron staircase on the left. It leads to something like a separate, raised room for guests. They call it a *darwaza khana*. It's where they first welcome guests to their home.

They rubbed the blood of the poor lamb on our feet. Entering the house with the blood of an animal on my feet? I didn't know what it meant, but it sure freaked me out. I immediately wiped my shoes with a wet cloth and went in. As soon as I entered the main part of the house, I got another surprise when they lifted the curtain, revealing the backyard on the right. It was a huge area like a vineyard. Various flowers and trees were visible. I've seen pictures that my aunt and grandmother had taken here, but I didn't know that it was actually the backyard of their homes. It looks like a warm, comfortable house. Hopefully, we'll have a good time here.

CHAPTER 9

Aunty Nuriya

It's been almost three weeks since we arrived in Afghanistan. When I look back on our vacation so far, except for the traumatizing encounter with those Taliban guys, I can say that our time here has been a fairly positive experience. The number of people I've met is astonishing. I can't believe I have so many relatives—more than I had ever imagined before coming here. Up until now, we haven't really left my grandparents' homes. They even opened a usually locked backyard gate that separates the two houses so we can go back and forth freely without having to go around to the front. Before we return to Moscow, I want to meet more girls like Birishna. I'm so curious about her.

I understand that the flow of visitors never ends. We're going to spend the rest of the days as guests for everyone. For example, if we go to one aunt's home in the evening, we must go to another aunt's home for lunch the next day. I'm tired of eating. It just seems weird to prepare so much food every day. By the way, we stay with women all the time. No one here watches the news. I don't have the internet. I'm living in a country where I don't even know what's going on out there in the rest of the world.

I'm in the room on the second floor of the house. Actually, there's no real second floor in this house. They just call it the upper room. I think it's the right way to describe it because there's a spiral staircase out there and it has nothing to do with the first floor. When I come into this room, I always feel like I'm in another world. It's different and beautiful. My Aunty Nuriya, Mom's younger sister, always comes here to attend to me.

I'm starting to like her. She didn't bother me in the car on the day we arrived. But I don't really find her very interesting or bright because she's always talking about men and getting engaged. She keeps checking her phone and trying to show me photos of various people. She assumes I'm going to be interested in them. I don't understand why I would have to mess with any of them when I won't be staying in Afghanistan forever.

The upper room has two windows on one side. Their frames are painted white and have large glass panes. There are three or four curtains hanging back to back on the windows so the sun won't damage the carpets. When I look outside, I can see some children playing. I can also see my grandmother's lovely garden. My paternal grandparents' house is similar to this one. The exterior architecture of both houses suggests how well my two grandfathers get along with each other. At the same time, it's clear from the different flooring and specific items inside the houses how my two grandmothers are not exactly best friends. Their rivalry can be seen in how both of them try to reflect their individual identities inside their houses through distinctive paint colours and other aspects of the decor.

Young girls who visit with their families try to be friends with me. Some of them seem hardworking and intelligent, while others try to impress the mothers of young sons—in other words, potential husbands. In Afghanistan, most marriages are based on money or convenience. It's really interesting. However, I still don't understand how they call such a loveless marriage a marriage of logic.

Fortunately, my aunt finished her phone call. She turned to me and said, "Afsun, I need to see my boyfriend right now."

"Well, see him then."

"But you know, I can't. Will you help me?"

"How's that?"

"If you say you're bored at home and want to go to the bazaar, they'll let you."

"But that's a lie."

"No ifs or buts. Do you want to spend all your time in Faryab in this house?"

"No, of course, but—"

"Come on then."

Actually, it was a good idea. After all, it's perfectly normal for my twenty-five-year-old aunt to be in love with someone and think about marriage, and it's none of my business. I also thought it would be nice to see the bazaar and the markets there. Another thing I was curious about was all of the restrictions imposed on women in Afghanistan. They say it's impossible to have a boyfriend here. But, perhaps it *is* possible, after all ...

"Aunty!"

"Yes, my dear Afsun?"

"Does Grandma know you have a boyfriend?"

"No, of course not. Would you tell such a thing to *your* mother?"

"Yes, of course I would. I think she should know."

"But then you'd have to die," she laughed. "You must be insane. If I tell my mother, she'll marry me off right away to anyone she chooses for me."

"But my mom is not like that."

"Your mother, Gulnur? Believe me, she'd also do that. In terms of behaviour and mentality, your mother is the same as your grandmother."

"But my mother has always said if you love someone, you can tell me."

"She must have said that so she can take immediate action when you make the mistake of telling her."

We were both silent. As usual, my aunt had messed up my mind again.

"I think it's better not to think about this matter since I don't have anyone I love anyway."

"But you can tell me, Afsun. I can be a good friend and keep secrets for you."

"I don't have that kind of stuff going on in my life, Aunty."

"Well, fine. Now run to Grandma for permission!"

"I don't know what to say, and I can't convince her in front of all those people."

"I'll call her then. You don't have to convince her. Just tell her you're bored. That's all. I'll take care of the rest."

Aunty Nuriya and I went down the iron stairs, which were warming up in the sun. The staircase circled twice, like part of a DNA helix. Near the bottom on the left side was a kind of cement ledge and a hallway leading to one of the rooms. More than twenty pairs of shoes were lined up there. The number of shoes indicated that tea and candy would have to be served to guests at all hours of the day. I've done this many times. I tried to carry around thirty cups of tea on a big tray. With all that weight, you must lower the tray close to the women sitting on the floor, but without tilting it. By the way, I've never seen any armchairs inside the house. Instead, people sit on carpets and a beautifully embroidered mattress laid out on the floor. The mattress is also used as a single bed at night. That's where the visitors were sitting.

It was a challenge to serve tea to the women sitting on the floor, especially for a tall person like me. The pressure to hold the tray steady while also leaning forward paralyzes your waist. Sometimes the women would get up, and kiss and hug me, saying, "Oh, this is Gulnur's eldest child." Anyway, I loved this task of serving tea despite its difficulties.

My aunt was pulling the curtain in the hallway. Suddenly, my Aunt Maryam, one of my father's sisters, showed up. She always looks at me as if to say, "You don't love me, do you?" But I love everyone. I just can't always be with the same person all the time. I have to divide my attention.

"Maryam, do you know where my mom is?" Aunty Nuriya asked. "Could you please call her from inside?"

Aunty Maryam squinted and said, "Okay."

Aunty Nuriya was holding her phone in one hand and placing her other hand over her heart. Her excitement was palpable.

Catching her breath, Grandma hurriedly joined us.

"Here you girls are," she said as she looked at me. "My dear, my beautiful granddaughter, how are you?"

"I'm fine, Grandma. I'm just bored. Can I go out?"

"Where are you going to go?"

"I don't know. Maybe to the bazaar with Aunty Nuriya ... if you don't mind."

"I'm glad you're asking permission. Just give me a minute. I'll have to consult the others. I'll ask your other grandmother too, and you'd better ask your mother as well, my beloved Afsun."

The others? My mother? My other grandmother? Really? Why does this simple shopping outing have to become so complicated?

I hadn't seen my mom since this morning, but I finally found her. She was mad at Aunty Nuriya. I think she knew my aunt had made up this whole "I'm bored" story. As usual, many other women were with her. My uncle's wife, whom I had just met, and the young girls, who were always hanging around, were there too, of course. I didn't like some of their sarcastic comments, such as "Oh, Miss Afsun has arrived at last. She finally remembered us."

Sometimes I want to say, "Look, I'm not here for you! Do I always have to pay attention to you? That's not what I call love and respect." But never mind. I must keep telling myself to be patient with these women in my family.

I sat next to my mother. Everyone else was sitting close to each other in a row smiling. One girl was leaning on someone else's leg and another one on someone else's back. On the surface, it seemed like a warm, cosy atmosphere, but what I don't like is that the majority of these women spend most of their time squabbling and gossiping about their husbands.

"Mom, I need to talk to you."

"Okay, girl, tell me."

My mother put my head right against her face, inhaled deeply, and kissed me on the head. This feeling of intimacy between us was one of the best feelings in the world.

"Mom, I really needed this. I love you." She smiled.

After a while, I said, "Can I go out with Aunt Nuriya? My grandmother said yes, and I want to get permission from you as well."

I tried to say it quietly, discreetly. However, I think everyone heard me. Zarlasht, one of the girls sitting near us, said, "Oh, I was also planning to go to the bazaar, so I'll come with you."

Instantly, Aunty Nuriya intervened. "No, Zarlasht. Stay where you're sitting!"

The others started laughing, but she deserved it.

Finally, my mother said, "Okay, girl, but watch out. You can't walk easily in a burka, so be careful. Don't fall anywhere."

"What? A burka? Mom! I'm not wearing it! Aunty, I'm sorry, but if I have to wear that thing, then I won't come after all."

"Please, my sister Gulnur. We won't go too far from the house. Afsun could just put on a head scarf. Let the girl take a breath of fresh air sometime."

My mother smiled and said, "Well, make sure to take my big veil, at least."

"Okay," reassured Aunty Nuriya.

As we escaped from the room, my aunt gave me a wink.

"Let's get out of here quickly," she whispered. "Otherwise, other women will try to join us."

I wondered how many places require permission. It's like we're asking for a pass to get out of prison for a day! We went to my aunt's room (the room that's always locked on the right side of the hall). Previously, they only allowed Asra and me to enter it to sleep. Aunty Nuriya gave me the black veil that my grandmother wore, and she put on another dress and a lot of jewellery. Then she sprayed on more perfume than I would ever use in a whole year. We both took our slippers. I liked this hijab style. It was airier and kept me cool.

My aunt was wearing a burka, but somehow it looked different on her. She wore it in a way that I wasn't used to. She knew how to free her hands on both sides to reveal her jewellery.

My grandmother said at least five hundred times, "Girls, watch out. Come home soon, and take this, take that." Thankfully, Aunty Nuriya managed to evade her mother's demands and we finally left the house.

As soon as she walked out the door, my aunt took a deep breath.

"Everything alright, Aunty?"

"Will you stop calling me Aunty? It makes me feel too old. I have a name, dear Afsun. You can just call me Nuriya."

"Okay, dear Nuriya."

"I see you catch on quickly," she replied with a laugh. "I was just about ready to give up and say never mind about my name."

When we left the house, there were two blocks in front of us, one of which was the first street we came to from the vineyard. I remember. The door through which we always welcomed guests faced there, but my aunt chose another path that day. It was a long and tiring walk.

"Aunty, which way is this?"

"Now we're heading towards the Afghankot school. There's a rickshaw stop there. We're going to get on one of them and go to the bazaar."

"Well, you said it was near."

"It's close but let's not walk anymore. We have many things to do this morning, and we have to get back by lunchtime. I can't see my darling enough anyway …"

"Well, that's up to you."

"Look, Afsun, everyone's looking at you. See that kid in the car, our neighbour Sadaf's brother. He can't take his eyes off you."

"Why are they staring at me? Do I look weird?"

"No, dear. It's because you're beautiful and extraordinary."

I didn't know what motive was behind my aunt's comment, but it certainly made me feel uncomfortable. Sometimes I don't like the way she behaves.

"No. Please stop exaggerating," I insisted.

"Really, they don't look at anyone else, just you. All eyes are on you on the street."

"Well, I think it's disgusting," I replied. "Why don't they just mind their own business? Both the young and the old are gawking shamelessly."

Even a man around the age of my two grandfathers made crude remarks to me. The way some of them looked at us and their harassing comments reminded me of Farkhunda for a moment. What they did to her despite her black hijab. Those disgusting, brainless men.

I don't know how we got to that rickshaw stand, but it was one of my fastest walks. It was about 11:00 a.m., and there were little girls between the ages of seven and twelve pouring out of a multi-storey school. Obviously, their four-hour school shift had ended. Suddenly, the street was filled with little girls in black school uniforms with white head scarves. Some were well groomed, while others were dressed in dirty old clothes that made them seem unlike school children. I couldn't resist taking out my phone to snap photos. They looked like bees buzzing all over a big street, the children coming out of a school with blue walls. The photo couldn't be more beautiful. My photo taking ended abruptly when my aunt pulled me by the arm and told me to get into the rickshaw.

With a smile, she said, "Come on, photographer tourist! Let's go."

"Aunty, look at those kids. How beautiful they are!"

"You know, our whole family has graduated from this school. Your mother too."

"So, shall we go in then?" I asked innocently.

"Oh, my God! If we do that, we won't have time for me to see my boyfriend. Shall we call Nimat as well then? Maybe he can join us."

I really wanted to visit the school, but my aunt was in a hurry.

"Well, Aunty, call him then," I said smiling.

"Yes, let's do that. Then we may call my father and brothers as well! Girl, how naïve you really are. Come on, we're late."

It was my first time riding in a rickshaw. I saw one on the roadside for the first time when we were passing Mazar-i-Sharif on the bus. It's like a national vehicle in this area. You can find it everywhere—a colourful, interesting vehicle. Whether it's an actual car is debatable. It has three wheels. Passengers get in through the only door at the back. I call it a door, but rickshaws don't have a conventional door. It's just a quadrilateral hole. Each rickshaw owner shapes his own details, including colourful curtains and other decorative features. There's not much in it either, just a fifteen-centimetre-long board as a seat on either side. The distance between the two rows is about seventy-six centimetres. It's fairly inexpensive—thirty afghanis (about thirty cents)—and the money is paid when you reach your destination.

"Come on, Afsun, we're here."

"Is this the bazaar, Nuriya?" I asked as we got out of the rickshaw.

"Yes, what—you don't like it?"

"No, I thought it was something else."

"Oh, it is. This place isn't your Moscow," she laughed.

"Why are you making fun of everything? I'm serious!"

"Yes, Afsun. This is Faryab. Actually, all over Afghanistan it's like this. Look at those rows of shops right over there. Together, these buildings are like a little mall. It's limited to mainly jewellery stores on the left, fabric and tailors on the right, and two or three dress shops in front of it. By the way, there are also small shops selling shoes and accessories. If we get tired and hungry, we can get snacks at the kiosks on the street. There are some other shops where we can sit down and eat. They have separate areas for men and women."

"Thanks for all this valuable information, Nuriya."

We were both laughing. My aunt's smile was expressive even though I couldn't see her face clearly. I could see only a little bit of both eyes from behind the burka's screen, and sometimes I could see her eyebrows.

"Hey, Miss Nuriya! Where's our brother-in-law?" I teased my aunt who was on the phone with her boyfriend.

"Wait, wait," she answered briefly.

Her tone suddenly changed. In fact, speaking in a coy, flirtatious way, she turned into someone else.

"My darling, your love has arrived … Are you at the store? Any customers there?"

From that sentence, I suspected her Nimat was a shop owner. We turned right on the first street. There were two or three shops on the left. Then there was a two-storey sales centre. A white sign read "Brothers Sales Centre." We left the level of the bright, sunny street and descended a staircase. It was hard to get down those stairs to the first level of the sales centre. Some watchmakers and other tradesmen were standing in their doorways and waiting for customers. These men kept staring at me. During all this time, I never saw a woman without a burka. I seemed to be the only one whose face was not fully concealed. Maybe that's why I was attracting so much attention. We entered the first shop.

CHAPTER 10

Family Personalities

I don't think the fact that I grew up in a cold country like Russia explains why I have a different appearance from others in Afghanistan ... I mean I guess I'm quite tall. My skin is whiter. My hair is lighter, and my eyes are blue. People from Northern Afghanistan who have Turkic roots are already different in appearance. They also have a distinctive language and culture. However, there must be some other reason to explain why I attract extra attention from strangers. I'm not sure what it is yet.

In Afghanistan, though, the concept of a woman's physical beauty is slightly different. Being tall and having big eyes, long hair, white skin, and a long nose are the main criteria. Also, surprisingly, having some extra fat is considered the most valuable quality. When people refer to someone as "very beautiful," they use "white and chubby" as compliments. Since I'm not chubby, I guess my height, hair colour, and complexion stand out and compensate for my skinny build, so I sort of live up to the local beauty standards. Maybe this is why everyone stares at me.

Anyway, today when I was out with Aunty Nuriya, I almost got into a fight with her. First, we walked into a shop with coloured lights. The proprietor was a man around forty-five. I didn't see anyone else in his shop.

"Is this your boyfriend?" I asked impulsively.

She didn't answer. She was looking at the clothes on the racks without looking at the guy. I noticed some shiny dresses on two mannequins. There were no price tags, meaning that any interested customer would have to approach the owner to ask for the price.

"You're seeing him for the first time, aren't you?" I whispered. "I'm sure you're also surprised that he's so old. Let's get out of here."

Aunt Nuriya began laughing. "No, Afsun. I've known my boyfriend for five years."

"But this guy's my father's age," I replied. "Look, he's even wearing a ring."

She started laughing even more, and I started to feel uncomfortable and angry.

Then she said, "Of course, this man isn't him. I entered this shop randomly. People would get suspicious if we went immediately to my boyfriend's store. I don't even know this guy here."

"Aunty Nuriya, you really are the devil."

"I know, dear."

We didn't notice the proprietor had come up behind us. He said in a low voice much too close to my ear, "Are you looking for something special? Tell me. I can help you." We hurried out of the shop.

We entered another shop. The proprietor of this next one looked more suitable as a boyfriend. He was young, handsome, and well groomed. He was wearing a clean, white perahan tunban. He seemed to recognize us because he stood up as soon as we walked in. Yes, apparently, he was the famous Nimat.

"Welcome," he said.

My quirky aunt simply replied, "Thank you." She sounded so artificial.

Then Nimat turned to me. "You must be Afsun, aren't you? My beautiful niece, welcome first to Faryab and then to my shop."

"Thank you." That's all I could say in response.

I don't think Nimat is a decent human being. On first impression, his mannerisms, behaviour, and remarks seemed insincere. He was talking like a lazy student who was running away from literature class and pretending to look cool and sophisticated in front of girls. His tone of voice showed that he had a pretty high opinion of himself. I almost laughed at him. When I think about Nimat, I must remind myself to try to be unbiased, but the truth is I don't trust him.

I moved to another corner of the store. I tried to make myself busy by browsing through the dresses, but I could still hear their voices. They were both speaking in an artificially polite tone, saying things like "how are you" and "what have you been doing lately?" Then I heard him make a comment about me!

"She looks much older than her photo. So, she's already sixteen. The girls her age here still look like kids."

When I heard that remark, I felt my anger rising. *If sixteen-year-old girls here are considered kids, then why are they being forced into marriage with strangers?*

Then my aunt drew me into the conversation. "Yes, this my niece. She looks like her father, doesn't she?"

After a few minutes, Nimat said, "Shall we do what I wrote in the message?"

"Which one?"

"You don't remember that we were going to hug?"

He had barely finished his question when three female customers entered the store. Aunty Nuriya rushed towards me.

"So, did you see anything you like?"

"No, Aunty—sorry, I mean Nuriya. Where did these women come from?"

The women seemed to be lingering too long, so Nimat got rid of them by saying, "Sorry, I'm not the proprietor, ladies. We're just waiting here for a friend."

After the three women left, my aunt approached him again. This time he embraced her over her burka. I think hugging is the most comforting thing in the world. We do it to make the person we love feel closer. I felt sorry for them. They had been in a relationship for five years, yet they were still surrounded by fear, seeing and touching each other through the barrier of a burka. I couldn't understand why they weren't married already. I had to know.

"Enough, my love," whispered my aunt. "Careful. Someone might come in."

One of Nimat's hands was on her neck. His other hand was on her leg. Even though I felt sorry for them, I thought their behaviour looked disgusting. Some people are always wondering what others are doing, who's talking to whom, who's having an affair—even who's texting whom. Maybe that's why the salesmen in the surrounding stores kept looking at us suspiciously.

A few men and women were coming towards this shop. I called out to my aunt, and she nervously put her burka back in order. Approaching me from behind a mannequin, she pretended to be a normal customer.

"So, Afsun, how is this dress?"

By that point, the shop was full of new customers. We had to leave. As we were moving towards the door, Nimat approached us with two bags in his hand.

"Girls, please give these to my mother."

"Okay, brother," said my aunt as she took the bags from his hands.

I felt like I was in a movie full of intrigue, secrecy, and romance. When Nimat noticed the customers coming in, he suddenly started addressing us as his sisters. Smart tactic maybe, but giving us gifts was not a good idea. I thought he was sneaky, making up lies. He seemed to lie too easily.

We left the shop and walked quickly towards a rickshaw stand. I noticed something else on the way. Men were looking lecherously at women's feet and making vulgar comments like "Pinky feet, oh so nice!"

While we were riding in the rickshaw, my brain was busy. I couldn't stop thinking about the disgusting behaviour of some of the men here, like that guy in the first store who suddenly came up from behind and asked, "Are you looking for something special? Tell me. I can help you." In fact, if he had taken his creepy eyes off us, maybe we would've ended up buying something from him.

✥ ✥ ✥

Thankfully, not all the men around here are undressing women and girls with their eyes. For example, my grandfather—that is, my dad's father—is the exact opposite of those men on the street. I guess it's obvious that he's the family member I love the most here. From day one, I knew he was special. One night, when I went to his house, the two of us talked about various things while the other relatives were chatting in another room. I liked his open-minded view of the world. I still recall what he said to me that night.

"The more pressure you put on a person, whether it's a man or a woman, the worse it's going to get. No matter how good that person is, you have to let him or her make mistakes and learn from those mistakes—otherwise, they'll continue making mistakes. In Afghanistan, we are often very wrong. In the name of our faith, we have imprisoned our women at home or wrapped them in burkas so that 'no one will see them.' However, some women do whatever they want to do under the burka, since they think that no one would know them anyway. And some disgusting men are aroused even by the sight of a woman's hands or ankles visible from the hems of her burka. The men who assault women try to cover up their own filth by hiding behind the cowardly excuse that the devil made them do it.

"Girl, every person will make different mistakes at different ages, and it's up to us, the parents, to educate our children, to reassure them, and make them learn from their actions and decisions so they don't make bigger mistakes. Human beings are flawed. God is the only one who never makes mistakes. People don't learn to get up if they don't fall down. Maybe I didn't explain this concept well enough to your father, uncles, and aunts when they were younger. No matter how careful I was, they were so subjected to their mother's ridiculous limitations that they were more influenced by her ideas. People who are fighting for their lives in this country have succumbed to their own prejudices. They have ruined their lives by preoccupying themselves with what the neighbour, the friend, the relative might think about them. My heart aches when I hear about domestic violence, especially the persecution of women and children, and the unprovoked beatings. It's hard to even admit that this happening in my country. The injustices here always hurt my heart, but I believe that in order to end the war, poverty, and ignorance in Afghanistan, we need to correct our mindsets."

I remembered that beautiful conversation with Grandpa Raz as I thought about Aunty Nuriya's situation. I mean what my wise grandfather said about the need for honest communication in families and the freedom to make mistakes so you can learn from them.

On the way home from our shopping excursion, my aunt remained silent. As soon as we got home, Grandma (Mom and Nuriya's mother) asked, "What are you holding in those bags?"

"Dre—"

"What kind of dresses did you buy?" she demanded.

"Oh, Mom, let me show you. They're hard to describe. You have to see them."

She pulled out two dresses: one an evening dress, the other a colourful, floral-patterned shorter dress for hot days. "Wow, look how beautiful they are!" my aunt exclaimed. "Look, Afsun. I couldn't appreciate the true beauty of these dresses in the light in the store. These dresses are gorgeous, aren't they?"

"Yes, Aunty."

My cousin Zarlasht couldn't hide her resentment over the fact that she hadn't been invited to join us on our shopping excursion. As she began to rummage through the bags, a small slip of paper fell out. I think she was a little suspicious of my aunt, and she was going through the bags to find something incriminating. Luckily, she had grabbed the bag so fast she didn't notice the piece of paper. I tried to divert her attention.

"Zarlasht, I wish you had come with us today. I liked the bazaar."

"Nuriya was jealous in case you liked me more," she replied.

I tried to reassure her. "Another time I'll go alone with you, Zarlasht."

The rivalry between Nuriya and Zarlasht had begun. Using my toes, I discreetly dragged the fallen slip of paper towards myself, picked it up, and held it tightly. At that moment, my grandmother cornered me.

"Girl, what's your aunt up to again?"

"I don't get it, Grandma."

"I saw that piece of paper. Someone gave it to your aunt, didn't they?"

"I don't know."

"I can understand by her eyes. I don't like it."

I couldn't tell my grandmother the truth or that love wasn't a bad thing. Plus, I knew how Aunt Nuriya would react. She'd never accept it, so I had no choice but to lie.

"No, dear Grandma. There's no such thing. That paper was the receipt for the dress. I took it before Zarlasht could see it. You know their relationship isn't very good these days. They argue for no reason. I thought if Zarlasht saw the receipt, she'd start her rude remarks like 'the price is too high or too low.' You know her."

"I hope you're not lying because I can't read."

"Of course not, my sweet grandmother. Have I ever lied to you before?"

This conversation ended with my lie. While I regretted having to lie to my grandmother, I was happy to save Aunt Nuriya from her mother's harsh words. I guess there's no reason to lie. However, considering there were benefits and drawbacks, I shouldn't have thought too much about it.

Asra and Aziz were sitting in another corner of the room playing on their phones. I guessed they were mad at me. I hadn't spent much time with them in the past days. For sure, they needed me. The last twenty days had taken us far enough. I got up and approached my mother.

"Mom, we want to have siblings' day today, so I'm asking you not to let anyone go upstairs to bother us."

Winking at those who were sitting there, I whispered, "My brother and sister are angry with me." Everyone was smiling. I assumed they were impressed by my behaviour.

I walked towards Aziz and Asra. "Come on, guys. Will you come with me?"

They both got up without saying anything. I sensed they missed those days when it was just the three of us. Aziz is very skinny. I grabbed him by both arms, pulled him up, and hugged him. We followed Asra to the upper room. That room was my home now. Once inside, I put Aziz on the top mattress and closed the door. Asra sat on a *taqcha* in front of the window. Since there is no cooling or heating system in houses in Afghanistan, they make a taqcha, a small recess in a thickly constructed wall. Sometimes they make windows in it, or duvets and blankets are placed there. Anyway, that's where I like to sit most of the time to write, putting my head against the window and stretching my feet.

I sat next to Aziz. At first, none of us said anything. It seemed that we had forgotten how to chat with each other as siblings. So, I began.

"Hello, dear guests, I am your captain, Afsun Raz. Today I will remind you of the rules and purpose of our flight. Our plane is departing from Kabul to Moscow. Please avoid putting on a sour face or raising your eyebrows—and keep silent during the flight! Beep!"

They both started laughing and raised their heads. Asra now came down and sat close to us on the floor. Thankfully, I was able to make them both laugh.

"No, Ms. Afsun, you've misrepresented the situation," Aziz declared. "Dear passengers, when I was in the washroom, the co-pilot, Afsun, made an inaccurate announcement, so I am here to correct what she said. I am Aziz Raz, your greatest captain. Our route is Kabul–Moscow. We ask you to spend time with each other every day, not just in difficult times, and if she does not do so, hit her on the head with a pillow."

I couldn't stop laughing, but Aziz's pillow already came shooting at me, indicating that he was mad at me for going to the bazaar without him. Our laughter was not over when Asra, the mother of rational words, began her announcement.

"Dear guests, with all due respect to these two flight attendants, I am your chief pilot, Asra Raz. We are happy to serve you on the flight from Kabul to

Moscow. If I forget you during the flight, save yourself with the parachutes under your seats and make sure that everyone will go their own way."

"What kind of speech was that philosopher?" Aziz asked.

"You can't make fun of me by calling me a philosopher!"

The three of us were having a lot of fun now. Our laughter and intimacy grew by singing those ridiculous pilot speeches. I hugged my brother and sister tightly for a few minutes.

"Hey, heroic pilots!" I said. "How's it going in the homeland?"

"Boring," answered Asra.

"No, Asra, it's not boring at all," replied Aziz. "Look, we don't have to do homework. We eat the food we want. We receive a lot of love and attention from everyone. I don't know about you guys, but my dad's friends always buy me chocolates and drinks. It's heaven for me here. I don't want to go back to Russia at all."

"Gluttonous Aziz," said Asra.

Then Aziz turned to me. "Afsun, my sister, tell our sister—who's been mixed up at the hospital—that she should say my name correctly instead of pronouncing it like an alien."

"Aziz, I wish *you* could be an alien," Asra shot back. "You'd probably be smarter."

I needed to change the subject or else there was going to be a fight.

"Asra, how's the holiday going? Could you study?"

"No, sis, it's not good to study all the time, so I took a break. It's been five days and I'm living my life."

Aziz quickly intervened. "So, you mean you want to say that you're no longer a nerd?"

"My brother, don't worry. I'm still a nerd, but you're too lazy to ever be a nerd."

"Well, my dear sister, you seem to waste your intelligence on fighting. I wish you'd use that intelligence for better things."

There couldn't be a better way to get Asra angry. I missed these sibling spats, but I decided it was time to change the subject again.

"Aziz, how's Dad? Is he asking about us?"

"Yes, sis, sometimes. He even entered your room when you were sleeping and kissed you."

"Really?"

"Yes. When I woke up to go to the bathroom one night, I saw him."

"Wow!" said Asra. "So, Dad didn't forget us, after all."

"Are you crazy? How could he ever forget us?" replied Aziz. "He's always looking at his phone, talking to people all the time. Of course, he's tired. Sometimes our friends and relatives stay here until late at night. You know, sometimes I can hear the voices in the middle of the night, even until morning. We're in a different and special situation now. We need to show some patience. My father needs his family and friends, and finally, they have this opportunity now after fourteen years."

I was proud to hear such thoughtful words from my young brother.

"Yes, my wise Aziz, you're right. We must be patient."

Then Asra added, "We're here for a while, so we have to tolerate situations we don't like. We should just try to enjoy the beauty of this country."

At that point, we began singing our fraternity song, "One, two, three: power." Aziz was on my left, Asra on my right. The three of us fell asleep together.

Since it was extremely hot, there were swarms of mosquitoes in the room. Also, dozens of flies were buzzing around almost every lamp. It's really hard having electricity only every other day, especially in this heat. Sometimes when I wake up late at night to go to the bathroom, I notice that the light doesn't turn on, making a trip to the bathroom rather tricky and unpleasant. What's worse is that many rural areas don't have electricity at all.

When I woke up, it wasn't clear what time it was, but it was pretty late in the morning. They were banging on the door. As I recall, we were going to visit the home of Aunty Maria, one of our father's older sisters. Asra was absorbed in a math puzzle, but when she heard the voices, she went straight to the door. It was Mom. It felt good to see her. I was still rubbing my eyes.

"Girls, get ready! We're going to your aunt's place in the evening."

"Good morning, Mom."

Mother approached me and said, "I'm happy to see you spending time with your brother and sister. Thank you, girl."

I'm so happy I had fun with my siblings and got my mother's appreciation.

CHAPTER 11

With Beloved Grandpa

My Aunt Guljan, who's a year older than my mother, is one of my favourite people. She is innocent and kind. For example, she ironed all our clothes and brought them to us. It was totally unnecessary, of course, but it was her way of showing us she was thinking of us. She wanted to do something for us. I was so touched.

Unfortunately, Aunty Guljan couldn't spend much time with us because her husband is quite controlling and grumpy. Even though we can't spend much time together, I love her. While Mom was busy chatting with her, I kissed Asra and asked her to get ready. Then I woke Aziz up and prepared myself. We continued to follow Aziz's motto. It became the fraternity song for the three of us. "One, guide; two, intelligence; three, IQ! One, two, three—power!" Just to clarify, Aziz thinks of me as the guide and Asra as the symbol of intelligence. Since Aziz is often in competition with Asra academically, he gave himself the label "IQ." So, all together, we represented power! Although having a motto as siblings is kind of childish at my age, I'll continue to say it when I'm with my siblings, perhaps for the rest of our lives, since it seems to make my brother happy.

We had a late breakfast and spent some precious time together. The entire day, in fact. My beloved Grandpa—I mean my father's dad—was waiting for us in the backyard. My first impulse was to take a picture with him. Whenever I walk up to him, I hug him spontaneously. He gives me a sense of security and strength whenever he says, "Afsun, don't worry. Your grandfather is always behind you."

Aziz ran up to Grandpa and said, "Grandpa, can you take us around in your magic car today? Otherwise, Aunty Nuriya will steal my sister from us again."

Everyone who was sitting there on the sofha in the backyard laughed at Aziz's remark.

As if he had been looking for some kind of excuse, my grandfather turned to Grandma and said, "Lady Saliha, my dear wife, unfortunately, my car was acting up a bit yesterday. Of course, if you have too many passengers, the car will be weighed down, and the bottom will hit stones on the road. I think I can go only with my three grandchildren tonight."

"But there are only a few cars left," Grandma said. "How will we all go?"

Grandpa had an answer ready. "I'll ask the neighbour's son to help transport some of you, but only the elders will go with him. I will take my three grandchildren in my car."

Everyone was laughing as I recorded the best scene in the world on my phone. My grandfather's speech, his narrations, and his jokes were precious.

My maternal aunts and paternal aunts, the married ones, all left together. Then my parents left in another car. Grandpa went inside to pray and we three waited for him. We were the only ones left in the house with him.

Slowly, he pulled up the curtain and said in a hushed voice, "Is everyone gone?"

We laughed, wondering what was going on. "Yes, Grandpa," I said. "It's been a long time since we've been without a big crowd of people in the house. We're the only ones left here."

"Good, good …"

"Grandpa, were you hiding?" asked Aziz. "Oh, you're so funny."

"Yes, my grandson. If we had gone with them, we wouldn't have the opportunity to visit the city, and we wouldn't be able to eat Faryab's famous ice cream. To be honest, it would be difficult to buy ice cream for so many people!"

Whenever he made a joke, he laughed in a soothing tone. We walked to Grandpa's car. I had Aunty Nuriya's full-body cover sheet in my hand. Aziz got in the front seat. Asra and I were supposed to get in the back.

Grandpa saw what was in my hand and said, "Look in the room on the left side. There's a bag on the kitchen door. Take what you find inside it and put it on instead of whatever you have in your hand and come back to the car."

I immediately followed his instructions. What I found inside that bag surprised me. It was a delicate headscarf, similar to the kind of scarf women would wear in a "normal" Muslim country. It was lovely.

Grandpa also had instructions for Aziz. "And now, Mr. Aziz, go back to the house and lock the door. Give the keys to your uncle who lives next door. Then get back in the car."

Aziz got out and did as Grandpa had instructed. That's when Grandpa turned off his phone and said, "You girls don't have your phones with you, do you?"

"No, Grandpa."

"That's great."

When Aziz returned to the car, my grandfather played the old music tapes he had found. He had a 1992 station wagon. I love travelling by car. And if the driver is my favourite grandfather, my joy is at the maximum level. Aziz and Asra were also super happy to be on this outing with Grandpa. It was fun to listen to those nostalgic songs he loved. They added colour to our ride through the cobblestone and paved streets of Maymana. We passed small buffets and shops with yellow lights. Friendly vendors were selling colourful fruits and vegetables on the roadside.

At one point during our wonderful ride, Grandpa said something that stuck with me: "Sometimes be happy for no reason. Be generous with your laughter. For example, feel free to laugh right now!"

I listened to my grandfather. First, I uncovered my hair and tied it in a high ponytail. I felt the comfort that came with the fresh air. I was like a bird that had just been released from a cage. I felt like the happiest girl in the world. It's hard to explain. It was an unusual feeling, maybe like an innocent person who was serving a life sentence but then is suddenly released from prison after thirty years.

Looking at me in the rear-view mirror, Grandpa said, "Afsun, girl, your hair looks like your mother's. So don't go crazy and cut it."

That's when the Sarban track that we all loved started playing "Ta Ki Nabashi Hamdam Jan." I've enjoyed this song before, but tonight my grandfather started singing it, and then we all sang it out loud. I wish I had had my phone with me to record this moment.

That evening I felt like I was the happiest of princesses and the luckiest of the lucky ones. The city centre is very small. We went through the same streets maybe two or three times and continued to listen to music. There's only one park in the entire town. Since the park is not too big, it took only five minutes to drive through it. In this province of around two million people, there is only a park in the city centre for children.

There's a school on the right side of the park. It looks similar to the school I saw with my aunt the other day. It's the same colour, but it has a different name. When we passed it, I read the school name as "Sitara." We stood in front of the school. There are no houses or buildings more than two storeys tall. There's a shop next to the school and the famous rickshaws waiting in front of it.

Some young men were standing outside the ice cream shop. They were joking and laughing. The window on my side was facing the school. They couldn't see me, but I think they noticed Asra and pointed her out to each other. Grandpa got out of the car and headed for the group of guys. They knew him because he used to be a teacher in the old days. A couple of them rushed to his side. They chatted with him for a while. Although I didn't know what they were talking about, it was obvious from their smiles that it was a pleasant conversation.

Grandpa got ice cream from the vendor and walked back to the car. The ice cream here is very different from the ice cream in Russia. If I call it "ice cream," my grandfather would object because it's different both in taste and shape. They call it *shir-yakh*. We were enjoying it when Aziz's phone rang. Grandpa was surprised because he had told us previously not to bring our phones with us. However, Aziz wasn't in the car at that time and had missed this request.

"Oh, it's my dad."

"Answer it then."

"Hello? Okay, Dad, we're coming. I'm sorry."

That's all he said. Then he hung up.

"Grandpa, my dad and others are worried because it's been an hour and a half since we left the house."

With a calm smile, Grandpa replied, "Oh, how well I did. They consumed my life, and when I got older, they didn't spend a day with me like this. Let me enjoy my precious moments with my grandchildren."

Then, looking at his watch, he said, "Come on, look how fast the time has passed. We'd better head back. Finish up."

I didn't want the night to end so abruptly.

"Grandpa, the night is longer. I wish we didn't have to go to that other house. It's been so good spending time with you. Let's go out again. Will you take us for another ride like this?"

"Yes, of course, my Afsun, the light of my eyes."

It's nice to be called the light of someone special's eyes. I was flying with happiness. The more slowly Grandpa drove, the better. By the time we got to my Dad's sister's house, the gathering would be almost winding down. It's like Grandpa didn't want to go there either, but we're in Afghanistan. We couldn't stay out on the streets too late at night. How many times did the police warn us, "Don't walk around with young girls like that, Uncle." My grandfather relied on his old pistol, the heirloom of his youth. He usually carries it with him when he goes out.

We were headed for my aunt's house right behind Sitara School. When we turned left onto the street, there was a hospital. As far as I could read, it was the Afghan-Turkish Friendship Hospital. We arrived at Aunty Maria's house while I was still trying to read the Persian signage. Actually, I still haven't sorted out all these aunts and uncles on my mom's side and all the aunts and uncles on my dad's side. There were seventeen of them, and it's even harder to remember all their children and grandchildren. I'm bound to mix them up. When we were in Moscow, the relatives used to phone us. I feel guilty because I avoided talking to them back then. I used to make up excuses about schoolwork. It was hard to remember all their names, and many of them looked sort of the same.

As we approached the house, we noticed more than fifty people standing around. The older men I saw on the street reminded me of a scene in my father's wedding video. When we saw the crowd, my grandfather turned sharply into the alley.

"Excuse me, girl, you know I'm fine with it, but I don't want your father and uncles to get mad, so you should wear your headscarf."

"Okay, Grandpa," I replied as I put on my new headscarf.

My grandfather lowered the window and said, "I'm sorry, guys. We're a little late."

My uncles—I mean my father's brothers—were standing near the door. I don't know why Grandpa seemed kind of intimidated by his own sons. We got out of the car smiling. There was a big crowd. As usual, everyone was gawking at us. I felt so self-conscious. It was like we had just landed from Mars.

One of the young boys whispered to another one, "Look, those girls are Uncle Ismat's daughters from Russia."

Is this how they welcome their relatives? They stared at us so shamelessly as we walked the twenty metres from the car to the house. They looked as if they were eating us.

When we entered the house, another surprise awaited us. The house was crawling with people, from the children who plucked the flowers to the girls standing in the hallway trying to bring tea and the women washing the plates. It was like a wedding atmosphere. It wasn't clear exactly how the house was designed architecturally, but it looked big and cool. From what I could see, there were people we didn't even know. They were all waiting for us tonight. We stood at the doorway and glanced around. I had assumed we were going to have a small dinner party among our family members, but that night there were more people than I had ever seen at my grandparents' houses.

A few of the women walked towards us. Since there were only women inside, I took off my scarf. Although the dress I was wearing was made in Afghanistan, it seemed to stand out as uniquely attractive. I got the feeling that maybe everyone was looking at me because I was wearing it for the first time. I had pulled my hair back in a ponytail. It was simple but looked nice. All of a sudden, I heard a somewhat familiar voice in the crowd.

"Oh, look, girls, my friends are here. These are the girls from Russia."

I couldn't see her face, and her voice was unclear in the clamour of multiple conversations and children running around. After looking at Asra and taking a deep breath, we began greeting everyone one by one just as we had done on the first night.

"Oh, Aunty, oh, sister, how are you?"

We kissed and hugged each other, but it felt insincere.

By the way, the girl who introduced us as her "friends" was my cousin Zarlasht. She came to the gathering with a lot of her friends, so I responded quickly.

"My dearest Zarlasht, it's good to see you. I missed you. Come here, let me kiss you."

Asra was a little surprised at first when she witnessed me being that familiar with Zarlasht, but I did it on purpose. Zarlasht would have felt embarrassed if I had complained to her in front of others about the weird way she had introduced us. I decided to treat her warmly.

When I asked Asra to be polite, she started acting like me. That's why we were praised. However, since we didn't even remember the names of all the relatives who came streaming in to meet us, we started to speak in the same artificially friendly manner as everyone else. We moved to another room. The only person I knew among the women there was Aunty Maria, the aunt who had invited us.

As soon as she saw us, she said, "I was afraid you'd never come, Grandpa's daughters!"

"Sorry, Aunty. It's Grandpa's car's fault that we're late."

I really loved this aunt. She was down-to-earth and kind-hearted. Asra and I hugged her for several minutes to make up for being late. I asked her where my mother was.

"In the next room," she replied. "Go there. Everyone's already asking for you."

I was afraid of that when we walked into the room. I knew everyone would stand up to welcome us with a kiss. Sometimes the elderly women would also get up. It was so uncomfortable. Aunty Nuriya was there as well. I could feel the anger in her eyes. I didn't think I owed her an explanation or apology for enjoying a relaxing time with my grandfather.

The room was almost like a wedding hall, fifteen metres long. As expected, we felt like objects on display. I suddenly wanted to walk back out the door, but there was no chance to escape. I started greeting the young girl on the right first. I think she had just gotten married. She was dressed up as if it were her second wedding tonight. She was in a long Indian dress and wore a lot of jewellery and heavy makeup.

With Asra right behind me, I started the obligatory greetings, one by one from the right and turning 360 degrees, passing my mom. Finally, we finished making the rounds. When we walked back and sat down next to Mom, everyone from the left started asking their standard questions again, "How are you? Is your mother good? Is your father okay? Is your brother okay?"

Now, as I write this, it sounds funny. Even so, I love this big family atmosphere. Mom is sitting right there in the room, yet both the young and the old ask me and then Asra the same questions about all my family members—including my mother. I don't mind greeting them all, but going through this mechanical routine with more than fifty people is exhausting.

In the early days, I would answer the questions with one simple thank you, but now I was following what my grandmother taught me. She said, "You're a young woman, so you have to ask them the same questions in return. 'How are you? Is the family okay?'" Luckily, I was saved from this monotonous chain of questions when music began playing.

I like to dance, but I don't think everyone has the ability to dance well. Dancing is an art. Only people with talent can catch the precise rhythm. When I was in Moscow, I applied to join the school ballet group. Along with journalism, ballet is one of my favourite activities. In fact, if my grandfather were my father, I bet I would've started ballet a long time ago. I wished the girls here were learning ballet in school. Maybe it would help them block out the negative energy in their lives. I mean the deprivation and torture of girls in Afghanistan. Unfortunately, however, the people who brought this war here are ignorant when it comes to music and dance.

It's a sad fact that some of the people who walk to holy places such as mosques and *madrasas* claim that music and dance are evil. They actually warn parents to keep their children away from so-called demonic activities. The same powerful people are hypocrites because they dress little boys as girls, make them wear bells, and force them to dance in front of them. They even engage in kinky relations with these poor boys under the name *bacha bazi*. I've read a lot of disturbing articles about this sexual abuse of children.

For me, dancing is the best way to clear my head, and that's why I was dancing for myself. I think those who forbid it are trying to connect people to the "pattern of fear" they've established. Maybe they're afraid that dance and music relax people, helping them forget about their stress for a little while. Those people with power make it their mission to use fear as a weapon to keep the less powerful under their control. Leave them uneducated and ignorant, and intimidate them with threats. But as long as people live in ignorance and fear, those "religious" sex traffickers will have no trouble doing what their religion forbids and covering it up. As my beloved grandpa once told me, a number of so-called mullahs in countries like Afghanistan don't want people to read, gain knowledge, or improve themselves. They want to keep people in the dark, but it wouldn't be easy to fool educated people.

By the way, dancing to local songs is a lot of fun. That's what we've been doing every night since we got to Afghanistan. One of the songs that was played tonight is one of my favourites. As I listened to it, I put my head against my mother's shoulder, and I noticed Aunty Nuriya coming towards us. I thought, *Oh that's great. I really feel like dancing*. My aunt walked me to the centre of the long hall. We started dancing opposite each other. I enjoyed dancing with her. All the guests, including those from outside the room, clapped along to the beat of the music. Many people were dancing. Sometimes when I read what I've written, I feel like I'm describing a video clip. Every frame feels that way when I read it. I can actually see us dancing.

There are some interesting things about dance in Afghanistan. For example, here in the Uzbek region of Northern Afghanistan, there's one dance performed by two women. After shrugging at each other, they dance with one hand up and one hand down. It's probably one of the most interesting dances I've ever seen. One woman wears a white local dress like an old man, while the other wears a long dress and big headscarf like an old woman, her head covered with only her eyes visible. They pretend to be a married couple and clap with wooden spoons. You have so much fun that you forget your troubles for a while, forget how quickly time passes.

Eventually, I understood that it was time to go. I don't know how three hours flew by in that atmosphere, but it was finally time to go. When we set off for the house, the burkas, which seemed as heavy as mountains, exacerbated our fatigue. Fortunately, in the city, we were allowed the right to step outside with only a hijab instead of a burka. My mother, Aunty Nuriya, my siblings, and I all came home and had a happy ending to a long day. I went to my aunt's room and fell asleep immediately.

It's a shame to walk around here in pyjamas or something comfortable that you wear to sleep at night, but I guess the relatives don't complain too much about us because we're guests. That night I lay on the floor in a large area, enjoying my sleep like a newborn baby.

After that night, we visited close relatives—aunts, uncles, and cousins—for a full week. It was amazing. I love these huge family gatherings with local music, games, dances, and traditional food, such as Uzbek palaw, that dish I can never resist. It's one of the must-haves, among other dishes, as a main course for both lunch and dinner.

Every day I learn new things about my homeland. Agriculture, including raising livestock, was the main livelihood of the people here. It was known as a "fathers' occupation," but it ended due to the wars. Carpet weaving, a "mothers' occupation," remained the only source of income for many families. In other words, it's the power of women that enables these families to survive. Physically strong men have to migrate to neighbouring countries such as Iran, Pakistan, Turkey, and Europe to find work. They have to cross borders illegally and travel thousands of miles to earn money to send to their families. On the way, they face the threat of landmines, the brutality of human traffickers, and punishment or deportation by immigration authorities of each country.

In almost every house I've visited, I've seen women weaving colourful carpets by hand. Even pregnant women and those with young babies continue their weaving job. It takes months to complete each carpet. I realized there are thousands of stories behind each one of those exquisite hand-made carpets we admire in the market. When I was proudly browsing among carpets from Afghanistan during an exhibition in Moscow, I didn't realize that those gorgeous works of art were created by the women of my own Uzbek region and perhaps some of my own relatives. My respect for the strong women of this country has grown even more.

CHAPTER 12

Betrayal

The other night Asra was sleeping with Mom. I went to Aunty Nuriya's room. She started asking me personal yet interesting questions, mostly about things that made me feel awkward. It was weird and inappropriate.

For example, she came right out and asked me, "Do you want to have a boyfriend here?"

"I really think I have to love someone in order to choose him as a boyfriend," I answered.

"Then love someone."

"It's not something that happens instantly just because you want it to, Aunty Nuriya. Can we just skip this subject? You have the internet. Can you please give me your Wi-Fi password so I can chat with my classmates in Moscow?"

"Do you want to talk to a boy?"

"Is that important?" Her questions were starting to annoy me.

"If it's a boy, okay."

"Oh, Aunty, sometimes I think you're too playful."

"But I'm serious, Afsun."

She was saying all this in such a pretentious, teasing tone that it was as if her Nimat were right next to her. Her imagination seemed to be flying. Who knows what she was thinking about me just because I grew up in Russia. Anyway, I didn't like her behaviour, and I wasn't afraid to tell her so.

"Nuriya, you're really naughty."

"I know," she said. "Forget Wi-Fi. Why don't you have internet connection?"

"Well, the SIM card we bought from Kabul doesn't work here, so I thought I wouldn't waste money since we'll be leaving shortly."

"But it's not expensive. You can buy a SIM card for as little as thirty-nine afghanis."

"Really?"

"Yes, I have four or five of them. Wait a minute, I think I have enough on my AWCC SIM card to use at night. I'll give it to you."

"Thanks!"

"Here, it is."

My aunt put her card into my phone, and eventually, I was back online. There were a lot of text messages, followed by news on Tolo and other Afghan television networks when I pressed the YouTube quick notification button. First, I started responding to the texts. Aunty Nuriya was busy with her own phone, as usual. I had received a lot of messages from my classmates. They were all worried about me. I had a message even from my classmate Peter. I was surprised because he had stopped communicating with me after I refused to go out with him. He sent me a message when he didn't see me in the class group chat. I wrote back to him and a few other friends. I included some short videos and explained a bit about what's been happening here. Because I love Afghanistan so much, I think I encouraged them to come here. A few short videos and pictures I posted were liked by everyone in the group in a very short time. I started to receive comments, such as "you're in a dreamy place—let it be fun."

I already know I'm in a dreamy place. This is what happens in a dream. People try to find some way to be happy amid the misery of their lives. They try to focus on an intimate and beautiful time with its pain and sweetness … I love the natural world here. It took me nearly an hour to read and respond to all the messages. Then I wanted to concentrate on the news. A lot of things had happened in less than a month. I needed to catch up.

There are only three days left of our stay. We had talked about it previously, but recently, no one has been saying anything about our trip back to Moscow. I rarely see my father more than two or three times a week. My mother never seems to be around either these days, so I ended up leaving a message for her on our family group chat: "My beautiful parents, we haven't been able to be alone with you in your own country. It's hard to even see you now. I was afraid to talk to you in front of other people because what I want to say is private. We've been here for almost a month, and we're almost out of time. It's stressing me out a little bit, so let's talk."

It was 11:00 p.m. when I wrote the message. My father responded around midnight. However, all he wrote back was "My beautiful girl, how did you get access to the internet?"

When his reply came in, I was already asleep. When I read his message in the morning, I was furious. There was absolutely no mention of what really mattered. Immediately, I asked Aziz to find and fetch Dad. He found him in the garden.

I've really missed my dad. It's been almost a month, but we've never been able to sit alone and have a real conversation. Whenever I hug him, my maternal grandmother opens her eyes widely and watches me from afar. I don't understand her disapproval, but I don't care because I don't think it's wrong for a daughter to hug her own father.

All of us had a lot to talk about, but since I was the one who had proposed this family discussion, Asra and Aziz let me have my turn first.

"Dad, we love you very much," I began. "When we see that you're happy here, we're happy to be in this beautiful country. But as I wrote in the message, my concern is that school will reopen soon, but we still haven't heard anything about when we're leaving for Russia. It's been stressing me out, so can you share your departure plan with us? In the meantime, before you ask that unnecessary question about my internet access again, I'll tell you. Aunty Nuriya had an extra SIM card. She gave it to me so I could communicate with my Moscow classmates."

My father reflected on my words for a while, mulling over what he should say.

"Are you guys bored with this place?" he asked.

"Dad, you know, that's not the point. You know how much we love this place, how accustomed we are now to our grandparents and other relatives, so please don't change the subject. Let's talk about our school life!"

"Okay, girl. Look, your mom's coming. Let's ask her about it."

My mother approached us with a smile.

"Oh, so I see you're having a family meeting without me."

It was good for my mom to come here too. I guess she's on less medication for her migraines now—and she's less angry.

"Mom, we were going to talk about what I wrote on the family chat, and I wanted to call you, but I didn't want to bother you as you were in deep conversation with my aunt."

"It's all right, girl."

Everyone was beginning to leave the room, staring at us as if something important was happening. It was obvious that we were going to talk about something very serious.

"Guys, your mother and I have talked a lot about it, but whenever I get the chance at night to come here, you three are always asleep already. We haven't had an opportunity to tell you about our decision until now."

Then Mom said, "We didn't spend much time with you during this visit because we were in a rush to catch up with many relatives, but your patience and sincerity have made both of us happy and proud. Well, guys, before we got here, we were afraid that you'd have problems here and you wouldn't fit in. Thank God that didn't happen. Both the men and the women in our families realize that you did not grow up here, yet you are decent and harmonious. The positive comments that we hear make us feel proud. I especially thank you, Afsun, my daughter. You have taken good care of your brother and sister while your father and I have been busy."

Asra reacted. "Why are you speaking now like a politician talking to party members?"

"Wait, Asra!" I cautioned.

Then Dad said, "Children, you know the problems I was having in Russia. Although Asra and Aziz were born there, they could not become Russian citizens. None of us has any legal status there. As a result, we can no longer return to Russia."

My siblings and I were in absolute shock. We were speechless.

"Your mother and I have been thinking about this for years, and that's why we've been arguing. Our disagreement has made life unpleasant for us for months. Now we will experience good and bad days in Afghanistan. I understand how you feel, but I just can't explain everything to you right now."

In a trembling voice, Asra asked, "Did you plan this before we left Moscow?"

"Yes, since the day I lost my job."

"You lost your job?"

"Yes, girl."

"Why didn't you tell us that before?"

"I didn't want to tell you."

"But, Dad, life doesn't move forward according to what you want or don't want!"

"Now, I think you'd better shut up, my daughter—before you get slapped in the face!"

However, Asra, was too upset to shut up. While I remained silent, she couldn't hold back.

"You've found a good way for yourself, but have you ever sat down and thought about the future of your children? I was elected to the Club of Geniuses this year! Have you thought about that? Mom! What's Dad saying? Okay, we understand you want our support on this, but you've already made such a big decision already, and for once, you don't even share it with us and ask for our opinion! We were going to face it anyway, and your decision wasn't going to change, but we had things to do one last time in Moscow! Wouldn't it have been nice if we had planned this move together before we got here? Maybe I wouldn't have studied like an idiot day and night just to get into that damn Club of Geniuses! Oh, do you want me to tell you something else? Everybody here knew that we were going to stay here, didn't they? Is that why they were looking at us so weirdly when we were like idiots, telling everyone, 'We're leaving soon, and we're going to miss you so much'? Everybody knew the truth, except us, right? We're old enough to wear burkas, but we're not old enough to be informed about life-changing decisions concerning our own lives, are we? But we're old enough to get slapped in our faces!"

Dad's reaction was scary. He became redder and redder. I thought he was going to explode. When I looked at Asra, I understood she wasn't finished. Although I felt the same degree of rage and frustration, I knew my parents. Whatever arguments we presented were futile. The only thing that might've changed the situation was if Dad beat Asra up in front of everyone.

I decided to diffuse the tension. Thinking fast, I stood up, took hold of my siblings' hands, and said firmly, "They did what they wanted, and so they proved how much they care about us."

Then, glaring at my parents, I said, "Good luck with your decision, harmonious couple!"

We went to the other room. Asra couldn't control herself. I made an eyebrow-raising sign to my aunt and grandmother who were trying to get close to her because what we felt wasn't just pain and shock. It was as if we had suddenly fallen from the sky.

Still holding my siblings' hands, I turned to my grandmother.

"Grandma, let us be alone for a while, please."

My voice was shaky because of the knot in my throat.

Grandma said, "Okay, girl."

As we walked to the upstairs room that I always enjoyed being in, my feet were trembling. When I had almost reached the last step, I looked down at my parents. I saw something that hurt more than anything. The two of them were relaxed and laughing as they were chatting with young Aunt Zarifa, Dad's little sister who's around my age. How could they be so lighthearted right after Asra's outpouring of raw emotion? Were they trying to show off to the relatives that they had the situation under control—as if our reaction to being uprooted from our life in Russia was no big deal?

My heart felt squeezed. They had no idea what they were doing to their own children! They didn't even worry about Asra's condition. They probably thought that we're just kids and we'll get over it in time. When I realized the cruelty of my parents, I could see that they were no different from Birishna's parents and many others here.

I went into our room and locked the door. Asra, Aziz, and I spent hours in a corner discussing what had just happened. We talked about how our parents didn't really care about us. We had tried as hard as we could in a foreign country, but all our efforts have been wasted. Sometimes the human brain can't handle a traumatic event, and you think of all the possible ways to cope with it. First, you hope it's just a bad dream. Second, if it's real, then your brain becomes locked because you feel extremely insignificant.

At the end of a silence that lasted two or three hours, I was deeply moved by the rush of tears flowing from Asra's beautiful eyes. She was weeping uncontrollably. I forgot my own pain as I consoled her. As if that weren't enough, Aziz unleashed his sadness and frustration too. He had a lot to say. No one else could understand us, but the three of us understood each other.

We were suffering, feeling the same mix of emotions. Even if the idea of living in Afghanistan had once been a dream for me, now was not the time. Mom and Dad could have waited until after all three of us finished high school.

What about all the years we studied in Russia? All the time we spent there? I speak Persian, the official language of schools here, but my brother and sister barely speak Uzbek. Which school will accept them with this level of language? Asra just completed the eighth grade and Aziz the sixth grade. Well, let's suppose that we end up resettling in Afghanistan. If they study the language for a year, maybe it won't be that hard at their ages. But what about the bright future waiting for Asra? Her school in Moscow prepared her for international physics and mathematics competitions. She worked day and night to get into the club for gifted students.

Despite all this hard work, our parents decided to transplant us here permanently without even asking us once! Couldn't they have found a way for us to stay in Russia and at least finish high school? We came here willingly. We love Afghanistan, but we never agreed to stay here for the rest of our lives. They disregarded our future. Is it impossible for them to turn away from the wrong decision they made?

I knew the reality of the situation. I've been doing a lot of research. We can't leave the country alone because we're minors. We're not Russian citizens. We do not hold our own passports. All our immigration document are with our parents. If we go to the Afghan police and present our case, they won't pay any attention to us. Plus, one of my uncles, Dad's brother, is the police chief here. Obviously, nobody would ever take our complaint seriously. After researching these matters and thinking them through, the only logical way I found to survive was to keep my brother and sister together and make sure things didn't get worse. It would be best to talk about it once again with our parents calmly and rationally.

Aziz's tears had soaked my legs, and he fell asleep in my lap. Asra brought a pillow for him and arranged a place for him to sleep comfortably on the floor. I lifted him up and put him on his makeshift bed. Asra and I sat in front of the window. Even the view from the window we used to open to admire the back garden was now empty.

It was dark. A darkness that intensified our sorrow. Barely could we see each other. Asra's swollen eyes and relentless tears reminded me of Birishna. I stretched out my legs. I asked Asra to turn around, opened the hairband on her long braided hair, gently untangled her hair, and told her that she could rest her head on my leg. I began to massage her head. I knew she found it soothing. Now my own tears were flowing, but Asra was unaware of them. I wish I could figure out a way to alleviate her misery.

My mind returned to a recent episode in Russia, to a time when I was on a school field trip. There was a very bad storm on the way back. When it got dark, our bus broke down. We were stuck on a rural road near a forest. In the darkness, we heard the howling of wild animals. Even when my classmates were crying, I pretended that nothing had happened, but then our teacher began crying too. Her tears shocked me. The fact that even our teacher couldn't conceal her fear meant it was far more serious than just a difficult situation. I thought there was nothing more we could do to save ourselves, nobody left to protect us. Perhaps our teacher knew for sure that we were going to die. However, help finally came and everything was fine. The whole ordeal probably lasted less than an hour, but it seemed like eternity because of our incredible despair.

I guess the situation we're facing now can't really be compared to that school trip in Russia. During that trip, we had two possibilities. Either wild animals would eat us in the middle of the forest, or we would wait to be rescued and drive away in another vehicle. But in our situation today, there's no chance of anyone coming to rescue us. What I realized is that I should stay strong for Asra and Aziz. I shouldn't cry as my teacher did. My brother and sister are already in trouble. I need to fill this void they've fallen into. I need to be supportive. If I'm not, they'll become obsessed with negative thoughts.

Asra began talking.

"Afsun, it's over, isn't it?"

"Don't be silly."

Her wheezing was getting louder.

"You know we'll find a way, right?" I said.

"What way are we going to find? Come on, tell me!"

"I don't know yet, Asra, but I believe we can do something. I believe we can save ourselves, and most importantly, we can do it together."

"Do you really believe we can do it?"

"Yes, Asra, of course, we can. In the worst case, even if we can't get back to Moscow, I believe we can do good things here, and we'll achieve something meaningful. Look, in Russia, you've always wished we could do something to help girls in Afghanistan. Maybe all these troubles are an opportunity for us. Together, we can try to do good work for girls who can't go to school and for women who are victims of domestic violence."

"Sis, let's think about ourselves first. Look what happened to us! You know what girls here go through in order to study! Have you realized that to go to college, we have to get permission not only from our parents but from all our relatives—I mean, all the men? Afsun, I'm not used to such a system, you know. Even in Russia, I would freak out when there were any kinds of sexist arguments. That's why I've always focused on my schoolwork. Now I must get the approval of all the men in the family who haven't even held a pen in their lives, who haven't been to school a single day, whose minds are all about segregating men and women? All these years I've spent studying for my future goals, and now I need to ask for their approval to go to school? You already know the answer. They'll say no just because we're girls. Afsun, this is suicide for me!"

"Please don't say that. Even the thought of suicide is not normal."

"But that's the situation we face right now, isn't it?"

"Asra, as hard as it is, there must be something we can do. Think about it now. Don't give up hope. All I'm asking you right now is to think about what we can do. That's what I'm doing. Look at Aziz. He's also in a tough situation. Mom and Dad didn't even have a second thought when we stood up against them. I don't think they care about our brother either. He's younger and doesn't deserve this! We need to be strong and support each other to find a solution. I'll contact our former teacher, Ms. Olga, for some advice. Don't worry."

Asra didn't say anything more. She really needed to think and cry by herself. I was too busy thinking to cry. I needed to figure out what we were going to do, where we were going to live, what our school life was going to be like.

While tossing around thousands of possible scenarios, I felt a sharp, intense pain in my stomach. I looked at Asra. She had fallen asleep with her head in my lap. I carefully laid her on the floor and stood up. I took one of my mother's sedatives from my bag, but I knew I had to eat something before I took the medicine. I opened the door very slowly. My beloved grandpa was sitting there on the floor and leaning against the wall. He looked sadder and more helpless than we were.

"Granddaughter, are you all right?"

I forgot my own misery for a moment and sat next to him on the floor.

"Of course, I'm not good, Grandpa. Why are you waiting out here? You should have knocked. Have you just been waiting here for us all this time, my dear grandfather?"

"They weren't going to leave you alone, so I waited here because I didn't want them disturbing you by banging on your door unnecessarily. Sometimes the cure for some troubles is just time and being alone to think."

"I wish I could do something else to help my siblings."

"But you've already done something useful. Look how beautifully they're sleeping now. They're both relieved to be alone. And how are you, dear Afsun? Are you relieved? Why aren't you sleeping?"

I didn't think his questions really required answers. At the same time, I didn't want to hurt him.

"I'm fine, my dear grandfather. I just wanted to look for my parents."

"Well, come on, we've got a lot to talk to you about, but now is not the time. There are certain things I think you should know. I'll tell you at the appropriate time."

"Okay, Grandpa. Do you want to sleep here tonight? Come in. I'll make room for you."

Grandpa and I entered the room, and I created a space for him to sleep. He had missed the prayer time by waiting for us at the door. I immediately brought the prayer rug and laid it down. I kissed him before he started his prayers.

Leaving the room, I said, "I'll be right back."

Talking to my grandpa gave me strength. I could see how much he sympathized with us. This man was our biggest supporter here.

When I went downstairs, it was clear that there were fewer guests than usual tonight. Without the women, the men of the house had finally earned the right to enter. My Uncle Nazeem and Aunty Nuriya were sitting on the sofha in the big backyard that my four grandparents shared. I quickly went to the outhouse to avoid them for a little while. Even if they called out to me, I wouldn't turn around because one more word about my father's decision was going to trigger more pain.

When I searched for information on what could be causing this stomach pain, I learned that stress could be a big factor. That's why I knew sedatives were a good solution. The outhouse was next to the storage shed for firewood at the end of the house courtyard. There was a water tank right in front of it. I washed my hands and face thoroughly and went back to my aunt and uncle. This was the first time I would talk to my uncle so closely.

"Hello, Aunt Nuriya. Hello, Uncle Nazeem."

"Hello, Afsun, how are you?"

"How can I be okay, Uncle? You know what's going on."

"Come sit down."

"I have to look for my parents. I'll be right back."

I found my Mom and Dad inside the house. They were sitting with my two grandmothers and my maternal grandfather. My grandfather looked sad.

"Come, girl," said my father.

My mother looked a bit worried.

"Mom, don't worry about my siblings," I said. "They're asleep. Grandpa Raz is with them. What you told us earlier wasn't easy to hear, of course. We were in shock."

Mom's mother invited me to sit down, but I replied, "Uncle Nazeem and Aunty Nuriya are waiting for me in the backyard. I must get back to them. Then I'm going to bed. We can sit down and talk tomorrow."

When I left the room, they began talking behind my back.

I heard my grandfather say, "Few people can bear the pressure and pain of this girl. How calm she is. Bravo."

But what I was going through inside wasn't about being calm or cool. I was just making an effort to get the pain off my shoulders, a pain I couldn't bear.

When I walked back, I noticed my aunt was no longer there. Just Uncle Nazeem. He was still waiting for me.

"I'm glad to see you, Uncle."

"Me too, but I'm sorry to see you looking sad. You're sad about it, aren't you?"

"About what?"

"About what happened—"

"Let's not talk about it, Uncle Nazeem."

"You're right. I'm sorry. So, how do you like this place? Are you starting to get used to it?"

"Depending on your point of view, it's one of the most beautiful places for me."

"It's good to hear that," he replied. "I admire you. It's great that you're standing up to your family. Your altruistic attitude is commendable."

"What I do for myself improves me, and what I do for my family comforts me. I don't call it altruism at all. Family members have common rules to follow."

"That's why you've become my favourite among all my nieces and nephews."

"But we haven't spent much time together, Uncle Nazeem. We don't really know each other well yet."

"I've watched and followed you from afar."

I sighed deeply.

"I'd like to talk to you more, Afsun, but you're obviously tired, so go to bed now. By the way, are you hungry?"

"I'm a little hungry, Uncle. I'd better eat something because I need to take some pills soon."

"Come with me."

He went to his room. I was waiting at the door. He came out with juice and a lot of biscuits.

"I've got these."

"Thank you, Uncle. Shall we eat together?"

"Yes, of course."

I sat down and ate four biscuits. I was as hungry as a wolf. We talked a little bit while we were eating. He told me about himself. I don't even remember what he said exactly because I was so tired.

"Uncle, I'm going to go to bed now. I'm so exhausted that I'm having trouble understanding what you're saying."

"All right, Afsun. Good night."

"Good night."

I took two painkillers with juice and forced my way up the stairs. I stepped between my grandfather and Asra who were sleeping on the floor. I remember tears streaming down my neck until I fell asleep.

When I woke up under the effect of the medication and fatigue, it was dark. I felt like I hadn't slept at all that night. My eyes wouldn't open. I could hear my grandmother's voice by my bedside.

"Get up. Go get some food. Come on, please."

There was someone else with her. I could barely see. It was my mother's voice I heard, so I got up and asked about Aziz and Asra. Uncle Nazeem had taken them for a ride, which was a good reason to love my uncle.

"I'm sorry. I don't understand why I slept so long."

My mother stood next to me. Kissing me on the head, she said, "I understand, girl."

It was nice to hear this simple statement from her, no matter how much she really couldn't understand. A person who understands should think before taking action, and if she still does it even though she understands it, it's not really understanding at all. It's pretending to understand.

My mother patted me on the head.

"Let's talk, girl."

"But please tell me something that makes sense this time, Mom."

"As long as we lived in Russia, we tried not to worry you, but we had serious problems. We lived there for many years, but we didn't get any legal status. We went there first through visitor visas. Then we applied to the UN High Commissioner for Refugees to try to go to America, Canada, or a European country as refugees. Contradictions emerged between the first statement we made when we applied and the statement we made later when they called us for an interview. They wouldn't believe us, and our case was put on hold. Even those who applied much later than us were processed within a few years and went with refugee status to Western countries, but we just waited with no results. We were totally worn out during this time. We weren't able to return to our country, yet we had no status in Russia. And we couldn't get refugee status in another country. Your father was having psychological problems. Our marriage went through a rough period. At one point, we even talked about divorce. Finally, we decided to come back here. It wasn't an easy decision, of course. We've been discussing this plan for months. In the end, without losing my sanity, I became convinced—and now we're here. Unfortunately, we have no right to return to Russia. We don't have visas. When we applied for refugee status, they warned us, 'If you go back to your country, you will lose your refugee claim status here.' I'm afraid we've burned our bridges. As soon as our passports were stamped at the exit, we gave up everything we had built in Russia."

"Mom, why didn't you tell us about all this before we left Moscow? At least we could've come here psychologically prepared."

"Anyway, it's done. It's too late. You've got a lot of work ahead of you now, Afsun. You need to get yourself and your brother and sister together to prepare for your new life in this place. My God, girl, we *can't* go back now."

CHAPTER 13

Take Deep Breaths

I'm confronting painful truths. I'm still mad at my mom and dad. I feel extremely cheated, betrayed. At least they couldn't hide their plans from us any longer. But I have to be reasonable and calm now. Instead of crying and whining, I need to support Aziz and Asra. They need me.

I didn't talk to anyone for a while. Then I got up, ate something, and forced myself to smile. It was good for me to know the truth, so I decided to stand strong and upright. I convinced myself that I could do positive things after all. Besides, no matter how hard it was, I was no different from any other girl here.

I went into the bathroom. Although I've always been a person who likes to shower with cold water, this time I preferred hot water. I stood under the shower for what seemed like hours. The hot water gave me the comfort I'd been longing for. I took out a dress I had bought in Moscow. It had a red and yellow floral pattern. I like colourful dresses. I ironed it and then combed my hair. I used body moisturizer and straightened my eyebrows. That's how I started pampering myself in small ways. It's the first time I've ever put on so much perfume. I wanted to give my hair a different shape. I put some of it up on my head, made a ponytail, and left the rest free. That was one of my favourite styles. I will flash my watch and jewellery. Even if I have to stay here now, I will express myself through my choices of elegant earrings, bracelets, and necklaces. I will remain stylish, strong, and brave, not as I did a month ago. I'll be as I want!

Maybe my life was just beginning. I don't know if I would've recovered so quickly without my brother and sister. Whether I'm actually suppressing my anger or experiencing pre-storm silence, I'd rather have it remain just a question for now.

When I looked at my photo gallery on my phone, I came across a photo captioned "We're going to be friends forever." It was a photograph of the article I wrote with Yulia and Sergei at school. Perhaps we will remain friends forever but from afar.

Before leaving the room, I thought about what I had to do. I was going to pretend as if nothing had happened.

I'm going to take three deep breaths, and when I get out of this room, I'm not going to remember this whole thing anymore. *Come on, Afsun! You can do it! One, two, three* ... I opened the window and inhaled the fresh, oxygenated air, filling up my lungs. From that moment on, it didn't matter what happened. I had to stop crying and complaining to ensure a good future for the three of us. Even if it seemed impossible, even if what Mom and Dad did to us was unfair, I had no choice but to face our new reality and stand strong.

The guests were already arriving. I was surprised to see a young girl standing at the hall door. She looked very much like my aunt's boyfriend, Nimat. Maybe she was one of his sisters. I just passed her and greeted the guests in the room. I embraced them dutifully, one by one. I could play a tall, skinny but strong girl tonight. When the welcoming formalities were over, I left the room and asked Grandma to call my mother's brother. I picked up Mom's phone and went to a quiet corner on the far side of the room.

"Hello, my sister." he said.

"Hello Uncle Nazeem. It's not my mom. It's me, Afsun."

"I can hear it in your voice. Tell me, uncle's rose, what is it?"

"I was going to ask you something if you have time. Can you get me an internet package?"

"It's late now. I don't think the shop is open, but I'll try."

"Uncle, do you know where Asra and Aziz are?"

"They're with me."

"Have they eaten anything?"

"I forced them, a little."

"I'm waiting for you, Uncle. Thank you for taking care of my brother and sister."

"Don't drive me crazy, girl. It's not like we're strangers. Hang up now. Don't worry. We'll be there soon."

I hung up with a smile. I felt relieved that Aziz and Asra had at least eaten something, even if it was forced.

When I approached my grandmother (Mom's mom) in the kitchen, she had to make a negative comment about how I was dressed. Lately, she's been tough and unpleasant.

"Put your headscarf on! Just because your parents made a mistake, you think you can do anything you want now! Cover up like a woman!"

"Grandma, what have I done?"

"You're a grown up now! Look at the clothes you wear shamelessly! Look at your hair! Who are you trying to show yourself off to?"

After a month of so much sweet attention, what caused her to start such a sudden verbal attack? It was as if they were waiting for us to find out the reality about not returning to Russia before they revealed their true opinions about us.

"Grandma, let your ears hear what you're saying! You have to understand that you can't talk to me like that!"

I could say only that much. My voice was shaking. I was surprised at myself for being so bold. I turned and just walked away. She was saying a lot of things behind my back, but I couldn't hear anything—or maybe I didn't want to hear. If I spent my time listening to her, I would fall apart. What I'm angry about is that she should look at her own daughters before she criticizes me. Many of the clothes my aunts wear are lighter and more open than what I wear. There's nothing obvious about me. My dress isn't too open or too short at all.

My grandmother herself was an educated and well-dressed woman. Maybe in time, I'll find out why she was acting like this. That's why I told her—in a very short sentence—to watch out. I wonder if I was being disrespectful. I wish I hadn't talked back to her so harshly.

Since we're definitely going to stay here now, if I get caught up in this kind of friction with either of my grandmothers, I'm always going to be sad for no reason. I may have been subjected to unfair accusations and even humiliation, but I should have stood strong and not wasted my energy. Inevitably, I dwell on such incidents, and let them upset me. Even though I've lived outside the country, I have lived properly, stuck to my own values, paid attention to my head and clothes my entire life. I'm never going to stop wearing the clothes I like. Besides there's nothing exaggerated or inappropriate about the clothes I wear here. Even my mom dresses like this sometimes, so why did Grandma criticize me?

If something like this had happened in the early days, I would've laughed it off, but realizing the situation I'm in now, I was deeply affected by my grandmother's words. While I was still obsessing over it, I heard Aziz call out, "Sister!"

He ran towards me through the open outer door. Behind him were Asra and Nazeem.

Aziz and I hugged each other. This was exactly what I needed. I felt more relaxed. Asra had a bag in her hand. They had bought me the same kind of food and drink they had enjoyed earlier. I noticed my uncle standing still where my grandmother stood. I think he noticed fresh tears drying in my eyes, and he suspected that his own mother had upset me.

I embraced my dear siblings and inhaled their scents deeply. Then I told them to go to Mom and hug her. I know my mother well. She never runs away from trouble. Although she was acting like she didn't care about anything, I could sense the storms going on inside her, as if someone had taken away all her hopes.

As I watched Aziz and Asra, Uncle Nazeem came over and asked, "Is it time to speak, strong leader?"

"My grandmother asked me to help my aunts. I couldn't help them earlier today, so now I must help them get dinner ready."

"You're still a guest, and yet from what I've seen, you're one of the hardest-working people in this house, so we'll tell my big sister right away. She'll take care of it. You come here."

He called out to his eldest sister. She appeared within seconds, her hands covered in yogurt.

"Sister, I'm going to spend some time with Afsun," he announced. "Take care of our mother. Afsun won't be available to do any work tonight."

"Oh, okay. That's fine, my brother," she replied obediently.

This interaction struck me as odd. It bothered me the way she seemed to bow down to her much younger brother. *You're busy with housework, yet you drop whatever you're doing and come running to your brother who is ten years younger than you. Your younger brother is not your superior, not your boss, but he gives you orders, tells you what you can or cannot do.* I can't accept this behaviour towards women. In Afghanistan, fathers, husbands, and brothers inevitably decide everything. Often even mothers are afraid of their own sons. What is this? I want to call it love, but how mutual is that love? Never could I adopt this kind of mentality with my little Aziz.

Sometimes when my cousins asked their mother's permission to stay at their grandparents' home, I would hear the mothers say, "Go ask your brother. I can't ask him. You ask him." It's illogical! The eldest brother has higher authority than the mother? Why can't women have the same authority as men? Some mothers say without hesitation, even proudly, "My daughters are afraid of my son like a dog." This situation saddens and frustrates me. Also, I can't understand girls and women who allow themselves to be beaten up by the men in their family.

"Come on, Afsun," said Uncle Nazeem. "Let's talk. Let's go upstairs."

I sense that my uncle loves me. We connected in such a short time. I think one of the girls visiting my grandmother's house has a crush on him. As she walked past us, she smiled and said, "When will *we* be able to be so close to you, Nazeem?"

"Whenever you want," he replied.

The efforts of girls here to find a husband are hilarious. I was stuck in the middle of this ridiculous flirtatious conversation. I laughed at my uncle. So he pinched my nose and winked.

"Most of these girls came over here for me," he boasted.

"Ha, ha. Even Justin Bieber doesn't have your self-confidence."

"Who's that?"

"Never mind, my uncle. Let's go upstairs."

"Anyway, you should've called one of those girls."

"I've got work to do. You can stay with the girls if you want, and I'll go to work."

"I made a joke, sweetheart."

Uncle Nazeem and I went upstairs. When the women were indoors, my beloved grandfather would sometimes come in and a lot of the girls—except my cousins—would rush to cover their faces. My grandpa would never look inappropriately at girls the age of his grandchildren. However, the same girls were not in a hurry to hide their faces when they saw Uncle Nazeem. It was as if they were more informal and relaxed about the "face-concealment" rules when they were near a *young* man.

CHAPTER 14

Uncle Nazeem

We made our way to my favourite room. The noise of the children playing outside was annoying, but when my uncle entered the room, he turned on the light and closed the windows.

"I think you just have to close the window," I said. "You don't have to turn on the lights. It's still bright enough in here."

"You're right, girl. You're smart."

We both laughed. The light switch was to the right of the door, between the window and the door. When I turned off the light, the atmosphere was ready for sitting and chatting in front of the window.

Uncle Nazeem leaned against one side of the window and I leaned against the other. We were sitting across from each other. He opened the bag next to him and handed me the SIM card he had just bought.

"A friend of mine has a shop. I called at the last minute. He waited for me and I picked it up, but it's only for the ROSHAN provider. It's one of the lines that works well for internet service. I also bought five gigs of internet. He wouldn't even give me a chance to say thank you."

The SIM card was in a red bag with the word YARAN written on it. Uncle Nazeem looked into the bag for a second time and pulled out two books: a Persian-Russian dictionary and a book titled *Kelile and Dimne*.

"Uncle, you've surprised me. Thank you very much."

"In fact, the truth is that all I bought for you was the SIM card. It was your dad's father who gave me the money for the books. He's the one who asked me to buy these for you."

"How come?"

"Your grandfather called me. He asked me to buy these books for tonight. So I said jokingly, 'Give me the money first.' Anyway, he took care of it. He's thinking about you."

"My dear grandpa, I have no doubt that he is always thinking of me."

I was so moved that I could feel my tears starting to well up. Uncle Nazeem suddenly changed the subject.

"Never mind all this, Afsun. Tell me about your conversation with my mother earlier. Why was she angry with you?"

"I don't really know. I thought everything between us was fine. Then suddenly, she started looking me up and down and complaining about my dress."

"Were you upset?"

"Of course I was. Her behaviour and words were too harsh."

"Don't worry about it. My mom's a little different, and sometimes we have a hard time dealing with her moods. Sometimes she enjoys upsetting others."

"Uncle, please don't say that about her. She's your mother."

"I know she's my mother, dear Afsun. I think you need to understand something, or I'm worried it's going to hurt you a lot too, one day. My mother likes to rule people. I learned that once I left home and got out of town. First, she approaches you gently, as if she likes you, and then she begins to manipulate you with ugly, negative words. She acts in such a way that she makes the other person feel guilty. She has such a talent for it. She knows how to provoke a reaction in people close to her to feel powerful. Even though she's sometimes mean to people and blames them, she herself is the root of her problems. She wants to control everyone. She tries to make things the way she wants them to be. On the outside, we seem to be a decent, harmonious family. Most of the girls around here want to come to our home as brides. But look at my sisters-in-law. Has one of them ever come to have a conversation with you?"

I never thought about it. He was right. None of them has really come to start a conversation with me.

Uncle Nazeem continued. "Well, two of my sisters-in-law became teachers. First, my brother Gulagha got married. His wife graduated with an economics degree. She achieved very good scores. She worked hard until the last day. She was the daughter of a respected family. Her father was a university professor, and he let her go to college. Everything was going well in her life—until my mother saw her. At first, she seemed to support my brother's interest in this girl, telling Gulagha, 'Oh, look at what a diligent girl she is, and so beautiful and good.' Then she made plans with the girl's mother and finally got her wish. As for my sister-in-law, her first year was good. Everything seemed to be going smoothly, but my mother directed everything. My sister-in-law didn't have a chance to talk with her friends. My mother decided how she should dress, what she should eat, what her child's names would be, which nights she would go to bed with her husband. My mother made all the decisions for my sister-in-law's life!

"While continuing in this way with her first daughter-in-law, she established the same pattern of behaviour with her second daughter-in-law, who was only eighteen years old when she married one of my other brothers. Both my sisters-in-law used to be strong, beautiful girls, like angels. They were normal people who could make friends, but my mother turned them into robots that only she could program. Now they're two powerless women who have no idea how to be independent. They just do whatever their mother-in-law says. The reason I'm telling you this is because you're not like my sisters-in-law—and thankfully, you're not like my sisters. I know it sounds harsh, but you need to continue protecting Asra and Aziz from my mother. You mustn't let her put you in the same position as my sisters-in-law. Look at your own mother. She has never been allowed to live with her own thoughts. Even when she was in Russia, my mother tried to control her. Your mother was used as a toy by her own mother and your father—and even by your other grandmother."

I couldn't believe what Uncle Nazeem was saying. My ears were wide open as he explained his mother's psychological condition.

"What I'm trying to tell you now is that you should be careful with these people. Don't be too confrontational with my mother. At the same time, don't take what she says too seriously. If you go against her, she will poison everyone's minds against you: your cousins, aunts, and all your relatives. She'll introduce you as a 'naughty person.' After that, you know, they'll wear you down together. In fact, this kind of behaviour can pass from generation to generation of women in some families, but in my mother, it's a serious problem. If I'd noticed these signs of abnormal behaviour sooner, I could've done better to help her. Nuriya is in a slightly better condition, and actually, my mom's doing much better now than five years ago. I took her to Pakistan for treatment. Her psychological condition was not good, but she would never agree to see a doctor for that purpose. That's why I convinced her by telling her we were going to see a doctor for her foot ailment. When we left, the psychiatrist asked questions for hours. As an interpreter, I helped with my intermediate English. She even found the doctor's questions ridiculous. At one point, she said, 'It's not like that. Enough is enough. Stop questioning me about my family.' Ordinarily, the doctor wouldn't let me in, but he allowed me because I was there as her interpreter-translator, not her son. So, after a few sessions of interviews and various tests, the doctor diagnosed my mother with a high degree of bipolar disorder.

"We had a thirty-day visa to Pakistan. Even though my father didn't want us to go, I took my mother with my own money. We were staying in a hotel, and I was running out of money. I told the doctor about the situation. He gave me a prescription for the medication she needed and instructed me on how to behave to handle my mother's condition. If we had done what the doctor advised, my mother would be seventy percent better in a year. When we got back, I spoke with family members in front of my father and my brothers when my mother was not present. As soon as I began explaining what was going on, my father reacted by slapping me in the face. Actually, it wasn't really a slap. It was more like a hard punch. He hit me in the eye and said, 'How could you take your mother to a psychiatrist?' I tried to reason with him. 'Dad, listen, Mom needs to get better for her mental health, so she needs to get her medication right, and we need to do what the doctor says.' I said this in pain and shock, but the situation escalated.

"My eldest sister looked at my brothers and said, 'You're still sitting here listening to this guy talk about your mother's life? Shame on you! There's no such thing as a family secret. God knows who else he's told. Who knows what else will come of this!' I wanted to respond to my sister, but I didn't have a chance to talk. Stirred up by my sister's words, my brothers took me into the middle of the room and beat me. Only Nuriya tried to stop them, but they pushed her away. After that family drama, I stayed away for a while. My friends and I rented a room in Mazar-i-Sharif so that my years of preparation for university would not be wasted. The room was near a centre with car mechanics. Nine people shared a four-metre-long room. I had five choices for the test, and I chose psychology. This department was a newly opened branch in Afghanistan. Few people select psychology as a major, and those who do, usually don't end up working as psychologists. Anyway, I was quite well prepared for the exam. I studied away from home for a year and a half. My goal was to become a good psychologist in the future.

"On the day of the exam, everything started normally. The questions were fairly easy, and I made the most of my time. As the end of the exam was approaching, I thought to myself, 'You did it!' Then the guy behind me asked to borrow a pen. When I went to hand it to him, I felt some liquid was flowing. It turned out that the pen was leaking. Black ink had spread onto my exam document, invalidating it! From that moment, my dreams were shattered, and nothing went well in my life. I couldn't tell anyone what I thought anymore. Others mocked me relentlessly, sarcastically calling me a psychologist. It was such a tough time for me. So, Afsun, instead of cheering you up, now look where our conversation has led."

"But why didn't you just get another exam document?"

"In Afghanistan, a single document comes from the exam centre for the people who will take the university exam. The candidate's photo is on it with some code numbers. If anything happens to that document, you lose your right. Afsun, don't worry. Our time here is going to be fun. There's nothing to be afraid of. I've had some great memories in Faryab, of course, and I'd like to share them, but now we don't have time. I didn't say all this to scare you. I just want you to be careful. Don't let anyone hurt you or your siblings."

"Why are you talking like that, like you're going away somewhere?"

"Because I'm going to go ... Joke!"

"No really. Tell me where."

"The truth is I'm going to join the army. I'm going to be a soldier."

"Oh, really? That sounds cool."

"Yes, well, I'm going to be a commando. That's why I'm off to Kabul early tomorrow morning. I don't want to work for my father anymore. As long as I stay here, I will grovel like my brothers. If I stay here, I won't be allowed to marry the girl I love, nor will I have an opinion for myself."

"I think you made a good decision, Uncle Nazeem."

"It's good to hear that, but don't tell anyone, okay?"

"But if you leave, they'll wonder where you are."

"They won't even notice I'm gone for a few weeks."

"Uncle, did you just say 'the girl I love'?"

"No," he replied.

"I heard you say it. So, good. There's someone here you love."

"Yes, there is, actually. How did you know?"

"Do I know her? Show me her picture, please. My aunt showed me someone."

"What? Nuriya?"

"Yes, Nuriya showed someone."

Now he unlocked his phone and showed me a picture.

"Her name is Anosha. She's a sweet girl with blonde hair."

"Where did you meet her?"

"We've known each other since my brother's wedding, and I tried so hard to connect with her. Finally she fell in love with me too. I wanted to get engaged, but because her father was a drug addict, my parents wouldn't let me. They said stupid things like 'Forget about us if you marry this girl.' It was cruel to blame her. But now I'm ready to face the wrath of my family. The problem here is that my parents are the ones who have to go to her house to ask her parents for her, or they won't allow the marriage. Anyway, I'll wait until I can persuade my family members to accept her. Actually, since Anosha's father is a drug addict, I have an advantage. At least, no one else will want her before I get back from the army."

Uncle Nazeem was funny and different. It felt good to listen to him. Now I'm no longer angry with my grandmother. Now I'm going to block out the negative things she says and just try to be nice to her.

"Afsun, are you on Facebook?"

"Yes, of course."

"Good. Look at Anosha's page. She's taking a computer course, and from there she gets online and writes to me. She knows about you. You can write to her. You'll be friends. Her personality is very similar to yours. I think you'll like her."

"That's good, and thank you for trusting me."

After we installed my new SIM card, I wrote to Anosha. She wrote back right away.

"Uncle Nazeem, why did you wait so long to come and talk to me on your last night? I wish you had stayed with us."

"The house was too crowded. I didn't want to disturb you—until today."

We hugged, laughed, and tried to cheer each other up.

Everyone has a different story, no matter what their outer appearance is. What a long, troubling story some people have. I was wondering what other family stories I was going to hear as long as I stayed here. Uncle Nazeem turned on the light, and we took photos together. Then we went downstairs to join the others. We didn't talk to each other much more that night, but later, I texted him to let him know that he couldn't leave early in the morning without seeing me once more.

I entered the room where many women were sitting. Aziz had fallen asleep there, so I guided him to the room where I was going to sleep and went back to sit with the women.

"I love my mom's mom," I said spontaneously in front of everyone—including my other grandmother who was sitting a little farther away.

Anyway, I went directly over to my maternal grandmother and said, "I'm sorry, honey-mom, but I think I know what I'm doing. However, if there's anything you want to say to me, you can say it in a fair way. I spoke the way I did earlier for your own good."

She looked at me as if she had heard the word "sorry" for the first time.

Although she didn't say anything, she touched my hand. At least, this little gesture suggests that things are okay between us for now. I guess I hadn't offended her as much as I had feared.

My heart still aches for Asra. She was sitting in a corner and seemed to be crying. I had to do something for her as soon as possible.

It was finally bedtime. Aunty Nuriya was happy to stay with us, and as usual, it was late.

"Afsun, come on, it's time to go to sleep."

It was 1:45 a.m. when I got a text from Uncle Nazeem saying, "I'm leaving at 5:00." I wanted to see him one more time before he left. At the beginning of his journey, he was not supposed to feel lonely and hopeless. It was already late. But if I fell asleep, I wouldn't be able to get up in time. If I put my phone on alert, everyone would wake up. Aunty Nuriya and I sat by the window and chatted for a little while. Then with the help of the light from outside, I read *Kelile and Dimne*.

I read until around 4:30 a.m. My aunt had fallen asleep with her phone on her chest. I could go out and wait for my uncle now. First, I tried to get my aunt's phone off her chest, and I came across a scene like a movie. Her phone was on and Nimat was still listening to her. I left the room quietly, leaving her phone next to her.

My uncle's last message to me caught my attention: "You go to sleep, my dear. I'm going to leave a little early because my father will go to prayer at 5:00, so don't let him see me." Fearing I was too late, I was so upset. But then a man wearing sneakers appeared through the trees. I knew he was Uncle Nazeem, so I approached him. We hugged and promised to write and call each other.

"Afsun, I'm glad you're here. You've made me feel happy. Your siblings are in your care. Also, take care of yourself. I trust you. Whatever the circumstances, you will succeed." He was wearing only a backpack and a local black shirt, with a Kandahar shawl on his back. Uncle Nazeem was medium-sized compared to other men, but he really was one of the most handsome men I've ever seen here. When I saw him off and returned to the bedroom, it was impossible to fall back to sleep. With my headphones on as usual, I started listening to nostalgic songs and began crying. Remembering my uncle's words, I couldn't hold back my tears. I prayed this wouldn't be the last time we saw each other.

As the sun was rising, I could hear my grandmother talking to my grandfather. Then I drifted back to sleep. I got up at noon. I learned that Uncle Nazeem had called and told his family everything. I think it was a good decision letting them know. Apparently, his mother is used to his behaviour. It was his second time leaving. But when I saw my aunts and family members crying, I knew it was worse than I thought. There was a high risk of soldiers losing their lives due to adverse security conditions in Afghanistan. It is said that more than one hundred soldiers are killed daily. Even more tragically, when they fight on the frontline, they are often captured and slaughtered en masse by the Taliban because of the lack of reinforcements for immediate support. When I found out, I started to worry a lot, but I trusted Uncle Nazeem. I prayed that nothing bad would happen to him before he could have a chance to be with the one he loved.

CHAPTER 15

Ramadan

We are well into the month of Ramadan. All the *suhurs* and *iftars* have been very beautiful, especially with a lot of people. Although these traditional meals at sunrise and sunset are enjoyable, they're sometimes a bit of a struggle to prepare because of the power outages and the oppressive heat. Also, some of our relatives are not very understanding. Worst of all, I have to act like I'm fasting—even on my "special days." I woke up one morning and discovered that my period had started. I got a glass of water and a leftover date. Aunty Gawhar, Mom's older sister, came to the iftar that night, and she stayed with us for the night. When she saw me drinking water, she reacted.

"Oh, girl, don't you fast?"

Next, her mother-in-law started to attack me without understanding, without listening.

"Don't you know they raised heretics in Russia? Look at her. She's as big as a donkey, but not fasting!"

"Sorry, I'm already enjoying my fast," I replied, "but I have my period, and I don't think it's appropriate for me to fast on these days!"

Both women glared at me.

I get very emotional and irritable when I have my period. Also, I was really tired after catching up with my siblings. It was tiring to listen to Aziz complaining about how hungry he was. However, he wouldn't accept it when I said he was still too young for fasting. Asra, on the other hand, was a little better at it. When I looked at her, I saw a strong girl who could take care of herself. Even if she wasn't particularly interested in the welfare of others, she was taking good care of herself and maybe doing the right thing for the situation we were in.

Unfortunately, even our religion has not been properly explained here. They tend to overdo it to the extent that tolerance and humanity have been forgotten in Afghanistan—the birthplace of Mawlana, the famous philosopher and poet of the thirteenth century and a symbol of love, respect, and peace.

We had a special guest tonight: one of the greatest religious scholars of Faryab. He is one of my father's uncles. He came with his whole family. Everyone was busy all day preparing a feast. After the fast was broken, all the men here sat close to this person to listen to his inspirational words. I wish we women could have listened too. I hear he has some powerful messages, but as usual, we had to remain in a separate area.

We prepared dinner from morning until the time of the iftar. If it had been up to me, we would have served only soup and a main course because the power was out, but when I walked into my grandmother's kitchen this morning, I saw they were making incredible preparations in a small kitchen. Actually, it's not small, but it seems too small for a family of twenty.

There wasn't enough space to accommodate all the food, and in the hot weather, the little window in the kitchen wasn't enough to let in light and ventilate the room. There was a small door running from the kitchen to the bread tandoor. Working in the heat of boiling boilers and fatty dishes, on top of the natural heat of the season, was extremely stressful! I've never seen a chopping board and a work counter in any of the kitchens here. We were hand-chopping onions and herbs. Since there was no table, we had to sit on the floor for hours to make the pastries. I felt like my back was going to fall off.

Despite all the challenges, I didn't complain because the girls and women here are so friendly. Sometimes even the neighbours come over to help. I enjoy doing household duties with team spirit in a warm family atmosphere. I think one of the biggest reasons I love this place is the solidarity I sense among the women.

We spent only two iftars in our own houses (my paternal and maternal grandmothers' houses). For all the rest of nights of Ramadan, we were invited to the homes of other relatives. Each dinner was lively and enjoyable.

Knowing how difficult it is to prepare a meal in hot weather, I offered to help the women in the kitchen wherever we were invited.

One evening after dinner, one of my younger cousins approached me.

"Afsun, sister, Aziz is crying."

Aziz was in my aunt's room. Normally, he doesn't cry easily, so I was so afraid it was a serious problem. Before the guests had arrived that night, my grandmother asked me to wear the dress I was wearing when we went out of town. It was a long, black linen dress. I was too late to help in the kitchen. Two minutes before the inauguration, I went and put on the dress. Although I was wearing underwear, of course, I didn't have time to put on a pair of pants under my dress. However, I assumed my legs wouldn't be exposed because my dress was quite long. I was extremely hungry while the prayer was being recited. I was also ready to faint from thirst. In my rush to get to Aziz, I tripped and fell when I was walking through the narrow doorway between the two houses.

The first thing I remember is that my legs were open and I wasn't wearing any pants under the dress. I hit my knee pretty bad, and it hurt. Even then, what I was worried about was whether someone had seen my bare legs. I got up with the speed of light and looked around. The only person around there was the orator's daughter. It wasn't clear exactly how old she was, but she was giving milk to a little girl in her arms. She saw me, and when I made brief eye contact, she smiled, but I moved on quickly without looking closely at her face. I was afraid I'd be humiliated if she told anyone my legs had been visible, but the more important thing now was Aziz. He wasn't weeping when I got to him—probably, the other boy had exaggerated—but he was definitely upset.

"My Aziz, what happened to you?"

"Nothing, sister."

Unlike Asra, Aziz would normally tell me everything, so as soon as I looked him in the eye, he started opening up about what had happened.

"The imam was talking to my father before the iftar, and he looked at me and said, 'Son, how old are you?' I said, 'Almost thirteen.' Then he asked me if I've been circumcised! I was so embarrassed by the way he asked that in front of everyone!"

"He didn't say anything bad to you, actually. Don't you think it's time?"

I can't forget the look on Aziz's face. He looked terrified but so sweet.

Apparently, on the day of Eid, the imam saw Aziz with my father once again and asked the same question in front of the crowd of men.

"Aziz, my son, you didn't answer last time. Have you been circumcised yet?"

Obviously, Dad was embarrassed and ashamed. Aziz was already a teenager. Normally, boys in Afghanistan are circumcised right after birth or no later than five years old.

My father confessed, "No, brother, he hasn't been circumcised yet."

Everyone started laughing at that point, and then the imam said, "We need to do it now, as soon as possible!"

Grandpa Raz, who witnessed the whole scene, announced, "We will have a circumcision wedding for my grandson next Friday!"

Immediately, he began making preparations for it. Here in Afghanistan, the circumcision is celebrated like a wedding, so it's called a "circumcision wedding." Later all the details for the event were discussed: the menu, the guests, the venue. There was also talk among the women about the entertainment. That part of the planning was the most fun: the choice of costumes, the group dances, the music. Everyone said it was important to make this circumcision wedding a huge event, since our family was one of the most prominent families in Faryab. Others would expect us to celebrate in a big way. A fun-loving team of nieces and cousins was assembled to help organize everything.

My favourite grandfather entered the kitchen while I was washing the dishes. The other women had gone to practise their dances. I'm glad I had volunteered to stay behind and wash the dishes so that my aunt could go to the other room with the girls for dance practice. With water from the tank in front of the kitchen, I washed the dishes in two large basins. Anyway, I had this chance to chat with Grandpa Raz privately. I dried my hands and hugged him right away. He was the one who taught me many things.

Although we had a big, respectable family, there were some things about our family that I didn't approve of. For example, I had a conflict of opinion with family members about education. Especially among girls, there was always a warped logic that men should work and earn money so we women can enjoy material things. Also, it infuriates me that our education isn't talked about much. Mom once said I'd be starting college in the future, but no one has much idea about the details of how that's going to happen.

Tonight I wanted to talk to my favourite grandfather about school.

"Grandpa, how will our school issue be resolved?"

"Now don't worry too much about that. Have fun for now. I'll deal with it. Don't worry, my dear girl. I know people in the education department. I'll get information from them."

Grandpa's positive energy and confident answers relaxed me and helped alleviate the great burden on my shoulders. I felt safe and secure around him. He was a man who found solutions to every problem and showed the right direction.

"Thank you, Grandpa. I'm glad to have you. Please let me know about school."

"Of course. Go inside, and I'll collect the dishes."

"No, Grandpa. You don't have to do that."

"I'm not like your father, who refuses to do chores in the kitchen."

All the women were busy with specific tasks in preparation for Friday's big event. At my maternal grandmother's house, huge pieces of fabric were being laid out and sewing machines were whirring in the middle of the big room. At my paternal grandmother's house, the young women on the entertainment team were continuing their menu planning and dance practising. Turkish songs are indispensable for entertainment and especially girls' group dances in Afghanistan. I walked into the room and started watching them. They danced so well. I wanted to join in, but I didn't want to risk disrupting their rhythm.

Many of these girls carry a burden of sadness and suffering. They have experienced huge losses and troubles, but when immersed in certain environments, they can enjoy themselves, at least for a little while. I saw that they were trying to be happy and strong, as if nothing had happened. They could laugh and appreciate little things. Initially, I thought they were pretending to be happy, but when I spoke to Sultan, one of my younger aunts, she said that people here could soon forget their pain and cling to life again.

Recently, on a sunny day of Ramadan, I was washing dishes in the kitchen with Aunty Nigar, one of Dad's sisters. I'll never forget what she said to me that day.

"Afsun, we women in this country grow up suffering from childhood. We must face social oppression and ignorance, as well as the negative impacts of an ongoing war. Women and children suffer the most. If what happens to us happened to people living in a wealthy Western country, they would never be able to tolerate it. They'd probably commit suicide. On the one hand, we live in hell because of the war. It robs us of our loved ones. On the other hand, social pressure and forced marriage at a young age destroys us. Domestic violence already begins as soon as we come into the world as 'girls.' When a child is born, the family must be prepared for two situations. If the baby is a boy, there's a feast, and if the baby is a girl, there's an atmosphere of mourning.

"We have a lot of problems, but we have to forget quickly, even if it's hard, or we'll miss out on the beautiful things in life. For example, they married me off at a young age against my will to someone who was a stranger to me. Maybe in other countries, this is a crime, and when you complain, the government holds your hand and rescues you, but justice doesn't happen here. They're forcing little girls into marriage when these girls should be in school. Nobody has the courage to object. Girls who dare to defy the decisions of their parents and grandparents are either killed or handed over to their families by the authorities if they file a complaint, and the file is closed. Then the names of these girls are tarnished forever. Everyone in the community turns their backs on them.

"I know exactly what happens to young women who dare to stand up to their families and leave home. They end up tortured, raped, and/or killed. I know some girls who have committed suicide to escape. Other women just shut up to avoid the fate of those brave girls. Our parents keep trying to find us a rich husband, and we go along with it. Of course, a few other families in this city are as 'civilized' as our family, yet we fail to speak out enough to help those other girls. As a result, dear Afsun, nobody really improves the situation directly. They just pretend to do so or make superficial attempts for Western media. Even some of those 'women's rights defenders' who appear on TV use photos of poor Afghan girls on their literature so they can get project money from foreign countries and promote their own public images. But the girls here still feel abandoned. They're still being forced into marriages. Most of them still can't go to school.

"I must admit that some girls and women manage to save themselves, but their ratio is around one in a thousand. It's really like a dream to be like them. I used to want to be like Sharifa Azimi, a woman leader in Faryab. I worked hard, even attended a meeting and gave a speech. Everyone loved it. But when I wanted to go on the second day, my brother, the 'educated one,' was furious. First, he cut my hair. Then he transferred me to a different school. In one day, I lost my school, my circle of friends—and my self-esteem.

"I witnessed my poor cousin getting killed on her wedding day simply for yelling, 'I don't accept it!' I know the reality of this place. Even several years after my cousin's death, my aunt never wore any colourful dresses. She never laughed again from the inside. She died from her grief and was buried with her daughter. Pity the woman who feels she must hide her pain from others.

"All the women here have psychological problems. I'm no exception. But look, when it's party time at weddings and circumcisions, we put on the gold jewellery we accepted from our despicable husbands so that we can show off to other women. And anyone who sees these women at parties would assume they are the happiest women in the world. Sadly, some of the Afghan girls and women who suffer domestic abuse have such low self-esteem that they believe they deserve it. They've been brainwashed into thinking that men are just naturally in charge of everything, and women should obey their rules without any objections.

"If anyone wants to save this country, they need to provide psychological treatment for everyone first. The people need to be freed from generations of backward thinking. Our community elders need to see the truth about how damaging their narrow ideas are. Our society can change only when our families are ruled with love and respect instead of fear and pressure. In my case, I was too scared. I knew what would happen to me if I dared to protest. Maybe I was a coward, but if I hadn't conformed, I'd be dead by now. Sometimes I wish I were dead. Then I wouldn't have to think about all of this again and again. I realize that death is not a solution either. Then I just sleep hugging my gold bracelets and bow to my fate.

"When my father, your dear Grandpa Raz, got older and each of my brothers grew up and became strong, he didn't get much of a say in anything. That's why even my uncles and brothers make decisions about us. Out of respect for my father, they at least inform him about their decisions afterwards. I think my father is no longer able to fight against all these men alone."

I realize that most of the girls here actually think like my aunt, but they don't have the power to fight. Although sometimes it might seem like I've forgotten what happened to us, I'm not really silent and passive inside. I'm just trying to stay strong to protect Asra and Aziz.

✢ ✢ ✢

We've been preparing for a full week. Aziz seemed worried when I went to the hair dresser early this morning, so I talked to him. His cousins said the procedure would hurt more because he's older. Plus, it's not a doctor who performs the circumcision operation. He searched online about its risks. I tried to cheer him up and sent him off to find Dad.

I didn't really want to go to the hairdresser, but they said I had to go as the "circumcision boy's" sister. Every woman here has prepared at least three dresses for different parts of the event. I just brought one dress. I went to the hair salon with Aunty Nuriya. It seems that everyone had taken a shower in the early morning because I could smell the shampoo in their hair. There were about thirty girls. Each of them showed the hairdresser a picture of a model they had identified, saying, "I want to be like the woman in this photo."

The salon was near our house. My aunt knew the salon staff quite well.

The owner looked at me and asked, "What style do you want, Russian girl?"

I didn't like people treating me like an outsider, but I understand their reactions. My clothing style, my mannerisms, my looks, and my pronunciation set me apart from other women here. In their minds, I am a Russian girl. And thanks to Aunty Nuriya, whenever she introduces me to anyone, she starts explaining where I came from even before saying my name!

"Begum, you can prepare Afsun's hair like mine."

"But Aunty, I don't even know what kind of style you're planning to get."

I didn't like it when they started putting makeup on my aunt. I knew that if I wore such heavy makeup, it would damage my skin. Also, it's not suitable for a girl my age. I stepped away to call my grandpa.

"My granddaughter, don't get stressed," he advised me. "Explain to your aunt that you don't have to be like all the others."

His words calmed me down. Maybe I could have managed this situation without consulting him, but he was the one I trusted the most now. I needed his opinion to be sure about everything. Maybe I was just looking for an excuse to hear his voice.

I walked back to my aunt.

"Do I have to wear makeup, Nuriya? I prefer to look natural."

"Why? Don't you like *my* makeup?"

"It's not that, Aunty. It's just that so much makeup is inappropriate for someone my age. Probably, they won't even agree to apply heavy makeup on a sixteen-year-old girl."

The salon owner started laughing and said, "This girl really doesn't like makeup! Girl, I'm going to prepare a bride tonight—and she is also sixteen. What do you say to that?"

Luckily, Aunty Nuriya intervened.

"Afsun, you do what makes you feel comfortable."

"You're not mad, are you, Aunty?"

I had my hair straight and simply blow-dried. I wore my long black dress from Moscow, and I had just a little eyeliner on. All the other girls who came and went looked at me. I bet they were probably thinking, "What an idiot this girl is." But I was comfortable following my own style.

That day, around 11:00 a.m., still feeling sleepy, we arrived at the wedding hall. Even the stairs to the fourth floor were full of people. I couldn't understand why some families in this country would invite over a thousand guests to a circumcision wedding while other families in the same country were struggling to find decent food and shelter.

In our long dresses, we carefully ascended the dusty stairs. The young men seemed to be waiting for our arrival. They didn't take their eyes off us for a second. As soon as we walked in, we took the burkas off and put them in the bags we had brought with us. The videographer was filming without giving us a moment to adjust our clothes. I reacted by saying, "Wait a minute. Please let us pull ourselves together first." I almost got run over in the crowd. However, while I was dancing with the other women on the dance floor, I put the hot and busy day behind me. The special celebration began at the wedding hall with only women, but it continued later at the house where the men were already enjoying music and an impressive array of special dishes.

When Aziz arrived, two of my father's younger brothers put him on their shoulders. Just before they took him inside for the actual surgical procedure (witnessed by the men only), Aziz noticed me and called out, "Sis, come here quickly!" I approached him, and he whispered in my ear, "Hide my money in my bag. I don't want to risk dropping it." It was so funny. I took the money he'd been gifted right away and followed his request.

When they brought him back downstairs and out into the courtyard afterwards, he looked like a groom in local white clothes and with a traditional cone on his head. Some of the guests were video recording him. Others were clapping. It was crowded. Neighbours, relatives, and friends arrived to congratulate him.

Despite how stressful it was, the entire event went smoothly. All night long, everyone ate, danced, and celebrated. At least, it gave many of the women an opportunity to forget about all the negativity in their lives and just have fun for one evening. Now I can say I've officially witnessed my first circumcision wedding.

CHAPTER 16

Settling In

Half a year has passed since we arrived in Afghanistan. During that time, we've had many memorable days, both sweet and bitter. I find myself thinking a lot about Birishna lately. I have no idea what's happening in her life now, since I haven't been able to return to the vineyard. Now Taliban militants are close to the entrance of the city. We can hear the sounds of helicopters and fighter jets. Day by day, this country is becoming more unstable.

Aziz and Asra have started taking Persian language courses. Today we had a good time together, creating an intimate atmosphere. Remembering what Uncle Nazeem had said about his mother, I advised my siblings to treat our maternal grandmother patiently and warmly, like a friend.

From today, we'll have our own home. They went to pick out the new house. Grandpa Raz is taking us with him, and now we're waiting to hear back. He said he'd return after lunch. My uncle sent me a photo of a four-walled lot, and I wanted to ask Grandpa about the location.

I took off my hijab veil. The headscarf was a Herat burka especially prepared for me. They had asked someone to send it for me from Herat—as if it mattered where they got that dungeon curtain. I didn't want to wear it. "Dear, you listen to your father now," my grandfather had advised. "Take these burkas, but don't worry. You know that as long as I'm alive, no one can force you to wear them." That's why I was sure I wasn't going to wear that new burka again.

When we got into the car, Grandpa looked at us and said, "My dear grandchildren, guess what neighbourhood your new home is in?"

"Afghankot?"

"No."

"Baluch khana?"

"No, Aziz."

"Zargar khana?"

"No, Asra."

"Grandpa! Then where is it?" we all demanded.

"My dear grandchildren, I never really wanted you to go to another house. I wanted you with me. I told your mother, but she didn't accept that. I guess your mother is right. Every family should have their own home, but don't think you're going to get rid of me. Save a room for me. I'll see you seven days a week. Your grandmother may divorce me." He began laughing.

As we listened to Sarban songs playing at a low volume in the car, our warm conversation and laughter told us how wonderful life was after all.

"Oh, by the way, your house is located very close to the school I chose for you. It's right between Afghankot and Ghond 35, in a very good spot. I'm sure you will like it!"

"Grandpa, is that close to you?"

"Although we couldn't find a house for sale on our street, it's not that far from us, maybe only ten minutes on foot. Pretty close."

When we drove from my grandparents' house to the Afghankot School, we saw a boys' school just to the left of the street. From there, we turned left and went up a little. Less than a year ago, there were people living in houses where streets now exist, but the municipality expropriated those homes because they were in the way. Remnants of some of the former structures were still visible. On the side streets that ran right through the middle of the houses, the homeless were living in tents. There were multi-storey buildings as well. I saw some unfinished new buildings just up ahead. Only two houses caught my eye. When I was dreaming of going to school in the near future, I thought I'd walk these streets like a normal girl of Faryab, not a guest anymore.

Turning to Grandpa, my mother asked, "Is this really a good place?"

"My dear, now whether or not you will feel comfortable here will depend on the relations with the neighbours and your environment," replied Grandpa. "Even though this district is considered the centre of the city, most of the former houses here have been destroyed, as you can see. Now, I don't know what to do with this little area that's left behind, but I doubt we could've found a better place. There's a public university, a boys' school, and a girls' school in your immediate vicinity."

When we turned to the right, we entered a narrow dirt road. That's where Grandpa parked the car. I didn't know which of these doors was ours, but the first door on the left looked a little different and warm to me. Grandpa was waiting for one of the workmen to open it, but then he turned around and opened the first door on the right, a big, green iron door with a little pattern of red flowers on it. I could see a view of big stones and few trees through the open door.

Aunty Nuriya was next me.

Slowly, she said "You know that house over there, two doors down, that's Nimat's house." She seemed thrilled to announce this fact to me, but she seemed to be speaking to her Nimat.

Our new home was one of the houses being built to replace the older houses demolished for the road construction. They had chosen to build new houses afterwards, and it didn't matter what they looked like now. I could see the end of the street through the door. There was a small mosque, a light green and white minaret, and a large shrine next to it. I wasn't sure what it was, but we were going to live here now, and I was going to see it anyway.

We saw the land but did not go inside the house yet. The neighbourhood seemed warm. As soon as the neighbours saw the car, they came over to welcome us. Some of the children were barefoot. Some of the women had come with dough on their hands. That's exactly why I love this country. When most of the people wake up in the morning, they laugh despite their poverty. If they lose their children, they try to overcome it by saying, "God give us patience." There must be good and bad people everywhere in this world, but in Afghanistan the good ones are special. Sometimes you feel closer to them than to your own family. There are also bad ones, of course, very bad ones. They could be the most brutal. Living here is sometimes a miracle. Maybe the circumstances have put them in this position. I don't know, but there seems to be more sadness and tragedy than good things about living here.

When we were getting back into the car, the neighbours gathered around again to say goodbye. They were all very friendly. All the young girls I met went to Afghankot High School, the school near our house, so I guess that's where we're going to start our education in Faryab.

We went to get our pictures taken and receive IDs. When we got home, an old man was waiting for my grandfather at the door. Grandpa handed the man our IDs with some money.

"Kids, good luck. You're registered in school now."

"How? What's going on, Grandpa?"

"Nothing to worry about, Afsun. They're going to call you for a test. Then you'll start with no other obstacles."

I witnessed what could be done with irregularities and bribery. Normally, we would go in person to deal with any bureaucratic matters. It was interesting to just hand over the IDs and get everything sorted out almost instantly. I didn't know who that old man was, but I was sure he wasn't involved in something legal.

"Grandpa, why did you give that man money?"

"Now, my dear, you don't know much about Afghanistan. When I was young, I used to think that I'd do all the paperwork by myself without having to pay someone. I remember the times I would be running around for a month just to get an ID. I was so tired of hearing 'give me money or a cup of tea, brother' everywhere I went. When I got angry and protested, they would get more aggressive and find a thousand excuses to delay my work. I'm not in the mood to fight any longer. You're right. Maybe I should've done things the regular, honest way, but the schools are going to be opening soon. I don't want you to face any trouble or delays. Maybe what I'm doing isn't right, but I ask you not to act like me when you're in a situation like this."

I learned something else from Grandpa Raz. Even if the person you're dealing with is young, you have to explain in a logical way what you're doing. You can't assume she or he is just a kid who's too young to understand. According to my grandfather, although I was young, I was gaining experience by listening to him and taking advantage of his wisdom.

CHAPTER 17

Turning Seventeen

Today I'm officially seventeen. I woke up at my maternal grandmother's house with my aunt like every morning. Back in Russia, I used to celebrate my birthday with my classmates every year. I thought maybe it wouldn't be celebrated this year because birthdays aren't so important in Afghanistan, so I took a slice of one of the little cakes I bought from the market and made a wish. Then my favourite grandpa and I went for a car ride. It was fun to ride through the entire city with him. The pleasure and serenity I felt in such a short time was precious.

On the way home, I was starting to feel like the family was up to something. Everyone was acting a little suspiciously. It was obvious that Grandpa was planning a birthday surprise. Every minute he was on the phone, he'd answer quickly, "yes, yes," so I wouldn't understand. I pretended I didn't understand. I suspected my grandfather was trying to make me happy. I was touched by his effort to orchestrate a surprise for me. It was probably the first time in his life that he was planning a birthday celebration.

When I got home, my suspicions were confirmed when I saw my cousins dressed up and walking around the garden. Ordinarily, my father was against such birthday celebrations. He called birthday parties a custom of the infidels, but I learned later that they had prepared a nice surprise at Grandpa's request. Actually, my cousin Zarlasht eventually spoiled the real surprise by texting me about it. I still don't understand what her motive was.

My father's negative attitude didn't mean he didn't love me. After all, until two years ago, he was a normal man who even celebrated my mother's birthday. However, ever since some of his friends started coming and going, my father began calling everything a sin. The only person who dared to challenge him was his own father. Grandpa Raz stood up to my father's new extremist ideas and at least managed to subdue him a bit.

It was a complicated situation—we were trying to experience happiness and deal with the psychological problems of some family members at the same time. Under the pretext of work, Dad has been going to Dawlat Abad and Andkhoy districts recently, sometimes staying away for weeks. It was obvious there was something else going on. Normally, my mother would have questioned this kind of behaviour, but ever since we got here, her mind has been busy with other things. Before she got married, there was this guy she loved, one of the neighbours. He lived next door to my grandmother. Now that guy is married, and my mother spends her time feeling jealous of his wife when she should be taking care of my father.

I went to my aunt's room in the evening. When I was there, my favourite grandfather knocked on the door. In his hands was a traditional Afghan Gand dress.

"My dear, put this on and come to our house right now."

"Okay, Grandpa, but why?"

"Let's make your grandmother jealous," he laughed. His smile was full of excitement. It warmed my heart to see him so happy for me. I put the dress on right away, and I left my hair uncovered and loose—something I hadn't been able to do for a long time. Then Aziz knocked on the door.

"Sis, can you give me your phone?"

"Here you go."

I got that too. They figured they were going to take photos, and they wanted to keep them on my phone. I prepared myself quickly, sprayed on perfume, and left. I appreciated that they had planned something for me, but all my life I've been wondering about next year's birthday: my big eighteenth birthday. *Who's going to be with me? How am I going to dress? What will we do at the party?* I've always dreamed of it being so special.

I put a big blanket over myself and headed to my paternal grandmother's house. They had turned off the lights.

Aziz was standing at the door, and he said, "Sis, go into the living room." He still assumed I didn't understand what was happening.

When I entered the hall, I encountered a scene that seemed straight from a fairy tale. It's like the sultan had a daughter, and everyone did their best to make her happy. That night, I saw my mom's sisters, my dad's sisters, my mother's brothers, my father's brothers—and all my cousins. In short, everyone was there. Then Grandpa declared that his granddaughter was entering her new age for the first time in Afghanistan, so she would not feel alone. In Russia, I had never experienced such an elaborate birthday party. I would gather with my family of five and a few friends at home or at a bakery. We'd just cut a little cake. I didn't know if it was normal here, but I wanted to give a speech because I adored my Grandpa Raz wholeheartedly, and what I wanted to say for him was always inside me.

"Sorry, I want to say something," I announced. The music was muted. At that moment, the strange looks I received from Uncle Ezzat, one of my father's many brothers, bothered me a little. Nevertheless, with a little embarrassment, I turned to Grandpa Raz. "Thank you all for not leaving me alone tonight. Grandpa, I'm glad you're here. Dear Grandpa, your presence gives us great power. From time to time, maybe we've been unhappy, even heartbroken, about not returning to Russia, but I've never regretted being here. That's because of you. All we think about is living happily and peacefully with you, Grandpa. I'm glad I have you in the seventeenth spring of my life, and now I have a wonderful big family, and you're on our side."

When it came to presents, everyone brought something for me. The most common gift—but definitely *not* my favourite—was money. Receiving money was something I didn't like at all, in fact. My Uncle Rashid, the police chief, gave me US $100 (approximately 6,000 afghani). It's common here to use American dollars. He made a show of it to everyone. I felt embarrassed because that amount of money is what the average teacher in Afghanistan makes in one month. It seemed far too extravagant as a birthday present for a niece he hardly knew. My uncle's gift and his intense interest in me made me feel uncomfortable and suspicious.

A gift should come from the heart. It shouldn't have anything to do with its material value. It should remind you of the giver and something pleasant whenever you see it. Something that warms your heart and always stays in your mind. The words are also special for me. They represent attention and attachment. Even if it's ordinary, it's nice to be loved, but it's even better to feel special. For me, the meaning of the gift is measured by the sincerity it contains. I've thought about this matter since I was around ten years old, but a lot of my thoughts like that seemed to make no sense to people in Afghanistan. Few people know or celebrate their birthdays here anyway, so to protect myself from disappointment, I kept telling myself not to expect anything from anyone.

There was another issue almost from our first day here. I really didn't care about it before, so I didn't even write about it here in my journal. But now I have to write about it. What's becoming increasingly annoying is that people from all over the neighbourhood seem far too interested in me. At first, I thought nothing bad could ever happen to me as long as Grandpa was with me. And then when Uncle Rashid said he wouldn't give his niece to anyone, I was happy. This uncle of mine, the police chief, is a respected member of our family, and I was reassured that he'd protect me. At the same time, I'm suspicious about the constant talk of Subhan, his eldest son. He's twenty years old. Marriage between first cousins is common in Afghanistan. I pray they aren't planning to match him with me.

My dearest grandfather was the last person to approach me after everyone else had presented their gifts. He seemed to understand exactly what I was thinking. He knew what I liked and didn't like. He approached me gently. He had a piece of carefully folded fabric in his hand. It was white with some Afghan stitching on it, but because it was yellowish, it was obviously old and used. I remember that for Aziz's circumcision wedding, my cousins worked for days on sewing local dresses with the same hand embroidery that was on the cloth in my grandfather's hands. As far as I know, it was one of the most difficult and elegant stitches called "ash stitching," a job that required patience, skill, and time. I wanted to examine the piece in my grandfather's hands, but he started explaining it first.

"My dear, Afsun, this is a piece of embroidery made by your grandmother sixty-five years ago. Here we call it *kadifa*, a kind of shawl. Girls usually learn to embroider it when they're thirteen, and when they get engaged, the groom is sent home with it as a symbol of engagement. I first saw your grandmother at our wedding, and I fell in love with her. I have wanted to use this special shawl for the rest of my life, but I was afraid that if I used it every day, it would become too worn out. That's why I've used it only on the most meaningful days of my life. It was on my shoulder on the days my children were born, the days each of them started school, on your father's wedding day, on the day my first grandchild Zarlasht was born, and most recently, during Aziz's circumcision. I give it to you with the hope that you will always wear it on your happiest days and share my special memories. It might be the most financially worthless of the gifts you've received today, but it means a lot to me. I want to give this to you, thinking it will have the same value for you. Of course, the years are passing quickly. I won't be with you for the rest of your life. On your next birthdays and special events, I hope you'll remember me whenever you look at this piece. You'll always feel like I'm there for you. Even if I'm not alive, it'll be there for you with all the good memories. I wish this kadifa that has witnessed my most precious memories will bring happiness to you too, girl."

I couldn't control my stream of tears. I was speechless. Grandpa touched me deeply with the most beautiful gift in the world. He is the most beautiful human being in my life, and this kadifa will now be my most treasured possession.

✢ ✢ ✢

Our house is finally finished. Grandpa has been a little tired lately. My father didn't want to take us to check the house, claiming that workmen were still there. I didn't know what our house was like, but we were going to find out when we got there. By the way, we wrote tests yesterday so they can decide which grades we're going to be placed in. I'm not a big fan of studying. Everyone knows that. There are different things that attract different people, and one thing that didn't attract me was studying and competing for the highest scores.

Asra worked very hard to prepare for the exam. I know it wasn't good to cheat, but since the teacher knew my grandfather, she gave me a little help by allowing me to take a glance at my notebooks for the exam. I needed that boost, especially in subjects in which Asra was better than me. Now we're both going to Sitara Girls' High School to see the results of our placement tests.

Let's see how many subjects we've passed. According to the system here, when you come from outside Afghanistan, you can take as many exams as you wish and move to the upper class. It was right next to where Grandpa and I went out and had ice cream. On the day we entered the school, Asra and I bought ice cream and decided to go inside without any stress. Shiryakh, that famous local ice cream, was now reminiscent of my grandfather and his positive energy. I entered the school with that energy.

Several girls came to check the results. Among them were academically strong girls who wanted to skip classes or had never attended school, but who eventually qualified to go to school. They taped the exam results to the wall. As much as I didn't want to seem too excited, I couldn't help feeling curious and impatient. My heart was beating rapidly. We waited because it was crowded. At the end, the crowds dwindled. Some girls walked away happy, but many were upset. Finally, we were able to get close to the wall to look for our names. The list started with the first-grade results, then the second, third, fourth, fifth and sixth. Aziz just passed. He made it into the sixth grade. After all, it was suitable for a student his age. We kept reading. Sixth, seventh, eighth, ninth. Both Asra and I were deemed ready for the ninth grade. Although it was an appropriate level for Asra, it was a step down for me. I'd be two years older than most of my classmates.

I called Grandpa, but he didn't answer. He must have been busy, but for the first time, my call went unanswered. Next, I called my mom. She was so happy.

Asra and I have a noticeable height difference. I think I'm quite tall by the standards of this place. I used to tease her by saying, "You're always studying hard, so you're not getting taller." Now, however, we were in the same grade.

I called Uncle Zafar, one of my father's younger brothers, to drive us home. That week, Aunty Nuriya went to the market with us for our school clothes. We received black fabric for uniforms, school bags, white headscarves, shoes, and the usual stuff for school. I couldn't really help my mother with the housework anymore. I had to study, and my mother would ask me for help only when she was stuck in some of her chores.

The day we took the new fabric to the tailor, my mother said, "Girls, at least, you don't have to go to school in a burka. The white headscarf of the uniform is enough. I took care of your uniforms myself. Anyway, the school uniform here is right below the knees, and if it's any shorter, you're not allowed in the school. And the cuff of the pants should not be less than a hand span—otherwise, you can't go to class."

We were relieved that we didn't have to wear a burka and black cover sheet. It was enough to wear a light chador to school. I showed the tailor a stylish school dress I had seen on the internet. It was used in Iran, and it was a little longer and more convenient than what my mom and school required. Everything was ready now. We moved into the new house, but we felt drained from the intensity of overlapping events over this last month.

We're going to spend our first night at the new house. My grandparents are here tonight. We already have three bedrooms: one for my parents, one for guests, and one for the three of us. The architecture of the house is unusual. It used to be attached to the wall at the back and had a concrete partition just below the windows. The workers left only a square gap around the trees in the garden of the house and poured concrete everywhere else. When we entered, we saw an unfinished kitchen and toilet on the left side. I'd say it's a warm house with architecture unique to this place. Actually, I like it. I also enjoy sharing the same room with my siblings ... I'm only one day away from our first day of school. I'm so excited!

Grandpa was supposed to pick us up for the first day of classes even though he had caught a cold. He has been coughing lately. That's why we haven't been able to spend a lot of time together lately. When he came home with us, he said he'd take us to our school. I was happily expecting to see him in the morning. The photo on my phone's home screen is the one my grandfather and I took the night we went out for shir-yakh. I love falling asleep while looking at that photo. That's what I did that night. I was excited about starting school. In fact, I fell asleep while looking at my uniform and the photo of Grandpa.

The phone rang. Asra touched my hand. When I woke up and saw the white walls and the big window, I knew I was in our new house. And Grandpa was there. I got dressed at incredible speed. Aunty Nuriya taught me how to wear that light headscarf in school. Aziz is still in middle school, so he doesn't start class until the early afternoon. He was still asleep when we were leaving. I took my bag and heard Asra screaming.

"Afsun it's 7:00 already! We're late! Run!"

Grandpa was waiting for us. He was dressed in white. I ran and hugged him, as usual. Oh, that smell! Don't ask. He smells so good. If I ever make a perfume, it will have my grandfather's scent, and if I ever fall in love with someone, I'll choose a guy just like Grandpa.

"Are my beautiful girls ready?"

"I'm excited, Grandpa."

"I wanted to wear that special kadifa," he said, "because today is one of the happiest days of my life, but I couldn't wear it because it's with a new owner now."

We laughed and set off quickly. Then I suddenly remembered something.

"I have to run back home, Grandpa."

"Why, girl? Did you forget something?"

"I forgot to say goodbye to my parents. Wait here. I'll come back right away."

"Okay, girl, but come quickly."

I left my backpack in the back seat and ran home. My parents were just waking up.

"Good morning, Mom."

"Good morning, Afsun."

"We're going to school now. I'm here to kiss you."

Then my father looked at me and said, "Is that how you're going?"

"No, Dad. Actually, I'm going to wear a T-shirt and jeans like in Russia."

"Those times have passed, and your grandfather spoils you too much. He doesn't even bother to ask us anything."

I kissed my mom. Dad pretended he didn't want a kiss. I really couldn't figure out this whole transformation. When he was in Moscow, this man used to text one of his brothers, a government soldier, "You're fighting for your country. I'm proud of you." And now he's telling the same brother, "You're getting your salary from the infidels. Quit your job." The way he treats us now and his long beard scare me.

I waved to my grandmothers through the window on the way to the car. The moment we got in the car, my grandfather's condition broke my heart. I was surprised to see Uncle Zafar behind the wheel. Grandpa was sitting next to him. His health problems had weakened him. Though I noticed it, I pretended everything was normal. The car moved down the streets, turning left and right. All I could think about was Grandpa's condition. I prayed that it wasn't anything serious.

As we got closer to the school, I saw a mud-brick security room right at the entrance. The school gate was in shades of green. We were coming for the first time because my grandfather had already taken care of all the papers for our registration. When we walked through the door, I noticed two girls in black uniforms on the right. They had blue pieces tied on their arm and a registry in front of them. Outside, just to the left, there was another mud-brick room that looked like a security room.

Grandpa led the way with Asra and me right behind him. There were classrooms on both sides of the school. The students and teachers peering at us through the windows seemed interesting. Since Maymana is a small city, when you talk to people, you find out that you've got some kind of connection, even kinship, with everyone. Since we've been here, after all the hospitality, weddings, and parties, everyone has seen us and knows who we are. I've heard some people have been making fun of us, referring to us as "Grandpa's Russian daughters."

Just across the street from the door was a water tank with UNICEF written on it. It stood on iron feet about twenty metres long. The water from there was flowing down into pipes. Some of the girls were drinking water from plastic bags, and some were drinking it from their palms. I think the middle building was the one with the big classrooms and the teachers' room. Grandpa and I stood right in front of the stairs leading to the building in front of that water tank. A skinny woman of average height came out. Probably, she had seen Grandpa through the window.

"*Haji sahib*, welcome." ("Haji sahib" is a common nickname used to show respect to an elderly male.)

"Hello, dear Headmistress. I've brought my granddaughters."

"You've done well, Afsun and Asra, haven't you?"

"Yes, Headmistress."

"How's Aunt Saliha?"

"Thank God, she's okay."

"Girls, wait a minute, and I will direct you to your class."

The headmistress seemed quite friendly, but after she left the room for a few moments, we learned she was considered a dictator. I saw girls running away as soon as they saw her. I guess it's supposed to be that way.

"Girls, the headmistress is your grandmother's cousin," Grandpa said. "Watch your step. She knows us."

"Hmm ... how great that is," I said.

"Oh, if you think she's going to help, you're wrong. Girl, this is one of the teachers who failed your aunt."

"This is our chance!"

The headmistress came back before our remarks about her ended.

"Haji sahib, you can go now," she told Grandpa. "School ends at 11:35. You can come to get the girls then."

"Have good lessons, my daughters," said Grandpa as he turned to leave. "May God give you clarity of mind."

"Bye, Grandpa."

Then the headmistress said, "Come on, girls, follow me."

We walked to the left together. On both sides of the one-metre hallway were classrooms. These ones were worse than the ones we had seen earlier. Some had blackboards, and some had whiteboards. There was a wooden classroom attached to the exterior wall of the middle building. The classrooms on the other side were even worse. They had covered the roof of the classrooms with tents to protect them from the rain. We entered through the fourth door on the left. Girls were sitting opposite each other in the whiteboard classroom. Tablecloths and pencil holders were used meticulously to try to beautify the classroom, which was in very bad condition. The classroom was small, no more than four or five metres long, but extremely clean and neat.

The girls looked like flowers in a tiny, ruined classroom.

The headmistress banged on the open door.

"Mualim Sahib Zarghuna," began the headmistress, respectfully addressing our teacher, "if you'll excuse me! These girls are Afsun and Asra. They are two hardworking new classmates from Russia."

"Oh, from Russia?" murmured the other students. Obviously, the word "Russia" piqued their curiosity.

"Yes, girls from Russia. If anyone interrupts me, I will punish you! So, girls, where's your classmate Parisa?"

"Headmistress, Parisa's brother has passed away, so she's not here today," said our teacher.

"Oh, that's right. I'm glad you reminded me. We're going to her home today to offer our condolences. I don't want to hear anyone fighting with these two new girls, okay? They're both calm, polite girls who won't cause any trouble, so don't cause any problems for them. I hope that's understood."

Turning to Asra and me, the headmistress said, "Girls, this class is one of our best and most successful classes in school. At your grandfather's request, I'm handing you over to such a hardworking class. Parisa, the class leader is absent today, so I'll tell her about you. She'll help you out when she returns. Come take your seats."

"Thank you, Headmistress," I said.

All our classmates had their eyes on us as our teacher said, "Please don't be shy. You, the little one, come on. Go over there and sit next to that blonde girl. And you, tall one, come and sit here next to Najia."

My heart was pounding fast. The first lesson was biology. I didn't make a sound until it was over. We were sharing a one-metre table with four girls, so I felt squeezed. The room was extremely hot. It was all overwhelming.

It was break time after a heavy class. Many of the girls approached us to welcome us. They seemed genuinely warm and friendly. Filled with curiosity, especially about Russia, they had one question after another. The hours flew by. For the first time, I didn't want school to end. Everyone wanted to help in a different way. From day one, Asra managed to make the teachers like her with her intelligence. She deserved it. She gave very smart answers to all their questions.

The school day ended so fast the first day. The last ones to leave were Asra and me with our new friend, Firuza. She is the girl who was sitting next to me. She helped me a lot today. Firuza seems to be a diligent student. She was ranked as second in the class.

Parisa, who did not show up today, is the top student in the class. Therefore, despite her young age, she's like a teaching assistant. I heard that her five-year-old brother died last night as a result of electrical shock. They said he accidently touched the electrical wires when he was playing in their home. I haven't seen Parisa yet. It must have been a very sad day for her. May

God give her patience. How can a person bear the death of a little boy, the death of one's little brother?

Electricity service to some provinces in Afghanistan came a little late. They still import electricity from neighbouring Uzbekistan and Turkmenistan because the country doesn't have its own energy sources. Consequently, many houses, including my grandmothers' houses, do not have a proper system. Electrical wires pass dangerously over walls and trees to reach the houses. In fact, many people have become fatally caught in the wires that pass along the roofs of houses.

When the three of us reached the door, some of our classmates hadn't left the school yet. Someone rang the bell five minutes earlier, and the headmistress had refused to dismiss the students. Firuza told us that there was a bell in the tree by the drinking water tank. Some students would hit it with a stone or iron bar when no one was around in order to confuse everyone about the dismissal time.

Uncle Ezzat, my dad's younger brother, was waiting for us at the door. I noticed the headmistress speaking to him and then quickly looking around for us. We walked over to them.

"Afsun and Asra, you can both leave now," said the headmistress.

Then Uncle Ezzat asked, "How was school today?"

"Good, Uncle."

"No one has been abusive or rude to you? No one has fought with you?"

"Of course, not," replied Asra. "They can't act like that."

Laughing, my uncle remarked, "They're going to be afraid of you, aren't they?"

"It's not a matter of fear, but what have we done that would ever make them fight with us?"

"Normally, on the first day, new students are not treated very well by the others. I think it's the same everywhere in the world."

"That might be true, Uncle, but our classmates are very kind."

"Yes, I heard. The headmistress told my father that she was going to put you two in the best class, but be careful and try not to break your promise to your teachers."

After a short conversation in the car, we arrived in front of the house. Time was running out now. I was a little drowsy. The dusty, warm air of the tiny classroom had been oppressive.

I immediately prepared Aziz for his shift of school. Dad was supposed to drive him, but I think he forgot. I called him a couple of times, but he didn't pick up. I was getting mad. I tried to comfort Aziz, reassuring him that Dad would be coming, but knowing my father, I suspected he probably wouldn't be arriving home in time. Children passing by our house were dressed like Aziz in a uniform consisting of a blue shirt and light brown pants. I opened the outside door of the house slightly and saw a boy with a shaved head. He was about nine or ten years old.

"Brother, what school do you go to?" I called out to him.

"Abu Ubayda School, sister."

"What time does your class start?"

The boy looked at his watch and realized he was late. He began running and shouted back, "Sister, it starts at 1:00! I'm late!"

Aziz understood and turned to me. "Afsun, I know Dad isn't coming! Look, I'm already too late! I can't go to school today!"

"Don't make excuses, Aziz," I replied. "You can still go."

At the same time, I had no idea how he was going to go. My aunts and my mom were busy fixing curtains inside the room. Asra was doing her homework, and she promised to do my homework, too, if I did the dishes. I looked inside. Since I was still wearing my school uniform, I could just go out like that, so I ran to my mom.

"Mom, since Dad's not here yet, I'm going to drop Aziz off at school. I'll be right back."

"But you don't know the way, girl."

"I know, Mom. Don't worry."

"Watch out. Don't let your father see you like this on the street."

"What do you mean, Mom? Anything wrong with how I look?"

This wasn't the time to argue. I grabbed my white headscarf and went back to Aziz.

"Are we ready, school runaway?"

"I'm ready, sis."

To look more like a schoolgirl, I also took my backpack. I was going out as a guide for the first time here. We left the house like two siblings walking down the streets of Moscow with no adult accompanying us. We had to turn right, and then there was an asphalt road on the left side. I knew there was a school on the right at the end of that street. But that street was very long, and all the alleys looked similar. As soon as we left our little street, we saw shops selling gasoline and oil stuffed into bottles. I've always loved the smell of gasoline and the smell of new books. It's fun for me to inhale the crisp smell of the pages of new books never opened before, and sometimes I even smell newspapers just for that scent of fresh newsprint.

CHAPTER 18

A Fateful Day

We were off our own street. I'm now used to the looks I receive from strange men when I'm out in public. Even if a young schoolgirl walks by with her parents, most of the men look at her brazenly, even some men old enough to be grandfathers. For them, girls and women are nothing but objects to satisfy their lust. We were walking fast, up the middle of the street with various shops. Almost every market sold homemade yogurt. There was a bloody butcher's market at the end of the street. I was scared to walk past it. More worrisome was how I was going to get into the boys' school. A large number of boys of different ages were entering the school. There was a river between the school and the street, and a bridge to cross it. I've seen different food and junk food vendors on both sides.

"Sis, this is the school," Aziz announced.

"Yes, my dear brother, this is it."

We crossed the bridge. Before I even got to the school grounds, I noticed some young men waiting outside. We walked briskly to the entrance. Two students were standing behind a table, just as I had seen at my girls' school.

"Hello, good afternoon," I said.

One of the guys started laughing. "What kind of pronunciation is that?"

"Excuse me, what's so funny?"

The student next to the first one started laughing and mimicked me sarcastically. Both of them were so busy making fun of me that they were no longer listening to me. Maybe they didn't take me seriously. Or maybe if I hadn't been wearing my school uniform, they would've reacted more respectfully.

AFSUN BEYOND THE VINEYARD

As they laughed at me, I couldn't hide my frustration and embarrassment. I held Aziz's hand tightly. It was clear that they were going to continue giving me a hard time. At that moment, I remembered Farkhunda's case. Most of the young men who attacked her were like these two in front of me: extremely impulsive. They acted without understanding the subject, without listening, without thinking—just for the sake of a reaction.

They kept us waiting for about five more minutes until the last group of students entered. Then I heard a voice behind me. It sounded like one of my many uncles.

"Hey, why don't you answer the girl properly?" asked the stranger.

The boy with the eye glasses replied, "It's none of your business, fisherman."

I had to look back and find out who this person was who came to my defence, but I was too scared. I could hear the young man in the back approaching.

"This is a reflection of the level of their culture and manners. Sorry, sister."

The boy wearing glasses retorted rudely, "What's your problem, man?"

"Well, when I tell the principal about your behaviour, then you'll soon find out what's going to happen."

Aziz turned away. Not only was the afternoon sun bothering his eyes, but the whole situation I was facing made him uncomfortable. My heart was pounding. It felt like flames were shooting out of my face. It was a situation I had never experienced before.

The young stranger was dressed in a white shirt and black pants. Turning to me, he asked, "Are you okay? What do you need?"

I knew I had to speak now. I had to respond right away so I wouldn't reveal my fear.

"Yes, yes. I'm fine, thanks. I just brought my brother here for his first day of school. My grandfather has completed all the paperwork. I just have to drop him off at his classroom."

"Okay, let's find the school administrator's office. Please come with me."

Even though I tried to act like a local girl, it was obvious that I wasn't from here. My movements, mannerisms, and pronunciation marked me as an outsider. I was sure of that now. The mocking laughter from behind us was still making me furious. I held Aziz's hand tightly. We walked behind the young stranger as he made his way to the school building. He seemed as kind as he was handsome. When we got up the stairs, he stopped.

"The room opposite you is the school administrator's office. I think you're scared, so I'll come with you."

I didn't say anything. We entered the room. When he walked through the door, I saw that he was very relaxed and familiar with the teachers there. They all seemed fond of him.

"These are two new friends: a brother and sister. They want to see you."

They call the principal "*sar mualim*" here. He was a gentleman with white hair and a physical disability.

"Hello. Come in, girl. How can I help you?"

"I'm here to drop my brother off for his first day of class. I have his documents."

"Has he signed the attendance book yet?"

"No, but he passed the exams. He is supposed to go to the sixth grade."

"Well, then, let's not lose any time. That second teacher is the counsellor for our class 6A. He'll take your brother to his class right away so he doesn't miss anything. You get the paperwork finished."

The teacher got up. Turning to Aziz, he said, "Come, son."

Aziz has had a growth spurt recently. He is now like a young man. He doesn't like to look childish, and he doesn't want people making a fuss over him and asking him a lot of questions.

When I went to give Aziz's documents to the principal, I turned with a smile and said, "Have a good class, Aziz."

Aziz always says that when you laugh, your stress subsides. That's why I wanted to reassure and comfort him with a warm smile. I handed the papers to the principal. He asked for Aziz's I.D. and four photos. My grandfather had filed them all. I don't know why he didn't complete the registration for Aziz as he did ours. Maybe it was because we were girls, or maybe he didn't know these guys.

The principal began to write down Aziz's information in the attendance book as he recited it aloud: "Name: Aziz. Father's name: Ismatullah. Grandfather's name: Haji Raz Bay."

Suddenly, the principal stopped writing.

"Are you the children of Ismat from Russia? The grandchildren of Raz Bay, the iron dealer we know?"

"Yes," I answered.

The teachers and the principal looked at each other.

Then one of the teachers said, "After the prayer today, the imam made an announcement."

Everyone was looking at me, but I didn't understand what they were talking about.

"Sir, I'm sorry. I didn't catch what you said."

"Your grandfather has passed away, girl."

I couldn't find any words to respond to what I had just heard. I sat there frozen. I only wanted to scream and beat up whoever told me this. Whoever started this rumour is a liar!

"I wish you hadn't said anything," said the principal. "Obviously, she doesn't know."

Suddenly, I found my voice and began freaking out. "What don't I know? Can you tell me something, please? What did that teacher just say?"

I felt like boiling water had been poured on my head. I clamped my two hands together and squeezed them with all my might, my fingernails leaving traces on the skin of my hands. I couldn't feel anything anymore.

"We don't know exactly," responded the principal. "The imam just announced his death after the call to prayer today."

I looked at my phone. It was 1:45 p.m. Asra had called three times. Aunty Nuriya had called four times. I had muted my phone before coming here. *They were calling because I was late. There couldn't be anything else going on. But they wouldn't call seven times around the same time. Grandpa himself dropped us off at school this morning. It's impossible. No. My grandfather's fine. The people in this office are just teasing me like those kids at the door.*

I looked up. My eyes were burning. The guy who brought us to the principal was looking at me with a confused and dull expression. I got up.

"Do you need anything?" asked one of the teachers.

"No, I just want to go home."

A conversation was going on around me, but I wasn't listening. I kept looking at the door. Suddenly, I got up and darted into the hallway. My right leg and my left leg were in a race with each other. I don't even know how I got out of the school building. Those two obnoxious guys were still at the door. One of them said, "Look, I told you. This girl's going to cry easily."

I got out of the school grounds, but I couldn't remember the way to our new house. Right or left? I turned left. It didn't matter which side of the street I was on. I just had to get home to see my grandfather. I had to prove wrong what those people at the school were saying about him. *Wait for me, Grandpa! Wait for me!*

As I turned left, I noticed what looked like my own school up ahead. The sun was beating down on me. As soon as I saw the school, a signal entered my brain. If this school was truly my school, I should go right. A few moments later, I realized I was standing next to the tailor's shop in front of my own school. That's when I felt a hand hitting me on the back of my shoulder. Impulsively, I turned my head and got a hard slap on my face. My eyes closed. This was the guy who had helped us at Aziz's school. He slapped me again. I was stunned.

"Crazy Fatma, walking down the street alone! I'm going to tell Mom! My friends make fun of me because of you! 'Look at Firdaws. Look how his sister walks on the street like a crazy person!' Where were you going?"

I understood why he was doing this. I needed him to help me find my way now. In a whisper, I told him my home address so he could lead me there, but I had to keep pretending that he was my older brother. Otherwise, people on the street would suspect something different and lynch us.

He grabbed me by the arm and said, "Come on, sister! Let's go home."

My brain wasn't working properly. There was no sign of life. A girl who lost her way in the middle of an unfamiliar street in Northern Afghanistan didn't know anything. If we had walked back through the alley, we would've had to walk a long way and put up with the scrutinizing stares of strangers. It would have been too hard to maintain our theatre all that way. Continuing to pull me by the arm, the young man kept walking back the entire route that I had previously taken by mistake. We were taking a short cut. I remembered having come this way once before with Aunty Nuriya, but I kept quiet. When we got out of the area of my school, we were no longer within sight of others, so he left my arm free.

"I'm sorry I had to act like that, sister. I'm going to take you home now. Don't worry. I hope everything's fine there."

After the guy spoke those kind words, he distanced himself from me. He made me feel better. Although I no longer felt frightened, I was disoriented. The street ended near two trees, and we had to enter another street. He approached me and said, "Look over there. That street in front of us is the address you gave me. I'm going now. Goodbye."

He turned to leave so quickly I couldn't even say thank you. I caught a glimpse of his face as he walked away. Then I ran to my house. They had locked the door. No one was home. The unpaved streets were filled with small stones, gravel, and dirt that hit my feet hard. The pain was more than I could bear. My lips were dry. My throat felt stuck. I was like a dehydrated animal desperate for a drop of water in the desert. But now seeing the door locked, I felt like I couldn't move on. My energy was depleted. I leaned against the door. I thought to myself that if I call them, someone will pick me up. I remembered this a bit late, but I couldn't call and tell them to take me to Grandpa's house because I wasn't prepared to accept the news I had just heard. Now I was thinking of just telling Mom that I had come home but the door was locked. I would simply ask her where she was so I could go to her.

I pulled out my phone. There was the familiar sweet picture of my grandfather on the screen. I called Asra. It took her a while to answer. At first, I thought she was busy visiting somebody with the rest of the family, so she couldn't hear her phone ringing right away. Storms were building inside me.

Finally, Asra answered the phone. "Hello, sis."

In the background, I could hear screaming and wailing. Yes, it was my grandmother's voice. The sounds of a lot of people wailing.

"Asra! Where are you? What are all those voices? Tell me! Tell me what happened!"

"Sis ..."

"Tell me! Why are you silent now? Say something!"

"It's Grandpa ... Grandpa's gone ... He's left us."

Her words squeezed my heart. Then my heart seemed to stop beating.

God! What kind of pain is this? What kind of test is this? A test of power and strength? My only hope, my only real support in this world, the man who made me smile, who gave me confidence and peace, that man cannot be gone! No, it's not true!

I still refused to believe it. I kept telling myself that they were all making a cruel joke. What about his recent voice message? "Afsun, it's Grandpa Raz. Look, I'm going to ask Uncle Ezzat to pick you up." How could Grandpa leave us? He had taken us to school in the morning. He said he was a bit ill, so he didn't drive. The day before, he had said to Dad, "Don't bore my grandchildren. Let them go to school in uniform." He was the one who always cheered me up and made me feel happy. Now there was just a weak girl who was waiting at the door.

One of the neighbours, an overweight woman, came out to talk to me. I think her husband had also heard the news from the imam. Everyone heard it because it was a small city, but I wasn't going to accept it. *He's not dead. He hasn't left me alone. He's going to stay with me. I'm going to become a psychiatrist or a journalist, and he is going to protect and support me. We are going to work together to help the children here.*

My neighbour raised my head gently. I looked at her with tears in my eyes. People's eyes are so beautiful. It's like everything's dawn. The unique beauty of the pupil, its dilation and shrinking according to our emotions. One of the common ways to express emotional pain is through the eyes.

My neighbour lifted me off the floor.

"Did you call your family?"

"Yes, someone will come to get me. My uncle."

"Okay. Until then, come wait at our house."

Our houses were very close to each other, only about two metres apart. I couldn't stay at home doing nothing, so I went to her place and waited there. All I knew was that I was lost and confused. There were people coming and going at my neighbour's house. Everyone was talking about the same thing: Haji Raz, my grandpa. They asked my neighbour if she was going to attend the funeral. It was after 2:30 p.m.

She brought me a glass of water. Then she prepared herself to come with me.

"Look, we'll wait five more minutes, and if your uncle doesn't show up, I'll take you there. The other neighbours have already left for—"

She hadn't even finished her sentence when Uncle Ezzat's car stopped in front of the house. I ran to it and got into the back seat. My neighbour got into the car with me. I looked into my uncle's eyes. Now I knew for sure that it was true.

"Uncle, what happened? Is it really true?"

"Unfortunately, it's true, Afsun."

He was in tears. His face was red.

"Uncle Ezzat, I don't know how this could happen! Grandpa dropped us off at school this morning!"

"Unfortunately, he had a heart attack."

"Uncle, I can't believe it! I'm crying, but I can't accept it!"

"I know your grandfather was your only hope here, and I'm sorry we're not as close to you as your grandfather was. Sorry we didn't understand you enough in your difficult situations."

As soon as we entered my grandparents' street, I encountered a sea of people. It was like the whole of Faryab was there. Women in burkas were wailing in front of the house. I stood at my grandmother's door. I entered quickly, but it was too hard to get past all those people. My grandmother's house was full up to the door. Eventually, I made my way to Grandma's room. The heartbreaking crying, the voices of the crowd—these sounds are never going to leave my brain. It was hard to reach where my grandmother was sitting among all those women. They wouldn't even clear a path for me. It was like they were sitting on top of each other. Everyone there knew how much my grandfather loved me and how much I loved him. I couldn't hold my body up anymore. My legs were ready to collapse. I don't know how I ever got through.

They had put the body right in the middle of the room, inside a big coffin. Those who entered the room approached the coffin and put something on it. Then they returned to their places. Almost everyone was dressed in white or black. Women were wailing and shouting. My father's sisters kept crying out, "Dad, where are you?"

My grandmother was screaming repeatedly, "Oh, how can my heart hold this pain!"

I couldn't take it any longer. I approached my grandmother and the coffin. Grandpa's face was visible, his eyes closed. I could see his white beard, but they had covered his chest with a piece of white cloth. My heroic grandfather looked like he was sleeping. He was in an eternal sleep. I sat as calmly as I could, trying desperately to hold myself together. I put my hands and face close to him, but they didn't let me touch him. I stayed by his side all day, all evening, and late into the night. Some people came, some left, some spoke, some fainted from crying. Of course, that's what would happen when such a good person dies.

I sat there, trying to ignore all the reactions. I heard my father, the mosque imam, our elders, men, and women, all say, "Afsun, it's enough. Go to the other room." I didn't allow my mother and my aunts to grab my arm and force me to leave. I was going to stay there as long as I could. Finally, in the middle of the night, it was just Uncle Ezzat and me left in the room. My grandmother's blood pressure had dropped from the sadness, heat, and crowd. The rest of them had to prepare food for all those people who came and went.

This is a custom I don't like in Afghanistan. Your beloved one is dead, yet the people who come to offer condolences stay almost twenty-four hours—and you need to prepare food and serve them?

My Uncle Ezzat tapped me on the shoulder.

"Come on, Afsun. You go home. I'll stay."

"I want to talk to Grandpa, Uncle. Please leave us alone."

"No, a young girl should not be left alone near the body. God forbid something happens."

"Body? He is my Grandpa, not a body. Even though he can't talk to me, Uncle Ezzat, I have a lot to say to him. Please, please! One last time! This is all I ask from you. Please!"

When my uncle realized my determination, he couldn't stand it and burst into tears.

"Okay, girl, but only five minutes."

"Uncle, you and Uncle Ashraf were with my grandfather. What exactly happened today?"

"Please don't tell anyone about what I'm going to tell you, Afsun. Promise me."

"Tell me! What is it?"

"As your grandfather was breathing his last breath, he was uttering your name. You must know how much my father loved and trusted you, so I'm telling you that life will be even harder for you now. Your father has been helping the Taliban. We found out yesterday. Your grandfather followed your father after he dropped you off this morning. On the way to Almar, he saw a Taliban militant talking to your father and giving him money. When he got back, they argued in the store. Eventually, your father admitted the truth. Your grandfather was very angry, but he seemed normal when he came home. Then he fell to the ground. All he said was, 'I promised Afsun everything was going to be okay.' Girl … only four other people know the truth. The only reason I'm telling you all this is so you can take precautions accordingly. If anyone finds out about your father, the government will arrest us all. I won't be able to come to you anymore. I'll lose my job and my life. But don't worry. We're talking to him. Maybe we can convince him to give up these activities."

Uncle Ezzat walked to the door. My grandfather's room was a long room with one window. That's where we celebrated my birthday. He danced the first dance of his life with me that night. I walked to the door after my uncle left. I locked the door so that no one else could enter, and I closed the window.

✣ ✣ ✣

In Afghanistan, they give the body to the family. My Grandpa can stay in his own house until he's buried. Ordinarily, they would've buried him immediately, but because one of my father's brothers is in Mazar-i-Sharif, they waited. They'll bury Grandpa when my uncle arrives in the morning.

I stood by the door. On the right side was the portable air conditioner. It was working at its highest setting to mitigate the smell of the body. The cool air blowing out of the air conditioner blew through my black school dress. I approached my grandpa. I had missed him all day, but I knew I couldn't touch his face. I lifted the layers of white fabric covering him one by one. There were more than ten pieces laid out on the top base. The last piece was between my hands and my grandfather's face … I lifted it. His eyes were open, unlike how they were the first time I saw his him earlier. I was scared, but if I left the room, I'd lose my last chance to talk to him.

"Grandpa, you're alive, aren't you? Look, even your eyes are open, and you've seen me all day, but you just haven't gotten up. I kept crying because I thought you were joking. I thought you were going to get up now. Everyone's going to be mad, but they're going to know you're alive, and everybody's afraid to come near you tonight. They treat you like a dead man, like you're going to scare them, when they fall asleep. You'll come to their dreams, or goblins will attack them. They are scared like crazy. How could it be, Grandpa? Didn't you tell me that you were going to protect me, that you were going to be there for me until the end? What happened, Grandpa? Why did you give up? Look, there's no one around. Why was it such a sudden death? I'm stuck on my own. I don't even know where to go or what to do. You just kissed me this morning, Grandpa. You said you were proud of me. You said I'd take care of my brother and sister. What's the matter now? You've stopped taking care of me. How can I move on? Who's going to take care of me? My mom who's too busy being jealous of her ex-boyfriend's wife? My dad? I'm not even surprised by his work with the Taliban. It's been obvious since the day we arrived. His willingness to forcibly cover us with burkas, disappearing for days, not looking at me with love anymore, and finally changing so much. I didn't tell you, but the terrorists who got in our way the first day we arrived gave him their phone numbers and they talked with him outside the bus. I suspected then, Grandpa. Maybe it would have been better if I had told you, but obviously your heart couldn't have handled it then.

"Forgive me, Grandpa, but just so you know, I don't have the strength to go on. I don't even know what to go on for. All I care about is Aziz and Asra. I was glad we came to Afghanistan … I'm pretty sure I said that before. Grandpa, look, my hands are touching your face, but you're like cold glass. I don't have the heart. You know how bad I am, and you know how sorry I am … You're alive for me, Grandpa, so maybe I'll fool myself with this. At least, I'll relax thinking that way. Grandpa, I don't know how to go on, I don't know what to do in a difficult situation, you know? I don't know at all. I'm so confused. I don't know how I'd be if I couldn't talk to you right now. If only I could extend my time with you, the lovely man who drove us around in his car and played Sarban songs is gone.

"I was calling you in troubling times and using you as an excuse to pour out everything. I was coming to you to ask how I was going to live with my father. And you'd be mad at my father. So, you could stand it to a certain extent, but now you've left me. Grandpa, look how they're banging on the door. Before, you'd be the one standing at the door in situations like this, protecting and comforting me. Now I'm going to open the door before it gets messy, Grandpa. I'm going to kiss you for the last time. Maybe this is the last time we'll see each other face to face. Grandpa, aren't you going to tell me to kiss you without making your face wet? Look, my heart prefers to cry instead of beat. It's my tears making your face wet now. I can't hold them back. You rest in peace, Grandpa. Those you left behind will find their way. I'll come to you when I'm lost. I'll talk to your grave even though I can't see your face. I want to dream about you. We'll talk a lot, Grandpa. Ask God for patience for me. I love you, hero of my life."

I had a lot more words to say, but I didn't have time. Uncle Ezzat was pounding on the door non-stop. I said my final words by kissing my grandfather. Then I carefully replaced the pieces of cloth over him.

"Why did you lock the door, Afsun?"

"You've come back too quickly, Uncle."

"It's been an hour."

"Couldn't I have stayed here alone tonight?"

"Of course, not, my girl. The imam won't allow it."

We returned to our positions: my uncle on Grandpa's left side, me on the right side. Uncle Ezzat looked at me. There were tears in his eyes. He couldn't help it.

Seeing his tears, I thought about another phrase that Mr. Ivanov often recited in our literature class in Moscow: "It's hard for a man to cry; he lives his pains in himself." I knew that everything in literature was taken from real life.

I brought a pillow to put right next to my grandfather. I didn't know what was coming out of my mouth anymore. My vision was blurred by a wall of tears. My tears were streaming down my face. They were creating a knot in my throat. All I could think about was how I was going to endure the rest of my life here without him. I put my head down and drifted to sleep still talking to him.

My grandfather was reaching out, extending his hands towards me, and we left the room together in the middle of the night and went to Russia. That's the dream I had last night. Since my grandmothers came in the morning and started crying, my dream was cut short.

Around 8:00 that morning, they removed Grandpa from the room and put his coffin on the bier outside. I didn't have the strength to go out. I called my brother and sister. They weren't around yet. I had asked my uncle to pick up Aziz from school yesterday. I didn't know if he picked him up or not.

My eyes were dry now. I heard women talking. They were talking about me. "She stayed by the body the entire night, so she might have been possessed by a genie."

Looking in a mirror, all I could see was the face of an exhausted girl. I screamed and cried. Storms were brewing inside me. I was trying to find my brother and sister. Finally, I found them both in a corner. Aziz came towards me. That's when we actually started crying together. I knew they were devastated—just like me. Grandpa was their only reason for staying here.

My father arrived with the imam to take the coffin away. In those few minutes, the sound of crying filled my ears. They will bury Grandpa in the vineyard in the village of Oncha Arlat where we stayed when we first arrived. The family cemetery is there. They're going to put his body in the ground now. We're going there today or tomorrow, and there's an entire week of condolences called *fatiha*.

My dad disappeared again, so I called him, but he didn't pick up. Along with Aziz and Asra, I went upstairs to Grandma's room. I cried incessantly for hours. I needed this release. Around 2:00 a.m., my phone started ringing. I was so tired I could barely reach the phone even though it was under my pillow. It was my dad calling, so I quickly answered it.

"Did you call me, Afsun?"

"Where are you, Dad?"

"I'm home, where are you? Where are your brother and sister?"

"We're at Grandma's upstairs room. Mother, Aziz, and Asra are with me."

"I'll be there then."

Another night without sleep. I sat around waiting for my dad. Everyone else stayed asleep. I went to the door. It had rained a bit. I inhaled the fresh smell of the wet soil. It's like my grandfather was everywhere. Sitting on the stairs, I waited for my father. When he came up the stairs, he was wearing a black local suit. His collar was torn. In the moonlight, I could see his black beard mixed with dust.

"Afsun."

"Dad, are you okay?"

"I'm okay, daughter."

It had been a while since I heard the word "daughter" from his lips. He didn't look so good. The person who befriended murderers of countless young men—the person who caused my grandfather's death—was standing in front of me. At that moment, I could say that I hated him.

"Dad, sit here. Everyone is sleeping inside. We had a rough day."

"My father is dead, Afsun."

"Your father? Your father?" I couldn't contain my anger.

"Are you out of your mind?"

"It's normal to be out of my mind when I hear that you're helping the Taliban, Dad!"

My bold remark struck a nerve.

"Your Uncle Nazeem said so? That jerk!"

"No, Dad, Uncle Ezzat told me. He told me how you broke up this family."

My father was looking at me like he was going to kill me, but if I didn't express myself, my own heart would explode.

"How come, Dad? How did you change so much?"

"Living according to Islam is not changing."

"But the Taliban kills people!"

"You don't understand, girl. Never mind, this is not the time."

I felt like my father was stuck in a situation in which he was so confused that maybe he didn't even know what to do or what he really wanted.

"What's going to happen now, Dad?"

"I'll try to get it together, girl."

My father went to where I had been sleeping, so I went to my aunt's room.

I can't tell you how miserable those nights were. I actually thought I couldn't manage my grief and anger, and my youth seemed to be in vain.

CHAPTER 19

There's a Way

The next day we went to the village of Oncha Arlat. They buried Grandpa on the hill at his vineyard, the big hill that I insisted on climbing in those early days in Afghanistan. Everyone went there first. I stayed home and tried to find Birishna, She had come to help us with the chores in our vineyard. I went into the kitchen. I recognized her from behind.

"Birishna!"

"Afsana!"

She was crying, but I could tell how happy she was. She was wearing a black headscarf and black dress.

"How are you Afsana? You've lost your grandfather. My condolences."

I hadn't told Birishna about my grandfather. I didn't get a chance, so she didn't know about my special bond with Grandpa Raz. She thought it was just a normal loss. She was making a fire in the kitchen. When she saw me, she stopped what she was doing, filled the kettles with water, and called her sister. She spoke Pashto to her, I don't know what she said. Then she grabbed my arm and took me to the back of the kitchen.

"Afsana, I know this is not the time, but my husband has also passed away."

Even when she cried, it was obvious from the twinkle in her eyes how happy and relieved she was by this loss in her life.

"Maybe it's a sin to be happy when someone dies, but I'm glad."

I laughed for the first time in the last three days.

I could hear my aunts crying, "Father, my father," as they returned from the hill.

"Birishna, do you know my grandfather's grave?"

"Yes, I went on the first day. I prayed."

"Take me there, please."

There was a big ceremony called *khatim-e-Quran* at noon, and all the relatives and acquaintances were going to read the Quran.

Birishna washed her hands. Without being seen, we went up the hill. I was wearing the dress my grandmother made me wear. It was the hill we went up the first day I met Birishna. We just needed to go out a little farther. I saw my father from a distance. He was at the grave. I didn't know why he was still sitting there, but as soon as he noticed us approaching, he got up and went down the other side of the hill.

There was no name on the grave yet. I remember my grandfather used to say, "As you pass through the cemetery, pray for all graves without names, and when you feel your heart beating, then you know that a person you love is there under that soil."

First, I prayed for all the dead. Then I walked to the spot where my father had been sitting. The graves were quite close to each other, not even half a metre apart. I noticed the graves of children. They looked like little hills made of soil with white stones above them. Birishna also sat down. She hit two stones together. She said it's believed that the dead person will hear you like this. My grandfather's grave was easily noticed. The soil was still damp and loose. A piece of green fabric was flying over a board. I couldn't hold on. No one could understand my pain, and I couldn't explain it. I could open up freely only when I was with my grandpa.

My heart was racing. I remembered my grandfather saying, "Even if I die, I will live in your heart." Maybe what he said was true. I sat down to avoid being seen.

"Hey, Grandpa, are you comfortable in there? I'm holding myself back too much, so I don't say anything bad, so I don't commit a sin, but I can't bear to be abandoned like this, Grandpa."

I put my head on the gravestone. I closed my eyes. Even his soil was peaceful.

"Afsana, are you all right?"

"I'm okay, Birishna. I mentioned you to my grandpa. He said he could help you. He also said, 'You can cause good things for that girl.' Look, now it seems I've lost my way, but I'm not going to upset Grandpa. I'm going to be strong."

"But you're already strong."

We got up and said goodbye to Grandpa, but as long as we stayed here in Oncha Arlat, I was going to come back. I started talking to Birishna while I was walking.

"Tell me what happened."

"My husband is dead. May God forgive his sins. Amen. But I am still not free. My father can still give me to someone else. They're just waiting for one year to pass from my husband's death. Then I'll have to find some other way, or it'll be the same story again."

"Oh, Birishna! I understand you so well now. But don't worry, there's a way, I hope."

"God is big."

✢ ✢ ✢

They're going to split my grandfather's inheritance right after the khatim-e-Quran. I was doing the dishes with my aunts when my Uncle Ezzat came in.

"Put on your burkas!" he said. "The imam is on his way here. The inheritance will be divided before the elders."

Less than half an hour later, they called me. The imam had arrived. Wearing a burka, I entered the room. My aunt and grandmother were already there in their burkas. I went over to sit with them.

"Khoja imam, this is Bibi Afsun." (I understood that Grandma used "Bibi" in front of my name as a form of respect for women.)

"Now that Bibi Afsun has arrived, let's move on," declared the imam. "First, I would like to read the will of the deceased Mr. Haji Raz that he wrote before he died last Friday." He proceeded to read aloud from the will.

"My dear granddaughter, Afsun, I couldn't tell you that I felt my death was imminent, and I don't think I have much time, so don't forget what I told you. I leave the new building I built on the way to Maymana Airport, including its land, to my granddaughter Afsun, Ismat's daughter. I bequeath this inheritance by my own request and desire. Afsun may use it whenever and however she wishes."

I knew he had a lot to write for me. However, since he knew in what kind of environment it was going to be read, Grandpa wrote only briefly a message he knew I'd understand: "Don't forget what I told you."

The imam turned to one of his students and said, "Write it down son. The newly built house on the way to Maymana Airport belongs to Bibi Afsun."

As soon as the imam was finished, my uncles and aunts started arguing. I heard one of them say, "I don't know how. She just got here from Russia! How could he give it to her? We are the ones who've been serving him his entire life! How come he saw this girl as special?"

They couldn't tolerate the fact that my grandfather had singled me out. They could have that house if they wanted it. I mean, Grandpa left a lot of his other property to them. Why were they so focused on that one house? They argued for about an hour.

Finally, the imam concluded, "Sisters, gentlemen! Your father put his fingerprint under the writing. You can't change it. I want you to respect it."

Everyone shut up for a while. Under the burka was a girl who had lost herself among her grandfather's last words.

As the meeting was drawing to a close, one of the imam's students placed a document in front of me. It's called a traditional or custom deed. It's even more important than the state deed. If that piece of paper is not certified with my fingerprint, the government wouldn't give us the deed. So I put my fingerprint underneath the text, and the imam asked all of us for halal (agreement) and left the room.

As soon as the imam was gone, I grabbed the document and removed my burka. There was no one left but the family. I felt all their eyes on me. They were looking at me suspiciously. I wanted to say, "It's not my fault! It's not like I forced Grandpa to give me that house!" If it weren't for Birishna, I'd refuse this inheritance right away. *Wait! Did I say "Birishna"? Yes, that's right! I will give that money to Birishna's father. He won't marry her off to another old man. Birishna could move to the city and go to school.*

I heard my relatives mumbling about me, suggesting I had tried to get close to my grandfather only for selfish, materialistic motives. But I knew that the bond between my grandpa and me was genuine. I knew why he had left that house to me. He knew that I would use it in the best, most meaningful way. But I couldn't do anything yet. I couldn't sell it or even live in it until

I turned eighteen. I thought about it the entire night. Some brilliant ideas entered my mind.

Before 6:00 in the morning, Birishna's father would usually go up to the big hill. I remember Birishna telling me that. I left my room around 5:00 a.m. and headed past the canal. I had only the deed and my phone with me. Birishna's mother came to milk the cows early every morning. I went to her. I wasn't even thinking about the aggressive dogs anymore. All I could think about was preventing Birishna from experiencing the same dehumanizing fate. Three women were there milking cows. I got closer.

"Good morning, sisters."

One of the women said to the others, "Oh, isn't that the girl from America?"

"No, sis, from Russia."

"Oh, that's it. How are you girl?"

"Good, thanks."

"What are you doing here at this hour? The sun hasn't even come out yet."

"Who's the mother of Birishna?"

The woman milking the black cow turned her head and responded, "I am, daughter."

"I want to talk to you."

"Okay, wait a minute. I'll finish milking."

"Please, it's urgent."

She didn't really understand what I was saying. The words I used were what I learned at school, and with that pronunciation, it was really hard for a peasant Kochi woman to grasp. She got up, hung the bucket of milk on a tree branch, and said something to the other women in Pashto. Then she came over to me.

"Tell me. What is it, girl?"

"I'm sorry, but I need to talk to Birishna's father."

"What's going on?" she asked in bewilderment.

"Please, let's go before your husband leaves, and you'll hear it."

"Come on then. Our house is behind that little wall."

I approached the mud wall through the grass and thorns that rose up to my legs. Their house was small and crowded. I got there before 5:30 a.m. Everyone seemed to be awake. They were having breakfast. A few young men were there, but what surprised me was that none of them looked up at me. I saw Birishna from a distance. My presence alarmed her, but she couldn't get up. I don't know why. The women sat on the floor separately. Some men were sitting in the tent outside. I went fast. Her father was sitting there too. He was the only old man, so it was obvious he was her father.

Her mother spoke Pashto again with her husband. I don't know what she said. Their dogs were approaching me like they were ready to attack. Birishna's mother was trying to protect me. I was terrified. I could barely hold the phone and the deed document in my hand. Birishna's brothers came and calmed the dogs down. Then her father finally approached me.

"Hello, Uncle," I said. (In Afghanistan you can call any elderly man "uncle," and any elderly woman "aunty.")

"Hi, girl. What are you doing here?"

"I have something to talk to you about, and I'll tell you once Birishna is here."

"Come on then. She can join us."

After the other men had left, her father motioned to Birishna to come over to sit with us, and I began explaining my proposal.

"Uncle, this is the deed to the house that my grandfather left for me. I know that due to financial difficulties, you arranged a marriage for Birishna. Her husband is now dead. If you promise right now to let her go to school instead of forcing her to marry anyone else, I will give you this house. Look, it's worth a lot. It's a brand new building built on a huge property near the airport …"

It was obvious how shallow and money-hungry Birishna's father was. He responded without any hesitation.

"When and how?"

"I'll be eighteen in seven months. I can't sign over the deed to you until then, so you'll have to wait."

"How can I trust you?"

"Look, Uncle, her husband just died. Based on traditional law, you can't marry her off in eleven months. I'll be back in seven months, not eleven months, so don't worry. I have no reason to lie to you, and you will not lose anything anyway."

He looked at his wife and said, "All right, then. It's a deal."

"Oh, by the way, I'm going to sign an agreement with you before I give you the house. Birishna will own fifty percent of the house, and she will stay in the city and go to school. You will be the one to sign this agreement."

"No way! Can you tell me the price of this house first!"

"I don't know the price either, but Khoja imam said it's worth no less than ten million afghanis."

The man's eyes opened wide. Never could he imagine this amount of money in his life. He looked confused.

"Okay, girl. I want her to study anyway."

"Then let's give the house to an orphanage. Let's get Birishna to go to school here."

"No way, thank you. You can go now."

I laughed.

"Don't worry. I'll keep my word, Uncle. Just take care of Birishna, and give me your phone number. We'll be in touch."

"Okay, girl. I'll take care of her like a flower. Don't worry."

I got his phone number. I was really disturbed by how much this guy loved money. His palpable greed reminded me of my cousins, who stared at me the other night in the same way. We said goodbye. While I was talking to Birishna, he was talking excitedly to his wife.

"Your daughter did something smart for the first time."

"But it's *your* house," Birishna insisted as I got up to leave.

"It's not going to solve *my* problems, but if this deal saves *you*, I'll be relieved. I'll call your father and ask about you often, my dear friend, Birishna. Goodbye."

"Goodbye."

CHAPTER 20

Back to School

It's been two weeks since my grandfather passed away. We're home now. There are specific traditions here during the period of mourning. If someone dies in the house, it's forbidden to turn on a TV, listen to music, and dress in colourful clothes for up to a year. And one cannot attend a wedding or any other kind of social event involving dancing and fun. Asra and I have been absent from school for two weeks now. However, since this restriction doesn't apply to boys, I sent Aziz to his school. The headmistress of our school came to Grandma's house yesterday. She said we should go back to school or we'd fail. That's why I was preparing tonight as I did for my first day. My school uniform smelled dirty, so I washed it. I packed my books and other stuff in my bag from the night before. Asra did the same. Then we recited the Quran and went to sleep praying for Grandpa. My father has been very quiet and calm lately. I think he feels guilty.

The sound of the alarm clock woke me up this morning. I imagined Grandpa coming to pick us up as he did on that first day of school, but we went to school on our own for the first time. Asra and I calmly left the house without speaking. We didn't say anything until we had passed Aziz's school. Nowadays people keep saying I've changed a lot physically. Especially in the last year, I believe I've grown taller. Some people call me "stork." I'm probably the tallest girl in school. Apparently, it's no longer appropriate for me to leave the house without a burka. That's what I figured out from the way people look at me whenever I walk down the street without one.

We entered the school, but my eyes were searching for Grandpa. Class hadn't started yet, and the other students had their eyes on us. I held Asra's hand tightly, as if we were in danger of losing each other. The looks were so strange. The girls were gawking at us as if we were from outer space. We entered our classroom. Only two girls were there. They were the two students designated to clean the classroom that day. We moved to where we were sitting the first day, left our backpacks there, and then went outside to explore the school grounds for a few minutes. We walked around the schoolyard until class started.

Although it was a small school, it was obvious there were several students. When we got back to the classroom, everyone had arrived. The leader of the class, the one that the headmistress had mentioned on our first day, was there as well, but I didn't know which girl she was at first. The attendance was being taken, so I took my seat.

A young girl with almond-shaped eyes was standing with an attendance book in her hand. She looked at me and said, "Welcome." I just responded with a little smile.

When I sat down, she looked at me again. All the others were shifting their gaze between her and me. She winked at a girl named Maryam, who was sitting next to me. Then she began calling out the names.

When it came to our names, this girl with the almond-shaped eyes said, "Afsun and Asra, you have not been in the classroom for fourteen days, and if this goes up to forty days, you will not be allowed to write the exam. I know you're new, but please watch out. You'd better provide a valid reason for the days you're not here."

"But my grandfather passed away," responded Asra.

The girl—who we realized was Parisa, the class leader—looked intently at Asra with her head up.

"My condolences. When?"

"Thank you. He passed away two weeks ago."

"Look, little one, my brother is dead too, but I stayed home from school on the day of the funeral only. The reality is that a relative dies here every day. A family funeral is not a strong enough reason for fourteen days of absence. If you live in this country, you should know that we don't have time for mourning. Anyway, I wanted to inform you because you're new."

Parisa went about her business as if she were the teacher.

Firuza, one of the girls next to me, whispered, "You've taken Parisa's seat. They've reserved those desks for the top three students."

"It won't happen again, will it, Afsun?" added Parisa.

"Sorry, I didn't know."

"Also, you don't know how to answer properly when somebody says 'welcome' to you?"

Maybe she was right, but I didn't like her tone. She seemed so cool and smug. I got up to move to another seat.

"No, you can stay there for now," she said. "I'll sit here."

As the hours went by during that first day back after our absence, I noticed fierce competition in the class. Asra's smart answers caught the attention of the other girls. They were already comparing her to the top students in the class. At every turn, four or five girls almost got into a fight to be the first to answer the teacher's questions. This behaviour was something I didn't mind since I'm not too competitive when it comes to school.

Our first lesson that morning was literature, and the teacher started with a poem. Every teacher who came in understood that we were new. We received the same personal questions as we got on the first day we stepped into the school. They were especially curious about our life in Russia. Most of the teachers knew my aunts who had once attended the school. In general, the students and the teachers were nice to us.

The first poem we read today wasn't from the book, but it was one I needed to hear. I don't recall the exact lines, but it meant "Tonight, don't bother yourself with yesterdays, the other days, and past problems. I swear, it's a punishment to remember the pain of the past …" The verses that followed were similar to this one. It was the first time here that I felt sparks from literature. In fact, I can say that I began to understand the meaning of literature and poetry just when the test of my life was beginning.

On the one hand, the second day of school was normal with warm weather. On the other hand, the increase in terrorist attacks on schools was alarming. I remembered my grandfather saying, "My dear, always get out of school last because they usually make explosions when there's a crowd at dismissal time."

Several schools, classrooms, and extracurricular classes in Afghanistan were the targets of attacks. That's why we waited to leave until most of the other students had already left the building. I was standing in front of the big door, just as I had stood on the day my grandfather passed away—the day I lost my direction and didn't know which way to go. I waited until 11:40 that day for Grandpa. This entire city reminds me somehow of my grandfather.

At our school, students of different class groups learned in thee-hour shifts. The first group was high school students from 7:00 to 11:30 a.m., then elementary students from 11:30 a.m. to 1:00 p.m., and finally, middle school from 1:00 to 3:00 p.m.

The elementary classes had started, and we waited until the school officials told us to get out. The moment we left, it was so hot that the sun was reflecting on the asphalt. We heard the voices of children reading the alphabet from inside and the clamour of the rickshaws passing through the street. We left the school grounds and moved on. I was going to say it was just another ordinary day, but then I came across the guy from that day Grandpa died, the guy at Aziz's school who helped me find our new house. For a moment, we exchanged glances and he smiled. He was standing in front of a store with a few other young men, but he was following us with his eyes.

"Afsun, why is that guy looking at us like that?" Asra asked.

"I don't know," I replied.

"I'll go and smash his face now."

"What else, Asra? It's really not your business."

"Hey, do you know him?"

"From where would I know him?"

Maybe it wasn't exactly a lie to answer her question with "from where," but I said it to mislead her. The guy seemed very sympathetic and kind. I wanted to thank him for that day, but I didn't know how. We moved on.

"Afsun, don't you think that girl Parisa is unnecessarily cool?"

"How?"

"I don't know. It just seems she tries to control the whole class as if she were the teacher."

"Maybe she's just doing her job the way it's supposed to be."

"No. she should know her place. After all, she's still just a student and probably younger than me."

"Did she cause any harm to you?"

"She can't. I just don't like her attitude."

We both laughed. I admire Asra's energy and reactions. She's always been a defender of her rights. I've always liked this quality in her. I've always stood by her.

As we walked through the front door of our house, we could smell Mom's cooking.

"Asra, how much I missed that smell."

"Me too, sister."

I almost shed tears of happiness. It was a comforting feeling. The last time there was such a surprise was when we were still in Moscow. Sometimes Mom used to welcome us home from school by having a special meal waiting for us.

"Girls, wash your hands and faces immediately. The food is ready."

"Okay, Mom. Right away."

Lately, we've had warm family moments like this. We missed and needed them. Such moments give us positive energy. We quickly washed up. Mom served the lunch on the floor in the area behind her bedroom and next to the living room. Aziz was also ready. We sat there with smiles as we ate together.

Suddenly, Aziz began talking. "Sis, I'm going to school with the neighbour's son. We met the other day."

"Okay, my brother, but let's meet your friend first."

Mom was smiling throughout the meal. I can't tell you how comforting her smile made me feel. It is one of the most beautiful feelings in the world, when everyone is together and happy. The time was running so fast.

After we had all finished eating, Mother said, "Kids, I have something to tell you."

Whenever I hear that opening line, my heart skips a beat.

"Are we going back to Russia?" asked Asra excitedly.

Mom laughed. "No, sweetie. I'm starting out as a teacher at a private school."

"But how, Mom?" asked Asra. "You don't have an undergraduate degree."

"It doesn't matter because it's a teaching position for the third grade. My sister works there, and I'm going for an interview this afternoon."

"That's great, Mom," I said. "You're finally getting out of your routine of sitting at home."

"Yes, but your father hasn't answered the phone yet, so I'm going to go talk to the school first, and then I'm going to tell him."

Then Asra said, "My father doesn't care about us anymore. When did he ever bother to let us know what he's doing? Don't worry too much, Mom. You've found a good job. Don't ever give up." Like me, my sister was angry about my father's latest situation.

Aziz's school time came. Mom started to prepare for her own school, and Asra and I collected the lunch dishes.

"Sis, my friend's here now. I'm leaving," Aziz announced.

"Wait a minute, Aziz. Let me see him first."

Asra and I went together to the door. There was a restless-looking boy at the door. He seemed about fourteen.

"Hi, Afsun sis."

"Hello, young man. What's your name?"

"Khuda-dad, Afsun sister."

"How do you know my name?"

"My sisters were talking about you as the new neighbour. Everyone knows who you are," replied the boy with a laugh.

"What grade are you in?"

"Grade eight, sister."

"Well done, brother, but be careful, okay? I'd appreciate it if you both go back and forth together, and no going anywhere else after school without asking."

"Okay, sis. Don't worry," replied Khuda-dad. Turning to Aziz, he said, "Let's go, buddy."

After they left, Asra said, "Afsun, doesn't that kid look a little different? There's just something about him that makes me feel uneasy."

"You're right, but I didn't want to embarrass Aziz by saying something about him, so when he gets back from school, I'll tell him to watch out."

That day, after my mother went to school with my aunt, my father finally returned home. I warmed up the food. As soon as he came out of the bathroom, he asked me about Mom's whereabouts.

"There's a new private school where her sister works. Mom went there to apply for a job."

"Who did she ask permission from?"

"Is she a kid who needs to get permission, Dad?" Asra replied. "She called you, but you didn't pick up. You've been gone for days, and you're coming now and questioning? You come home in the middle of the night, your clothes and face full of dust. It's not clear who is doing what. Let the woman work."

"You're talking a lot, Asra. This isn't Moscow," retorted Dad.

"Wherever we are, you are my father, but you must listen to us sometimes. We must listen to each other!"

"Watch out what you say, my daughter. I'm afraid I'm going to put you under my feet instead of listening to you."

"Look, I'm not Zarlasht, and you're not my uncle, Dad. Let's be civilized and solve things with dialogue."

"Civilization is not about defying one's father or doing whatever you want. Get out of here now! I won't let my eyes look at you!"

Now one thing was clear about my father. He was not behaving normally these days. Asra went into the kitchen and slammed the door.

Looking at me, Dad said, "Well, aren't you going to say anything?"

"But I've told you before. Don't scold my brother and sister so harshly, Dad."

"But she's being rude."

"We used to argue with you like this all the time. You're the one who gave Asra the courage to stand up for herself. In Moscow, when she got into a fight with her classmates at school, you said, 'Well done, girl! That's right. You're not going to give up. You must defend your rights.' Look, she's defending her rights now. What's changed? Nothing—except for your attitude and behaviour, especially over the past three years. What were their names? Abdullah? Anyway, you had some friends. They started calling, telling you, 'Fight for Allah's way' and then ... I don't know, Dad, you started acting differently after you began associating with them. It's not Asra who has changed. She remains daddy's daughter just as she was three years ago, but you're not the same person. She won't change that easily anymore. She needs to join the Taliban just like you in order to change."

Looking at the ceiling, he sighed deeply.

I went up to him and said, "Dad, I'm sorry. I know you didn't want it to be like this."

"Girl, I do this for our religion, for our family!"

"Dad, thank God we were Muslims from long before, and we still are, but these people you've been hanging out with lately are definitely not true Muslims. They've distorted Islam. They don't represent any religion."

"We fight against those who are sinners and who are paid by the unbelievers!"

"Even if they are sinners, it's none of our business, Dad. You believe in God, don't you? If they have sinned, then let God punish them."

"Do not speak like this or you will disbelieve. Of course I believe in God! Do you hear what's coming from your mouth?"

"Okay, Dad, I'm sorry. My point is that the people who truly believe in the existence of God leave the sins of others for God to deal with. Who are we to judge? Who gave us the right to punish 'unbelievers'?"

"You can't say that! God has ordered us to kill them."

"Dad, do you remember? One day, when you were walking past Saint Basil's Cathedral in Moscow, you said, 'If our parents were Russians, we would live as heretics.' And then you laughed, saying, 'In their eyes, we're the heretics.' Back then, you had a broad, moderate outlook. I'm still repeating that today, Dad. Religion is a matter of individual choice. We cannot kill anyone's son, especially the Afghan soldier, just because we think he doesn't believe. Then which of them is the infidel for God's sake? On our way here that first day, the man on the bus prayed together with you in Balkh Province. He was a soldier. Didn't you see it yourself? They killed him later right in front of us. Then they tried to justify the killing by labelling him a heretic. Look, didn't you work in Russia and receive a salary there?"

"I earned what I deserved with sweat and hard work."

"Doesn't an Afghan soldier or civil servant ever sweat? Or do you think they're getting paid without working hard? The conditions are even tougher here. Did you work and get paid in Russia in tougher conditions than the work of Afghan soldiers who fight on the front lines without food or water?"

"Afsun, you don't know that."

"So, tell me then, Dad, if there's anything I should know."

"I've … I've killed two people. My hands are tied."

"Let's escape and go back to Russia then."

"While I was killing them, I was video recorded under the Taliban flag, so I can't go anywhere anymore. If those images come out, they won't leave me alone. They will find me even in Russia. Plus, I'm already happy because I'm in the way of my religion."

"You're deluding yourself, Dad."

"Your words can't deter me, Afsun. I'll go to war in a month. I trust you, so I am leaving the house is in your hands."

"You trust me, but you don't let other girls like me go to school and gain knowledge."

"The girls' concern here is to go to school to find a boyfriend."

"You also once fell in love with a girl named Tanya. It's normal to love someone."

"I was ignorant. It was a mistake."

"People are already learning from their mistakes."

"But those people don't pay for their sins by fighting in the way of Allah, like us."

"Your arguments are so illogical, Dad. You can't even imagine."

We had this conversation in the backyard. I rested my feet against the stairs.

"Dad, let's say you're dead."

"I don't die. I become Shaheed, a martyr."

"What's going to happen to us?"

"You and Asra will get married. Eventually, Aziz will get married too, and he will take his mother with him."

"But you once said to me, 'Don't marry someone without loving him. Happiness is the most important thing. If you marry someone you don't want, you won't get along, and then it'll get worse.' Don't you remember saying that, Dad? Now would it be the end of the world if your daughter married someone she loved? So, you're going to blame the school because your daughter went there and happened to fall in love with a boy in her class? Are you going to kill them both because they loved each other? Do you realize how you've just connected two unrelated subjects? Recently, your friends burned down Almar districts schools. Then they burned the Akshay

School. I don't know what those Taliban guys put in your head, but you're making irrational statements, Dad!"

"Shut up now! There is no boyfriend allowed for you! I was a heretic then. How I wasted my life in Russia. Your uncle wants you as a wife for his son. You will marry your cousin Subhan! That's all."

"What? My Uncle Rashid, the police chief? Your own brother? I thought you claimed he and his policemen were heretics. I thought you said his government salary was *haram*, forbidden. What you're saying gives me goosebumps. Look how inconsistent and convoluted your words are! You contradict yourself!"

"There's a lot I could say now, but it's too late, Afsun."

"Give up, Dad. Please!"

"No, it's impossible."

A motorcycle stopped at the door. Before leaving, Dad threw a shawl over his shoulder and said, "I'll come back at night."

It was obvious how much he regretted the situation, but he didn't know how to untangle himself. It was hurting him. The more I talked to my father, the more I thought about him. And the more I saw Asra and Aziz, the more worried I became. I was devastated. Unfortunately, I lost my father when he was alive. After he put the entire family in such a dangerous situation, I suffered as if I had no father. During this stressful time, I don't think he ever wondered how we were. He never called or asked about me. How could he even look me in the eye again?

Your father dies. Everyone knows you're without a father. You cry. You go to his grave. You talk to his soul. At least, there's something that you look at and yearn for. In time, you'll say, "There's no cure for death." Then the reality will hit you like a stone in your heart. But like me, you don't live in fear every second that something will happen to him. And the most painful thing is that while you're still wondering about him, you keep telling yourself that he doesn't even care about you, and you try to accept it.

CHAPTER 21

New Developments

Back in Moscow a few years ago, I made a "friend" in my class. Honestly, when he asked me for an eraser, a classmate said, "Look, I think this guy likes you," so it started like that. Our sweet glances continued for a month, and the only so-called sin we committed in this love story was sitting in the same place and talking during the break times. One day he went to the dining room before me. I saw he was busy laughing with another girl. I walked over and poured my chips on him. Not satisfied with that, I took the bottle of Coke in front of him and poured it on his head. Then, for a week, I wandered around ridiculously with the idea of having been betrayed. I cried melodramatically and threatened to commit suicide as I had seen in movies. Looking back, I think I was just trying to get attention. One day at school, I even attempted to hurt myself by drawing on the vein in my wrist with an iron ruler.

That day, Mr. Ivanov, my literature teacher, asked, "Afsun, why are you doing this? Don't you have dreams? Think about your future. Study and look ahead, girl."

With the absurd psychology of adolescence, I responded as if I were speaking from the script of a movie like *Titanic*.

"Teacher, do you know what the most painful and intolerable situation is?"
"What is it, Afsun?"
"The death of someone you love."
"Did someone die, Afsun?"
"I wish he were dead," I replied. "I buried him breathing."

In response to my performance, the whole class said, "Wow, good job, girl."

I found myself bragging as if I'd done a great job. At that time, I thought I knew more about life and love than any of my classmates. They just didn't understand me. One day I even told my mother, "Mom, I'm fifteen now and I understand life better than anyone else." I thought the guys my age were stupid or psychotic. They didn't appreciate me. I couldn't believe that a boy I had "dated" for a month was laughing with another girl, and I was suffering because I thought he was cheating on me.

In my first days in Afghanistan, I met Birishna and listened to her tragic life story. It transformed me. I realized then that I had been feeling unhappy in the past for such embarrassingly trivial reasons. I was too self-centred back in Moscow. I'm actually in a better situation than most girls my age. My heart was in pieces when I spoke with Birishna. When I looked at my own life, I understood that I was never thankful for what I had.

Maybe it was my right to live freely—to study and to live a life without war in a country like Russia—but I didn't understand it then. Maybe that's why God said, "Afsun, there's no such thing as rights. If your parents are with you and you lead a normal life, you're lucky. If you weren't born and raised in war, you're lucky. If you're not hungry and you find something to eat, you're lucky. If they didn't force you to marry someone you don't like, you're lucky. If you have all this and you're still not thankful, you have to stay in Afghanistan to understand it."

When you try to get the right to education again, when you try to understand how a piece of bread is earned, when you try to achieve good living conditions, and even when you find someone you love and build a happy family, that's when you deserve all this. If you really think you deserve better, then you should run and work harder. However, running won't be easy either.

In my most miserable days, I buried my grandpa, the person I had been breathing with. When he died, I lost my way, and I searched everywhere for him. In desperation, I spoke to his lifeless body. They took the most important male figure in my life out of the house in a coffin, and even when I was talking to his soul, I didn't begin thinking about suicide. I didn't say I was unlucky and helpless.

My father has definitely joined the Taliban. How bad this group is doesn't concern me right now. All I know is that my father, who used to prepare meals in the kitchen and sing with us, has become a person who beats us and condemns us to the burka. He now calls people whores and infidels. Despite my immense sadness over his transformation, there's no idea of suicide in me. On the contrary, I keep telling myself, "This family needs you. You must be kind and stay strong."

Even with all my current hardships and disappointments, I haven't used the word "unlucky" in months. Maybe the last time was in Russia when Mom used to cook. I'd complain sometimes and say, "Dad, we're tired of my mom's cooking. Take us to a restaurant."

☩ ☩ ☩

It's been twenty-eight days since my father announced he'd be going to war in a month. Although the circumstances here are stressful, life is going on fairly normally. Same streets, same school. The guy who helped me at Aziz's school stands on the street every afternoon waiting for me to pass by. I'm getting closer to Parisa, the young class leader. Asra is competing with her and challenging her. My mother is working as a teacher now. All these new developments have brought us some happiness. My mom goes to school every day, and my dad doesn't seem to mind since her students are very young children, and no men are around. From our recent father–daughter talk, it seems he has accepted the situation. I made new friends at school, and a new girl came from Kabul. She dresses differently and talks about her boyfriend all the time. She's someone who tries to attract attention with her cool attitude. Aziz goes to the mosque in the morning for his Quran lesson. Asra goes to math and physics classes in the afternoon, and I sit at home until Mom gets here.

I'm not always waiting here alone, though. Aunty Nuriya often gets permission to stay with me, but I think it's a pretext just to be close to Nimat, who's a neighbour of ours. She watches for him at the door. Whenever she gets a signal from him, she takes the risk and runs up to the guest room of his house. Then she comes back to us before Mom arrives home. I don't know what my aunt is up to over there, but I don't like it. I still have my doubts about that Nimat.

Starting next week, I'm going to take literature classes. Literature is now my new passion. Especially at night, when I read the poems of Hafiz and

Mawlana, I become more interested in Persian. I also inhale the smell of the pages while I'm reading novels.

My father isn't coming home. As a cover, in case someone ever asks about his job, he opened a mechanic's shop. However, we found out he wasn't going to his shop either. He had a boy working there. Tomorrow is Friday. If Dad decides to leave, he'll come home to pick up some of his clothes first. My grandmother (Dad's mom) never goes out because she's still grieving. We've been visiting her every Friday for a few months, but it's frustrating when she wails all the time and cries out nonsense, such as "Find your grandfather! He loves you! Call him! Maybe he'll come back!" Whenever she cries out like this, I'm reminded of the day of the funeral. The only development that comforts me after the repeated pain and shock is that the guy who helped me find my way home the day Grandpa died stands every day in front of the school and smiles at me as I walk by.

I watched a movie once about soldiers in a battlefield who are short of bullets and food. They choose someone in their military unit to go to the city to find supplies. The soldier takes the train to the city, gets all the necessities, and on the way back, while waiting for a train at the station, he suddenly sees a beautiful girl singing. All of a sudden, he forgets about war, forgets all his troubles and losses. He sees a beautiful new world in her eyes. There's a brief moment when he makes eye contact with the girl ... Then he hears the sound of the approaching train. He boards the train and returns to painful real life ... But that fleeting moment of eye contact is worth everything ... Sometimes I feel like that soldier.

We have literature class three days a week, and the themes are interesting. I've been able to make good friends lately. As I said, I've become quite close to Parisa, and she has been very kind to me. Sometimes she even sits down with me and helps me understand difficult subjects. The girl who moved from Kabul is called Rona. She has also become a close friend of mine. Our friendship was smooth at first, but now she's jealous of my friendship with Parisa. In fact, she childishly says, "You should pick either her or me to be close to you." There was a disagreement between the two of them, and now it's inevitably my business too.

Rona is from a wealthy Kabul family. She's also quite attractive and well groomed, but she knows it and wants the entire school to revolve around her.

Although she's a bit arrogant, everyone wants to be friends with her, but for some reason, she gravitates to me. She has been to our house many times, and I feel a connection with her. I told her I wanted to take a literature course outside our regular school, and she agreed to attend too, even though she doesn't like literature very much. She just wants to spend more time with me.

The literature course takes place in the Chahar Samavat area near the city centre. I haven't been there yet, but we're going to go together after school. Only Fridays are the weekend in Afghanistan. Starting this Saturday, after school, six days a week from 11:30 a.m. to 12:30 p.m., we're going to attend the classes. I'm excited.

By the way, I called Birishna's father three times. He answered twice, and she was with him only once. When I spoke to her, she sounded very happy. Recently, Dad told Aziz, "Afsun should sell her grandfather's house and give me the money to start a business." Aziz doesn't know what Dad is really doing, so he said, "Sis, please give it to him."

I can't tell my young brother the truth about his father's Taliban involvement. If I tell him, I know it'll have a negative effect on him. I fear he would no longer devote himself to his lessons. That's why I mentioned Birishna to him. He saw her with me once. That day, I felt Aziz had grown up, as he approached me and said, "I'm glad I have a strong sister like you."

I don't know how strong I am, but lately I've been putting a lot of time and energy into trying to keep my family together. I'm not going to allow my father to ruin our lives too. Nothing will happen to my father if I take good care of my brother and sister, visit my grieving grandmother frequently, focus on my schoolwork, and keep my promise to Birishna.

A lot of this may be normal, but the subject of Birishna really scares me. One night I even dreamed her father married her off to someone. In the dream, she said, "I trusted you. I believed your words, but my father sold me out." Even though I didn't remember all the details of my dream, I understood the possibility that I couldn't keep my promise to her. It happened in a dream, not in real life. Nevertheless, it upset me.

The twenty-ninth day is over. It's getting hot. I sat outside until 10:00 p.m. and waited for my father. I thought maybe he gave up going to war and he would find a regular job. My grandfather left behind land and shops. If

Dad ran them, maybe he would become successful and give up working with terrorists. I keep hoping.

I've done my homework. Our living area in the garden is very large. It starts from the guest room to my parents' bedroom, with the wall extending from the street. I turned on the guest room light, left the window open, and went to sit against the wall outside. I was writing in my notebook on my lap. There was a stream of light coming from under the door. Everyone was asleep. That's when the doorbell rang. I knew it was my father. I ran to open the door. He had someone with him, a big man with a black beard. He was sitting on a motorcycle, and he had surma around his eyes. His posture was similar to my father's recent posture.

The stranger turned to my dad and said, "Her hair's exposed! Who is that?"

"My daughter. Sorry, she was in a hurry," answered my father.

"Well, teach her to dress like Bibi Fatma and Bibi Zainab. If she refuses, then you'll take care of her."

For the first time, a strange man was being rude to me in front of my father, yet my father remained silent. The man was insulting me, yet my father was bowing down to him without saying anything. I couldn't believe how deeply Dad was brainwashed. As if to please this guy, my father hit me in the face and closed the door so quickly that it injured me in the forehead near my left eyebrow. I was bleeding.

Instead of worrying about my injury, he blamed me for having answered the door.

"Why did you open the door?"

"Who else was going to open it at this hour, Dad?" I said.

He shut up because he didn't have an answer.

"Why weren't you wearing a headscarf?"

"There are no strangers in the house right now."

"Why are you opening the door like this?"

"How else could I open the door at this hour, Dad? Seriously? I was waiting for you! Did I do anything wrong, or did I dress inappropriately? All that can be seen is my hair. I'm not going to go to bed at night wearing a burka. Three women and a little boy were all alone in the house late at night. Why are you bringing strange men to our home at this hour anyway? Never mind, Dad, never mind. I wish I hadn't waited up for you. If I had gone to sleep instead, then who would have opened the door for you?"

He kept quiet, sat next to the water tank by the tree, and washed his face.

"Dad ..."

"What?"

"Are you going to war tomorrow?"

"How do you know about that?"

"You told me yourself."

"Yes, I'm going. I hope so."

"Can't you just give up? We're alone. Look, there are thieves around here. We're scared here until you come at night."

"Your Uncle Zafar will come at night to stay with you."

Even the tears in my eyes, my bleeding eyebrow, and my broken heart could not change his mind. He believed he was doing something for himself, a man who couldn't even defend himself, a father who couldn't protect his daughter, who had become a member of an organization in which nobody really understood whom they were working for. He seemed like he was guided by remote control, like a soulless robot. He had nothing to say. Although he couldn't even look me in the eye, I sensed from his voice that he missed me. Maybe if he sees his daughter, if he can look into my eyes, he'll give up. Maybe if he smells me, he'll remember the peaceful, old days and say, "My sweet girl, how good you smell. Come and hug me."

We held each other's hands as he said, "You're a young woman now. I can't be a *mahram* to you any longer. Only a husband can hug or kiss you now or accompany you in public—not your brother, grandfather, or uncle like before, not even me."

"What? But that kind of rule doesn't make any sense at all. It's not written in the Quran. You're still my father. How can you no longer be a mahram? It's normal for a father and daughter to show affection towards each other. Do you really believe it's shameful to hug your own daughter just because she's an adult now? For God's sake! Look at me, Dad. Look at me! I feel like a girl who betrayed her family and ran off with someone. Please don't abandon us! Dad, please don't do this ... We'll do whatever you say as long as you don't leave us!"

He was trying to let go of my hands. At that moment, I didn't know whether I'd ever get a second chance if I got angry and let him go. I held onto his hand with all my might. The kitchen had two little steps, and my father sat there. So, I sat right on the floor, holding his hands. He put his head down and never lifted it. His face wasn't fully visible because of his bushy beard. He hadn't shaved in months.

Eventually, I let go, and I held his face in my hands. I used to do this often, and then I'd wait for my dad to kiss me on the forehead. He had lost a lot of weight. I could feel his bones. His hands used to be soft, even without any hand cream. I used to say, "Dad, I'm jealous of such beautiful hands." There was nothing to be jealous of anymore, not even his presence. I raised his face. Around his eyes was that black surma that Taliban guys wear, so he went to wash his face. The whites of his eyes were bloodshot. From the light of the little lamp hanging in the distance, I could see his veins protruding. We were eye to eye. I stared into his eyes. Gasping for three or four breaths, I reached out to place his hand to my bleeding eyebrow.

"My daughter, my Afsun. My beautiful girl."

That's all he said. Tears were streaming down his cheeks. Maybe he was regretting what he had lost, but he was so brainwashed he didn't even have a choice between his children and the Taliban anymore. He was ready to do whatever the organization ordered him to do.

I put my chin on his two knees and hugged his legs. Just as he was about to say something, Mom's voice came from inside. She had gotten up to go to the bathroom. Maybe she stopped my dad from speaking as himself for the first time lately. I could hear my mother's footsteps getting closer. I wish she hadn't interrupted us.

Dad got up right away, saying, "I chose the right direction, and you need to grow up."

That's not what his tears said, though. With the distorted way the terrorists interpreted Islam, they had turned my father into a different person.

"Oh, good to see you, father and daughter."

"Afsun fell just now, and her eyebrow opened up a little bit," my dad quickly explained. "You need to watch your step, Afsun. You're a big girl now. Watch out."

My first impulse was to stir things up by revealing the truth, but I thought about my mother's weak health. Actually, I wanted to tell my mom everything because I was going to save my family, but my dad wasn't going to give up. My mother would have been hospitalized for nothing, and I would have ruined my mother with the dream of saving the family.

As he walked into the room, I said, "Dad, it's halal to kill people, burn schools, cut roads, and rob. But is it forbidden to look your own daughter in the eye?"

I wanted to scream. My heart was burning, and now I had lost my father. I knew that it wasn't Islam. As far as I know, Islam is a religion that preaches love, peace, and respect. I wish those terrorists had read the life of their prophet first. How easy it was for the Taliban to pit a father against his daughter and to present a daughter as "bad" to her father.

I'll never forget my grandpa's nostalgic reflections on life in Afghanistan in more peaceful times. "My beautiful granddaughter," he said, "it wasn't always like this around here. It used to be a very open and tolerant place. I remember in the 1960s and '70s, a large number of foreign tourists used to visit our country. I met a Canadian hippie couple at that time. They visited the Bamiyan statues and came to Northern Afghanistan. We hosted them here in our village. They even stayed at our home for a couple days.

"Back then, we didn't have today's narrow mentality. In fact, our society resisted radicalism for a long time—despite the 1979 Soviet invasion and the beginning of the war. Even until 1992, the entire crew of public bus drivers in Kabul were women in their beautiful uniforms. Plus, over seventy percent of school teachers were women in their uniforms and their heads uncovered. Unfortunately, for the sake of the war between the West and the Soviet Union, they radicalized our society under the name of jihad. Since then, our customs, traditions, religion, society, and lifestyle have been condemned to extremism. Now we are surrounded by ignorance and terrorism under the name of Islam."

I understand Grandpa better now. He was so wise. I miss him a lot.

When I woke up on the morning of the thirtieth day, the blood from my head wound was on the pillow. Aziz went to the pharmacy early in the morning and bought bandages. They prepared eggs and milk for breakfast with Asra. Normally, breakfast in Afghanistan means only sugar tea and bread. They woke me up. After a great breakfast, Dad left. He was going to get something for Grandma, and then we were all going over to her house.

During breakfast, I forced a smile, telling my brother and sister not to worry. I appeared to be listening to what was being said at the table, but my mind was wandering off. I used to have good conversations with my dad. He used to have a sense of humour. We used to laugh together about many things, including the makeup worn by some of our relatives. And then my father would end by saying, "Enough is enough. We're going commit a sin by badmouthing others."

My brother, sister, and I share a room, but it's not big enough for three people of growing age because it's even smaller than my room in Moscow. We laid three mattresses on the floor against one wall to sleep. My feet reach the window. In the morning, when the sun rises, it warms my feet and then my body. There are two bathrooms in the house, but none of them have toilets. The only toilet is in the courtyard of the house by the door. At night, it's difficult to walk that far in the dark. Going to that toilet alone at night is scary, so we wake each other up and go together.

These days, we are more than siblings. We are each other's best friends and literally each other's protectors. At first, I was jealous of Asra and Aziz because I thought my father and mother showed more interest in them and loved them more. However, the three of us grew up fast, and those feelings of insecurity dissipated. Even our arguments became enjoyable. We no longer had a father who hugged us every day. We no longer had a mother who showed her love openly or made cakes for us. Therefore, we had no reason to be jealous. We had a lot of fun together. Mom still prepares food, but during the meal, there's a lack of laughter, joy, and comfortable conversation. We especially miss Dad's affection and energy.

Our family life is, perhaps, pretty ordinary. We follow the same routine, eating similar meals every day. The four of us have fallen into a comfortable rhythm. Also, over the past year and a half, we've all been fairly healthy. It's a comfort to know that the eggs we eat come from the chickens in our garden, the milk and dairy products we consume come from the cows we feed, and the fruits and vegetables we eat are grown in our own garden. All we lack is that old family bliss when we felt secure with our parents.

One morning during breakfast, Asra began examining the yolk of her egg.

"The yolk of the eggs we got from my grandmother's chickens is orange not yellow!" she said, prompting laughter.

"Don't you know egg yolk is naturally orange?" Aziz responded.

It was fun to hear such sweet discussions between the two on science matters. Afghanistan's positive impact on my two siblings, who once argued by throwing pillows and paper at each other, can be found in the subjects and logic of their arguments now. In fact, they are both researching more and trying to provide evidence to substantiate their claims.

The bread and other baked goods here are more delicious and appetizing than what we used to eat in Moscow. Bread is called nan. It's delicious to open it up, dip it in the frying pan where the egg is still cooking, and eat the soft, scattered yolk with the egg white. I was popping the last piece of bread into my mouth when my mom came in. She wasn't sleeping in pyjamas anymore. (She used to lie there all day sometimes wearing whatever she was wearing.)

"Good morning, kids."

"Good morning, Mom," we all responded.

Pointing to me, she remarked, "I see you're having breakfast with your new mother. My shoes have been thrown on the checkers." In other words, she was telling us that she's been forgotten, no longer needed.

Aziz laughed as mother came to sit between Asra and me. She looked like she had just showered. Her hair was still damp.

"Who prepared the eggs?" she asked.

"I did," responded Aziz.

"It's not a man's job."

"Well, Asra prepared the milk and bread, so I cooked the egg."

"Don't let anyone see you doing chores in the kitchen, my son."

"Let the world see that I'm helping my sister," he said. "I'm not ashamed of it."

My mother's glum face brightened a little, and she smiled.

Asra, Aziz, and I had recently formed a solidarity movement among ourselves. We supported and defended each other. We used to bang our hands together and shout, "That's it!" It was Aziz's idea. He was fairly strong and mature for his age. I was sure our precious unity and time together helped us move on.

There's a saying among girls in Afghanistan that if you're good with your brother, you have an advantage in moving on with your school life. Some girls have even said that their brothers had positive or negative influences on their love lives. For me, it was important for the three of us to get along well, strengthen our bonds with each other, and have a successful school life.

In reaction to our joyful sense of camaraderie after Aziz's proud statement that day, Mom said, "I see you three have formed a little gang."

I enjoyed a good laugh with my siblings when she said that. Later the three of us chatted by the window while Mom finished her breakfast. My siblings pretended to be doctors examining my head wound. Then they carefully applied the bandage. As they worked hard to make sure it didn't hurt, I rested my head against the gap in front of the window. Thinking about what happened last night and what Dad was doing with his life hurt me far more than the wound on my eyebrow.

I had mixed feelings when Asra said, "The operation is over. Let the assistant check the wound." She got up to bring the little mirror.

Then Aziz said, "Wow, you exaggerated a small wound by using such a big band-aid."

At that point, Mom announced that it was time to leave. "Come on, guys. If the surgery is over, tidy up and we'll go to Grandma's place."

"Okay, queen of mothers. Right away," responded Asra.

When I got up to gather the breakfast dishes, Aziz intervened. "Sis, you straighten up the room. Give me the tray. I'll take the leftovers to the kitchen. Asra can do the dishes."

"What? You left the hardest job for me," complained Asra. "We'll wash the dishes together, my brother."

"Just joking," said Aziz. "It's only a few dishes. I'll do them. You guys go and get ready."

I picked up our bedding from the floor, placed the plates on the tray, and handed the tray to Aziz. I was thankful to have such wonderful siblings.

After cleaning up, I ironed all the clothes we were going to wear, and we all got dressed. Since we were still in the period of mourning, we could not wear any colourful clothes yet. I wore parts of my school uniform since almost all my other clothes were light or patterned. After the sixth month from Grandpa's passing, these restrictions would be lifted. Until then, however, listening to music, watching TV, and laughing loudly were prohibited. Such activities were perceived as disrespectful to the deceased.

If my grandfather were alive, I'm sure he'd kick everyone out of his house who screamed and cried out at his funeral. He wouldn't overwhelm people with rules that restricted their freedom for six months. I knew he wouldn't approve because he was a person who wanted people to be happy, to laugh and live their lives freely. He didn't like to see anyone crying or suffering. When my aunts and sisters-in-law came to visit my grandmother on Fridays, they would walk through the door screaming and lamenting. I think what they did was nothing more than emit negative energy and give my grandmother headaches. It was as if they thought that their love for Grandpa could be measured by the volume of their screams in front of others.

It was frustrating when the wife of one of my father's brothers squeezed me on the day of the funeral and said, "You should cry more loudly 'oh Grandpa, oh Grandpa!' to show everyone your grief."

I was the only one who stayed with my grandfather's body that night when he was sleeping there like a king in his coffin. I didn't necessarily have to scream dramatically to express my sadness. My expression of grief wasn't a performance. Some of the other women in the community were literally counting who attended the funeral, who fainted, who tore her hair out, who cried more, who scratched her face. They were taking account of and comparing all the displays of grief. In fact, they continued to gossip about the funeral and its aftermath, sometimes even at our school. Some of our classmates told us what they had heard about our family from their mothers and neighbours. My own cousins were outrageously catty, talking about me behind my back at the khatim, the ceremony of accepting condolences.

"Oh, she got the best house our grandfather left. She doesn't need to cry and has nothing to worry about anymore."

Finally, we were all set to visit Grandma. My mother wore her dark green dress and white headscarf again. Even those clothes were now giving off negative energy. We sat on the mattresses laid out on the huge sofha outside. Since Mom and I were wearing burkas, the thick layers at the back were like an extra cushion for us when we sat on the floor. Asra had her black cover sheet on. Aziz came and sat next to me. He gave me a kiss and his sweet smell gave me energy. We sat there waiting for our ride.

"The doorbell is ringing," Mom said. "Come on, Aziz, go open the door."

"But I just sat down, Mom," he replied. "Let Asra answer the door."

Without objecting, Asra, wearing the appropriate clothes that would please her father, went to the door. It was Dad.

He had a lot of food in his shawl. He went into the kitchen and left it all there. Then he stood at the doorway of the kitchen and suddenly decided he needed to reprimand Aziz.

"You've become a big boy, yet you ask your mother for a pacifier. You're sitting on your sister's lap without shame, like a baby."

"What's wrong with that, Dad?" I said. "Don't exaggerate it."

I felt sorry for Aziz. He looked so defeated and embarrassed. I think Dad's comment made him feel as if he'd given up his manhood.

"I came here in your uncle's car. Come. He's waiting outside."

I stood up abruptly. I don't even remember how I put on the burka. We left right away. They came here in my grandfather's car. Two of my father's brothers had grasped the car as their own right after Grandpa Raz died. But those are two sons who did not deserve that car. The back of the car was full of food. My father and Aziz shared the front seat, while mother, Asra, and I sat in the back seat. Uncle Ezzat tried to start a conversation with us. Of course, he asked how school was going. I waited for Asra or Aziz to answer when it came to school because both of them were real students. Literature was the only subject that interested me in school.

"It's good, Uncle Ezzat," Asra responded. "I passed the exams."

"What were your results?"

"Well, I'm ranked second in the class."

I hoped that they would change the subject because if they asked me about my ranking, it wouldn't be fun to say I was in tenth place.

"Dear Aziz, what about your results?"

"I came fifth, Uncle, but you know my Persian is not very good."

"Anyway, well done to you."

As my turn was approaching, my father suddenly changed the subject.

"Haji brother, we need to find a good mullah for this Aziz. Besides his schoolwork, he has nothing to do."

"There's a mosque just up the street from your house. A lot of kids are studying there. Send him there."

"You're right. I'll talk to the imam."

I knew that mosque. I saw it the first day we came here when I was in the car with Grandpa. They called it Haft Shaheed, which means "seven martyrs." There were even tombs in the courtyard of the mosque. The sides of the tombs were old and eerie with turquoise walls and green window frames attracting attention.

When we arrived at Grandma's house, my little cousins were playing near the front door. We got out of the car. The first thing that caught my attention was that the gate between the two houses was closed. This sight upset me because that gate used to be kept open so we could go freely back and forth. After my grandfather died, the two houses were completely separated. Only the main doors at the front are used now to go from one house to the other. That day, similar to the past Fridays, was spent hearing the voices of my aunts screaming, crying, and groaning to exhibit the extent of their grief.

While I was washing the dishes, I couldn't help thinking about my father. That's when he and my uncle entered the room. They called everyone in the house. The sun was about to set as we all waited for Dad to start speaking.

"You know, we've had a hard time lately, so we couldn't get together and talk. I'm going to Pakistan to take care of my mechanic shop and grow the business. It'll take about a month to get the car parts from there. I have a few more friends to accompany me. They'll be right back to pick me up. So, I am leaving. Give me your blessing."

My grandmother responded first. "You're going to work, and God bless you."

"Mom, you know the circumstances. Anything is possible."

"God forbid, son. Come here."

My grandmother was sitting on the stairs in the hallway. My father went over to kiss her hand. She hugged him. They sat next to each other for a while. Almost everyone had found a place to sit.

Asra and I were the only ones standing. Asra looked at me.

"Sis, what's going on?"

"Nothing, hon. It's all about what you can see."

My father's obvious lie is making the situation harder for me. I can't even tell my brother and sister the truth. The Taliban's attacks on the city centre, on the one hand, and the bombardment of the army's jets and helicopters, on the other hand—all of this violence was costing hundreds of lives every day. Now I was going to live every night of the war worrying whether my father is alive or dead. While my siblings and most of our relatives are assuming that my father is safely in Pakistan, I will be the one burdened with worry after each incident involving the Taliban. While I was thinking about all this, I realized everyone else in the house was saying goodbye to my father. They gave him good travel wishes—along with requests for items they wanted him to bring back from Pakistan.

The wife of one of Dad's brothers remarked, "God, destroy those who have started this war. As a result, people are going to other countries to gain a bite of bread." I used to hear a curse like this from almost everyone, every day, but I was the only one who knew that my father was one of those who was engaged in that war. Hiding this reality hurt.

Dad looked at his mother and said, "Mom, while I'm gone, Zafar should go to my house and stand over the children, or even stay there at night, okay?"

My grandmother replied, "Of course, son. Zafar usually stays with his friends. At least, he gets picked up by them from the street."

My parents spoke to each other earlier, I believe. He had convinced my mother that growing the business would improve our family's financial condition. Still believing that Dad was off to Pakistan for work, Mom stood in the corner of the house and wept innocently for her husband.

"Have you packed my clothes, Gulnur?" he asked her.

"Yes, I did," she replied.

Then my father turned to his mother and said, "Mother, why don't you come over tonight so the kids won't feel any emptiness when I'm gone."

My grandmother wanted to stay with us, actually. She hadn't been out of the house for weeks, as she waited every day for people coming to offer their condolences.

I was surprised when Dad said, "Look, Mom, if you're concerned about people gossiping, no one would misunderstand. Don't be afraid of the neighbours. Wear your burka. Nobody will recognize you. Even if someone sees you, it's your son's house you're going to, so who cares."

I liked my father's behaviour towards his mother, trying to make her feel better. Even though he was brainwashed, sometimes he reverted to his old self.

AFSUN BEYOND THE VINEYARD

Grandma still didn't answer either yes or no. Uncle Zafar told her she'd better go when she had this opportunity. It was sad that a woman of her age would need to consult so many other people about such a simple decision—even getting permission from the sons she raised.

We packed up to go home. My father went to my maternal grandparents' house as well to say goodbye. We got into the car, but since Grandma was with us too, either Asra or I would have to sit in the trunk. Although I could barely see with the burka on, when my uncle opened the trunk, I spotted my grandfather's favourite music cassettes in there. As soon as I saw them, I volunteered to be the one to sit in the trunk.

While sitting there, I covered the cassettes with my burka, and when the car started moving, I put them in my bag one by one. Grandpa's cassettes were of no use to anyone else, but they meant the world to me. They gave me strength. When we got home, my father and mother went to their room to say goodbye to each other for the last time.

My grandmother, who had locked herself up in her house for several months, was finally venturing outside. This was the first time she'd come to our house since Grandpa's death. I was happy to take her away from the house of mourning to clear her mind. While Asra and Aziz sat next to my grandmother, I went to the kitchen with my Uncle Zafar to prepare dinner.

When I asked Grandma what she wanted to eat, she replied, "My dear, make some warm soup, and put tomatoes in it. That's enough."

Uncle Zafar said, "I'll come with you. See if there's anything missing."

As my uncle walked me into the kitchen, he said, "Please call your Aunty Nuriya and invite her to come over."

"It's late Uncle. How can she come at this hour?"

"I'll go get her."

"But her mom won't allow it. As you know, her mother doesn't have a good relationship with your mother."

"If you call her, your grandmother will allow it."

This was the first time Uncle Zafar was asking me for anything. I didn't know why, but I didn't want to reject him, so I called. The phone's ring tone was Farhad Darya's song, "Salaam Afghanistan."

"Allo?" answered my grandma, Nuriya's mom.

"Hi, honey mom. It's me, Afsun."

"Peace be upon you, my dear Afsun. How are you?"

"Good, my dear honey mom."

"You went to your other grandmother's today. Couldn't you have stopped by?"

"Grandma, you know the whole family was here. I couldn't get out of the kitchen until tonight. I was already doing the dishes until I got into the car. And my dad's leaving. I'm so sorry that I couldn't make it to see you. There wasn't enough time. Sorry."

To show her reaction, she called me "Jogi." Actually, this is a name given to a "gypsy" in Afghanistan, but it's used to refer to a person who talks a lot in order to make excuses to convince someone.

"My sweet grandma, can Aunt Nuriya come to visit us tonight?"

"Now? It's late. How will she get there?"

"Yes, I know it's late, but Uncle Zafar is here. I'll send him to pick her up."

I could hear Nuriya in the background. Obviously, she had been listening to our conversation. "Tell that bastard black snake to go and pick up his mother."

Her mother intervened and said, her tone now changed, "My dear, Afsun, it's late. Not now. Maybe another day."

"Okay, it's up to you, Grandma."

After I hung up, Uncle Zafar asked curiously, "What did she say?"

"My grandmother said no. I knew she wouldn't allow Nuriya to go out at this hour anyway."

"But I heard Nuriya's voice. What was she saying?"

"Nothing."

"Please tell me," he said anxiously.

"Well, she implied that she doesn't like you."

I had no idea why I said that, but I felt like he had a strong crush on her. He usually looked at her, and even when he was driving us somewhere, he would hold the front seat of the car for her so no one else would sit there. However, my aunt never seemed to like him. Besides, she already had a boyfriend.

Zafar's chance of marrying Nuriya was zero. Since my two grandmothers disliked each other, they would never allow it. That's why I didn't want to give him any false hope.

Asra came towards us and turned on the lights in the garden.

"Oh, I see you two are here having a good conversation."

We laughed as she joined us.

"I called mom's mom to ask if Uncle Zafar could go pick up Aunty Nuriya to come over here tonight, but she said it was too late."

"So, our uncle misses his old love," Asra commented.

"Old love?" My curiosity was aroused.

Of course, Uncle Zafar wanted this topic of conversation to stop right away.

"Don't exaggerate it, girls. Let's do our job in the kitchen."

"You and the kitchen? From what I've seen, you don't even lift your glass."

I started chopping onions and tomatoes while Asra did other things. It was my opportunity to ask her about her earlier comment.

"What's the love story of Uncle Zafar and Aunty Nuriya? Please tell me."

My uncle overheard me and said, "Change the subject, girls."

Asra laughed and continued. "Look, let me put it this way ... Uncle Zafar, please don't stop me. Afsun won't tell anyone. Well, a long time ago, our uncle and aunt were in love, like Layla and Majnun. They'd had feelings for each other since childhood. In the last year of high school, our uncle revealed his love and made a proposal. Aunty Nuriya accepted, but then she went off to college. She ended her long love story by saying, 'There's no such thing as us any longer. Goodbye, Zafar.'"

"You told the story like a journalist, my dear sister," I said.

We laughed, but it's weird that my aunt never told me about something so significant. She usually told me everything about her love life. She even said that Nimat was her first love. I even knew what she was eating each morning, so I was surprised that she managed to hide something this big from me.

My uncle turned to me and said, "Afsun, now I'm going to ask you something. Please tell me the truth. Is there someone in Nuriya's life right now? I know she talks to you."

"I don't know, Uncle Zafar. We don't talk about that stuff."

I knew my aunt wasn't very good at romantic relationships. After all, a person who doesn't even remember a twenty-year relationship wouldn't consider a short-term one as true love.

"I don't know, girls. Your Aunt Nuriya is flamboyant and spontaneous. She broke up with me without a reason. I wish I knew why."

It was clear that my uncle still loved her. "I think your relationship was beautiful when no one knew," I said. "Look, if your mothers had known about you two, maybe they would never have let you get married. Then you'd be more upset. Maybe it's good that you broke up."

"But is it that easy, Afsun? You know how they say, 'I sacrificed my life for someone.' That's exactly what my experience was. Even when I was a kid, I was always looking out for her, watching her not to get hurt, not to fall when she was playing. When I got circumcised as a child, I cried for Nuriya to come to me, and my mother refused. She was mad at me and wondered why I was so persistent about having Nuriya there. I used to walk her to school in the morning when unrelated girls and boys are not supposed to be seen together. It was considered unacceptable, but I wanted to be there for her every chance I got. I did all kinds of outlandish things to impress her to the point that I couldn't make any other friends. I'd forget everything and everyone when it came to Nuriya. No one wanted to be friends with me anymore."

As he opened his heart to me, his eyes began tearing up. It was obvious that Uncle Zafar was trying hard to win her back. Maybe they broke up because of my aunt's arrogance. After all, when you care about a person more than he or she deserves, it can be too scary for that person you love, or you end up being taken for granted. The initial excitement and challenge of the relationship fades, and the person you love gets bored and leaves. I think my aunt didn't deserve that much love and attention. While I was thinking all this, Asra summed up what was in my head.

"Uncle, I think I know you and my aunt. She's not a bad girl, but I'm sure she doesn't deserve you. I'm asking you to watch out for your next relationship. Don't be too eager. Some people can't handle it if you come on too strong, seem too interested. Loving too intensely can sometimes be overwhelming for some people."

"That's right," said Uncle Zafar. "You've presented a valid analysis, my dear Asra. I'm reminded of a saying: 'Every pot will find its own lid.'"

I saw another side of a family member that night. I couldn't trust my aunt anymore. Actually, I've noticed before that Aunty Nuriya is sneaky. I remember the night my cousins sat down with us. Without knowing anything, she said, "I think Afsun loves someone." It was just something she fabricated to stir things up, to get a reaction, or to see if any of my other cousins were interested in someone. I see now that she used me for her own selfish games. I didn't reveal too much to her after that evening. I know now that when she was describing herself, my aunt was lying on her innocent feet. According to her, she was living her life as if she were an angel—with caution and without mistakes. She has never mentioned her past connection with Uncle Zafar. The thought of never being able to trust her again weighed on my mind.

Uncle Zafar sat with us that night until we finished the cooking. We laughed, cried, and talked about my grandfather. Best of all, we refused to believe my grandfather was really dead, so we declared, "Although his body has been separated from us, he will live in our hearts as a young Raz Bay and will always be remembered and loved beautifully."

About half an hour passed. We were closing the pot and washing the vegetables when my dad emerged from his room. It's been a while since he said he was going to Pakistan. Since he wasn't really going there to build his auto mechanics business, he could have left anytime. He had a little bag in his hand and left behind the bag my mother had prepared for him. A Taliban militant didn't have to bring wedding photos or nice clothes. My grandmother came to the door behind Aziz and Mom.

"Come on, girls, let's go out too," my uncle said.

As soon as Asra and Uncle Zafar went out to the yard, my father took me aside and said, "Afsun, you wait. Let's talk alone."

We couldn't communicate properly with each other anymore, and I wasn't telling anyone exactly what I wanted to say and what I was thinking. When my father came back inside, I backed down. We walked in, and he closed the kitchen door with the glass window. I could tell from my mom's curious gaze outside how much she wanted to hear this father-daughter conversation. My father dropped his bag to the floor and got straight to the point.

"Look, girl, when I said I was going to Pakistan, I could tell from the look in your eyes that you didn't believe me. There's no end to this road. War can be anything. Maybe we will end up going to Pakistan for weapons and ammunition. What I'm asking you to do is not tell anyone about this. Be careful. Try to listen to what they talk about. Look, they all appear to be okay about it. They seem to believe that I'm going for work. Saying anything negative can't keep me off the road or help your family, so keep quiet."

As he left, he gently put his hand on my shoulder for a few seconds. He knew that my family was my weakest point, but it was different for him. He could easily walk away since he didn't seem to care about his family anymore. I recognized the long-haired guy waiting for him on a motorcycle. He was the one who criticized me the other night. While the family poured water behind Dad (a customary good luck ritual for a person who is leaving on a journey), I locked the door.

My dad got on the back of the motorcycle, and they rode off. The dust and soil on the back of the engine suggested what my father was up to. What if a man who didn't protect his family went and joined the war? Who would he protect? He couldn't even explain why he did it. I knew he was confused and in conflict with himself. I sensed it in the tone of his voice when he called me "daughter."

When we returned to the kitchen that night, Aziz was still standing at the door and there was music coming from the street. The sounds of children playing disturbed my grandmother. She and my mother rushed to another room as if trying to avoid the sound of people having fun. After all, they were still supposed to be in a period of mourning. They went back to the kitchen while Aziz and Asra were preparing the table.

"What is all that noise out there, Aziz?" asked Mom.

"Our neighbour Nimat got married today. They're celebrating his happiness."

"Which Nimat?"

"You know—that guy with the store, that creep who always stands on the street and tries to talk to girls passing by."

They all laughed together as Aziz continued.

"Yes, really! His brother goes to our school. He says Nimat has seventeen girlfriends. He even bought gifts for five of them on Valentine's Day. Stupid young girls are constantly around. It's disgusting that he talks to each of them as 'my love,' 'darling.'"

CHAPTER 22

Believing in Love

That night my father walked out of our lives. The same night, I learned something new about my Aunty Nuriya. While my father's situation is worrisome, I can't help thinking about my aunt's situation. What surprises and upsets me the most is that she chose to spend time with such a scumbag as our neighbour, Nimat. She used to visit us three or four times a week just to be close to him.

Every once in a while, she'd forget herself and show me a text message from him. "Look, Afsun. He wrote this, he wrote that, he wrote this, he wrote that ... He is going to marry me. He's planning a big wedding. He's making all the arrangements himself. He is already calling me his wife, my life. He said his family will come to ask for me by this fall."

Whenever I made any negative comments about her precious Nimat, she'd say, "Don't be jealous, Afsun. Nimat loves me, and he will marry me!"

Now I have only one wish. Even though I dislike him, I wish the wedding Aziz mentioned had been Nimat and Aunty Nuriya's. I wish they had hidden it from us because Grandma was mad at us for not visiting her today. Although I knew there was no such possibility, I still deluded myself in this way.

At dinner, my paternal grandma complimented me in her own way, heightening the tension in the atmosphere.

"Well, our daughter Afsun is grown up now. Look how she's prepared some delicious food. I think she's got her fortune open. Her Uncle Rashid has to think of something."

My mother's reaction was even more interesting. "You're right. I swear, it'll be nice."

Hearing such comments from the closest people in my life, especially after all we've gone through recently, was deeply disturbing. I felt like I'd been shot in the brain. Uncle Rashid was the police chief, and they kept hinting at his son Subhan.

Uncle Zafar was going to say something, but Asra bravely interjected first.

"No, of course not! No one can marry a girl who is only seventeen years old without her consent. Even here is Afghanistan, we are against these practices, so please don't talk about this matter again!" Everyone had already gotten used to Asra's bold and blunt remarks, however.

Then Uncle Zafar added, "Mom, you gave your own daughters to husbands when they were only thirteen or fourteen. You didn't even listen to my dad. Now it's time for this? Let Afsun study with a relaxed head."

"I made a joke, son."

"We know your jokes, Mom. You made a joke like that once in front of my uncles. I thought it was a joke that night, but the next day you and my sisters-in-law went to someone's house to check out a girl for me."

As the conversations continued, I collected the dinner dishes. Asra and I were washing the dishes when the power went out. When we finished the chores with the light of a gas lamp and cell phone, we returned to the room where everyone was talking about what was going on in their lives. I called Aunt Nuriya many times, but her phone was off. I stood next to Uncle Zafar and put my head on his shoulder. Asra joined us. Aziz fell asleep while sitting between Mom and Grandma. Asra, my uncle, and I were in the other corner.

My uncle's comments, connecting everything to Nuriya, suggested that he was still in love with her. Even in response to Asra's question to me, "Is the school uniform ready?"

It was funny. He said, "Nuriya looked so good in her school uniform."

At night, we four women slept in the guest room. Uncle Zafar and Aziz went to the other room. I've been wandering around all night. I've lost my sleep, thinking about how Aunty Nuriya had been hurt and deceived by Nimat. I know more or less what kind of ending is expected for girls who lose their virginity before marriage in this country. I've heard thousands of tragic stories. In fact, the groom's mother stands at the door of the bride's bedroom, asking for the bloody handkerchief to show to all her relatives. If there's no blood, they hand the bride over to her brothers and other male family members, kicking her out of the house. Finally, in some cases, they take the new bride out of her husband's house in the middle of the night to kill her and throw her body in a pit. Our neighbour's daughter-in-law was killed and buried secretly in the garden of their house. Weeks later, disturbed by the stench, neighbours called the police, and they found the body.

My grandmother insisted that she would select someone for Nuriya to marry. I shuddered to think about what would happen to my aunt if her parents and brothers ever found out about her and Nimat. I remember the conversation I had with her when she came to visit us a month after Grandpa's death.

"Nimat thinks I don't trust him," she said.

"Why?"

"Every time he insists on having sex with me and I say no, he says I don't trust him. But it's impossible for women to have sex before marriage in this country."

"But your reaction is normal, especially living in a country like Afghanistan," I assured her. "You can see what happens in the end to women who are suspected of not being virgins on their wedding night. After all, even if you trust him—and I don't think you should—hundreds of young women are being killed for such a reason. It's unfair of him to act like this, putting pressure on you, knowing the horrible outcome. Who knows? Maybe you won't even end up marrying him at all, so what's going to happen then?"

"God forbid! Why do you make such negative comments, Afsun? Don't kill me this way."

"Nuriya, I just told you the reality. I think you don't like the fact that I told you not to have sex with him."

"Oh, but he's so romantic! He's already making plans for our meeting next week."

"Then don't bother asking me. You'll end up doing whatever you have planned when you meet."

"I'm not sure if we will do it, but I am sure we're going to get married."

A few days after our conversation, Nuriya came to our house after visiting Nimat. I noticed drops of blood on the edge of her burka. I remember asking her, "Did you make that mistake?"

She headed for the bathroom without saying anything. I remember she was shaking. She stayed in the bathroom for hours. When Mom returned from work, Aziz accompanied my aunt home. She didn't say anything about it the next time I saw her, and I didn't question her. I already suspected she had made the mistake I feared she would make. I tried not to worry about it too much. I thought about my father instead. I had a lot to think about.

When I was little, I believed that the moment I closed my eyes, my second life would begin. When we went to sleep, the genies would get up and do what we did all day long. On nights when I slept less, I'd force myself to sleep, thinking it would be unfair to the genie who would take over my duties. If I had such thoughts now, I would feel so sorry for my genie who takes my duties over as I almost never sleep. If Grandpa were still alive, maybe I would talk to him about all this, and we'd figure it out together.

✢ ✢ ✢

I woke up to an unusual sound: the voices of both my grandmothers. I didn't even know what time my mom's mom arrived or why she was there. I was in a hurry. I had to gather up the mattresses we had used as a floor bed and then prepare for school.

School is where I can forget about my family stress temporarily and have a bit of fun. There was no literature class, so there was no favourite class that day. Rona and I hung out and the two of us casually toured the school. We both felt ourselves different from the other girls. I don't know where it came from—I mean, this need to try to show off and prove how cool we were. Anyway, I started to hang out with Rona between classes. I guess I was just trying to be like her when we were together. Maybe I had to forget about the problems and live my life. She told me about her boyfriend in Kabul and also about a certain boy she had just met here. Asra, Rona, and I left school early. It was the first time we'd left a little early, but we didn't want to be late for our poetry course.

The class took place in an old two-storey adobe-brick building. The instructor was an old man who read poetry nonstop. We had just entered the room when I caught a glimpse of the boy who came in after us. Then, just like Prince Charming of fairy tales, he approached me. I recognized him. He was the one who helped me at Aziz's school the day Grandpa died. He's the one who walked me home that day, the one who waited for me to pass by the same spot on the street every day after school. At that moment, he looked beautiful to me. Sometimes I thought he was the only one who could make me believe in love with his mere presence. Sometimes I even fantasized that he'd help me escape from this suffocating environment. I had a mixture of thoughts, in fact. I don't know. I just somehow felt connected to him. I had this instinct that he was someone I could trust.

He looked at me, closed and opened his eyes softly, and smiled at me discreetly. And then his friends, the ones I saw with him every day on the way to school, entered the classroom as the teacher began reading a beautiful poem by Fereydoon Moshiri. Since they were late, the three friends waited in front of the board for the teacher to give them permission to sit down.

Girls and boys our age are not allowed to attend the same class in any educational institution except for only two or three courses. This was one of them. Some courses permit this co-educational policy only because of the lack of students. Nevertheless, there was still segregation: separate, distanced rows between the girls and the boys.

It was not the first time I had heard that poem. My head was down, and I was taking notes about the important phrases, but my brain was still locked in that guy's smile as he slowly closed and opened his eyes. Whether his expressive blink was real or not didn't matter. I could imagine it was a message to me.

When the reading of the poem was over, the teacher called out to the latecomers.

"Where were you, boys?"

One of them answered, "My teacher, our friend, Firdaws, was waiting for someone in front of the school. She didn't come out, so we waited in vain and were late."

The teacher laughed and said, "I think you're talking about his special one that he keeps presenting all these poems to."

At that awkward moment, my guy intervened. Now I can say his name: Firdaws. I have just learned his name, his beautiful name.

"Teacher, I'm sorry."

"You don't have to apologize, Firdaws. Not everyone likes poetry anyway. The students who come to this class either have pains or like to buy pain through loving someone. I know that the boys who come with you endure this class just for you."

"No, teacher," said one of Firdaws's friends. "We come here because of you. We love you. You wouldn't believe how many of the questions that came up in the university preparatory exam were poetry questions. I just scored points on the exam because of this class." He laughed.

"Well, go to your seats. We have two new students joining us today. I don't know which one came under the other's persuasion, but welcome girls."

Rona immediately answered, "I find the class enjoyable, sir, but I must admit, it was Afsun who forced me to come here."

"Then Afsun is the one sitting next to you. Guys, let me name the subject of today's poetry as 'Afsun.' Everybody write something, but first, I'd like to ask Afsun to read the poem I was reading just now."

"Of course, sir."

"Wait, I think you just arrived in Faryab, or rather, Afghanistan, didn't you?"

"Yes, sir, I'm fairly new here."

"Where did you come from?"

"Moscow ... Russia."

As soon as I uttered my response, one of Firdaws' friends commented, "Oh, my God! We can't even go to neighbouring Iran from here, and she left Russia for here."

The teacher reprimanded him, saying "That's an unnecessary joke, Hasan." Then he continued speaking to me. "Your accent is sweet, Afsun. I'm sure you'll appreciate it yourself when you read this poem."

The teacher closed the door and sat down. The chairs didn't even have a desk attached to them, so I couldn't hold the book steadily. I was feeling nervous. In Afghanistan, there's a tradition of standing up when you want to read aloud or recite lessons, except Quranic lessons.

As I stood up, the teacher held out a sheet of paper and said, "Here you go. Read it from this paper. The print is clearer."

I approached slowly and took the paper from his hand. On the way back to my spot, I caught a glimpse of Firdaws, two feet away. I saw in his eyes the glimmer of a little boy eagerly awaiting what he loved. I could see the dingy curtains blocking sunlight from the green windows at the back of the classroom. I was sweating, but I had to start now.

I began by stating, "*The Alley* by Fereydoon Moshiri." Gradually, my voice became smoother. I got used to reading every verse. My reading got better and better with each line. Before that day, I would read poems silently or listen to teachers reciting them, but this time, I was reading a poem about love aloud with genuine emotion, with my soul. It's interesting how many times I've read one particular verse in which the poet speaks about walking past an alley on a moonlit night without the person he loves. Each time I read that romantic yet melancholic verse, I can't help thinking about Firdaws. I visualize him, like the narrator of the poem, waiting in an alley to catch a glimpse of me passing by every day.

Although the poem is long, it's fluid and engaging. All the poems I've read until now address only one side of love, but this unique poem opened up another dimension of the subject for me. I remember closing my eyes as I recited the last verse, feeling its intensity with my whole body as if I'd written the poem myself. I believe I recited properly. Anyway, everyone in the classroom was silent. I opened my eyes and glanced at the teacher first. He was leaning against the wall. He seemed to be contemplating the poem deeply.

All of a sudden there was applause—I think Firdaws started it. The teacher looked at me and said, "You read it magnificently, Afsun! Do you realize that?"

"Thank you, sir."

The lesson of that day continued with the teacher explaining what we should pay attention to in poetry. There were two people in the class who didn't speak until the end: Firdaws and me.

On our way home, Rona started asking questions as if she already knew everything.

"So, Afsun, I thought there was no one in your life. I thought you weren't in love with anyone."

"Don't be silly, Rona. What are you talking about?"

"What happened between you and my cousin didn't go unnoticed."

"What? Your cousin?"

"Firdaws is my cousin."

"Come on!"

"From the way he looks at you, it's obvious he likes you. And given the way you read that poem, I think you have feelings for him."

"No, of course not. It's not like that. I've seen him only once at Aziz's school."

"I'm sure it is," replied Rona. Then she began laughing.

"Oh, girl, we don't have a burka," I reminded her. "Watch out now. We don't want to draw attention to ourselves. Don't laugh in the middle of the street."

"Until what time will Asra be at her course?"

"She comes home around four, especially when it's math. She hangs out with Parisa. They go everywhere together."

"I don't like Parisa," said Rona. "She's such an annoying girl."

"Why do you say that? She's not doing anything wrong. Are you jealous?"

For a while, there was an uncomfortable silence between us as we continued walking together. Normally, we'd part at the crossroads of Char-Rahi-e Mualim, and I'd head out onto my street.

Rona finally broke the silence. "I'll tell you something, Afsun."

"Okay, tell me."

"When we first came here, Firdaws came to our home one day. He looked very cute and handsome. And since then, we started texting regularly. One night, when I wrote that I liked him, he got mad and never wrote back again. When he came to our home on Eid day, I asked him why he had distanced himself, and he said he was interested in someone else. When I asked him who she was, he left our place saying 'she doesn't even know how I feel.' Now I believe you're the girl he was talking about."

When I heard Rona's revelation, I felt roses blossoming on my face, and I analyzed everything in my own way. We met before Rona came here. Firdaws waited at the school gate every day before the holidays. When I heard his name or someone talked about him, my heart would beat fast, and I'd feel like I was floating on clouds like a princess in a fairy tale.

I've been dreaming about Firdaws ever since. He waits outside the school, and after we pass, he comes with us, nine metres back, to the course. Poetry days he reads the most beautiful poems in the world. His handwriting is also beautiful. He always competes against me in the contests held in the course, and he doesn't answer all the questions he knows, as if he wants me to win.

I think about him when I'm doing anything, almost seven days a week and twenty-four hours a day. I know it isn't normal to be so obsessed with someone, but I feel like I'm floating whenever I think about him. When I'm sad, thinking of my father and I'm on the verge of tears, I try to push those thoughts out of my head and replace them with thoughts of Firdaws.

I also remember Ali Shir Nawai's poem in Uzbek: "Don't worry, my beautiful, everything will be fine." Thinking about that poem and Firdaws is the only way I can fall asleep at night.

✛ ✛ ✛

I sensed that Grandma suspected from the beginning that Nuriya was already involved with someone. Another time when she wanted to give Nuriya to some man, she saw my aunt try to hurt herself by taking an overdose of blood pressure medication. No matter how angry she gets, my grandmother still has a mother's heart. She still has her weaknesses. Aunty Nuriya probably knew that she was on the wrong track from the start, so she kept refusing to marry someone else, but what's happened is done. It's too late. Next week is going to be the last "girl-asking" ceremony, so the women are going shopping.

When my maternal grandmother came to our house, she suggested I join them on their shopping outing. She noted that I have good taste. In Afghanistan, there's an engagement ceremony as the last step of asking for a girl. On that day, five hand-embroidered silk handkerchiefs decorated with gold will be given to the groom's family. My mother wanted me to do the hand embroidery on the handkerchiefs. She liked mine when I was doing it with my cousins the other day.

"Grandma, look, these handkerchiefs take a lot of time. Let me prepare them. If you don't like the embroidery, we can change it, but it's already a week away from the ceremony."

"Okay, girl, thank you. By the way, your aunt isn't speaking to anyone. Can you go check what's wrong with her?"

"Okay, grandma, I'll talk to her. Don't worry."

Asra stayed behind to close the door. I walked through the door inside to speak to Aunty Nuriya. I had wanted to talk to her for days. I called her many times, but she didn't answer. When I called my grandmother, she said Nuriya was asleep. I was worried about her.

I walked into the room. Nuriya was there. But for the first time, her appearance seemed unkempt, as if she no longer cared about anything. She was drained and depressed. Even though she was sitting all alone, she was wearing a headscarf. Usually, she wouldn't bother wearing one inside the house when there were no male family members around.

I didn't want to say, "I understand your pain," without having experienced that kind of pain myself. Although I had never been in her deplorable situation, it hurt when I looked at her with her head between her knees. She seemed helpless. I sat down next to her. For a while, we just stared blankly into space. Tears were streaming down her cheeks. She wept for a long time without saying a word to me. Finally, I spoke.

"Nuriya, why did you lie to me?"

"About what?"

"Why didn't you tell me about Uncle Zafar?"

No response. I tried another blunt question.

"Did you really do it with Nimat?"

"Did I do what?"

"You know what I mean. Did you sleep with him?"

The flow of tears couldn't stop. Her lips were red. She squinted and raised her head.

"Yes," she said.

I can't express how her confession hit me. Maybe it's a normal situation in Western countries, but it's an unacceptable mistake here. Since even I was in pain, who knows what emotional anguish she was going through, the deep regret and disappointment. One thing I knew for sure was that nobody in this country would marry someone who was not a virgin. Not even her own family would accept her if they ever found out.

I could have predicted the outcome of her story. As angry as I was with my aunt, I felt sad for her at the same time. I knew how much Nimat had hurt her. She had slept with him because she trusted him and didn't want to lose that bastard. She took the risk when she knew the consequences. She sacrificed her life because she loved him, but she did all this for an unscrupulous person. He was never worth it.

"What's going to happen next, Aunty?"

"I don't know," she answered.

"Do you know this guy who wants to marry you?"

"No, but from what I hear, he's very old-fashioned."

"Maybe if you tell him what you've experienced, he'll understand you like a real man and protect you from his family."

The knots in her throat were untied. Her tears began to overflow again.

"Come on, you know there's no man in our society like that."

"But Nuriya, what are you going to do about it? You know, there was no blood on Zarlasht's first night with her husband. Her virginity wasn't obvious. Do you remember what happened? Even in our house, it was a topic of discussion. My uncles, your brothers, said, 'If my sister was like this, I'd burn her.' I'm not saying this to scare you, but you have to do something."

Taking a deep breath, she replied, "I'm going to do it. I'm going to commit suicide."

"What?"

"I've already thought about it. We're not allowed to see each other until the wedding anyway, so I'll just invent some reason to be alone and I'll kill myself."

"Don't talk like an idiot."

"What else can I do, Afsun? I'm not interested in dying, but I have no choice. I'm finished. I see no other solution."

"Don't worry. We'll try to find a way out."

We hugged each other and I kept quiet. I didn't want to hear or talk about it anymore.

My grandmothers returned from the bazaar around 3:00 p.m. I didn't have the patience to sit and do the needlework on handkerchiefs during the day, so I decided to do it in the evening. I gave the easy part of my homework to Aziz and the rest to Asra to do for me. They were in the guest room with my mother, so I opened the beads in our own room and started sewing.

As I was working on the handkerchiefs, I heard a tap at the window. It was Uncle Zafar.

"What's up, stork?"

"Nothing much. Just embroidering."

"There's a busy homework session for the kids going on in the other room, and your mom's preparing for school, so I'll come chat with you if you're available."

"Come, Uncle, come."

As soon as he walked into the room, he laughed. "What preparation is this, girl? Is it for you? Is your engagement real?"

I smiled.

"No, we're preparing for my aunt."

"Which aunt?"

From the flickering of his voice, I could tell he already suspected something.

"How many single aunts do I have?" I asked.

"What? Nuriya's getting married? How could I not have heard of it?"

"Don't worry I found out only today."

"Who is she engaged to?"

"Believe me, I really don't know yet."

"That guy she loves?"

"Was there someone she loved?"

"That's what I heard when she broke up with me. Also, in a WhatsApp story, she once wrote 'heart N&N.'"

I was thinking my aunt didn't even have as much sense as a five-year-old child. I couldn't understand her ridiculous behaviour. It's a shame that she used the cell phone that Uncle Zafar bought her for her birthday to do something like that to further upset him when he was already suffering because she broke his heart.

I looked at my uncle. He was looking at me, his eyes reflecting his sorrow.

"Do you still love her?"

"How do you think I look?"

"Your heart hurts."

"Oh, stork," he sighed deeply, "I gave my entire life to her and look what she's done. I don't believe in love any longer."

"I think you should believe in love, since it hurts so much."

Clearly, he was still deeply in love with her.

"Uncle Zafar, I'll tell you something."

He knew it was something about Nuriya, so he got excited.

"Tell me stork, come on."

"Would you marry Nuriya? I mean if things hadn't turned out like this?"

"Are you crazy? Of course, I would do anything for my love."

"Now, will you do something to get her back?"

"If I understand why she left me, of course—"

"There are things I want to tell you, Uncle, but first I need to make sure you will keep this secret and show your humanity."

"Don't talk like you don't know me."

"I don't know anyone else I can talk to about this because it's an extremely sensitive subject. What I want to say is private, totally confidential."

"Afsun, I swear I won't tell anyone."

"I know that, but I want you to control yourself."

"Okay, come on, don't drive me crazy, please."

"My aunt loved someone else."

"But I already knew that from the beginning."

"The guy tricked her and got engaged to someone else."

"She doesn't know this guy she's supposed to be getting engaged to then? How could she accept it?"

"No, she doesn't know him. She hasn't even met him yet. Plus, which girl here can marry whomever she wants? Can you show me a marriage based on love? For Nuriya, it's a little different. She always wanted someone rich and handsome."

With a deep sigh, I got to the point.

"Look, the truth is that Nuriya slept with the guy she was seeing. In fact, he deceived her with the promise of marriage."

"Come on! Why?" asked Uncle Zafar, scratching his head.

"Uncle, this is the first time I've ever spoken to a man about such issues. Don't make this more awkward for me."

He held the sides of his head, sighed deeply, and stayed that way for several minutes. When he looked up, he was so angry there was fire coming out of his eyes.

"Then how will she get married?"

"I don't know. She talked about suicide today."

"She kept doing reckless, nonsensical things, and I warned her—"

"Uncle Zafar, don't talk like that. Everybody makes mistakes."

"She's done well. Let her move on. I don't care anymore."

I didn't know if I had done the right thing by telling him, but I knew he'd keep it a secret. I was sure of that anyway.

He sat and thought for hours in the dark. Even the lights in my parents' room were off. My uncle pretended not to care at first, but less than half an hour later, he started telling me how sorry he was. The tears streaming down his face summed it up.

"Please give Nuriya a call."

"What are you going to do? Do you care?"

"Let's see how she's doing."

"Her phone is off. Grandma might have taken it away from her."

"Then call your grandmother."

Luckily, my aunt picked up the phone and said my grandmother was a little sick.

"Ask her if anyone else is around," instructed my uncle.

"Is anyone with you, Aunty?"

"Who's with you?"

"My Uncle Zafar."

Suddenly, Nuriya burst into tears and said, "Say hello to him."

"He says hello too. What are you doing now, Aunty?"

"Nothing, I'm in my room, just sitting."

"Where's Grandma?"

"She's asleep, I've got her phone."

"Are you all right?"

"I don't know," she replied.

"Hello? Nuriya? Are you all right? Alloo …"

Uncle Zafar couldn't take it any longer.

"That's it!" he said as he grabbed the phone from me. "Hello, Nuriya, please speak up! What happened? Please say something!"

But he couldn't hear anything anymore, so he handed me back the phone.

"Look, she hung up because she knew I was here, or did she do something to herself? She didn't sound good. She didn't sound like herself."

"I don't know. I'm not comfortable either."

"If I leave and go over there, they won't open the door for me now, so Afsun, whatever the hell she's done, please pray that she stays alive! God, don't let her get hurt!"

"Don't worry. I'm calling my grandfather now."

On my third call, my grandfather answered the phone.

"Who are you calling at this hour?" he demanded.

"Grandpa, it's me, Afsun."

"What are you doing up at this hour?"

"I just spoke to Aunt Nuriya. She didn't sound very good. Would you look in on her? Is she all right? I'm worried."

"She'll be fine."

"Please, Grandpa, go and have a look."

"Okay, wait."

For around ten minutes, there was no sound at the other end of the line, and then I heard my grandfather arguing with someone.

"Are you an idiot, beating her like this? Why did you do this, you bastard?"

"Father, don't back up this shameless immoral girl! She'll destroy our family honour. All this started when you let her go to university. I heard her on the phone earlier. I also heard a man's voice. He was on the phone with her. I'm going to kill her!"

"Don't be silly. It was Afsun who called here. She's still on the line with me."

"Come on, Dad. It has already happened three times. Nuriya is always lying. She's definitely up to something."

I didn't know exactly what was going on, but I found out later that her brother beat her up pretty badly.

"Are you still there, Afsun?"

"Yes, Grandpa, I'm here."

"When he heard your aunt talking to someone at this hour, Nasim beat her a little bit."

"Grandpa, I'm the one who called Nuriya earlier. I swear."

Then I heard my grandfather talking to Nasim. "Look, son, it's Afsun. She says she was the one talking to Nuriya."

"Grandpa, I'm going to hang up now. Please tell my Uncle Nasim to call the last number Nuriya received a call from. If I don't answer, then he can feel free to beat or kill her. What are you guys doing? How do your minds work? What age are we living in?"

I hung up, and after two or three minutes, I got a call from my grandmother's phone.

"Hello?"

"Hello." It was Uncle Nasim's voice.

"Uncle, what can I tell you for beating her just because she was talking to me?"

"Who was the man next to you?"

"Who's going to be in our house at this time of the night?"

"I'll talk to you later. You're on the phone at this time of night."

Before he hung up, I said, "We're going to talk a lot with you, Uncle Nasim. Thank God, there's nothing I can't answer for."

I didn't have the patience of my early days here. I wasn't holding back anymore. I was just saying whatever was inside me.

"Your Uncle Nasim is right," said Uncle Zafar. "He might have heard my voice."

"But I didn't say anything about you, Uncle. I just told him it was my number."

I don't even want to think about what's going to happen to Aunty Nuriya. If they could beat her up severely only for being caught on the phone late at night, they would definitely kill her if her future husband's family announces she's not a virgin.

"Do you know that guy she slept with?"

"No, Uncle, I don't know him, so stop asking questions."

"It hurts. Even when we were playing as kids, I was cautiously watching her to make sure she wouldn't get injured. What they've done to that poor girl now."

"Can you forgive her?" I asked.

He kept quiet for several long minutes. Then he said, "I have to think about it."

"I've finished the handkerchief."

Uncle Zafar looked at it with a forced smile and said, "You've stitched it so beautifully. It will look good on that shitty guy."

"It'll look good on you, Uncle."

Tapping me on my shoulder, he replied, "Come on, show me a mattress, please. I'm sleepy."

CHAPTER 23

Something's Going On

In the other corner of the room, I laid mattresses on the floor for Uncle Zafar. We slept in the same room that night. In the middle of the night, he called out to me.

"Stork, I've made up my mind. I will marry Nuriya. I cannot watch her go dark."

I was relieved and thrilled to hear that. He finally said what I wanted to hear. We sat down right away to plan what we needed to do next. First, we had to convince my grandmothers. I couldn't go to school and my poetry course for a week because we were preoccupied with the engagement preparations.

Finally, on Friday, Aunty Nuriya and Uncle Zafar became officially engaged. Thank God the engagement ceremony was simple. Ordinarily, engagement and wedding ceremonies here are elaborate affairs full of fun, especially for the women. However, my grandma (Zafar's mom) didn't want it because her mourning period for Grandpa wasn't over yet even though several months had passed already. Since the ceremony was so simple, they only had to worry about "what people are going to say." I was glad to give my uncle the handkerchief I had carefully embroidered. Before he announced his decision, I remembered the night when I told him the handkerchief would suit him.

The engagement might sound easy now, but it has actually been complicated. I endured sleepless nights and my grandmother's accusations of "You did everything. You corrupted my son." I also had tears over my maternal grandmother's actions. Plus, I had to listen to Aunty Nuriya's regrets over her mistake. Finally, however, I was very happy for my aunt and uncle.

The only thing I've done for myself lately is texting with Parisa, the class leader. I asked her not to write down my name on the list of absentees over this past week. Luckily, she took my family responsibilities into consideration.

Parisa is probably the most reasonable and trustworthy person here, especially when it comes to class attendance. As the class leader, she is able to manage the students and use her discretion when marking someone "absent" or "sick," or when writing an excuse beside a student's name. Based on what I heard from Asra, Parisa was very helpful for the entire week of my absence. I felt grateful, and I told Asra, "No matter what anyone says about this girl, I think she's genuinely nice."

Parisa and I were spending more time with each other. Rona called me quite often, but we couldn't talk. She even asked Asra about me many times and came to our home on Thursday while I was out. Uncle Zafar told her I wasn't home.

That night, when Aunt Nuriya was receiving congratulations, I was moved to see her. She hugged me with tears in her eyes and said, "You saved my life, Afsun."

"Aunty Nuriya, I have one request to make. Please do not ever tell Uncle Zafar about Nimat. He knows the basic story, but he doesn't know the name of your former boyfriend. I don't want him to feel jealous and cause any trouble. Don't reveal Nimat's name no matter how insistent Zafar is. He might try to kill him. Then everything will be ruined."

As soon as I finished my talk with Nuriya, I noticed a text message on my phone. It was a number I didn't recognize. Apparently Rona had been texting me all week as well, and I couldn't respond to any of messages. I opened this message.

"Hi, Afsun, I'm Firdaws. I hope I'm not bothering you. I'm just curious. I'm writing because I haven't seen you all week. I asked Rona for your phone number. She couldn't reach you as well, so I was worried. Please write to me."

As I read the message, my legs were trembling. My heart was racing. I was so excited. I slowly got up and walked out of the room. All my aunts and other relatives had gathered. Although they couldn't play any music out of respect for Grandpa Raz, they were talking about their happiness. They also sent bundles of gifts to the groom's house. Everyone who came congratulated me too on my new "sister-in-law" and my new "brother-in-law" at the same time—even though they would still be my aunt and uncle. (Here someone who marries my uncle becomes a sister-in-law, and someone who marries my aunt becomes a brother-in-law.)

I went to the bathroom right away and locked the iron door. Bursting with excitement, my hands quivering, I typed a brief reply to Firdaws's text. "Hi Firdaws, I'm fine. I've got some work to do. Thank you for writing."

Although my message was fewer than twenty words, it took me almost an hour to compose it. Firdaws responded instantly. "Thank God I finally heard from you. I was really starting to get scared. Hope everything's okay."

Then I texted back. "Everything's all right. Don't worry."

After that night, our regular exchange of texts began. I texted him every night and every morning. My feelings for him grew more and more intense. Writing "good morning" every morning made my whole day go well. I don't know how acceptable it is for me to chat with a man when I'm only seventeen, but I've really needed his positive energy. He has been the only power source that can make me smile and spice up my life.

In the morning, Aziz was supposed to go to the mosque near our house for Quranic and general religious lessons. He was sleeping so sweetly and deeply that I could barely get him up. That's why I became an early bird. I also had to wake up my Uncle Zafar. He had been talking to my Aunt Nuriya all night. He was on his way to his shop around 6:00 every morning. Making breakfast, receiving Firdaws's "good morning" message, and going to school with that energy made my day full.

My life has been going on like this for two months. I called my dad the other day, but we didn't say much to each other. I've only been able to talk to him twice since he left. It was a relief to find out he was okay. Aziz spends more time outside of school hours at the mosque. My father asked the imam to make Aziz a *hafiz* (to learn and memorize the Quran by heart) in a year. That's why the imam was putting so much pressure on him, and I was concerned about that pressure. In fact, on late days, they would lay him down on the floor and hit him under his feet with tree branches or cables. How many times have I tried to prevent him from going there? But no one listens to me. My mother agreed to let him go to learn our religion and be close to

God. So, all I can do is help him avoid punishment by making sure he doesn't arrive late.

✢ ✢ ✢

It's two days before my eighteenth birthday. I've been sensing something weird about my family's attitude and behaviour lately. They seem to be hiding something from me again, and it's been going on for a month. Except for my brother and sister, everyone around here is acting strangely. My mother and Uncle Rashid's wife, an elementary school teacher, have started getting together more often. I find this highly unusual since they have never really liked each other very much.

Uncle Rashid is the police chief, and he has already made his intentions known. Now it's strange that his wife has been coming to visit us more often than ever before. She and Uncle Rashid have also been going more often to my grandparents' house. She has even begun introducing me to her inner circle. It's like prep season. My cousin Subhan and I seem to be at the same social gatherings more often than usual, and it doesn't seem normal for our family members to lavish praise on him.

For me, the comments of "time to get married" were getting louder. My anger was growing. One day, I snapped, "Enough! Don't make jokes like that to me or it's going to end badly."

I had a bad feeling. In fact, I didn't trust my family any longer. I realized that anything could be expected of these people. Now I had to find out what they were up to. That day, around lunchtime, I called my Uncle Zafar. I wanted to meet with him and Aunty Nuriya.

Normally, they'd say they weren't allowed to get together because of a new disagreement between their mothers, so they were told to get together only after the wedding.

I knew something was going on now. I was frantic. I prayed that the family wasn't planning for me what I feared they were planning. It was too much for me to bear. I called my Uncle Zafar again and asked him to come over.

"What's up, stork?"

"Will you come, please?"

"Okay, I'll be there in ten minutes."

Asra was going to her course. I went to the door with her. I was stressed. If they were plotting what I dreaded, then this life would be over for me.

Sensing my anxiety, Asra asked, "Are you okay, sis?"

"Oh, yes. Don't worry."

"Good. Watch out for yourself, sis."

"Asra?"

"Yes, my sister?"

"They're not going to force us to marry anyone, are they?"

"Why would you ask that? Of course not! You're stressing me out, sis!"

"But I'm already stressed out."

"What's the reason?"

"Nothing, sis. Forget it. Don't be late. Have a good lesson."

"Come on, tell me what's bothering you."

I wish I hadn't opened my mouth. Asra looked really scared. I didn't want to worry her about something I wasn't even sure about.

"Nothing," I assured her. "I'm just asking. Go to your class now. I'm fine."

As soon as Asra left, my tears started flowing uncontrollably. This life was wearing me down. There was no word from my uncle. He said he'd be here in ten minutes.

I'm sitting at the kitchen door writing now. For the first time, I'm going to be honest with myself. I'm trying to hold on, but I feel like my world is collapsing. I went through all these challenges to support my family. Even though I'm a girl in a sexist society, I did my best. This society and its people can be incredibly unfair. However, a girl who hasn't quite turned eighteen yet can't do anything.

I have already emailed all the authorities who might have the power to help us get back to our old lives. I've tried every possible way, but they haven't even answered. I knew that we had no legal status in Russia and no one could do anything for us. This life is so cruel. It's painful that our relatives have changed so much. I, Afsun, as a naïve girl, promise myself that if any of my closest relatives has gone behind my back, I will not remain silent and passive. They will face a completely different Afsun. I swear I will not be the same person anymore.

My tears were still streaming down my cheeks when the doorbell rang. Uncle Zafar arrived at last.

CHAPTER 24

Turning Eighteen

Finally, I turned eighteen today. I got up at 5:00 a.m. and went to the other room. I opened the suitcase that hadn't been opened in a long time. It contained important personal belongings. I took out my cherished kadifa that Grandpa gave me a year ago and that had witnessed his special days. As I put it in my black and white hard-leather bag, I cried for all the injustices, disappointments, and frustrations that had accumulated inside me. I felt sorry for those lost years, the days of my youth that I had to spend here.

I slipped into my favourite shoes from Russia. I also put on a yellow headscarf, yellow and silver socks, jeans, and a beautiful formal dress. I made sure to cover my hair with the headscarf, and I put my little Nokia phone in my leather bag. Along with my notebooks and the deed to Grandpa's house, I also packed a sharp knife in my bag. It was the knife we had used to sacrifice a lamb for Eid. Then I went to the room where Aziz was sleeping. The enclaves of his eyes were purple. I inhaled his scent deeply. I also went to kiss Asra and my mother, who were still sleeping. Wiping tears from my eyes, I inhaled each of their scents.

Then, enveloped in a burka, I left the house. No one would recognize me.

As soon as I left the house, I called Birishna's father. As we had previously arranged, they came to the city centre—Birishna, her father, her sister-in-law, and her brother who was literate. They were waiting for me in Chahar Samavat. I also called Firdaws. We were meeting for the first time in a different environment outside our poetry class. He came with his father's car to pick me up.

The minute we all gathered, we got into the car and went to the house I was going to sign over to Birishna. It was bigger, newer, and more attractive than the house we lived in. I was trying to get all the paperwork done as quickly as possible. After I entered the house, I sat on the sofha in the courtyard and took the burka off my head. I had a private little chat with Birishna. After I made sure everything was fine, I called her family members to join us and we all sat there together.

Despite her age, Parisa was very good at taking care of official bureaucratic matters. She'd done a lot of paperwork for me before for school stuff. Of course, Firdaws was very helpful too. I pulled out the documents we'd already prepared. I had four copies of each one. Birishna's brother had also called an imam and several witnesses they knew. Instead of signatures, I took fingerprints in front of everyone. According to the laws of this region, the deed certificate, which is called "The Orfi Deed," is given with the approval of the imam and the testimony of witnesses, who are known as "The White Bearded" (meaning elderly people).

I introduced Firdaws to the imam and to the witnesses there as my husband so that no one could object to his presence, and I sold the house as the owner of the house. If any violence or persecution were committed against Birishna, her father would be deprived of his right to the house. Firdaws was also authorized to resolve possible problems.

Birishna's father made a solemn vow in front of everyone. "I, who once gave away my daughter for fifty head of lamb, would not even touch her for such a large and precious house. Don't worry."

From there, Firdaws and I took Birishna to Gawhar Shad Begum Girls' School. School officials deemed Birishna's registration eligible for second grade. After a long break, we had a chance to speak with her privately. I wanted to make sure her father wouldn't hurt her again.

"My father is very happy now, so he's treating me well," she reassured us.

"Good luck, Birishna," I said. "You are now a schoolgirl. Please do not worry about being much older than the other students. When you're successful, you can skip grades and move on very quickly."

I hadn't covered my face with the burka at the school. On my way back, at the exit door of school, I saw a familiar face. It was Uncle Rashid's wife. She was a teacher there, and she spotted me from a distance. Looking at me suspiciously, she called out, but I pretended not to hear her. Without glancing back, I hurriedly got into the car with Firdaws and Birishna. But even after we drove off, I could feel that woman's penetrating stare.

I shuddered when I thought about my second mission, which I planned to carry out after we drove Birishna home. I checked the time. It was only 11:45 a.m., and I had some time left.

"How are you, the light of my world?" asked Firdaws.

"I'm okay."

"You don't sound good. You seem stressed."

"Can you stop the car in a quiet area?"

He thought about it first and then agreed. We headed for the Maymana city entrance gate. I remember that spot from the day of our arrival. Many members of our huge extended family came to greet us there that day.

We stopped right next to the hills in a place called Damqul. The car windows were closed. We were in a yellow and white 1997 Toyota: a common car here. A woman in a burka in the back seat and a handsome young man in the front. And there was no one else around. I was sitting right behind Firdaws, and he turned around to speak to me.

"Afsun, can you sit in the middle for a while? I can't see you where you're sitting now. I'm really curious about what you said to your mother. I mean how did you manage to get out of the house this morning?"

"Don't worry. She'll assume I'm at school."

"You dressed very stylishly today to save your friend Birishna's life. And the imam called you my 'dear wife.'"

We laughed. I was so stressed. I reached forward to touch his hand, which was resting on the gear shift.

"What are you doing, Afsun?"

I must have surprised him. I remember him always saying he was more reserved than me and didn't even want to hold hands yet. He'd even said, "I'm not going to touch you until we're finished school and we've gotten married."

However, I had to touch his hand to alleviate some of the overwhelming stress of that day. He wanted to take his hand away, but at the same time, he seemed to like my courage. I lifted the front of the burka to reveal my face. It was the first time we'd looked at each other so intimately.

"I love you, my princess," he said.

Just as I had seen in the movies, I suddenly allowed my lips to brush against his lips. We kissed gently. I closed my eyes. I'll always remember that one tender moment. I can only describe my first kiss as "the meaning of my life." After all, I was approaching someone who loved me and respected me, who genuinely cared about me.

The honking of a car horn suddenly broke the silence. Startled, I quickly pulled myself back in my seat and lowered the burka to cover my face. It turned out that the horn sounded from our car. Firdaws's arm had touched it accidentally. That's when we noticed soldiers rushing towards us from the hill. I thought immediately about Farkhunda who was lynched in Kabul. At first, Firdaws seemed locked in fear. I shouted at him, "Step on the gas, Firdaws! Step on it!" The soldiers opened fire towards the back of the car as we sped away in swirling dust and soil. Thank God, we got away in time.

It was lucky for us that almost all the cars in Faryab are old-fashioned unmarked Toyotas. They wouldn't be able to find us.

Firdaws was terrified, but he tried not to show it.

"Should I give you a ride home?" he asked.

"No, I'm going to school."

Despite the frightened look on his face, he still tried to smile at me. If anything happened to Firdaws, I would never forgive myself, but we got away with it.

CHAPTER 25

My Plan

He stopped the car in front of the school. There was a lot I wanted to tell him before we said goodbye. Long stories I didn't want to end. But I was running out of time, and the work I had to do was waiting for me.

As I got out of the car, I simply said, "I'm going to love you forever, Firdaws."

"Me too," he replied. But the look on his face told me that he was surprised by my bold steps today. Maybe he was trying to understand this sudden change in me.

I walked briskly to the entrance, but as I knew they wouldn't let me in at that time, I told the caretaker at the door, "I'm here to pick up my little sister."

I looked outside the school gate. Firdaws was gone. Clearly, he wanted to get away quickly to avoid getting caught. I knew they wouldn't find Firdaws in a city where all the cars looked alike. Nevertheless, I assumed he was consumed by fear.

"What's your sister's name?" the caretaker asked. "What class is she in?"

Instead of answering him, I turned around and left the school grounds. I had a plan to carry out that day. It was the day I was going to confront that slimy bastard Dastagir, who had traumatized Aziz and become his nightmare. We had exchanged messages before. I told the degenerate that I wanted to meet him.

He said, "When the imam leaves the mosque at 2:00, let's meet next to the building where the Quranic lessons take place. There's a little room there where we can have privacy."

When I contacted him again from the rickshaw I was in, he said, "The imam hasn't come out yet, so not today, my darling. Let's see each other another day."

Then when I said I was already on my way to see him and couldn't come back again, he said, "Okay, you come. I'll set this place up."

When I arrived, I was sweating. I looked at my watch. It was 1:58. I asked the rickshaw driver to stop in front of the house next to the imam's room at the end of the road. Meanwhile, when I looked at my phone, I saw some missed calls: two from Firdaws, three from Dastagir, and one from a number I didn't recognize. I called Dastagir right away.

"Where are you, my darling?" he asked. "I'm waiting. Come to Haft Shahid."

I took a deep breath and replied, "I'm already here. Walking over now."

As I approached the imam's room, I saw the creep in a dark green local suit next to the wall of the mosque.

As soon as he noticed me, he said, "Put your head down and follow me."

Slowly, with my head down, I followed him. We went into the imam's room. It was messy, full of religious books. Dastagir, who worked as the imam's assistant, was the one who prayed in the mosque five times with the imam, who showed himself as a gentlemen to the imam and other people. However, once the imam left the mosque, Dastagir opened his room and revealed his true monstrous self.

Sadly, the imam trusted him and handed over everything without knowing his true character. Mattresses with different sheets were laid on the floor. He locked the door, quickly approached me, and asked me to lie down. He was very tall, bearded, and pretty-faced, but I can tell you that the devil was inside him.

"Dastagir, wait. Not yet," I forced myself to say.

I don't know how I ever found the courage to maintain this act. I was suppressing my overwhelming hatred for this repulsive creature. I had just kissed Firdaws, and I promised myself that I would never allow anyone else to touch me.

"But we don't have much time, my darling. Someone may come," the scum replied.

"Wait a minute, please. Give me a breather. I've got an energy drink. Let's drink it first. Then we'll do whatever you want."

His eyes opened. He had nothing to lose.

"Okay, honey, but take off the burka and let me see your face."

"You'll see my face, but wait a minute. Come on, let's enjoy our drinks first."

Sitting on his knees, he finished drinking in seconds and started preparing one of the mattresses. I was waiting for the drugs I had put in his drink to kick in.

He was trying to lift up the skirt of his long dress and open his pants when I said, "Don't rush. Let me finish my drink."

He was sitting on the mattress waiting for me, but the moment he got up and tried to come towards me, he fell to the floor on his knees. Thank God!

I got up right away. He was lying down, unconscious, only one step away, but I couldn't afford to go after him in anger.

Running on a loop in my mind was one horrifying scene. It was a hot, sunny day, and I thought Aziz had gone to school before we returned from our after-school course. I noticed traces of blood on Aziz's pants when he came through the door. He was shivering in his white regional clothes and went to the toilet.

Some people in this country ridicule and condemn harmless gay adults in Western countries, yet the same homophobic bigots turn around and sexually abuse young boys and girls! In fact, last summer, two high-profile figures in Afghanistan were named for raping children. That's what sickens me. Thousands of vile degenerates who look like Dastagir are out on the street. They molest little children and make vulgar remarks to all the young women who pass by. They never leave us in peace.

I had to finish what I'd planned. I had been tracking Dastagir for months. I messaged him on Facebook to get his phone number. Now that hypocritical pervert was lying at my feet. He was in such a deep sleep that he couldn't possibly get up. I could have killed him easily at that moment, but it was better to give him a lesson he'd never forget. It would be a lesson for all the other child molesters who saw him.

I pulled the knife out of my bag. I thought about stabbing him in the chest first, but he deserved a different kind of punishment. I had to amputate his genitals for raping so many innocent children like Aziz. I stuffed a piece of cloth I found on the floor into his mouth so he wouldn't be able to make a sound. I wrapped another piece of cloth around my left hand. I then took some plastic bags I brought with me and wrapped them around both of my hands. I took off my burka.

With my left hand, I held his organ. I sliced it off with the knife in my right hand. Then I ripped off the devil's clothes and wrote on his chest: "PUNISHMENT FOR RAPING CHILDREN." I didn't know when and how I became so violent and fearless. I grabbed his phone and put it into my bag. I put the burka back on. I didn't know exactly how much time I had spent inside that room, but all of a sudden, I heard the imam knocking on the front door.

Oh my God! I thought it was the end of me. Fortunately, however, the imam walked straight into the mosque. I hurriedly picked up everything that belonged to me, put it in my bag, and ran to the street through the back door. The only thing I left was the plastic bag I had wrapped around my hand. It accidentally fell when I was startled by the knocking at the front door.

I looked at the time. It was 3:49 p.m. I had become a girl I didn't even know. With a bloody knife in my hand and sneakers from Moscow on my feet, and wearing jeans and a burka, I walked along the dusty cobblestone street. Nobody was there but me. I had nothing more to do. I slipped the knife back into my bag and called Parisa, one of the few people in the world I could trust. I tried three times. Finally, she answered my third call. I saw many more missed calls on my phone—from Aunt Nuriya, a few classmates, Firdaws, and some unknown numbers.

CHAPTER 26

Risking Everything

I knew Parisa was busy because she was leaving for Kabul tonight to start receiving a better education and pursue some of her dreams. Everyone knew that I loved and respected her as a determined and strong girl. She finally picked up the phone.

"Hello, Afsun."

"Hi, Parisa."

"Where the hell are you? Your whole family is looking for you everywhere. They're going to kill you."

"Don't tell anyone. I just need to talk to you."

"Where are you?"

I gave her the address where she could find me. I took the SIM cards out of both my phone and Dastagir's phone and smashed them. I was on the street where I passed the day my grandfather died and I met Firdaws. I don't know how long I waited, but the kids who ran down the street were talking about what had happened to Dastagir.

I noticed a splash of blood staining my jeans, and I could feel my whole body sweating. I deeply inhaled the smell of the soil I was sitting on. My mind wandered back to what had happened about three days earlier.

I was worried about my future and hoped my Uncle Zafar would come through the door saying, "Don't be silly. We're not giving you away."

My uncle arrived with Aunty Nuriya. As soon as I let them in, I asked, "Uncle, are they going to give me to Subhan?"

"Where did this idea come from?"

"Everyone's been acting so weird lately," I replied. "Subhan's mother comes to us with other women almost every day. She *shows* me to other women. Then they all go to my grandparents with my mom."

Both my uncle and aunt started thinking deeply. Clearly, they did not have time to think about my problems while they were enjoying their engagement period.

Before allowing myself to breathe and be comforted by them, I asked, "Uncle, Aunty, tell me please what's happening."

When I saw the tears welling up in my aunt's eyes, the fear and stress in my heart intensified. I thought my heart would stop. I just stood there. What I had dreaded was now happening to me. It was even worse than I had imagined.

Through her tears, Aunty Nuriya revealed what she knew.

"Afsun, the other day, your father's mother asked me for my engagement dress and an outfit that matched your size, but it's normal. Everyone's acting different these days. They won't tell me what's going on because they know you and I are close."

"What are you talking about, Nuriya? This is my life! You know what they're hiding!"

"I'm not sure, honey."

"Shut up. Neither of you, nobody did anything to help me! I'm here alone!"

My aunt was crying with me. I knew it was bad. Obviously, they both knew something more. My uncle looked at me in the same sympathetic way.

"Come on," he said. "Get up. We're leaving now."

"Where to?"

"We're going to our place."

I got up without protesting. My aunt hugged me all the way. We quietly entered my grandfather's house. I could hear the women inside, and I saw Subhan's car parked near the door. I followed my uncle and aunt upstairs to the guest room. Subhan and his brother were in the main room with a pile of white envelopes that looked like invitations.

As soon as he noticed me, he got up, excited.

"Afsun, welcome!"

I didn't even look at him. Then his brother said, "My sister-in-law is shy."

I got closer to pick up one of the envelopes. If the whole world had come together that day, they couldn't pick up the pieces of a girl who had burned to the ground. They left that girl on her knees with an invitation to an engagement ceremony she hadn't even been consulted about. They didn't even bother to write my name on the invitation. Since they're ashamed of girls, my name is irrelevant.

They had decided on my behalf, fearing that maybe I'd refuse. The invitations were going to be distributed in five days. They were prepared by the families of Rashid Raz and Ismat Raz to announce a major decision about my life, but without my knowing anything! I was speechless, helpless. I was in shock. All I could do was sob. Uncle Zafar and Nuriya also picked up an invitation and read it.

"Do you like the invitations?" Subhan's voice echoed in my ears.

Suddenly, what I was going through in this scenario flashed before my eyes and brought me tremendous pain. I had said to Birishna and other girls here, "I can't say I understand the pain you're going through. Your pain is much greater." Now I understood.

Uncle Rashid came in and said, "My dear Afsun, what are you doing here?"

"Hello, brother," said Uncle Zafar.

Uncle Rashid approached me. Putting his hand on my shoulder, he said, "My daughter-in-law, the bride, how are you?"

"What daughter-in-law? What bride? I have no idea what you're talking about. What are these papers? This is a nightmare that doesn't end! I thought you were protecting me, Uncle Rashid. What's going on here?"

He hugged me nervously and tried to grasp my hand, bringing it close to his son's hand. When our fingers came into contact, I quickly drew my hand away.

"What are you doing, Uncle?"

At that point, his anger rose to the surface. Men like him always use their anger as a weapon to intimidate people who oppose them, especially women.

"Actually, what are *you* doing, Afsun?" he demanded.

"I don't accept this marriage that no one bothered to ask me about."

Smiling slightly, he replied, "Well, it's not up to you. I've decided, and your father has accepted. Your mother has agreed. We were going to let you know today."

"Oh, I'll know today? Am I one of the random neighbours who can be ready to attend an engagement party in five days?"

"Behave yourself!" commanded Uncle Rashid.

Uncle Zafar felt compelled to intervene at that point, saying, "My brother, she's already in shock. Is this something to say to—"

Uncle Rashid slapped him in the face. "Leave the room now," he commanded, "or I'll shoot you in the head."

Looking Uncle Rashid in the eyes, I shouted, "You have a gun, don't you! You try to scare everyone with it, but you can't scare me, Uncle Rashid! I didn't accept any marriage proposal to your son! I don't accept it now, and I won't until I die!"

He smiled smugly. "Do whatever you can."

Standing in front of me was a man who would never understand no matter how much I screamed and tried to reason with him. I walked out of the room as if I were dragging my body. My Uncle Zafar took me home.

I continued to scream and cry in my room, realizing that, if I didn't put up a fight, I wouldn't have any more of myself left. I thought about escaping. If I ran to government-dominated areas, all the way to Kabul, my uncle would find me again. If I ran to Taliban territory, my father would catch me. What kind of hell was this? What kind of punishment? What a nightmare! Even if I tore myself apart, I couldn't end it.

Like me, Asra and Aziz didn't know anything about what was planned for them. How could I protect my brother and my sister when I couldn't stand up for myself? I had to choose. Should I opt for suicide? Or is it better to be strong and change a few people's lives or teach someone a lesson? In the name of feminism and human rights, many of those famous women activists in Western countries claim to care about the women of Afghanistan. They make speeches at conferences and in front of TV cameras, but they don't do anything meaningful to end the suffering of millions of girls here. Maybe the fire really burns where it falls.

But I've already risked everything to punish that monster Dastagir. I spent months trying to get Aziz back to his senses. Maybe my sweet brother will never heal completely. He has stopped going to the mosque—to forget things maybe—but whenever he sees that scum, he is dying inside. Even if days, weeks, or months pass, the embarrassment, pain, and misery—and the anger it stirs up in Aziz—kills me. When I saw him in agony and humiliation, I felt tortured. I can't control my emotions any longer, and I don't want to.

I always dreamed of my eighteenth birthday. I dreamed of it being beautiful and special. It shouldn't have turned out like this. Parisa even postponed going to Kabul that evening because of my condition. She finally found me. She didn't have to wear a burka because she is smaller and younger. She came out in a light headscarf. Once again, she showed up at my most difficult moment. I appreciated her genuine kindness, her friendship.

Uttering my name in tears, she grabbed my hands and pulled me up from the floor. There was a girls' madrasa in one of the alleyways I passed. We went there because Parisa knew the owner. There was a woman there named Bibi Zainab. Parisa told her, "We're going to sit here and talk for a while."

The woman pointed to a row in the courtyard of the house and said, "Go over there."

It's the first time I've told someone what happened. After opening up to Parisa, I felt an overwhelming sense of relief. I didn't know what was going to happen to me, but something inside me wanted to reveal everything I'd been keeping to myself all of these months. I needed to feel the lightness of a bird in flight.

CHAPTER 27

No Regrets

I asked Parisa for some paper and a pen from the madrasa, and I wrote some letters. The first one was to Firdaws. I wrote that I loved him and asked him to forgive me. I didn't have much time. I couldn't tell him everything. I couldn't even tell Parisa everything.

At 5:15 p.m., the owner of the madrasa said they were closing and we'd have to leave.

Parisa knew the basic story now. She was afraid that dreadful things would happen to me, so she said, "Let's go to Kabul together. The buses haven't moved yet. We have a chance."

She was desperate to find a solution for me. She suggested that we go to her house, but I couldn't get her in trouble too. I was aware of the challenges I'd face. It's impossible to travel a long distance without the company of a first-degree relative from your family—a male relative, of course. On the way, the Taliban would stop the bus. Then there would be thieves and perverts like Dastagir. Swarms of men like the ones who tortured and killed Farkhunda in Kabul were a potential danger everywhere.

Even though Parisa insisted, I refused to go. After all, even in Kabul, my situation would be no different. Once your name is smeared in this society, there's no salvation. I read about it on the news every day before I got here, what happened to those poor girls. Never could I have imagined I would become one of them.

Parisa kept pleading with me. "Come with me, Afsun. Let's go. I'll take you to my home. If you go to your house, they'll kill you. They saw you with a man outside the Gawhar Shad Begum School. You've been gone all day. It's been on everyone's tongue. 'They say she ran away with a man.' It's a mess, Afsun."

My angry and worried family members had been looking for me all day. I couldn't accept what was happening, but I knew it was all going to happen.

I don't have to hide myself. I didn't do anything wrong. I can get out of this mess. I must escape, but then there's my unstable psychological situation, the people whose lives I'm going to put at risk, and most importantly, my diary and stories at home ... My family must never read the stories in my diary, especially what happened to my Aunt Nuriya and Aziz. It's all written there in detail!

"No, Parisa. I must go home," I insisted. "My family must never read my diary!"

"Wait," replied Parisa. "I'll call Asra. Let's see what she has to say."

"Hello, hello?"

"Asra, hello, this is Parisa. I was wondering if Afsun has arrived home yet."

"Yes, yes, she's here."

"Good, that's good. Where are you?"

"We're all at Grandma's. Sorry, I've got work to do. We'll talk later."

I guessed that Asra lied to Parisa to protect the family's reputation. I knew they'd all go to our grandparents' house when there was a serious problem, so it was safe to go to my house. On our way, we saw people gathered in the street and police in front of the mosque. We rushed to my house and opened the front door. I went straight to the bathroom. That night, for the first time in weeks, the power did *not* get cut off. I handed my clothes to Parisa to throw into the washing machine. We were one of the few houses with a washing machine.

I washed myself fast. I had to write quickly—even if it was the last time. The story of my eighteenth birthday shouldn't be left unfinished. I put on the yellow and red floral-patterned dress that I brought from Russia. I wrapped my hair in a towel. Now as I write this, Parisa is sitting across from me, looking at me. I put my notebook in front of the window.

I'm officially eighteen now. From my experience over this past year, I can't compare this year's birthday to last year's birthday. Too much has happened between my two birthdays. But I don't regret anything I've been through. If I could go back and had the power to make a choice, I'd still choose to come to Afghanistan. Maybe it was a bad idea to live in Faryab. However, my father's mind was already made up, so even if I wanted to stay in Moscow, I wouldn't have been allowed to live there alone. Dad made all the decisions regarding our lives.

Asra will still find her way because she's a smart girl who wins awards. However, I can't say anything yet because they force girls who are only fifteen to get married here. They take away the dreams and ruin the futures of thousands of smart young girls in this country. Boys with extraordinary intelligence in Afghanistan can also become victims. Some boys are molested by corrupt mullahs under the name of bacha bazi. At the age of fourteen or fifteen, others are recruited by terrorists and transformed into killing machines. There are talented but poor children in Afghanistan who never have the opportunity to go to school.

Even knowing all these injustices, I wanted to stay here. I hoped that maybe I could contribute somehow. Even at my age, I tried to do something on my own. I prevented my Uncle Zafar from suffering. I saved my Aunty Nuriya from death and sexual slavery by going to Nimat's shop and stealing his cell phone so he couldn't blackmail her with the indecent photos he had taken of her. And I managed to save Birishna from a miserable fate. She no longer has to marry someone her grandfather's age. I can also say I sprinkled water on the burning hearts of kids like Aziz who were Dastagir's victims. And I saved other children from his evil by ensuring he could never harm anyone again. For all these reasons, I don't regret having come here.

If I hadn't come to Faryab, I wouldn't have met a wonderful human being like Grandpa Raz. I wouldn't have been able to change the minds of seven of the girls at our school who were destined for marriages before they could finish school. I'd return to Faryab to write about girls whose lives are much tougher than mine.

Finally, I would come back here to taste the feeling of love. I would come here for Firdaws, a man who proved to me that not all the men of Afghanistan are the same.

I'm actually glad I came to this country. If I had remained in Moscow, I might have become a fashion designer, which was my dream once. Maybe I would've become successful, but I wouldn't have learned to do little things to improve the lives of others. I've learned a lot here, and I'm happy for the good things I've done.

Now I hear my father's voice. He was missing for months, but now he is coming through the door. I'm going to walk bravely in front of him with my hair exposed, with my grandfather's kadifa draped across my shoulders. Even if the end of this road is death at the age of eighteen, I want to go with my head held high. My conscience is clear.

After I write these last lines, I'm going to give my diary to Parisa. She knows what to do with it. I pray that she gets out of the house before getting caught by my father.

Goodbye, Faryab!

CHAPTER 28

In the Courtyard at Dusk

This is Parisa writing now. As Afsun's close friend, I must continue telling her story.

As we heard her father approaching, I whispered to her, "Your father's coming. He's in the courtyard. What are you going to do?"

"Take these and hide over there," she said as she handed me two notebooks and the letters she had written earlier at the madrasa, including a letter to someone she loved.

She said she knew she could trust me. Her final words to me were "I love you, Parisa."

It was starting to get dark. Her father had probably turned off the main power switch. As she ran past my hiding place and outside into the courtyard, I caught a whiff of her favourite perfume, the one she told me she had received from that person she loved. The beautiful girl ran towards her father with her long hair flowing. She was wearing a brightly coloured dress and her beloved grandfather's kadifa.

Suddenly, I shuddered. Her father was shouting.

"You whore! Afsun! Come out here!"

"I'm already here outside, Dad."

I didn't know what she had written in those notebooks, but the way I felt and the situation I was in terrified me. I was still only fifteen. I wanted to protect her, but I felt helpless. I could do nothing but watch the injustice happening before me. My tears were flowing silently. Trying to suppress them created a knot in my throat. My heart was racing.

As soon as her father heard her voice, he ran towards her. Dusk had just fallen. It was too dark for him to notice me in my hiding place behind the curtain. However, through the window facing the courtyard, I had a clear view of what was going on out there. I used all my power to remain still and quiet.

He grabbed Afsun and knocked her down where a huge stone was embedded in the courtyard floor. She just lay there like an angel. He banged her head on the floor. The sound of the impact pierced my heart. Her hair, her face, her entire head was covered in blood.

Maybe if she had screamed, someone would have heard her and run to help, but she didn't scream. First, he beat her up pretty badly. One of the most beautiful and powerful girls I've ever met was dying in anguish under her father's feet.

Her father got tired and sat down. There was blood gushing out of Afsun's head. She still had her grandfather's shawl around her shoulders. Then her father sat down next to her. She looked up and asked to speak.

"Dad, I understand your anger, but will you listen to me for a minute?"

Her father's reaction was to punch her in the head again. Afsun was on the floor. She couldn't lift her head, yet she continued speaking.

"Dad, I'm going to help you, but you should listen first, and even if you want to kill me, I'm going to tell you how to do it. If you keep this up, they're going to arrest you. Listen to me, Dad—"

At that point, the monster pulled out a gun from his waistband. It was the sight of that gun that frightened me the most.

"I know my job. I will kill you the same way I shot infidel Afghan soldiers, the same way I shot thirty-five people in one place. You who run away with men, you disbeliever!"

Miraculously, although she was lying there bleeding, Afsun somehow managed to express herself coherently.

"Come on, Dad, I didn't … didn't run away with anyone, but everyone's going to question your honour. They're going to say, 'She did something bad.' If … if you want to kill me, take me to my room and kill me with a pillow in my mouth. Tell people I passed out and died. But, but … listen to me first. Please …"

How could she still talk like that? How could she still struggle like that to maintain her family's decency? She was unjustly beaten, in such horrible pain and blood, yet she still had the strength to try to reason with him. She was still concerned about her family. I couldn't look away. I was in shock, frozen.

"Who was that man you were with?" demanded her father.

Afsun laughed as she said, "Dad, I'll answer whatever you're asking, but … it's not what you think. Please, just calm down … Sit down and listen to me. I'll explain."

He turned Afsun's head towards the sky.

"No need. You're a whore. You don't deserve to live, heretic!"

Afsun started laughing again.

I'd known her for nearly a year. I had always thought she lived like a girl running away from her problems, but that night, for the first time, she was releasing her heartfelt rage and frustration with laughter.

"You've destroyed my life, Dad. I know you're going to kill me, but remember, I'd rather die than live to be as bad as you are. You never once asked how I was. You didn't even wonder. You've ruined our lives, Dad …"

Her laughter turned into sobs. She continued talking and crying in pain as her father kicked her. How her tone changed when she was hurting. That tone was breaking my heart.

"You have ruined not only us, but my grandfather, our future, and everything. I will never … never forgive you. And if my brother and sister found out what you did, they wouldn't forgive you either. I fought alone. I became a father and a mother to my siblings. You … you burned us, Dad. I'm afraid to leave Asra and Aziz to someone like you. I won't forgive you. I won't forgive my mother. I won't forgive any of you who put us in this situation. Maybe … maybe they'll remember me as a bad person, but I'll be taking that label to cover up your mess—"

Her breath was cut off. Although she was probably on her last breath by that point, she managed to say over and over again, "I hate you, Dad. I hate …"

He stood looking down at her and kicked her again. Afsun smiled as she wiped her bloody face and eyes with the back of her hand. She just smiled as she uttered one last time, "Dad, I hate you—"

Then her father covered her mouth with his hands and pressed down. His knees were on her body. She was struggling with whatever strength she had left in her arms and legs to push him away, but she was too weak. She couldn't escape. Suddenly, her long legs became limp, lifeless. She growled twice in agony. Never will I be able to remove that sound from my ears. Her father took his hands off her mouth. Afsun was motionless.

I was terrified. If her father came in, I'd continue hiding behind the curtain with her notebooks, just as Afsun had instructed. But I couldn't accept that she was actually dead. I was hoping that she was only playing dead, tricking her father in order to stop the beating—but unfortunately, Afsun didn't like this world enough to engage in such tricks anymore.

I kept watching her father. How many times did he put his hand on his daughter's heart and scream, "Afsun, Afsun? Can you hear me? Daughter of her dad, my princess, get up!"

He waved, grabbed her fingers, raised her arm, checked her pulse at her wrist.

"Don't do this to me, girl! Get up! Please!"

In a second, he had gone from a psychopath to a loving father.

"Afsun, girl. Look, your dad's here now. Please, please get up! I love you so much! Please, get up. I love you, dear girl!"

He began hitting himself on the forehead as he screamed, "God, take my life! I killed my daughter! Is it real?"

His speech was like that of a psychopath with a veil of blood in front of him. Where I stood, I was frozen, my tears dried up. My eyes were stinging as if hot peppers had been rubbed into them. I just stood frozen in front of the window.

For hours, her father sat next to her. I was able to text my family, who were probably searching for me frantically. I wrote, "My friend Afsun is dead. I'm fine. I'll be there soon."

I turned the phone off. I later realized what an odd death notice I had written.

Her father was still holding his head and wailing. Afsun, on the other hand, had become a white statue covered in blood. Her father's phone kept ringing. He didn't answer it. He just sat there crying without saying a word. Around 9:00 p.m., he lifted Afsun from the floor, held her in his arms, and carried her indoors. I remained hidden. It was still not safe to attempt an escape.

It was as if her father was pretending to be a father who loved his daughter and regretted his actions. For a moment, I thought about what he might do if he discovered my presence. He dropped her body on the bathroom floor, sat down, and continued crying. Then his phone started ringing again.

"Aloo, Makhdum Abdullah Sahib. Yes, yes … I don't need that kind of daughter … I'm out." There were noises. Probably, he smashed his phone.

Then he shouted, "Damn you all! You got my daughter killed!"

I don't know who the person on other end of the phone was, but I suspected it was someone who had ordered him to kill Afsun.

He walked into the room where I was hiding. My entire body was trembling. I knew he would kill me if he noticed me. He turned back through the door.

Looking at Afsun's body once more, he cried, "Your father is out of his mind. Forgive me!"

CHAPTER 29

Funeral

It has been days, weeks, months, and years since that incident, but I still have hiccups from the knots in my throat whenever I dream of her. I'm still trying to block out the memory, but it's impossible. For two years now, I've lost my way. I still wish I had sat down and hugged her more on that last day.

I looked slowly at Afsun. She was sleeping like an angel. I took her bag with her notes and the knife, along with all the other stuff she had entrusted to me. Making sure nobody would see me, I left her and made my way towards the door. I couldn't stay there any longer. Not until I approached the front door did I feel a sense of relief. Until then, I felt like somebody was behind me, holding me back. There are no words to describe the extent of my fear.

As I reached the front door, I looked back. My foot hit something on the floor by the door, and I think her father was in the bathroom outside. Ignoring the bleeding and pain of my toe, I threw myself into the street and started running as fast as I could.

I don't know which way. I don't know how. I just ran. When I looked back, her father was standing outside the front door. I don't know if he recognized me or not. I was afraid he wanted to run after me, but luckily, at that moment, a man he knew was passing by. He stopped and they hugged each other.

Despite my bleeding toe, I was running faster now. Everyone was looking at me, but I ran without paying attention to anyone. My tears soaked my hair to the ends with the power of the wind. At that time of the night, no woman was visible alone on the streets. I was thinking a thousand things. Fortunately, my house was not far away.

I don't know how I got to my street in only five minutes. Everyone who was waiting for me when I got home was furious because I'd been out from 5:00 to 9:30 p.m. I briefly explained to my family what was going on with Afsun. Nevertheless, I didn't escape a bad beating. Fortunately, no one had seen me with a guy—otherwise, that evening would've had a different ending.

I hid Afsun's things where no one could ever find them. Despite the pain of the beating I received, I didn't shed a tear for my own life. My only concern was Afsun. I didn't sleep until morning. I didn't want to talk. I didn't want to eat ... Every moment, my brain was preoccupied with the horror I had witnessed. An innocent young girl could be killed so easily.

Geography is such an interesting thing ... On the other side of the world, if a child injures the tip of his finger, the entire family will take care of it. Here we've always minimized such wounds to avoid intensifying the pain.

What a different thing childhood is in a country like Afghanistan. Even harder is being a woman. My testimony about the killing was considered invalid. First of all, according to them, I was a child. Second, I was a girl. Sadly, a woman's testimony is not accepted. This rule made no sense at all to me. Women and children are enduring the most difficult times in this land. Violence is being perpetrated against them daily. They are subjected to rape and harassment, and there's no objection to the forced marriage of an underage girl. However, when there's an incident like this one, girls are not even allowed to testify. Those powerful men don't believe what a girl sees with her own eyes. They claim that it couldn't possibly be credible, just because of her age and gender. At the same time, how come the same men don't object to marrying such a young girl? They expect her to give them children when she's a child herself.

✢ ✢ ✢

Early in the morning, the funeral was announced from the speaker of the mosques. Not until that announcement did I lose hope that she was still alive.

My aunt came up this morning to wake me up, but I wasn't sleeping.

"Parisa?"

"Yes?"

"Afsun is really dead."

I couldn't say a word. I just swallowed the news with tears.

"My mom says we'll go to her funeral."

I was scared, but since I wasn't going alone, I had to go for the last goodbye. I was in such a strange psychological state that I wasn't sure what to do.

I just said yes and glanced at the door of the room where the last of Afsun's memories were stored. For a long time, I couldn't look at the writing she had left in my care. I tried to forget, but I couldn't go thirty seconds before thoughts of Afsun filled my head again. I wanted to cry, but I was numb. I couldn't even cry. I couldn't pay attention to the conversations taking place around me. I just stared blankly at the walls.

My classmates and I went to the funeral. The only man I recognized among the men sitting outside the door was her father. People were talking, saying, "It's a pity her father wasn't here very often over all these months. He went to work for the family. Now how he weeps because he left his daughter alone."

The person who started the rumours that led to Afsun's death was her Uncle Rashid's wife. She was a teacher who stirred up everyone by saying, "Afsun has escaped with a man. I saw her at the school's gate with a guy. They were hand in hand."

Now that aunt was crying for her. "How did I know this would happen? I thought the girl I saw was Afsun, but in fact, Afsun was here at home. She fell down and hit her head, and no one was there to help her."

There were three people who were silent: her brother, her sister, and her mother who seemed to be in a coma. Both of her siblings sat next to the coffin and cried incessantly. They just kept uttering, "Afsun, Afsun, Afsun ..."

We barely made it through the huge crowd of people who had assembled at the mosque. My hands, my arms could not stop quivering. What hurt me the most was those women who gossiped maliciously. They were commenting without knowing anything, without knowing Afsun. I heard one of them say, "They caught her in bed with someone, so they killed her."

I remember weeping for months when I heard this outrageous slander.

I sat next to Asra that day and wept for hours. When I saw Afsun's face before they took her body away, she was smiling as usual. I still didn't believe she was dead. I thought I was crying, but I didn't have a single tear in my eyes.

I didn't even know how I felt. Actually, I had been through the funerals of other young people who were close to me: my five-year-old brother's funeral, a twelve-year-old classmate's funeral, and almost ten funerals of relatives.

But this time, I didn't realize how different things would be. I didn't know what was written in Afsun's notebooks. When I got home that day, first I cleaned that bloody knife from her bag and threw it away on our neighbour's roof. Realizing I was running out of time, I packed up. Then I left Faryab and everything here and headed for Kabul.

CHAPTER 30

Return to Faryab

I thought that getting out of Faryab would make me forget everything—that I'd never think about it again, that I'd study and finish high school in Kabul. I thought if I continued to be obsessed with Afsun, I couldn't become successful. That's why I resisted reading her notebooks. I assumed they contained the story of a rich girl whose life ended up tragically. She would probably be describing a fairly comfortable life in Russia. I guess I was deluding myself. Maybe I was avoiding reading her journal to avoid suffering more. However, after two years, I was finally able to touch her notebooks. Finally, I found the courage to read her writing.

Among the letters she gave me, I hadn't yet delivered the one she addressed to the guy she loved. The other letters, addressed to her immediate family members, were written more properly because she had probably written them the night before the incident. Unfortunately, she didn't even get a chance to give me any explanations when she handed me those letters. I had no choice but to read the one without an addressee in order to know who to give it to.

Coming to Kabul when I did to continue my education was a great opportunity. I felt lucky, and I was determined to succeed. I found myself in fierce competition at the best girls' high school in the capital. I did not want to disappoint all those people who supported me.

For the thousands of young girls who were deprived of their right to education and for my own future, the goal of "success" was my only option. I wasn't going to allow myself to meet the same fate as poor Afsun, Farkhunda, and many other girls here who were brutally murdered on the basis of a rumour. I had to study hard. Afsun's painful end was an enormous shock to me. I was a naïve young girl, and if I had gotten caught by her father, I could've lost my own life as well that night. She was sentenced to an execution without having a chance to be heard, and there was absolutely nothing I could have done to stop it.

Finally, high school was almost over. It was the summer of 2019, shortly before the exams. One letter and two notebooks were still there in a dusty bag in my room. In 2018, the last time I was in Faryab, I handed letters to each of her family members. There were no envelopes, just folded pieces of paper. I wanted to read what she had written, but I couldn't open them. I could only look at what was on the back. She had written personalized messages on the back of each letter. For example, on her letter to Aziz, she wrote: "There's nothing wrong with you. I'm always there for you. Feel my love, and if you love me, do good things for your family and yourself as a strong young man. I trust you. Don't betray my trust."

Afsun had folded each letter three times. Having run out of space, she continued writing on the back and in the margins. Undoubtedly, she had a lot to say to her loved ones, but her father didn't even give her a chance to speak.

When I went to Faryab on Eid holiday in 2018, I went to visit her family. I spoke with her mother and Asra. Their grief was still palpable. Losing a daughter and sister like Afsun left a profound void. I gave them her letters. They asked for the letter for Aziz, but at Afsun's request, I said I would deliver each person's letter directly myself.

Her mother may have had a lot to ask me, but she didn't dare to ask. From the grief in her eyes, I knew she was there only physically. Spiritually, however, she had gone to the grave with her daughter. I saw her for the first time when she came to our school to pick up Asra and Afsun. This woman sitting in front of me didn't look like that young woman I remembered. The other girls would refer to her teasingly as Afsun's "sister." They usually say that just to please the mothers, but in the case of Afsun's mother, she was actually quite beautiful. Now, however, her youthful beauty was washed out by her tears. She was still dressed in black, and I heard that every morning of Eid days she went to Afsun's grave and left clothes for her. I saw how a mother and a sister were devastated. Their loss had collapsed them.

How many times did her mother take deep breaths? I could feel her need to ask something, but she held herself back. Tears were welling up in her eyes. She was pulling on her nose and breathing deeply.

Finally, when Asra left the room to get tea, her mother released her tears and asked, "Did she have that idea? Why did she choose to commit suicide?"

"Suicide?" I never expected such a question.

I was already feeling ambivalent before she asked. Before I even went to visit them, I wondered if reading those letters would exacerbate their grief. Maybe they'd begin asking questions I couldn't answer. I worried that they wouldn't be able to handle it or they'd end up blaming me somehow. I couldn't live with that burden any longer. I waited a long time to fulfill my promise to Afsun.

Maybe Afsun was mad at me. Maybe that's why she hasn't been appearing in my dreams lately. In order to dream about her again, I had to hand over those letters. While I was thinking about all this, I wondered, *What am I going to say in response? Should I lie with my throat knotted in tears again?*

"Parisa?"

I had to snap out of my thoughts and give her an answer.

"Oh, um, no, she just said to me, 'I don't trust life. If anything happens to me, give these letters to my family.'"

"When?"

"Before the incident."

Her mother believed Afsun had committed suicide. Of course, this lie wasn't fair, but maybe Afsun wanted them to think this way. She didn't want to make her brother and sister's lives harder. Maybe she didn't want them to be burdened with being the children of a murderer and blaming their father.

I still didn't quite understand what was going on, so I couldn't really intervene to make things right.

Rona came that day as well for an Eid visit. Everyone's eyes were looking for Afsun. It was a relief to be with her family on the day of Eid. That's obviously why Rona was also there. Even though I witnessed the moment Afsun died, I was still looking at the door as if she would enter the room at any moment. I imagined she was still alive and one day we would meet. Years had passed, but I still couldn't accept her death.

We waited for Aziz for two and a half hours. Since it was Eid, he had gone to the prison to deliver food to his father. I didn't know why his father was in prison. I wanted to ask, but then I stopped myself because I feared it would upset Afsun's mother too much.

Finally, Aziz came home. He had grown a lot, standing taller than me. As soon as his mother called him and he recognized me, his face changed.

"Aziz, my brother," I said. He just looked at me awkwardly as if he didn't know what to say.

"My sister isn't here, so why did you come?" he asked.

"Your sister wrote you this. I'm sorry I'm delivering it late."

He approached and received the letter.

They all seemed to be lost, out of their minds, as if they couldn't ease their pain by thinking of an unknown death. Asra and her mother were reading their letters in a corner of the room, the guest room where they had sat for Afsun's funeral. The vacant expression on Asra's face—and on her mother's face—changed suddenly. The distance between Asra's eyebrows widened. After a deep breath, she began to kiss the letter. Her mother was weeping. Aziz sat down and cried for a while. He looked around like a medical intern visiting a psychiatric asylum for the first time. Everyone looked crazy. My heart ached.

I quickly left the room. Her mother, Asra, and Aziz were screaming and wailing, reminding me of the day of the funeral. I was also reminded once again of Afsun's last words to me. Coming back here to Faryab, to Afsun's home, gave me the courage to consider reading her two notebooks, but I wanted to wait until I got back to Kabul. I had to gather my strength first. I made the decision to read them when I felt ready, but I wasn't quite sure when it would be.

CHAPTER 31

The Last Letter

It was July 9, 2020. I was still trying to gather the courage to read Afsun's notebooks. They were still sitting there on my desk under hundreds of university entrance exams, but I never dared. Although I had decided to read them after my return to Kabul, I hadn't even made an attempt. I hadn't dared to touch them. Last year, I quickly picked up the letters and then put them away again. I was afraid I'd find out everything, get entangled in the past, and make myself too sad and distraught.

But there was nothing to be afraid of anymore, and Afsun, who had been in my dreams a lot lately, wasn't talking to me. She thinks I've forgotten her or that maybe I was not the right person to hand over her journals to. Finally, I risked everything. Those notebooks were going to be read. I wouldn't forget Afsun, and I wouldn't allow her to be forgotten by anyone else either.

I took the university entrance exam that morning, and I had to stand up after this stressful time. It would take three months for the results to be announced. I was ready now, ready to get rid of my nightmares, pay my loyalty debt, and get to know Afsun deeply.

First, I separated the books, took out the notebooks at the bottom, along with the last letter that stayed with me. Then I began reading every word. The first few pages were like any ordinary diary of a young teenager, but then Afsun's story became more intense. I continued reading and couldn't stop. I stayed in my room for days, surrounded by four walls. Since my big entrance exam was over, I had plenty of time to read while I waited for my results.

I struggled a bit with the first few pages because her Persian writing was not very good. Even so, I understood what she was trying to express. I proceeded to cry like crazy. As I kept reading, her writing got better. In fact, by the last few pages of the second notebook, I noticed her Persian writing was even better than mine.

Finally, I finished reading her two notebooks. Along with the truth about the events leading to her death, I also learned some important details about her life. Afsun should not be remembered as a weak, passive victim who killed herself to escape from the shame of being seen with a man. She should be remembered as a strong, resilient, and caring girl who paid the price for the mistakes of a mentally ill man who happened to be her father. She was a remarkable human being who struggled to maintain family unity. They had demonized a young woman who should be treated as a hero.

At first, I didn't realize that the man she fell in love with was Firdaws. I had helped Afsun with the paperwork for her poetry course. She once introduced me to him as her "classmate." However, when I found Firdaws—the guy to whom she was bound by such deep love—to hand him the letter, I was disappointed at first.

In recent years, I had no contact with anyone. I didn't have a phone or social media access for a long time because I needed to study and focus on my exams. I couldn't afford to get distracted. When I was trying to figure out how to find Firdaws, I went on Facebook, but I couldn't find even a trace of him. Then I turned to Rona. She was one of his cousins, but she and I had never been on good terms. She always seemed like an arrogant girl who looked down on the other girls. I had no interest in being friends with someone who didn't like anyone except herself, who flaunted her father's money with her expensive clothes and other stuff—and who had no success beyond materialistic things.

But now I had to reach out to her. I started searching on Facebook. Among Afsun's friends, I found Rona's account and then Firdaws's account. In fact, I should have understood their relationship when Afsun and Firdaws said we had to do something for Birishna, but I never thought of such things. I wasn't mature enough then to understand.

I wrote to him. First, I had to introduce myself by using a fake account, but it was unclear when he would ever reply. Having to wait is something I can't tolerate.

I made the message simple. "Hi Firdaws. I'm Parisa, Afsun's classmate. Please get back to me. There are some things we need to talk about."

I waited two hours, three hours. No answer. Then I started searching for information about him on his account. He was studying at the law school of Kabul University. This information made me happy. The fact that he was in Kabul meant I wouldn't have to travel to another city to deliver the letter. Two days after I sent him the Facebook message, there was still no answer.

I spent my days reading Afsun's journals over and over again and crying. I replayed in my mind the day I gave Aziz his letter, how he got so emotional. I had a thousand questions about him, as the kid seemed totally lost. First, they uprooted him from the country where he had spent his childhood. They took him away from his school in Moscow, his familiar surroundings. Then they forced him to attend religious lessons where he was raped and thus psychologically damaged. What names do they give to children who have been used this way in this society, causing them to lower their heads for life? How easily they could ruin human life in a society where even their families were embarrassed and still bowed down to the mullahs.

On the day Aziz was raped, they took away his emotions. During that traumatic time, Afsun was his only source of comfort. Aziz was still in his youth, but the only person he trusted, his protector, his hope, and source of power no longer existed. Who knows what else this boy has been through? The last time I saw him, my heart broke. He looked as if he were waiting for death to release him. How distressing it was to see a young teenager grow old fast when his voice was just beginning to deepen. No one else knew what had happened to Aziz. His sister had saved him. He would no longer be abused by that disgusting mullah. His sister had done everything she could to end this matter for life.

I haven't left the house for a week. For the third time today, I read Afsun's journal and checked my phone. Finally, Firdaws wrote back. "Hello, yes, I remember you. Why did you write it?"

I responded right away. "Where are you?"

"Can you tell me why you're asking?"

"I need to see you."

"I'm in Kabul."

"I want to see you. Actually, I don't really want to, but I have a letter that Afsun wrote to you. I want to give it to you."

"I'm done with Afsun. I've forgotten about her."

"It's a pity to hear that from you."

"That's what I thought, but she didn't really love me. What did she write?"

"I don't know. I haven't read it."

"Read it then."

"Do you allow me to read it?"

"It hurts so much. I don't want to go back to those days."

"Do I want to? Be careful what you write. Please speak properly about Afsun."

In fact, Firdaws hadn't said anything wrong, I was just too sensitive and upset.

"I have to think, Parisa."

Weeks passed without a word from him. I replayed everything about the incident day and night, even in my dreams. There was no one I spoke to except Afsun. In my dreams, Afsun is alone in white, in the blue sea. Then, she is dressed in black ... coming after me at school ... and when I'm running away from her house that night, she grabs me by the back and tells me not to leave.

I was out of my mind. I didn't know what to do. There was no message from Firdaws. The letter to him stayed on my desk for days. How many times have I tried to read it, but I couldn't. Sometimes you get caught up in a situation that you spend years trying to run away from, and you can't lift your head. I've been questioning why I had to witness so much pain.

Finally, I said to myself, *Firdaws let me do it. He doesn't want this letter anyway. Let's see what Afsun wrote ... even though I know it will hurt and make me cry and go crazy for days again.*

On an evening when the sunset was red, after another one of Kabul's regular power outages, I managed to light the lamp with a trembling hand. Then I unfolded the last letter.

CHAPTER 32

To Firdaws

Well, since you have this letter, then I'm not alive. Wow! What a pity. I don't know exactly what month or day it is as you read this, but believe me, I'd love to have these days in the future. If you took your university entrance exam, I hope it went well. If you haven't taken it yet, I hope it goes well.

Actually, what I'm hoping is that nothing is going to happen to me, and I will see and hug this lovely girl who is looking at me with her almond-shaped eyes tomorrow and get this letter back. She is sitting in front of me, staring at me with her gloomy eyes. Anyway, in case it's bad, I'll just keep writing. I don't have much time to tell you about my life.

My father, uncle, or someone else will come and find me any minute. If you're reading this, one of them has already killed me.

I just want to let you know that I loved you with all my heart. I don't know what you think, what other people think, or what gossip they spread. I won't be there to tell the truth and defend myself. All I know is that I loved you.

I loved you enough to even think about you the third day of my grandfather's death. Even from day one.

I loved you enough to think of you and smile even during difficult moments.

I loved you enough to record your poems and to think of you night after night.

I loved you enough to conceal my problems to avoid putting you in a difficult position.

I loved you enough even to be jealous of myself.

It's not really my job to love things, but loving you is different. I kissed you because I wanted to. I don't know about you, but it was my first and last kiss.

Live your life to the fullest, Firdaws. You're the best man I've ever met since my grandpa.

Since you're reading this letter, it means I'm not there anymore, so now I've already told Grandpa about you. Surely, he loves you and he is very pleased with you.

Thank you for everything.

Don't forget Birishna … Take care of yourself.

✧ ✧ ✧

Days passed and still there was no further word from Firdaws. But then he finally sent me a message. "Parisa, can you bring the letter today?"

"Okay, where?" I wrote back.

"You give me an address. I'll come."

I told him about a restaurant near our house, but I was so scared. It would be dangerous for me to be seen alone with a man who was not a close relative. I should not forget what happened to Afsun. I told him the address anyway because I didn't want him to go on thinking that Afsun did not love him. We decided to meet two hours later.

I got the letter, and as someone who hadn't left the house for weeks, I attracted attention. Everyone in the house was so happy that I was stepping outside. Nevertheless, it was still a problem for me to go out alone, so I took a walk and said I'd be right back.

He had arrived there before me. I had seen his photos on Facebook, so I recognized him straight away. He was sitting at a table towards the back. He looked so different from how I remembered him when we were students in Faryab.

Likewise, in recent years, I had grown taller and changed a lot physically. Even if Afsun were here, she wouldn't recognize me.

"Hello, Firdaws," I said as I approached him.

"Hello. Please sit down. Don't leave right away or they'll get the wrong idea."

"Okay."

We didn't talk for a minute. I just looked around. I haven't even spoken to anyone at home lately. I've only spent time reading Afsun's journals.

One of the waiters came to the table.

"Brother, what do you want?"

"Give me a cup of tea."

"Sister-in-law?"

"No, she's my friend, and she'll say what she wants herself."

"May you be lovers?"

Really? Do two people of the opposite sex who sit together in public have to be lovers? Unfortunately, this was still the mentality in Kabul. I couldn't understand it. If Afsun said she didn't understand this mindset, I'd say okay, but as someone who was born and raised here in this country, even I couldn't understand this ridiculous mentality.

"I'll have some water, brother."

After the waiter left, Firdaws took deep breaths.

"Don't worry, Parisa. They assume they can catch the customers' attention this way."

"I'm not going to think about it."

Suddenly, Firdaws said something that stunned me.

"Afsun betrayed me."

"You wouldn't be here if you really believed that," I replied.

"I was just wondering what she wrote to me."

"How could you believe she cheated on you?"

"We went out for a ride after Birishna's paperwork that day. We went up to the Maymana gate, and she asked me to drop her off at school on the way back. She was acting weird. She was nervous. She kept hiding her phone from me. She didn't go to school, obviously, as we all know, and then this happened … At first I didn't believe anything people said. Not for a year. But there was one truth. They saw her leaving with a man in front of the school, and it wasn't me. I had left her at the school, and I didn't even get out of the car."

I understood Firdaws. The distortion and fabrication of information and the spread of gossip could lead to confusion for everyone. Without really knowing the truth, most of them lied by claiming, "I saw them myself." I kept listening as he continued.

"I used to say to myself, 'I'll marry her whenever she wants.' My feelings for her weren't like those of any other teenagers. Since the first moment I saw her, Afsun was in my thoughts. She became my everything—in my dreams, my mornings, my nights, in every moment."

"I have little time, Firdaws, but believe me, you'll regret what you've said."

"Please tell me something I'm going to regret. I need it so much. Do you think it was easy for me? For the first year, I went to her grave every day. I wasted my energy, my time, my money. I didn't even take the university entrance exam that year. I was lost. Afsun's case wasn't like any other incident. She wasn't a random girl. Her innocence, the pain in her eyes ... I've been madly in love with her since the day her grandfather passed away. She was running down the street like a lost girl that day. I helped her find her house, but then I lost myself. Please tell me I'm wrong about the betrayal story. Please save me. I am doubting myself ..."

He had tears in his eyes. He was in anguish. I understood that there was as much love in him as Afsun expressed in her writing. He was as good as she described him.

"Firdaws, listen to me. Somebody saw her with you at that school when you both took Birishna to register. That's what finished Afsun. You're that guy they were all gossiping about."

Firdaws looked at me with painful regret.

"I'd love to tell you everything here in the first place, but I don't have time, you know."

He seemed embarrassed.

"She wrote you this letter just before she died. I think you should read it."

"Sure, thank you. I was just saying all this to fool myself. I never believed it."

"I know, or you wouldn't have come to meet me."

I handed him a napkin to wipe the tears from his eyes. His eyes had told me everything from the moment he said hello to me.

Unfortunately, I didn't have time to tell him everything. I got up from the table and left the restaurant, with Firdaws still sitting there. I began walking home. My tears came flooding back. I had many regrets concerning Afsun, but regrets would no longer help.

Today the village of Oncha Arlat fell to the Taliban. This is where Afsun's grave is located. The land where she sleeps is far away now ... It hurts to know that a handful of ignorant people who caused her death—or made the decision to execute her—are now walking on the land where she lies. But no matter what, I had to go there one more time. There were things I had to tell her at her grave. When I went to Grandma's house, I thought maybe there'd be someone to take me there. I feel lighter these days. I did what Afsun had asked. I could face her grave now.

Recently, my university results were announced. I got accepted to the department I had dreamed of for years!

I must fight and succeed for the memory of the seventeen relatives I have lost so far as a result of war, for the hundreds of young girls we lose every day—and of course, I must succeed in writing Afsun's story as she entrusted me to do.

But for now, I will go to Afsun.

CHAPTER 33

The End

My dear Afsun, I'm sorry it took me such a long time to visit you, but believe me, I wasn't ready to read what you had written until recently. You know, your death wasn't the only loss in my life, but it was the most painful. Since you left us, I've lost dozens of my friends in Faryab: Fahiza, Anar, Muzhgan, among others. In each terrorist bombing in Kabul, I also lost many classmates, especially my Hazara friends. It was hard for me to survive. You'd understand better. Honestly, I wouldn't be able to defend you and stand this strong if I had read your journal earlier. I needed to grow a little to feel ready for it.

Let me start sharing some news. I saw Aziz before I came to you. I don't know what you wrote to him in your letter, but it gave him strength. He has built a car by hand at the auto repair shop! It's beautiful. You know, he named it Pilot. I think he's feeding his dream of becoming a pilot. I believe you encouraged him, didn't you? Also, his English is incredibly advanced.

Asra doesn't wear a burka anymore. She has grown up a lot and looks like you. She wasn't like you back then, but as she got older, she became as beautiful and strong as you. Recently, she got accepted to go to an out-of-town university. She'll be leaving soon.

Your mother's fine. She's back to teaching now. I think she's recovered, but she still misses you a lot. She's lucky to have a daughter as smart as you. Even if you're gone, your letters got everyone back on their feet. Each one of them has been re-empowered thanks to you.

Your father was arrested, I don't know if you want to hear this, but I'm sure you were worried about your family, especially your brother and sister. I just found out why he was arrested. I was hoping it was for killing his daughter, but unfortunately, it wasn't. He got caught taking Taliban-produced drugs into the city. It also emerged that he was involved in executing government soldiers en masse. You see, he's going to be locked up for a long time for these crimes. Hopefully, he won't be having contact with your mom and siblings.

I know you didn't want me to come here in a burka, but I had to. It was hard, but I went to the prison to see your father before I came to you. I couldn't hold it in. I said, no matter what, he wouldn't recognize me with a burka anymore. Unfortunately, they didn't take him to the prison in Kabul. With the intervention of your Uncle Rashid, he's in the Faryab prison. I went there and told him I'd seen everything. I knew everything. Your father insisted that nobody would ever believe me. He said, "Your testimony is invalid. You're a woman and underage."

I replied, "If I wanted to tell anyone, I would have told them already. However, I wanted to remind you of what you are. You're your own daughter's killer. Afsun didn't forgive you, okay—and I will never forgive you either."

Your father is totally out of his mind, but now his evil can affect only him. I know you didn't mean for all this to happen. Your father was involved in illegal business, but now he's locked up and away from your family.

I'm sorry. I'm plucking out dried grass from your grave as I'm telling you all this. By the way, your grave is right at the foot of that hill where you met Birishna when you first came here. The tree you're lying under is that beautiful tree you mentioned in your journal. What a coincidence ... I read what you wrote. You know that Tolo News anchor you loved, Yama Siawash, well, they killed him recently. They put explosives under his vehicle. I'm sorry. Things are getting worse here, but I'm not giving up.

They may come to your grave. Maybe they'll take over more land, but I'll keep your story alive, dear Afsun. I will never forgive the Taliban who slaughtered you and thousands of our young people. My Afsun, unfortunately, the politicians have sold their graves and lands. They even sold out our children's futures. Taliban militants can travel around here now, but don't get sad. Their possession of these lands, their feet stepping on it, does not make us forget what they have done to us. Not to you, not to me, not to anyone ... They've taken over all the districts except the city centre. They closed the schools in regions where they now have control. I don't know what else they're going to do, but the schools for girls are closed. However, the schools in city centres are still open so far.

I almost forgot to mention, Firdaws is here in Faryab right now. Maybe he'll come to you. He's here briefly to check on Birishna. You know what? Birishna started her own business. Her father passed away, and no one can force her to marry anyone anymore. I am sure she'll come to you, and she'll tell you that you've changed not only her life, but the lives of many women. Birishna now has a carpet-weaving workshop in Maymana city centre. She has about thirty women working with her. She turned the courtyard of that house you gave her into an atelier, and none of the women that she's with need anyone else's financial support any longer. They make their living and support their families. She's still going to school in the city centre. In addition to Persian, she even learned to write some words in English.

Firdaws is studying law at Kabul University. I'm sure he'll tell you more when he gets here.

Your Aunt Nuriya and Uncle Zafar have twins. They live in the city of Mazar-i-Sharif and they're very happy.

You ended every bad thing in the best possible way, but we couldn't change that night. It was a nightmare for both of us. You were right. If your father found out I was there that night, two bodies would've been taken out of that place. The Taliban made the decision to execute you and made your father do it.

My cousin brought me here for a thousand afghanis. I can see in his eyes what I don't want to hear. He seems to say, "Come on. Get up. Let's go." A woman without a man can't go anywhere out of the cities anymore. They're making their rules again, like they did twenty years ago. God help us.

I have to go now, my Afsun, but I'll come back to visit you. Sleep peacefully.

> *İnna lillahi we inna ileyhi rajiun.* (Indeed, we belong to Allah and we return to him.)
>
> – The Quran, 2:156

I'll do whatever you want. Afsun, my friend, I won't forget you. I won't let them forget you!

(Oncha Arlat, Faryab, 2020)

About the Author

Khatera Tughra was born and raised in Faryab, Northern Afghanistan. Like her central character, she is a young woman with strong opinions. She has survived numerous death threats and school bombings and has witnessed incidents similar to those depicted in this book. Although fictionalized, her characters were inspired by various individuals she has known or heard about. Through her writing, she hopes to keep her homeland in the international spotlight and educate others on the need to restore democracy and uphold human rights.

Khatera's activism and stellar academic record were established by middle school. As an eighth grader, she took a university-level computer course held by the Norwegian Committee in Faryab. A year later, she became an instructor in that course and began writing articles on social issues for local publications as well as speeches for various politicians. Her writing helped her become an honourary member of the Afghan Journalists Safety Committee. She was also recognized by the Northern Afghanistan Human Rights organization for initiating projects for girls. Throughout her high school years, she garnered many accolades for both her academic achievements and her activities to support disadvantaged youth. In 2020, she was named "Student of the Year" by Afghanistan's Ministry of Education.

Khatera has also won praise for *Efsun*, the original Turkish version of Afsun Beyond the Vineyard. Published in March 2022, *Efsun* has already won four awards: Ankara Gazi University TÖMER Achievement Award; PEN International, Afghan branch, Success Award; Union of Afghan Associations' Creativity and Awareness Award, and the Afghan Embassy's Courage Award.

By the time the Taliban seized power on August 15, 2021, Khatera was already pursuing a degree in medicine in Ankara, Türkiye. Despite her devotion to her studies, she finds time to speak for those who can no longer speak for themselves. She is a member of the Afghan branch of PEN International and the International Development Association of Disadvantaged Groups.

When she's not studying, she enjoys volleyball, running, poetry writing, and chess. Already fluent in five languages, Khatera is working on perfecting her English. Follow her on Twitter, Facebook, and Instagram.

About the Illustrator

Rubaba Mohammadi is a young Hazara artist from a working-class family in Ghazni province, Afghanistan. Like Khatera, she has survived death threats for daring to defend the rights of girls and women.

Born partially paralyzed in a society that shuns individuals with disabilities, she was confined to her home for most of her life. Only after she received her first wheelchair in 2016 was she able to venture outside. Although unable to attend school, Rubaba managed to teach herself how to read and write. She also learned to express herself through the power of her pencils and paint brushes—held between her teeth. Even after her Kabul studio was destroyed by a grenade in 2020, she never stopped dreaming and drawing. She is known for her naturalistic portraits of famous people such as Justin Trudeau, and she longs for the day when she can see her work exhibited in galleries and museums around the world.

Addressing ten to fifteen-year-old girls for International Women's Day in 2020, Rubaba said, "If you really have an ambition to move forward, ask yourself what talents you have and what you should do to reach your goals." As she waits for official refugee status and passage to a safe country, she remains perseverant. Now in her early twenties, she says she'll continue to do what she loves regardless of the obstacles and dangers. Follow her on Twitter, Facebook, and Instagram.

Printed in Canada